For Grandma
Happy 90th!!!

May the perseverance and courage you've shown throughout your life in the good and not-so-good times, carry you into many more years filled with contentment and joy. I wish for you all the best in good health, peace of mind, and that love continually surrounds and keeps your spirit strong.

With love and respect,

Bart

# ON THE
# FRINGES

*"I know not with what weapons World War III will be fought, but World War IV will be fought with sticks and stones."* —ALBERT EINSTEIN

BRAD HUTCHINSON

ROBERT D. REED PUBLISHERS • SAN FRANCISCO, CA

Copyright © 2002 by Brad Hutchinson
All rights reserved.

No part of this book may be reproduced without written permission from the publisher or copyright holder, except for a reviewer who may quote brief passages in a review. Nor may any part of this book be reproduced, stored in a retrieval system, or transmitted in any form or by any means electronic, mechanical, photocopying, recording or other, without written permission from the publisher or copyright holder.
This book is a work of fiction based around real events and people. The names, characters, and incidents are the product of the author's imagination, or used fictitiously, and their resemblance, if any, to real-life counterparts is entirely coincidental.

Robert D. Reed Publishers
750 La Playa Street, Suite 647
San Francisco, CA 94121
Phone: 650/994-6570 • Fax: -6579
E-mail: 4bobreed@msn.com
www.rdrpublishers.com

Editor: Margaret Duggar
Book Designer: Marilyn Yasmine Nadel
Cover Designer: Julia A. Gaskill

ISBN: 1-8855003-98-6
Library of Congress Card Number: 2001117665

Printed in Canada

# Dedication

*For all the scientists who work tirelessly, often in the face of great adversity, to discover cures for deadly diseases.*

# Acknowledgments

I offer my profound thanks to my writing group for their honest critique and thought provoking questions that helped to make this story coherent. Also, I greatly appreciate the staff and students at Beyond Kung Fu for showing me that no dream is out of reach when you believe it is possible.

I owe deep gratitude to Victor Hugo, Fyodor Dostoevsky, and Ayn Rand for asking, and answering through their art, eternal philosophical questions. Their great virtuosity, infinite intelligence, and breadth of imagination gave me incredible insight to human nature and helped me to form my characters.

# Chapter 1
# Washington D.C.

Defense Secretary Harold Weaver sat at an elongated, polished table with four other men. They belonged to the Defense Science Board's Task Force on Readiness. A distinguished man in his mid-fifties, he was big, with a deep arresting voice. Grey lined the sides of his full head of black hair as though someone had touched the edges with white paint. The other men took notes as Harold spoke.

The thick, long fingers on his left hand formed an umbrella on the table looking like a bird-of-prey seizing command of the area. "I've asked you all to join me here today because we are failing to meet our objectives with regard to our peacekeeping role. With a new administration on the horizon, we must be persuasive and remind the incoming president that it's his primary responsibility to protect Americans from foreign aggression. It's important that we maintain military superiority over countries choosing to ignore human rights. Gentlemen, there is no one else on the planet that can carry the burden that peace and freedom require. Our current president has done well to deceive the public into believing that we no longer need a big arsenal anymore, and has chosen to direct National Security funds to social causes. The nuclear shadow that's been hovering over the world for over half a century continues to darken. Twenty-five nations already possess arsenals that could weaken our forces and leave us defenseless in the eyes of the enemy.

"The Pentagon is spending less on new equipment and weapons than at any time in the last fifty years. Russia has a nuclear arsenal that could destroy the United States in an afternoon. At the turn of the century, eleven developing countries had nuclear weapons, thirty chemical weapons, and fourteen biological weapons. And we have embarked on a massive disarmament!" Harold shook his head and he planted his hand flat on the table. "Gentlemen, give me the essentials," Harold said firmly.

Jason Walburg, Deputy Defense Secretary, rubbed his face. "It's not good, sir. The Navy is down significantly and for the first time in decades we don't have a single new-design aircraft in the development or production stage. Right now, defense budgets are a smaller percentage of the gross domestic product than any time since 1938, while in other countries like China, Iraq, and Iran they are on the rise. Tank procurement has almost disappeared completely. Over a third of all military personnel, has been cut." Jason looked up from his document. His face showed concern.

"Damn socialist. Aren't we fighting socialism?" Harold could feel his posture firm then as he relaxed, a long stream of air slowly escaped from his body. "What else do I need to know?" He made notes on the pad before him.

Ted Akerman spoke up, "We have it from the CIA that there is a powerful man with the rank of lieutenant general in Russia that seems to be rallying to bring back the old ways of the USSR. He has a great number of supporters. The people there are fed up with the violent crime, corruption, and the Russian Mafia. This man is persuading the people with slogans like the abolition of poverty, the achievement of general prosperity, peace, brotherhood … The economic collapse, he says, has more to do with the people who tried to run the system before, not communism itself. He's been very persuasive, rallying around the anti-American feeling within their armed forces. This and the political developments in Berlin that might lead to the communist party winning a majority vote have set a new stage for the defense of freedom. But even more worrisome is the fact that the Soviet Union, in trying to recapture their own power, has no means to regain the parenting affect they once had on despotic neighbors. We're dealing with a far more diverse group now. Contrary to the current president's position, we, since the fall of communism, need a stronger arsenal than ever, not a lesser one. An attack can come from just about anywhere. It's my position that only a firm commitment to self-defense, enforced, will protect this nation while limiting casualties of our men and women on the front lines."

"What does that mean to you?" Harold asked.

"Those countries that advocate the use of force against us, or any freedom aspiring country, must become targets of military retaliation from us. Which means our armed response must be perpetuated and devastating. We need an addition 7 billion dollars per year strictly to develop and put into place anti-ballistic weapons in all our stations around the world. The 1972 Anti-Ballistic Missile Treaty must not stand in the way of testing. It has to be understood that freedom will not be susceptible to errant missile launches by rogue states."

Harold flipped open a manila folder labeled "Nuclear Arms" and asked, "What are our nuclear capabilities?"

Jim Burns started, "Well, sir, as stated on page four of my brief, the Department of Energy closed the office in charge of ensuring long-term supplies of tritium. That radioactive gas decays rapidly, losing 50 percent of its radioactive charge over a twelve-year period. If it's not periodically replaced, our nuclear weapons will become inoperable. We're uncertain, or will be in the not-so-distant future, whether we can respond to a nuclear strike." He paused for a moment. "And, sir, we're pretty sure the Russians, the Chinese, and the whole Middle East know this."

"The President has been more concerned with releasing classified information to train and fund potential enemies, than he has been at keeping our arsenal reliable! We've been asked to protect our country and year after year after year they continue to under fund this department. It's a disservice to send brave men and women into the field with less than adequate means of defense!" Harold composed himself. "Okay, everybody, it looks like our country has been left in an unstable position. Let's draw up a budget proposal and a clear plan for meeting and sustaining our defense needs. It's our job to leave this military more capable than we found it." Harold waved the back of his hand to signal that the meeting was adjourned.

The four men got up, straightened their uniforms, and left the room. Harold stared blankly at his reflection in the table.

# Chapter 2
# Toronto, Canada

*... seven, eight, nine, ten ... one, two, three ...*

Through a white mist, Joanne entered a room of enchanting music to see a Prince ascend to the throne. His presence was exhilarating, confident, his elegance completely natural. She rose en points, stepping tour de force into the language of infinite images expressing the depth and passion of her innermost self. She was weightless and poised. Of all the beautiful women in the room, his celestial blue eyes were fixed solely on her, tracing and admiring her every movement. Joanne radiated joy, her eyes glistened and the brilliance of her dance sent vibrant energy outward. With light, elastic jumps she finished her technique and stood at the foot of his pedestal. The Prince stepped down, kneeled, took her hand to his face, and said, "I would bring peace into the world if this precious flower would stand by my side." The gateway to Joanne's senses was open as the floral gowns on the ladies came to life and sprayed whiffs of jasmine, rose, and lily of the valley throughout the room. Tchaikovsky's "Dance of the Swans," with its tinkling piano, chimed in her ears. She leaned forward, expectant. All that was left was a kiss and the taste of his lips ...

As her chin rose, a gust of wind drew in behind her tattered shawl and yanked it away from her face. Reality sent a piercing funnel of cold air down her spine and through her veins. She reproached herself for believing she could ever be so beautiful, so free. It was a dream that could never come true now. She lifted her hand and quickly pulled the cloth back so that only her eyes were showing; she could not be recognized, she would not go back. The windows of the building across the street reflected blazing yellow and orange colors of the afternoon sun. One by one the windows were extinguished by the growing shadow as the sun began to sink. The lifeless murky pools of glass mirrored the cold desolate feeling that embraced her.

Icy northern winds blew fiercely down Bathurst Street, pushing daylight into a dull gray. As predicted, the unseasonably mild January weather had changed overnight and a cold front had moved in with a vengeance. The quickness of the change left the roads glazed, dangerous. Water dripping from roof tops and window sills froze, leaving exceptionally long icicles, jagged rows of teeth everywhere, like the city had been trapped in the mouth of a giant shark. People wore thick winter coats, mitts and wool hats, and rushed from buildings to cars, feverishly rubbing their hands and bodies.

A woman, holding her daughter, stood in the bus shelter. Joanne was huddled in the corner, wrapped in many layers of clothes and an old worn out blanket. She stared hopelessly at the woman and her child.

"Mommy." The little girl tugged on her mother's coat. "She's cold." She broke free from her mother's grip and walked toward Joanne.

Her mother lunged and grabbed her. "Stand over here with me."

"But—"

"No buts. You know you're not supposed to talk to strangers."

The young girl huddled under her mother's arm. She held a blanket close to her body with faded designs of dancing cartoon characters, the thumb of her free hand, which somehow escaped the thick woolen mitten, planted firmly in her mouth. She continued to look with sorrowful eyes.

The bus pulled up and stopped with a hiss. The fumes tickled Joanne's nose and a sneeze was imminent. She fought the urge, too much heat would be lost. The TTC symbol, like Joanne's heart, broke apart as the doors swung open. A sudden pain stabbed through her lower body. The woman kept a nervous eye on Joanne while leaving the shelter. Just as she turned to get on the bus, her daughter pulled the blanket from her body and held it in front of herself. Joanne saw a look of confidence spread over her eyes and face. The girl pulled her thumb out of her mouth and with both hands, threw the blanket behind her. It landed just within reach. Joanne's body began to tremble. The hair on the base of her neck tingled, wanted to be unknotted, brushed, loved. She leaned forward, grabbed the blanket and took it in under all the other clothes that lay across her and held it close to her heart. For a moment she didn't feel as lonely and was almost hopeful. She pulled from her pocket a little wooden figurine Charlie had given her. It was so beautiful and having it in her hand made her less scared.

The wind made a mournful wail as it gusted outside the shelter and, seemingly in one blink of her eyes, the hostile veil of night cloaked the city with darkness. Warmth from the sun, what little it had provided, had been completely driven away by the wind, which left only the shadowed imprint of a sneer upon all that it had touched.

Joanne knew her face looked pale, her body undernourished, her eyes showing only disappointment. She would be a dancer, marry a tall handsome man, and reflect the beauty of the world through her movement, her eyes. Her body hunched over unnaturally and that pain in her lower belly was worse; Charlie was right, she needed a real doctor. She tightened her grip on the wooden figurine in her hand and counted to ten aloud, over and over again, until the pain subsided and a happy vision could be drawn through the fear.

A memory of her younger days appeared before her. Her father used to call her his little angel: she was cute, charming, exciting. She had him wrapped around her finger by the age of five. Curling his hands around his mouth, he would breathe heavily, simulating the sound of a huge audience while Joanne pirouetted around the house. "You will be the greatest ballerina of all time, my princess," he would say. She had believed him and practiced day and night, twirling, leaping, expanding her boundaries ... At the same time every night, he would sweep her feet out from under her, lift and secure her with a warm embrace, and tuck her into bed while chasing all the monsters away with a brusque scowl and a wave of his hand. She had been in the safest place in the world.

It was difficult to remember exactly when it was that his face became old, drawn. His eyes lost their shine and changed from a deep ocean green, a beautiful tranquil place she rested in often, to a dull gray. His jowls sagged and his shoulders dropped. Almost overnight his form changed from sharp, strong, vibrant, to round, weak, slothful. One day the paramedics came to the house and took him away. He never came back ... and then there was the funeral.

Joanne loved her mother, but she was different now. The life in her eyes had glazed over into an alcoholic haze and her moods had become unpredictable. "I'm not the type of person that can make it on her own!" her mother said as she introduced Edward into the house.

Joanne curled inward. With tiny burning stabs, cold air penetrated through the layers of clothes, freezing her skin as the temperature continued to plunge into the gloomy darkness. A bus passed without stopping. The wind became louder and whistled in between the tall buildings, swirling around the shelter, dipping its pliant fingers inside in an attempt to pry her clothing away from her body. It brought in litter from the street. A Styrofoam cup rebounded off all four sides, remained suspended in midair for a moment, then fell to the ground and was swept out into the night. Joanne clutched tightly to her blankets as the tremulous windows of the shelter rippled down her back. No matter how far she ran, how small a step she burrowed herself under, or how tightly she backed herself against a wall, it always seemed that Edward was right behind her, breathing down her neck. She could no longer feel the figurine in her hand. Somehow her arms and legs were unimportant now. Only a feeling of blood rushing to her mid-section remained.

"One, two, three, four ..." Joanne pushed the hurt away.

The wind cheered and howled as Joanne found her safe place. She had learned how to dissociate herself from pain by humming songs, counting to ten, praying; although it was difficult to remember any prayers ... she used to know so many ... It felt like years since she had been on the streets, a whole different lifetime. It was two and a half months. Her fifteenth birthday passed three weeks ago. But it was a nice birthday. Charlie made it special.

She could feel her face harden and become numb down across her cheeks toward her mouth, leaving only a small opening through which to breathe. She was now curled up in the corner of the bus shelter, taking up little space. The air entering her mouth sent a sharp pain over her teeth. She would not move for fear of putting out the last internal flame that was keeping her alive.

Her insides felt like the striking area of a matchbox as a flash of heat ripped through her lower body. More flashes came sporadically as streaks of fire. She shook violently with each.

She had stopped going to school as she could not handle the looks from her peers. When anybody looked into her eyes they would see the vile, crude, and vulgar girl she was. Indeed it was her fault. The seductive way she walked, the clothes she wore, her flirtatious behavior. *Please forgive me, sweet Jesus ...*

As she thought of Jesus, the vision of Charlie rose in her mind, brilliant. He was heaven sent. He protected her and gave her back her sense of life. She could see the brightness again, the eternal flame, as if her father had come back to take care of her. A warm feeling ran through her veins at the thought of his voice. It was deep, resonating, almost raspy. It tickled her when he spoke. Even when he was being serious, scolding her about what she should do, she could not help but smile. He was an endless well of comfort, replacing her pain with hope and joy. When she looked up at his opening arms and empathetic eyes, heaven had gates and God a face. The thinning thread of trust within her had woven into a thick heavy blanket as, slowly and cautiously, she confessed everything to Charlie. *I'm sorry Charlie, I know I promised, but when I saw my picture, I got so scared. He's too powerful!*

A newspaper slapped up against the door of the shelter, it flipped through many pages before one flew off and pasted itself against the window directly across from Joanne. The street light radiated flickering glimpses of the steel framed shelter over a headline that read: CRUEL, under which read in smaller type: MAN CHARGED FOR LEAVING HIS DOG OUT IN THE COLD ALL NIGHT. The page fell to the ground and Joanne bowed her head. *Jesus, forgive Edward, he could not know what he's done to me ...*

Joanne wrapped herself in a tighter ball position and counted, "One, two, three, four—" She stopped, unable to remember what number came next. It was strange, but she could smell her father's aftershave, musky-sweet, and the feeling of his face against hers. Her cheek twitched and she stopped shaking. She again felt chaste and pure as a tiny ballerina pirouetted around her heart touching it, warming it ... There was no sound, not even the wind. A power that was not her own had taken away the need to fight. *Daddy ... ? Charlie ... ? ... Jesus.*

\* \* \*

Melissa sat on her stool, back straight and eyes focused, facing an easel in the middle of her living room. As the morning sun moved across the sky, her shadow lengthened and narrowed, like a sundial, over the hardwood floor under her chair. Its magnified rays warmed her skin through the clear pane of glass that brought the city skyline and expanse of Lake Ontario into her studio apartment from the twenty-third floor. Being a corner unit, the window assumed the whole south wall and part of the east. She wore an old T-shirt sporting the faded image of a skill saw and oversized gray track pants, crimped to her waist by a shoelace.

One light hung from the ceiling directly over Melissa. It cast a defined stream of white light over her thin shoulders and across her arms, spraying its rays in between her long slender fingers. The shadow danced with her fluid motions. Her brush moved like a baton, graciously and smoothly at times, sharp and sporadic at others. She conducted a symphony of colors, melodiously portraying life on the streets of Toronto as a vehicle to drive her passion into a new romantic era.

Her only links to the outside world over the last two weeks had been a stereo system that was used solely to play compact discs, and her phone that was forwarded to a message service. This was her production time. The time she buried herself away for a month to crystallize the ideas that had formed over the last two.

The elegant sound of Bach resonated through her three-level studio apartment, bringing to the surface an uncorrupted innocence within her spirit. The purity of composition woven into the rich tapestry of vibrations, rose one level to the kitchen, then another level to her bed area, and back down, filling this open space with purpose, and giving Melissa a tangible sense of aesthetic control. A ceiling fan circled on low dispersing the smell of acrylic. She held her brush lightly in her left hand.

Melissa felt at times that she had been put together, blood, bones, and flesh in such a way that she was not entirely human, her body only a transmitter whose sole purpose was to take a moment in time and immortalize it into images. She was a conduit, but not a passive one. After tapping her subconscious she would painstakingly rid her visual concept of extraneous lines, colors, shapes, and characters before transferring images onto a physical surface.

The door beside her swung open. She looked over, startled.

"Sorry to scare you." John smiled uneasily and looked sympathetically into Melissa's eyes. His face did not display its normal contagious smile. All she could see were shadows of his strong features. There was a newspaper clenched in his left hand, his cobalt blue eyes were haunted by inner pain.

"What is it?" Melissa's head tilted to the right as she gently put her paintbrush down.

John handed her the newspaper. "Page ten."

Melissa flipped through to page ten and found an article near the bottom that would have been difficult to see had she not been hypersensitive to the issue. "Girl Freezes in Bus Shelter." It went on to vaguely explain where she had been found and blamed her death on the unusually cold night, the coldest night in over ninety years. There was no name, age ... anything of importance.

Her head sank, her arms fell loosely to her sides. John reached forward and embraced her tightly.

"Page ten, is that all she deserves, page ten?" Melissa could feel her blood pressure rise. "Couldn't she get into a shelter? Did nobody see her there? What's wrong with this city?" Melissa pushed herself away from John. "We stayed open, didn't we?"

"Yes. In fact we had over thirty stay the night and almost a hundred passed through. Jamie and Frank took shifts to make sure that all were comfortable. We borrowed blankets from the Salvation Army and served hot soup," John said reassuringly.

Melissa let anger overtake her. "Page ten! How the hell does this city expect to eradicate the homeless problem if it isn't brought out into the forefront? Who's going to see this?" She thrashed the paper against John and threw it down on the floor. "Isn't she a person?" Melissa clenched her fists needing to hit something. "Doesn't she deserve to be acknowledged?"

"It's okay, sweetheart, she's safe and warm now."

"What the hell do you mean she's safe and warm now? She's dead!"

"I'm sorry," John stammered, knowing that was the wrong thing to say. "I just meant ..."

Melissa's looked up to the roof. John pulled her body close again and said nothing. Melissa shook her head as he rubbed her back. "Damn, damn!" she muttered.

Over a minute had passed and John did not know what to say, how to console Melissa. Her arms hung loosely around the nape of his neck as her face rested easily on his shoulder. Her breath flowed across his collar, creating a moist warm feeling under his chin. He felt badly for her. At twenty-three, she cared more for the homeless than anybody he knew. Her paintings were incredible, even though he didn't quite get the meaning of them all. Melissa was considered a prodigy and her work garnered large sums of money. She directed almost all of it to running her soup kitchen, distress line, and pamphlets on where to go for what. John ran the operations and was happy to help. It was good experience since he wanted to run his own business one day. It wasn't a large shelter, but it could serve a lot of people in a short period of time. Melissa's artwork paid all the bills.

Her paintings, she had told him, "Depict conscience shifting scenes of life on the street." She had a natural ability to make the homeless seem worthy, important, and showed in tangible terms their potential. Her paintings portrayed street life as a gateway to a higher plane, a better place, that somehow they were less trapped by society. "Transcends the senses!" one review raved.

Art galleries from around the world paid huge sums to display and sell her paintings in their show rooms. This sparked interest with investors. The value of her work was, by all accounts, going to rise steadily in price.

Her parents were a part of this elite group. Not that they ever bought her paintings or even agreed with what she was doing. They felt Melissa belonged among people of her own class: high society aristocrats who gave money to the homeless but would never associate with them. They not only disliked what she was doing, they hated the fact that she was dating John, a blue-collar worker.

Melissa was such a rebel, John mused while holding her close. She would dress in old jeans and loose-fitting shirts and spend days on the street sketching out scenes. She worked in hostels and soup kitchens to immerse herself in the life of the street people. Then she opened a spot where food was served twice a day and acted as a shelter in emergencies. Initially, John paid little attention to this girl, but on the third sighting, he felt something stronger than he had ever felt before. Still, he could not explain that feeling.

John was a Natural Gas Fitter and gave a couple of hours two nights a week to help out in feeding and lodging homeless people. At his first meeting with Melissa he hadn't had the courage to speak to this unapproachable girl. It was not that she was stunningly beautiful, but her eyes held depth and intelligence, and somewhere in that world of hers was incredible spontaneity and charm; the essence of everything he had sought. John had watched her discretely for long periods of time as she worked. Her eyes had sometimes been an open display of acute awareness, letting in the world around her without bias. Then in the very next moment, as if suddenly aware of being watched, closed, detached with the power, at a side-ways glance, to make him feel unworthy to breathe the same air, as if on an evolutionary scale he was closer to an ape than to her. He remembered the apprehension while first approaching her. It had taken a week to build up his courage. Then one day she was sitting in a shelter sketching. Walking over to make his move, John felt like a glass pellet heading for a concrete wall. As he got closer, he felt the impending crash. The voice of his father rose in his mind. "Listen to your heart, my son. Do not turn away from its message, or its voice will fall silent. The fear of rejection can be more debilitating than the actual rejection. Take the chance!" Who could have known, he thought as he rubbed his hand across her back, that the daughter of a multimillionaire could fall for the son of a carpenter? He came to realize that her strong, stern demeanor protected something very soft and vulnerable.

Melissa looked up into John's eyes. "It's clear to me what I have to do."

John took a deep breath, looked up to the kitchen, and said, "I'm here to support you however you want." He paused, unsure exactly how to word what he wanted to say. He caressed her face with his hand and looked directly into her eyes. "You've done so much over the last few years, but people die all the time, you can't save all of them."

Melissa bowed her head resignedly. "Yes, I know, but I can't help but feel sad for people who die like this. It seems such a waste." She tightened her hug around John.

"Yeah," he said, empathetically rubbing her back.

# Chapter 3

"You don't scare me," Kelly said, one hand planted firmly on her hip. "You've done well at keeping people away from you, but I see through your repelling qualities."

"What do you know?" Charlie grumbled.

"You're just a grumpy old man who thinks he can *will* everybody out of his life. But you know what? I ain't going nowhere. You're not as dangerous as you'd have people believe. I saw you with Joanne." Kelly blew into her hands to warm them.

*You have no idea,* Charlie thought.

Charlie sat in front of Sick Children's Hospital on University Avenue. He was carving a miniature figurine out of wood. It was in the spirit of the Hutsuls, a fiercely independent group of skilled artisans from his native land. No, it was in the spirit of Joanne. There was something mystical in the little figurines he made, as if he exposed a new side of himself with every piece removed. Joanne had really loved the last one he made for her. It seemed she was always holding it.

He etched out another sliver of wood. The dark veins of his large hands looked ready to burst as he brought forward the Slavic faces of his memory. The lighted spaces of his mind had not dimmed as the coldness of age crept up and around him. He was seventy-five years old and his visions were more vivid now than they were fifty-five years ago, the year he discovered fear.

"Hey, Repellent, want something to eat?" Kelly held out half a sandwich.

"No."

Kelly shoved it close to his face.

"Will you go away if I eat it?" Charlie raised his hand as if fending off an attacker.

"Maybe, but if you don't, I'm going to stay and bother you all day."

Charlie quickly grabbed the sandwich and took a small bite.

Kelly smiled. "You know most people are afraid of you, but I see past those deep green ghostly eyes. I see a part of you that really cares for people—maybe not people individually." She laughed.

"I thought you were leaving." He looked at Kelly. She was thin and, from a distance, appeared strikingly beautiful, but on closer scrutiny her face looked as if it had weathered a thousand storms. Street life had hardened her.

"Here we go." Kelly let out a derisive grin as two well-dressed men approached. "It's like I have an extra sense for these guys."

Charlie knew exactly what Kelly was talking about.

"… and then she said I was heartless. All in front of the media. Bitch. She twisted my words. I never said we should drive the homeless out of the city completely. I'm just suggesting 'beggar-free zones'. You know, the downtown core, Union Station, Queens Park." One of the men looked back toward the government building.

They both stopped at the intersection. The other man pushed the button for the light to change.

"Yeah, it's out of control around here. All we need are vagrants hanging out on our front steps. Makes Queens Park 'unaesthetic'."

"'site!" Kelly yelled. She was now standing right behind the men.

Both turned abruptly. "What the hell?" one of them said as his hand flew to his chest. "Jesus Christ, you almost gave me a heart attack."

"'site, 'site." Kelly batted her eyes furiously.

Charlie watched and listened. This was a good distraction to keep him awake. He had only slept a couple of hours since Joanne had died and those dark hours were filled with specters of fears that hung over canyons of buried knowledge. He dared not drift into that abyss again.

One of the men dug into his pocket, pulled a coin out and handed it to Kelly. He turned back to his friend. "It seems to me the problem is, once given the money, the panhandlers turn around and buy things not conducive to their well-being. A voucher system has been brought to the table where they could only get certain products with their money and—"

"Then you create a whole black market like they have in the states with food stamps. I don't support that." The man pushed the walk button again several times. "Even they're changing that system."

Kelly tugged on the man's arm. "'site, 'site!"

He swatted her away. "What do you want?" He looked rigid, agitated.

"'site." Her voice turned soft and sympathetic.

The man again dug into his pocket. "Damn, I don't have any more money with me. Jake, give her something so she'll go away. Sounds like she needs glasses."

Jake opened his wallet and gave Kelly a bill. "My opinion," he started after replacing his wallet in his back pocket and turning again toward his friend, "we should make it illegal to give money. Because really, what do people down on their luck have to lose when asking for money? But the person giving has a choice—"

"Yes! Brilliant. Put the onus on the other foot. A wonderful thought. And if you look at it pragmatically, what value can we gain by fining people that don't have money? It would just tie up the court system worse than it already is. We can sell it to the public as a social issue. By stopping the handouts we prevent these people from buying drugs or alcohol and we've made the streets safer by political process. It would also induce these people to move on, maybe even leave the city completely. I'll draft a First Reading this afternoon. Where do you want to eat? I'm starved."

The other man looked down at his stomach bulge regretfully. "Maybe just soup and a sandwich today."

"I still can't believe what she said about me." He shook his head.

"Come on, Fred, it's politics. I'm surprised that you're so agitated. You'll be back in her pants in no time. And just think, now your wife will never suspect that you're sleeping with her."

The light changed and they made their way across the street.

Kelly shook her head and turned back to Charlie. "I love doing that. I make more money that way. You hear that conversation, Charlie? After all they said, they still gave me seven bucks. Man, I'm good." She went and stood by the corner.

Kelly had nicknames for everybody, some were endearing, though most were not. She could see people clearly, beyond intellect or position. Her spirit was radiant and vibrated outward through her eyes. She often said, "They've broken almost every part of me, but they haven't touched my soul." Charlie wished he could say the same.

Kelly had come up with the name "'site" whenever she had seen a politician. Charlie mused at how she could pick one out in any crowd or attire.

One day while in earshot of Kelly, Charlie saw a Member of Parliament walking along the street and said, "Parasite" under his breath. Kelly picked up on that right away and every time a politician came into view she would say, "'site, 'site" with her hand out as though going blind.

The front doors of the hospital slid open and Charlie watched, with great intensity, a man holding a boy's hand. They were joking and smiling. The man had a full head of black hair and dark lines under his eyes; the boy, of no more than ten years, was completely bald, with fat cheeks and wide trusting eyes. They approached where Charlie was sitting.

"... yeah, Dad, I really like the people here, they're lots of fun. I wish I wasn't so tired all the time though." He looked up at his father. "Am I ever going to be able to play like before?"

His father pursed his lips and tried, without success, to conceal his torment. He squatted and looked his son directly in the eyes. "I don't know for sure, Randy. I know that there are people all over this city praying for you, and with all those good thoughts, anything is possible. Your mother and I love you very much and will do everything in our power to make sure you get the best help available."

"I'll do my best too, Dad."

They walked away and Charlie could no longer hear them. He noticed that his thumb was rubbing deeply into the figurine he was carving. A thin bead of blood trickled across his palm. This was his pain, his torture for harboring the knowledge he had but could not release.

"Kelly!" a young slovenly man screamed from the other side of the road. He waved his hand as he made his way across. His hair had been spiked and gelled straight up into a rainbow of colors. He looked like a porcupine with two hundred and twenty volts running through him.

Kelly waved her hand for the young man to come closer.

He stopped when he saw Charlie. "You come over here."

Kelly looked down at Charlie and laughed. "I don't think he likes you." She walked closer. "What's up, Splinterhead?"

"You working today?"

"How much you got?" Kelly asked.

He pulled out a bunch of coins and bills and handed them to Kelly.

"Thirty-two dollars. All right, you get two passes." She walked to the street corner.

Charlie could see a group of at least six men with buckets of water and squeegees across the street, waiting. Kelly dug her hands into her jacket, made a quick snap in front of her chest, and pulled them out. Like locusts ready to swarm, the men gathered along the street. The light changed to green and Kelly opened her jacket, took it from her shoulders, and pulled it down around her waist; her bare breasts stood exposed, firm, ample over her ribcage. Unlike with Charlie, gravity was still a relatively nonexistent force where Kelly's body was concerned.

She walked slowly across the intersection. The light changed twice before any car moved. There were honks from cars behind the pack that could not see the half naked woman crossing the street. All the others waited patiently. The men were cleaning car windows as fast as they could move.

"Hey, you didn't pay to be here." A large man—the enforcer—pushed a tall, yellowing, thin man off the road and took his squeegee.

"You can't tell me where to work!" yelled the jaundiced man stretching his arm over to seize back his property.

"Would you like me to make it so you can't work at all?" He shoved him away and held the squeegee up into a striking motion.

The man left without incident and without his squeegee.

On reaching the other side of the street, Kelly pulled up her jacket and waited. The guys were still cleaning windows of the cars that got caught in the cessation of traffic. It had a ripple effect, causing a back up three lights down. With her jacket on, Kelly waited on the other side until the jam cleared to create a new one.

Charlie's vision blurred. He tried to keep his eyes open, but his head became a weight his neck and body could no longer support. He fell over onto the hard ground into a deep sleep.

… The naked body of a boy lay on a table and he could see a tumor growing on his neck and down into his chest. The boy's face was innocent, pure. In the flash of a thought Charlie stood on the threshold of this boy's future. He became a monochromatic beam of light that illuminated the root cause of the disease. The answer stood before him as an electronic frequency with the same resonance as the living virus. Charlie released it, discharging billions of glowing white vibrating soldiers through the infected area. Like tiny bolts of lightening, they devitalized the microorganisms that created the malignant tissue, without damage to healthy tissue allowing the immune system to repair the area. A euphoric feeling of victory surged through Charlie's veins. He had saved the boy's life.

The boy became physically and mentally powerful. A dark ominous feeling overshadowed Charlie's soul, as the boy's face grew malicious and cold, taking on the shapes of Stalin, Mao, and finally settling into the evil, sardonic face of Hitler. There was a U.S.A. flag pinned to the lapel of his uniform.

The vision faded to black.

Lightning ripped through the sky, illuminating a staircase entrance to a new dimension. Charlie's heart sank as he felt himself dip through the darkness, his stomach queasy from the motion. A blue luminous flame struck him, igniting a cool, eerily green glow around his body.

The feeling of boxes being placed over him and the smell of exhaust almost pulled him back to reality. "Sweet dreams." He heard Kelly's voice beyond the sound of footsteps. The cardboard shuffled and moved as his body shook. The nightmare took control, ignoring the weak, distant plea from his consciousness to stop the terror.

Seventeen thousand feet above sea level and 30 degrees below zero, Charlie glided though the air as darkness gave way to morning light. He felt claustrophobic and short of breath. An oxygen mask popped out of nowhere and hung in front of him ... taunting ... laughing. It remained just out of reach as Charlie hopelessly clutched for it.

Traveling through a mountain of cumulus clouds, he began to feel light, free, as though this dream was about to turn benevolent. His forward progress halted abruptly. A clock with no numbers, only a second hand that ticked increments away like a successive slapping of his face, stood before him. He hung still, in midair, not knowing which way was up or down. His head lifted and he saw the face of a giant mallet with MMM engraved on the surface: Mediocre Mind Management. It got larger and Charlie bowed with hopeless acquiescence. It struck him square on the top of the head, branding him as property of the state, and sending him toward the earth.

Plummeting through the clouds with accelerating speed he dropped, unable to escape gravity. He was whistling through the air when the ground stopped him. Two simple thoughts clashed together producing a heat so white-hot it set off a nuclear chain reaction. A blast resounded like the big bang of a new universe, but it was not, it was the destruction of an existing one. His form changed again. He became a giant ball of fire; infinite power shooting up from the earth at one thousand times the speed he had dropped in. He was becoming more alive as he climbed skyward, engulfing clouds only to spit them out into enormous white smoke rings. Energy resonated through him and he was caught between a feeling of exhilarating power and a helpless inability to stop. He was not just mass or light; he was a living entity of destructive power.

A fountain of heat four miles high became his form. From deep within he felt another surge of power. It shot out through the middle of his body creating a giant mushroom, increasing his height. Another explosion climbed its way through the first seething mushroom escalating him even higher until he was on the threshold of puncturing a wound through the skin of the atmosphere. He had more energy lodged within the chemistry of his mind. He could, by seeing from this perspective, garner even more. An equation so simple, *no, stop, please don't form it*, he pleaded to his ambition.

Charlie rolled over, knocking the cardboard boxes off his body. He felt the coldness but could not wake up.

Back to human form, he walked through the devastated area. He noticed a woman frantically digging her children out from under a pile of debris. Her hair fell out before his eyes. Charlie's heart raced as she looked over to him despairingly. There was not a building standing anywhere and he surveyed, with immeasurable pain, the mutilated corpses, smashed skulls, and stacks of smoking black charred bones that covered miles upon miles of land.

A boy was sitting on top of a pile of rubble smiling at him. He was not burnt and seemed unscathed by the bomb. A wave of happiness filled Charlie as he walked over to the boy. His clothes were clean and neatly pressed, his hair thick and black, his face beaming. The young boy stretched out his hand to Charlie in friendship. Eagerly, Charlie grabbed the boy's hand and shook it. As he pulled away, he looked down and noticed that he held, in his own hand, skin from the boy's hand and arm. The boy remained smiling with only tendons, muscle and bone showing from his elbow down.

"No!" Charlie shot up from his sleeping position, his clothes and blanket drenched in sweat. His body was shaking uncontrollably as he looked nervously at the people walking by in front of him.

One man slowed and stared Charlie in his eyes as he passed. "Loser," he said with righteous indignation. His head turned forward and he walked away.

\* \* \*

"Come on, Joe, you can tell me." Melissa wedged the phone between her ear and shoulder. She kept her voice soft, ingratiating.

"The information is privileged," Joe replied. "We've just contacted her parents and—"

"You know me, I won't compromise your position as city coroner. Have I ever broken your trust? For this to be an effective painting I need to know the circumstances. It's for a good cause and the painting won't be out until well after all the information is public knowledge, anyway."

"All right." Joe let out a breath of air. "What do you want to know?"

"Name, age, and cause of death to begin with."

"Well I pulled her dental files …" Joe paused.

Melissa cringed at the sound of dismay in his voice.

"Her name was Joanne, she was 15 years old, and she froze to death as stated in the paper."

"Yeah, I know, page ten." Melissa let out a breath and shook her head. "Damn, 15 years old, what the hell was she doing out there? Who are her parents?"

"Actually her parents are from the Bayview area. I'd imagine they'd have filed a report. I have to speak to Alistair down at missing persons."

"How long would you say she's been on the street?"

"I really don't know anything yet, Melissa."

"What's her family name?" she demanded.

"No, Melissa."

Melissa clenched her fist. "Sorry, Joe, I didn't mean for it to come out that way. Thanks, I'll be in touch. Now I have to call the papers …"

"Just remember, I've not spoken to you."

"Spoken to whom?"

"Right, Melissa," Joe replied.

"I just want to give it to them for their lack of coverage. Page ten! They're normally pro-active in this effort. What's with putting it on page ten?" Melissa stopped. "Thanks, Joe."

"Go get 'em, kid. Make 'em put it on the front page."

\* \* \*

"Ladies and gentlemen, over the next seven months there will be many foreign visitors, including diplomats, in this city as we try to secure the Summer Olympic games in 2008. A parade is planned on April 13th that the Mayor thinks will secure this bid." Gerald Benton, Chief of Police, stood behind a podium speaking to an auditorium full of police officers. "I want this to run smoothly. We have to be at our best for this, people, we'll be watched closely." Gerald looked up at the rows of men and women before him. "There will be a massive cleanup effort in the city for this event. Security is paramount. The threat from the anti-globalization movement is at an all time high and, as the world focuses on this city, they will be animating their discontentment.

"On the day of April 13th I've been asked to move the homeless out of sight. A good hot meal will be provided for them in another part of the city. We'll have to be gentle. There'll be resistance and protests. Let's get through this without anybody getting hurt, if at all possible. We want the hostels and churches to be on our side with this. The Mayor has committed to allocating unlimited funds for this effort." Gerald paused. "As a force we're well respected around the world. Be proud of that. On April 13th we'll show them why we're so good. There'll be lots of volunteer hours available; a little bit from everybody will make it easier for all. Of course there'll be overtime, too. There's no excuses for this not going well. It's important, let's be at our best." Gerald closed his note pad.

The officers left the room and Gerald went to his office. He looked at the newspaper on his desk. It showed a picture of the bus stop where Joanne had frozen to death and a headline that read: "GIRL FREEZES" with a subheading, "WHAT YOU CAN DO TO HELP Pg. 24."

There was a toll-free number at the bottom of the article where people could call in donations and an address where they could bring non-perishable food items and clothes. There was no name given to the girl and no age, only that she had frozen to death. Gerald was well aware of why the newspapers were hesitant in making this story a full-blown incident. He rubbed his face with his hands, shook his head, and thought, *Melissa's going to be a royal pain in the ass over this Olympic bid.*

# Chapter 4

The sun's upper extremity seized the horizon signaling an end to the soft quietude of morning darkness. Melissa, up before dawn to get a good start on the day, sat on her stool watching out the window with a paintbrush and paints ready on her easel. Light brightened where the lake met the sky until the blinding yellow sun peaked into view, slapping Melissa's face away from the window. Her eyelids pressed together revealing images spinning in transparent golden spheres. Wavelengths, like sunbeams in clear shallow water stretched from her imagination, through her arm, and into her hand bridging the distance between the abstract and the physical. She picked up her brush, dabbed her paint, and swept a line across the canvas. The patterns of form, content, and style would merge into a well-structured piece of emotionally charged art. The openness of her apartment and the view across many miles of Lake Ontario gave her the mind-space for truly creative thought.

Melissa sought something greater than she was able to express directly through her work. Her visions were more vibrant, detailed, and colorful than she could transpose through any medium she knew. Her motivation was to transcend her paintings to reflect more clearly the pictures of her imagination.

Feeling the fluidity of her body, her long slender arm brought forth the bus shelter where Joanne had died. As the rich image was appearing on the canvas, Melissa could almost feel the hard steel frame and the smooth cold glass. The sun moved across the windowpane as Melissa sat for hours adding thin layers of paint to the canvas, each layer giving depth and life to the scene. She was not hungry, tired, or ready to quit. *If only I had an idea of what this girl looked like.* She heard a key rattle and the door opened.

John smiled as he walked in. "Hey, beautiful." He was holding a cone shaped bag in his hand, obviously flowers.

"Hi, John, finished working already?" Melissa held a captivated eye on the purple bag.

"It is six o'clock."

"Already? I hardly made any progress today." She tried to stand up but her body was stiff. A faint whimper escaped through a breath of air as she pushed herself off the chair.

John grabbed her with his free hand and eased her onto the white futon, the only other seating available in the living room. If not for the bookshelves brimming over, and the clear view of the city on one side, and lake on the other, the place would look empty. John pealed back part of the wrapping.

"Oh, my ... ," Melissa gasped. In front of her was an eclectic blend of fresh Orchids, divided in bunches by green veins of gracefully arced branches. She could feel her body warm. John removed the wrapping so she could have a better look. "Let me see if I can name them all this time." She brushed her finger across the red ones: "Red Lipped Dendrobium's, very exotic," Melissa said sensually then ran her tongue over her upper lip. Like a visual magnet, the yellow in the next bunch attracted her eye: "Dancing Lady's, exquisite!" Melissa felt a sense of lightness flutter through her body. Struck by the pure white in the next blossoms, she said, "Royal Dendrobium's, radiant ..." She batted her eyes innocently toward John. The last bunch depicted how well John knew her. He didn't bring her flowers; he exposed the colors and contours of her soul. The lanky striped blossoms commanded attention, not only because of their visual impact, but also because from the flexible position sprung the symbol of unyielding power. "Tiger Tail Arachnis, wild and exciting!" Melissa pushed the flowers aside and kissed John on the lips then ran her tongue over the dimple above his chin. "You're so wonderful, thank you."

John smiled. "You're welcome." He stood up and went up to the kitchen landing. Melissa watched as he filled the vase with water, snipped off the ends and put the flowers in.

On his way down the eight steps, John said, "You can't just sit on that stool all day without moving, you know, it's not good for your body. You should stand up and stretch once in a while." He sat down and began to massage her shoulders.

"Not so hard, oh ... yeah that ... feels good ... not so hard!" Melissa's shoulders drew up sharply and John laughed. His touch was soothing now and she relaxed. "I know I get wrapped up in my work sometimes … Through all the things I do to give my life meaning, it's only when I see you that I feel complete," she said. There was a long pause. "Does that make any sense?"

John's voice was confident as he answered, "Perfectly. You can't live without me, I can understand that." John laughed as he continued massaging lightly. "It's great to see you, too. Did you see the papers today?"

"Only the Toronto Daily. I asked a neighbor if I could have the front page." Melissa pointed to the wall where it was pinned, showing the bus shelter in a large color photo. "And I called the others."

"Front page on two others. Good work, Melissa. Did they say why the story was so poorly covered?"

"Yes. The editors said that the news about the federal budget took priority over everything, a lot of controversy over hospital spending or something. The Government says the same thing every year and pats itself on the back for a great job. I'm sure they'll all get raises. What a joke! And the newspapers falling for that garbage." Melissa paused, turned her head, and looked out the window across the lake. Her eyes narrowed. "It still seems strange. The papers normally jump all over stories like this girl dying." She shook her head, took a deep breath and enjoyed the massage. "Anyway, getting the story on the front page is just a start. Something else has to be done. I'm not sure exactly what that is, yet." She pulled her chest forward and held her chin high. "I feel like I have a new surge of energy, purpose."

"Sometimes I think you put too much pressure on yourself," John said. "You can't single-handedly save the world, you have to take time for you."

"This is my calling, John, and I really think I can make a difference." She turned her head and looked at him through the corners of her eyes. "I've always felt that way. Since Stephanie died …" She turned and watched over the cold teal lake.

"Melissa, you've got to stop blaming yourself for that! There are things you can't control in this world." John's voice held a controlled balance of reproach and sensitivity.

"But …" Melissa could feel sad emotions starting to surface. "My father always said I was of his breed and I belonged with my own kind, but Stephanie showed me a different world than his and ever since, I've felt more comfortable with the less fortunate."

"Like me?" John said quietly, as though not meaning to be heard.

Melissa turned around and looked directly into his eyes. "I'm sorry if

I insulted you. There's my upbringing coming out again. You're not less anything!" She laughed easily. Melissa turned right around, pulled his face to hers, and kissed him on the lips. "There's nothing missing in you. I've never before in my life experienced the kind of love you have to offer. At home there were always conditions like, 'give me a hug and I'll buy you a dress, give me a kiss and you'll see a new car in the driveway for you next week'. I hated it, there was never any affection demonstrated just because you were loved." Melissa rolled her eyes. "That's why I started painting, it took me away to a different place, away from the prim and proper world of 'acceptable behavior'. Speaking of which, we're invited to go to dinner on my sister's birthday Thursday."

"Oh great, that sounds like fun." John's mouth crimped as his eyes shifted sideways.

"Please come with me." Melissa cuddled up to him, leaving the majority of the futon empty, and rolled her tongue over his Adam's apple. She could feel it rise then lower, sending a wave of heat through her body.

"I don't feel comfortable there, your parents and your sister, Ms. Pristine, always talk down to me." John squirmed as Melissa straddled him and held his face softly with her hands, kissing, teasing, arousing.

"Please come with me ... I'll make it worth your while." She nestled in as close as she could and ran her hand through his thick brown hair.

John was trying to remain unaffected as he replied, "I'd rather get hit in the head with a pipe wrench." He could barely maintain his serious expression.

She worked her way under his chin and found the spot that drove him crazy. She let out a long, hot, moist breath.

"Okay! I'll go." John firmly grabbed her arms as his whole body shivered. He pushed her just far enough away to be back in control. Her eyes were playful, predatory. He brought her close again and ran his finger lightly down the length of her spine. Her eyes widened and her pupils dilated as her chin rose, tempting his lips to mask the fleshy hollow of her neck.

An imploring half-smile crossed her face. "Take me," she whispered. She gasped as his strong, callused hand ran across the fullness of her breast. She fell into submission. John stripped away her loose clothing as Melissa unbuttoned his shirt and pants allowing him to slip out easily, quickly. She relinquished control, moving as he moved, breathing as he breathed, becoming one with his spirit, reflecting back to him all that he was, is, and could ever be, knowing it was she who brought out the best in him. Melissa's legs slid around John's slick body and clutched tightly, immersing him more deeply inside. As his lips pressed against hers, a passionate surge of primordial hunger flashed through her veins followed by an intense explosion. His thrusting sped, and another explosion flashed through her, then again as his wet body fell loosely over hers. She could feel his heart beating as he breathed exhaustively.

The union of the flesh, two electrically charged bodies entwined, made possible the exchange of thoughts and emotions through tiny bundles of light, seeds that would grow to illuminate and warm the soul.

Melissa kissed his neck and whispered, "I love you."

\* \* \*

The fading blue sky was a backdrop cut by shadows sharp as a razor's edge. The spire of a church supported a cross stretching up high, bringing heaven to earth. Two concave buildings, one slightly taller than the other, tempered the hard straight lines of the structures that spanned the horizon. They opened up exposing a dome-like pod. Soft arches smoothed the skating surface in front of Toronto City Hall over a multitude of people, young and old, skating in ovals.

Father Will Bower's exposed skin on his face numbed as he ate his brown bag dinner. Frigid temperatures overpowered a slight wind that was barely detectable save the swirling wisps of snow over the concrete underneath his feet. The warm transparent vapor leaving his mouth turned into a cloud almost immediately in the hard coldness of the day. As he sat on the wooden bench, he watched the skaters.

A coltish young man, in an attempt to impress a girl, aggressively dug his skates into the ice and moved with increasing speed, adroitly weaving in and out of the slower, less skilled skaters. On approaching the object of his desires, he turned sharply and stopped, sending a spray of snow high and far in front of him. The girl moved daintily and lightly like the whirling wisps of snow and stopped for fear of being bowled over by the boy. With the ease and balance of a professional he lifted one foot, smiled, and wiped the tempered shiny steel clean to reflect the essence of his youthful libido.

Father Bower sat not two feet away from a man lying on the bench curled deep within a sleeping bag. All that was showing was his nose and his mouth. A mustache and beard, frozen from his breath, protected his skin from frostbite. The cold wind brushed against Will's face and he could feel the hairs in his nose freeze as he inhaled. The sun was setting behind him and the clock tower bonged five times. It was a busy Sunday as people hurried by in both directions.

"Hi, Will." An old man with a deep solemn voice sat down on the bench beside him.

"Charlie!" Will replied. He pulled out half of his sandwich and handed it to him.

Charlie looked for a moment then took it. "I can't remember the last time I ate." He took a bite.

Will looked at Charlie and understood that he had suffered a great blow with the loss of his friend Joanne. "You're not doing very well, I can see that." Charlie's hair was gray, disheveled. His prominent forehead made his eyes appear sunken. His wrinkled skin clung to his cheekbones like a curtain to a metal rod. It was coarse and tough, like the skin of an elephant. His eyes were an ever-changing totality of who he was, traitors of a soul that tried to remain hidden.

"You haven't been sleeping well."

"No, dreams … even worse than …" Charlie looked at the remaining piece of his sandwich as if it were something foreign. He turned beseechingly to Will. "Why didn't she trust me? I wouldn't have turned her in." He threw the crust on the pavement in front of him. "She didn't belong on the street. I could've taken her away and made sure she was safe. Why did she have to run? Why?" His fists clenched tightly and his face turned cold and hard.

Will placed his hand on Charlie's back. Charlie looked over, his anger filled eyes telling Will that he was out of line by touching him. Will could feel his own heart quicken, but continued to stare into Charlie's eyes. If Charlie didn't want his hand there, he could brush it off himself.

"Listen, Charlie, Joanne loved you. I could tell by the way you spoke of her. She looked up to you like a father, you said that yourself. You played an important role in her life and gave her comfort in her last month. I know it's difficult now to appreciate, but you were a positive light in Joanne's life."

"The problem was, I turned my back for just a minute and she ran away. Why didn't I see those posters first? I could've hidden her—" He stopped, his look even more intense, but he didn't brush Will's hand off his back. "And let's not bring religion into this, I'm in no mood today!" His voice and face shook.

Will reflected on all the discussions he had had with Charlie about religion. Charlie was brilliantly creative with his views and knew the

Bible—New Testament and Old, all of the scriptures—better than anybody he could think of. His soul had been scarred somehow and this had tainted his hope for humanity. Will never pressured him about what had hurt him so deeply. If Charlie wanted him to know he would have told him. Other than that, they had become friends. It seemed strange to Will now that he had only known Charlie for a few months. The depth of their understanding far exceeded the length of time. There was something powerful about the way Charlie spoke. Words and their organization, the influx of his tone, and the passion that escaped the very essence of who Charlie was, gave Will an avenue to corral language as the vehicle of new thought. Indeed it all started with the word. As Charlie said, "There are over a trillion ways for a five-word sentence to unfold and in those five words is the meaning of life, waiting patiently to be illuminated." But Charlie wasn't thinking of meaning or life now, he was thinking of his friend Joanne.

"Her spirit here on earth still lives on if you hold her close to your heart. Don't let her die in your contempt and self-loathing. She deserves better than that from you."

"With all I know and all I can see, I couldn't help her, couldn't find her." Charlie pounded his fist repeatedly against his leg. "Why does the world always lose the good ones?"

Will wanted to give Charlie hope, to somehow take away his pain, but he was at a loss now. Charlie caged himself and closed his heart. He held onto his anger and sorrow as though it protected him. Will struggled to find a word, a gesture to help, but his mind drew a blank. A comforting presence was all that he could be now.

Charlie continued to speak of the unfortunate things that happen in the world, his voice directed into the middle of the square. Will kept his hand on his back until Charlie got up and walked away. He did not say goodbye. He just got up and wandered aimlessly, his feet heavy on the ground as though his shoes were metal and the earth below a magnet.

Will looked over at the Church and smiled. He remembered Charlie saying once that the spire should be truncated and opened up to allow the beauty of the universe to flow freely into the building. Peace and love was Will's goal. He would pass on that message to encourage higher understanding, acceptance, but most of all, tolerance.

Will was unorthodox in his beliefs and met with controvery for his views. It was not that he ever questioned the existence of God or that he should devote himself to any other pursuit. Will felt only that the origins in which the church doctrine began belonged to a world very different and unlike this one. He did not condemn new knowledge modifying old beliefs, as had been the wont of most religious reformers. In fact, he embraced reason as a systematic way to God. His admirable devotion and work ethic had put him in the good graces of the Archdiocese of Toronto and, just recently, into one of the biggest churches in Toronto, though he had run into opposition from other clergy for his methods and views.

He had one sandwich left in his bag, took a post-it note out of his pocket, and wrote "Manna from earth" with his initials below. Will looked at the man sleeping on the bench beside him. He placed the sandwich inside his sleeping bag so it would not freeze and when the man woke it would be the first thing he felt. Will made his way back to the church. He would come back soon to make sure the man had shelter this evening.

The statue of Jesus on the cross was suspended over him. He bowed his head and looked deeply into his soul for a way to help Charlie. He allowed his body to become a channel through which the light of God would shine out and into the world.

\* \* \*

Detective Terese Bolino, on the coroner's request, brought Joanne's parents to his office after they had identified the body. They waited for him.

"I can't believe this. She was so young." Edward shook his head.

"After her father died she was never the same," Julie said, her face scarlet and swollen from crying. "She became reclusive and started making up stories ..." Her voice quivered as her statement trailed off.

"Now, now," Edward said as he pulled Julie in close to his side. He turned to Terese. "Julie's been through an awful lot this past year."

"What kind of stories, Mrs. Woodrow?" Terese asked. This was a case to handle carefully.

Julie looked up at her husband, her eyes filled with shock and grief. "Just ... uh ... stuff like, her father was watching all of us and that I should act more like a grieving wife. She said he spoke to her and told her ... I don't remember. I ... I ... I did the best I could. Then she just ran away."

"I know this is very difficult for both of you." Terese looked at Edward and then to Julie with concern. "How long ago did she run away?"

"Ten weeks. I filed a report, Detective!" Edward rolled his eyes and shook his head. "Surely you've seen her picture."

"These are just routine questions, Mr. Woodrow. I have to ask them," Terese replied. It was important to get Julie on her own, to talk without Edward there.

"I'm sorry, we're just very upset. We did everything we could: we called the police within hours of her disappearance, we handed out flyers, and just a few days ago I hung up reward posters all over the city for someone to call." Edward held his wife tightly. "When can you release Joanne?"

"The autopsy isn't complete yet. When the coroner is done, you can—"

"Not complete!" Edward said too quickly. "I thought you said she froze to death. What else is there to know?"

"Sir, when the autopsy is complete you may take possession of the body, and not before." Terese raised her eyebrows.

Edward stepped forward and pointed his finger. "That may be just a body to you, Detective Bolino, but it was my stepdaughter. What's your badge number? I want to make a complaint on how this whole situation is being handled."

Joe entered the room. He looked at Terese, then at the Woodrows. "We've almost completed the autopsy of your daughter, there are just a couple of things I have to ask before we go any further." Joe noticed that Terese had taken out her notebook, written something down, tore off the sheet and stoically handed it to Edward Woodrow. "How long was your daughter missing?"

Edward snatched the sheet of paper out of Terese's hand. "Ten weeks. Is there anybody else that needs to hear this information? Because if there is, maybe we should wait until they come. I would rather not go through this a hundred times."

"I'm sorry, sir." Joe tried to keep his voice calm. "This must be very difficult for you. In order to finish the autopsy and get an accurate account of what happened, I will need to ask you just a couple of questions."

"Very well, I'll answer the best I can," Edward replied.

Julie began to cry hysterically.

"Maybe Detective Bolino can take your wife into the next room." Joe suggested. "These question will not be easy for her."

Edward looked concerned. "I don't know, it doesn't ..."

"Come on, Mrs. Woodrow." Joe gently took her arm and linked it to Terese's. He gave Terese a nod and shift of his eyes telling her to take Julie out into the waiting area. "I think it'll be easier this way," he said directly."Before your daughter—"

"Stepdaughter." Edward corrected.

"Excuse me. Before your stepdaughter ran away from home, did she have a boy friend?" Joe looked at Edward, studying his expression.

"No. Yes, I mean she often came home late." Edward seemed caught off guard. "Her mother asked her where she had been, but she was always evasive. I think she was seeing a boy from school. Why do you ask?"

"Well it seems Joanne has been sexually active and I was—"

Edward cut in, "I didn't want to say this while Julie was in the room, but before Joanne ran away she was acting very distant. I tried to talk to her on one occasion." A disturbed expression spread across Edward's face. "She screamed at me to leave, not only her room, but the house. I was very distraught at this since I was trying to encourage a healthy relationship with her." Edward shook his head. "Later I went into her room when she was out and found a test kit under her bed, you know, a pregnancy kit. I put it back and never told her mother. I wanted to talk to Joanne about it, to prove to her that she could trust me, but she ran away ... I don't know, maybe I was wrong."

"I see," said Joe.

"Would you let me tell Julie this?"

"Yes, I think that's best. Would you like me to be there to—?"

"No, I'll do it." Edward lowered his head.

"Thank you, that's all for now, Mr. Woodrow. I will carry out my duties as expeditiously as possible so that you may get on with the funeral proceedings."

Edward left the room. Terese entered a couple of moments later.

"Well, what do you think?" she asked.

Joe massaged his temples. "I'm almost positive she was abused. Was it Edward? Maybe. There's really nothing to support that right now, though."

"Let me know your progress." Terese made a note on her pad and left the room.

# Chapter 5

A raggedly dressed man with unmatched shoes doddered over to Charlie. "I hear they're planning a beautiful meal for us on the day of the parade." A cool white vapor left his mouth as he spoke. "They say there's going to be a television so we can watch it all. Maybe they'll let us stay to watch a Leaf game, if there is one that night. Wouldn't that be great?" He tilted his battered fedora in front of his eyes. He wore a wool knit beanie underneath.

"So I hear, Chris. We're being moved on that day so those parasites can pretend we don't exist in their wonderful clean city." Charlie always added subtle sarcasm as he spoke. It came naturally, especially lately, and was an important part of his fitting in with the general feeling of the homeless. It was relatively easy to fade into the sea of the unnoticed. *Stay as far away from a centralized government as possible*, he thought. Charlie blew into his hands to warm them. He was carving another small wooden figurine with his Swiss Army pocketknife. "Nice hat," he commented.

Chris' eyes screwed up and his forehead moved in up and down motions to lift and lower his hat. "Thanks, I just picked it up. It's like one I used to wear in the good ole days. Fits perfect." He looked toward the theater across the road. "Time to go to work. Look at all those people leaving." Chris pulled up his oversized trousers to stop them from dragging on the ground and made his way across the street. His motions were hurried, his movement slow.

Scattered numbers and equations flashed through Charlie's mind and pictures began to form. He shook his head, trying to disarrange the connections. First, numbers appeared. In circular motions they turned into equations: ten-to-the-power-of-eighteen seconds was followed by the unfolding of time and space; ten-to-the-power-of-fifteen seconds, earth had formed; ten-to-the-power-of-nine seconds, man's longevity; intervals between Charlie's resting heartbeats, one second.... Charlie saw a human being, generic, no sex, with ten-to-the-power-of-ten stamped on the hand over its lifeline. "Stop, I can't ..." He bowed his head with his hands clasped tightly over his face. He knew he was suffering from sleep deprivation.

He stood on the corner of Yonge and Queen when around walked Melissa, dressed in a black overcoat. Charlie knew who she was, but Melissa did not know him. *Look at her walk down the road like she owns it.* He was quite aware of her save-the-homeless mission. He felt repugnance as she walked closer. *She's a hypocrite, no better than the politicians whom she claims to loathe. She has the same self-righteous look and walk.*

Charlie kept his head down, trying to avoid eye contact.

Melissa stopped, opened her dainty black purse, and took out a two-dollar coin. "How you doing today?" She went to hand Charlie the coin.

"Fine," he said. Charlie held his hand out. He did not want to take her money, but felt she would become inquisitive if he refused.

Before placing the money in his hand she asked, "You won't buy booze with this, will you?"

"No, Ma'am, I don't drink." *None of your business.* He lifted his foot to show the hole in his boot. "I'm saving for new boots."

"There's a Salvation Army down the road. You should go there, I'm sure they can help." Melissa dropped the two-dollar coin in his hand. "Are you new around here? I don't recall seeing you before."

*No, just trying to avoid you,* Charlie thought and said nothing. He looked up and into her eyes for the first time.

Melissa's head angled up as though about to look at the sky, but her eyes remained fixed on Charlie. "Well, my name is Melissa." She paused as if waiting for a reply. He remained silent. "If you need assistance with anything, I can be found in one of the shelters or in my kitchen. Most of the people around here know me."

"Yes, Ma'am."

Melissa looked at her watch. "I have to go. I'll see you. Don't forget to go to the Salvation Army." She walked away. After ten steps, she stopped, turned around, and stared at Charlie. He felt the weight of her gaze, turned, and headed in the other direction.

* * *

"Terese, it's Joe." Joe held the phone with his shoulder as he pulled a notepad from his pocket. "There was a lot of pressure to release the body to the Woodrows, but I worked all night and got a comprehensive report from the autopsy on Joanne."

"What did you find?"

He took a deep breath. "I discovered that she was indeed pregnant and had had an abortion. Not a professional abortion, either. Man, she was a mess inside." Joe flipped through some notes. "It looks like she was in her first, maybe early second trimester. She'd had a D&C, but part of the fetus wasn't removed. And the wall of her uterus was perforated in the process. She would have died sooner, had the cold not slowed the rate she was bleeding inside. She must have been in a great deal of pain."

"My God …" Terese let out a breath of air. "Do you think it was his?"

"I don't know yet, but now we have DNA."

"Yeah, that's good, but *it is* Edward Woodrow—" Terese stopped as if catching herself. There was a long pause. "Thanks for the information, Joe. If anything comes up, you have my pager number."

"I'll give you a call."

\* \* \*

Melissa approached the church where the funeral proceedings for Joanne were being held. There were over a hundred people clamoring outside the gate, mostly activists carrying signs and shouting. A television crew was set up in the middle of the crowd and reporters were conducting interviews. There were more than twenty police around, and a squad close at hand with riot gear at the ready. Melissa noticed that there were a few people rallying and handing out pamphlets from a coalition-against-poverty group. No good could come of this, Melissa thought. She could feel the tension in the cold air and it seemed that some kind of confrontation was imminent. The path to the church was littered with protesters bundled up; some had made fires in garbage cans to keep warm. Melissa took a deep breath, and headed for the gate.

"Poverty is not a crime! We're repeatedly told, 'Toronto City Council has made homelessness a high priority,' but we're still being harassed by police who dump our knapsacks, confiscate our water, and kick us when we're sleeping!" Short puffs of air escaped the grim face of a young girl, of no more than twenty, as she shouted to a group around her.

Melissa made her way past.

"Did you know the deceased?" A man in a thick blue winter jacket held a microphone close to a woman with a dirty face, and unkempt hair.

Her clothes were stained copper brown.

"There but by the grace of God go I." She crossed herself. "Can you spare some change?"

Melissa walked right by the reporter, protecting her face from the camera with her hand. "Not right now, Steve," she said at his motioning for an interview. She hurried on through the crowd, keeping her head low and her pace fast. There was no time to stop and chat. The service for Joanne had probably started and Melissa didn't want to miss it. She needed to know more about her.

As she turned toward the gate a large strong hand seized her arm. Her body jolted to a stop causing her to almost fall backward. Regaining her balance, she thrust her arm forward, freeing herself from the grip. "Take your hand off me!" She turned to see Anton Strand, leader of the Coalition Against Poverty.

"Melissa, I've been trying to get hold of you." Anton's weathered, nut-brown eyes narrowed and his mouth twisted up with contempt. "You don't return your calls?"

"I have no time right now, Anton," Melissa replied.

"Come on, Melissa, we're both fighting the same battle. We could really use your help to defeat this government. Your visuals could be our call to action, images in our struggle against tyranny."

"No, Anton, we're not fighting the same battle. I've told you before, I will not be a part of your organization." Melissa studied Anton for a moment. The menace in his face had more clearly defined itself since she had seen him last. She looked toward church. "I have to go." She turned and started to walk away.

"Stephanie would be disappointed in you, Melissa."

Her forward progress had been halted again, this time by a force immeasurably stronger than the physical power he had used to stop her with his hand. It seemed that thick heavy roots had grown around her feet, securing her to that spot. Anger burned through the paralyzing feeling, freeing her. Like a whip, she spun around. "You son-of-a-bitch!" she said through clenched teeth as Anton stood smugly before her.

"Ah, there's the nerve that strikes an emotion." Anton paused, lifted his head, and looked at Melissa over the bridge of his nose. "She was one of us, you know. You didn't know that when you were friends, did you?"

"She would have never made allowances for violence. She may have been fooled by your colorful words and 'good intention' crap, that leads to nothing more than a gang of thugs who think that initiated force is justified somehow. You make demands, but have no means—"

Anton smiled derisively as he cut in, "Influence from your capitalistic father has clouded your vision, Melissa."

"No, Anton, yours is clouded by revenge." Melissa looked to the crowd that seemed to be getting louder and more forceful. It was difficult to see as the midday sun reflected blinding flashes off the reporters' microphones and cameras. She closed her eyes and winced. Slowly, she opened them and waved her hand to the shadows of aggression. "This is the right way, Anton?" she questioned with contempt. "People will likely be hurt here today."

"They will understand that we mean business!" Anton's eyes narrowed and his mouth firmed. "Our only goal is to eliminate poverty, and our pleas seem to mean nothing to this government of big business. Our words must be followed by action!" He spoke in a loud vindictive tone.

"Advocating the use of force to achieve social goals is a contradiction, Anton. All you'll do here today is make it seem like the homeless are responsible for the destruction you cause."

"Then what? I'm open to suggestions, tell me what else we can do?"

Melissa was stuck. There were no easy answers, but there were answers, and violence wasn't part of the solution.

"You're a better artist, Melissa, but Stephanie was a better person," Anton said, critically.

Melissa felt like spitting in his face. Not because he said Stephanie was a better person, that was true, but because he was using her now as a tool to engage her emotions and bring her to his level. Melissa took a deep breath.

"Melissa, there are no comfortable ways to bring about social change ... I will not allow more people to die on the streets without an organized struggle ... we will prevail over this government and then bond with the Anti-Globalization Movement!" Anton raised his fist with anger.

"Ah, I see, it's power you're after."

"Somebody has to lead the way, you have a talent that could help us bring about change. Those bastards in power carry out social crimes with the backing of the people, the corporate elite, and the media ... and call it democracy! Why do you think Joanne's story was so poorly covered until you called and raised hell to get it on the front page?"

Melissa did not reply, but her interest was piqued. She didn't like Anton, but felt he was intelligent ... actually, that's what scared her most about him.

Anton shook his head. "You have no idea, do you? You actually think it was you that made that happen, don't you?" He laughed, as though Melissa was gullible. "It's private tyrannies that control the distribution of information to the general population, and your last name had more to do with getting her story covered, if you can say that it was covered, than your cause. Coming from wealth, Melissa, I thought you would know that your work rides on the shoulders of your father's bank account. Without that you're nobody, with no voice, like the rest of us. Which is why necessary action must be taken!"

Melissa would not engage Anton in the way he wanted her to. He had no idea how hard she had worked to earn her own influence. "You know what, Anton? Anybody can throw a stone to get a reaction, but when you can do it with ideas, then you have the power to get a response conducive to your goals." Melissa walked away. She had put on a strong front with Anton, but when he mentioned Stephanie, the thorn of guilt pierced her confidence and insecurity bled through her. She struggled to keep her body from shaking. Why hadn't she known about her? They had been so close.

Approaching the church, Melissa saw a heavy wrought iron fence surrounding the grounds. There was a knot of people clinging to the black bars, shouting, holding up signs. Two large, well-dressed men were standing by the gate.

"Friend of the family?" one man asked as he lifted his hand for her to stop.

"Of Joanne," Melissa replied as though she had been a childhood friend. "Who are you?"

The man looked her up and down. "Hired by the family to watch the gate. You must have a pass to go in."

"I left it in my other purse." Melissa lifted her arms in a helpless gesture. "I would miss the service if I went back."

"I'm sorry, ma'am, I have my rules."

Melissa looked around and could see no way to get in. Damn, she had to find out more about Joanne. She stood there thinking of what to do when an object whizzed by her ear and struck the larger of the two men beside her. She looked back. Police were accosting people and physical altercations had broken out. The big man fell to the ground and his partner bent down to pick him up. Melissa snuck in behind them and inside the gate.

Without looking back, she hurried along the cut stone walkway and up the concrete steps. She pulled open a heavy mahogany door.

On entering the church Melissa was impressed by the grandeur of the structure. The simple, overreaching Gothic design made Melissa feel small and insignificant. Silently the door eased shut, taking away the wedge of light from outside as chambers of blackness rose around her. She stopped, unable to see anything. Ironic, she thought, that this doctrine had cloaked humanity with darkness for a thousand years. She tried to control her thoughts. She was not here to judge, she was here to find out about Joanne.

Lightly, a hand cradled her elbow. "Let me direct you to a place to sit. There's a seat near the front for one person." The soothing tone of a man's voice set Melissa at ease. She felt like she was on a moving sidewalk as he gently ushered her down the aisle. Her eyes adjusted to the twilight of the room and she could discern shapes. She slid into a seat as everything came into focus.

The stained glass windows that lined the upper walls subdued the natural daylight, creating a dim, contemplative atmosphere. She stared at a stream of white light. It was channeled through a clear glass block strategically placed between the stained glass pieces and reflected sunlight off a porcelain statue of Jesus and onto the altar, bathing the priest in a golden mist of incense.

"… for the Son of Man is going to come in the glory of His father with His angels; and will then recompense every man according to his deeds." The priest lifted his arms, light illuminating his surplice.

Quiet sobs came from the first two rows. Melissa stared at the casket sitting on a gurney in front of the altar, her fists clenched in her lap. She looked up at the fifteen-foot statue of Jesus and something about the design made her body relax. She undid her jacket and let out a quiet breath of air.

"I am edified and honored to give Joanne's Eulogy. I chose that passage because I thought it really spoke to the life of Joanne and her many contributions. Over the last little while, I feel I've come to know her quite well. I learned that at the time when her father was still alive, she was quite active in the church, and everybody who knew her could not say enough about her kind and loving demeanor. She had glorious dreams, one of which was to be a ballerina. She prayed to God every day that He show her a way to express His beauty through her movement. And she did, not just in her dance, but in her peaceful presence and love for all of God's creations."

Melissa listened with great interest; it was important that she portray the essence of Joanne properly in her painting. The priest was animated as he continued.

"As I spoke to her family, I was not surprised to hear that she was an A student and had many friends. Her infectious smile could lighten any room and made manifest the face of our lord. She was active in Ballet and was quite a competitor in school sports."

Why, why, why? Melissa wondered. She realized that there were as many reasons for being on the street as there were homeless people, but why Joanne? What was the answer to this problem?

"When Joanne's father died, she was hit hard. Every day she came in to pray and ask Jesus why He had taken her father away."

The moan of a woman came from the front row and Melissa could see her body shake.

"Her grief was strong and crashed in on her like a tidal wave. It seemed it was so severe that she stopped coming here for answers, and got to the point where it was too difficult to be at home. So she took to the streets."

The woman in the first row wept uncontrollably.

The priest paused for a moment and nodded his head in sympathy toward the woman, the lines of his face etched with sorrow. He continued, his voice a little stronger: "In her grief, she stopped her life of dancing, reading, and eating properly, but what never died was her commitment to God. In her state of depression we must understand the choices she made were not from sound thinking, and know that her deeds in this world are now being rewarded, as she is among the spirits of the saints; she has entered a glorified state. Let us pray for Joanne." The priest bowed his head, the light from the clear glass block splashing over his back, creating a glowing line around him. Everybody bowed as he recited verses from the Bible.

Melissa lowered her head out of respect. This was not her faith, and she had come here of her own accord, she would abide by their customs. She lifted her head slightly and peered at the people sitting in the front two rows from under her brow.

"… and God shall wipe away all tears from their eyes; there shall be no more death, neither sorrow, nor crying, neither shall there be any more pain; for the former things are passed away. And He that sat upon the throne said, Behold, I make all things new!"

The priest continued on with more passages and spoke of Joanne's contributions to the church and her achievements at school. Melissa watched the people. There were many in attendance, mostly young, students it seemed. Over a hundred for sure, she thought as she turned around to see many people behind her.

"Let us learn from Joanne." The priest held up a small statue of Jesus. "She placed this symbol of Jesus on her nightstand every night before she went to bed, but did not take it with her." His voice exuded an open fondness and his intonation was light, uplifting. "She left it for us, to let Him guide us. Let her be our teacher and give her early departure from this world, purpose. Be comforted by the fact that she is with Jesus right now, praying that we get through this most difficult time …"

*Where the hell was Jesus when Joanne was stuck in that bus shelter?* Melissa thought. *Damn, fifteen years old is too young to die.*

"Show people who have suffered great grief that you can rebuild your lives and come to terms with the loss. Let the grieving take its course and let us remember Joanne forever in our hearts and not allow this to interfere with our capacity to grow, learn, and, yes, experience joy!" There was a moment of silence. "She would want us to heal in that way." The priest crossed himself and stepped down.

It wasn't long before the front row began to clear, then the second, and third … until it came to time for Melissa to get up. They were stopped for what seemed like a long time, standing, waiting. The priest announced that everybody would have to be redirected out the back door as hostilities had commenced out front. The crowd changed direction. A line formed and started back toward the altar. It stopped again. Melissa was positioned beside the woman and man from the front row.

The man looked Melissa up and down and asked, "Who are you?"

"My name is Melissa, and you?"

"Edward Woodrow." He paused as if that meant something. "Joanne's stepfather. Did you know Joanne well?"

"We were becoming quite close," Melissa lied.

"You don't appear to be a street person or young enough to be a school friend." His eyes skimmed down her body, his head angling slightly to get a look at her bare legs. Slowly, his glance moved up and stopped at her breasts. "Are you a student teacher?"

She pulled her jacket closed. "No."

"How did you know her?" He stared into her eyes salaciously.

"I do a lot of work in the shelters—"

"Couldn't you see she was too young to be on the street?" Edward cut in. "Why didn't you call the authorities?" The anger in his voice seemed fraudulent somehow.

Melissa looked into his eyes and felt contempt for him right away. His posture of superiority did not impress her. "I think the question is, why was she on the street to begin with?" Melissa kept her voice low, but it seemed everybody around them was preoccupied with why the line was not moving and wouldn't have noticed them speaking anyway.

"She couldn't cope with the grief of her father dying. Did you miss the service?" Edward said, his tone imbued with sarcasm.

"No, I got it, I just—"

The woman beside him buckled at the knees and began to fall. He grabbed her and pulled her up. She cried hysterically. The line began to move. He looked back at Melissa with inquisitive eyes as he escorted the woman out.

Melissa walked on behind all the people and thought about Joanne. Things didn't seem to fit. As she walked out of the church she felt dirty somehow, like she had done something wrong. She pulled her jacket closer together and made her way home to get ready to go to her parents' house.

\* \* \*

Specimen trees, spaced just far enough apart so that the lush landscaping could be seen and admired, flanked the long winding driveway. John and Melissa got out of the car and walked up to the front door. Melissa loved her parents' house. It was perched gracefully on an elevated corner lot and was a blend of old world architecture on the outside and cutting-edge technology within. The exterior was a harmonious mix of brick, cedar shake, river rock, and stacked stone.

A servant greeted them at the door.

After taking off their coats, Melissa and John were directed through the main corridor. The ten-foot arches of the hall opened up to the over thirty-foot ceiling of the living room. The walls were imbued with tongue-and-groove paneling. Two wrought iron chandeliers hung from wooden beams and a hand-carved brick fireplace sat in the corner, emanating warmth. It gave a cozy feeling to this large area. Bold geometric patterns on a thick hand-woven rug covering the floor gave continuity to this space. Melissa and John eased onto a soft leather sofa.

John's pleasing, well-structured face was steeped with discomfort by the heavy expression in his blue-green eyes. Melissa locked her arm with his and rested her head against his shoulder, in thanks for his coming to Camille's birthday dinner.

"Dinner is served," said a man Melissa had never seen before. His shoulders were pulled back, creating a sharp, dignified form. He waited as Melissa and John passed by him en route to the dining room.

On the mahogany dining table was an Italian carved marble sculpture of Leda and the Swan. It was centered between a pair of Regency bronze candlesticks with white marble columns. Ten high-back chairs surrounded the table. Melissa thought about all the people who had been in this house as she was growing up: prime ministers, presidents, foreign diplomats, businessmen ... She was never impressed with their titles and even as a young girl did not like the way they spoke. It was nothing she could pinpoint other than that they never spoke directly about any subject. They spoke down to her, which she hated more than anything. But her father always made sure that she was at the table to eat with them even though her sister, or any other children for that matter never were. She thought that strange now.

"Come on, everybody, take your places." Melissa's mother stood by the head of the table.

A servant pulled out Melissa's chair and then John's. They sat. Melissa's father and mother, Philippe and Angeline, sat at the head and foot of the table and her sister Camille and her boyfriend, Dion, sat across from Melissa and John. The room was decorated with flowers, streamers, balloons, and colorful birthday greetings for Camille.

Melissa lifted her chin as a tapestry of aromas engaged her senses. The air was thick with jasmine and rose perfume worn by her sister. It reminded her of playing hide-and-seek in the summer garden. Camille and she would chase each other for hours, crouching, using the flowers and bushes as cover, and then jumping out at the last moment to scare the other one. They would laugh and laugh. Melissa's pores seemed to open as she could almost feel the warm breeze on her face as she ran. Often, to the heated reproach of the gardener, they would pull petals from the roses and taste them, like a velvet blanket spread across her tongue. Her mouth began to salivate. Fleeting scents of Peking duck caressed her memory until a door swung open. A servant, dressed in a plain black suit and pure white gloves, rolled in a cart of food. She was bombarded with a pungent fruity smell that momentarily arrested her thoughts. Another servant entered the room and they served the meal. John was last to be served.

"Oh, thank you very much," John said as a woman leaned over his left shoulder and placed a plate in front of him.

"So, John," Philippe looked in his direction, "are you still pumping gas?"

John looked at Melissa and raised his eyebrows as if to say, "See what I mean?" He turned and faced her father. "Actually, Mr. Belmont, you don't pump natural gas."

"You don't?" Philippe replied, his lips curved in an insolent, mocking smile. "Then what do you do with it?"

There was a pause, no noise at all. Everybody seemed to be keen for his answer.

"First I find the source, contain its energy, then systematically deliver it to areas that add value to people's lives." John stopped and continued to look directly into his eyes. "The same thing you claim to do with money."

Melissa watched John, who, before anybody else, began eating again. She expected some kind of smart remark. Her father was trying to make him look unworthy, but John had just scored big points. And not in her father's eyes.

Philippe shifted his head to the left and turned away from John. "Dion, any luck in the markets?" It was another question directed at Melissa, although Melissa knew that even Dion wouldn't be good enough for her in her father's eyes. And Dion didn't know it, but it was only a matter of time for him. Camille would be moving on soon, as usual at this stage of the relationship.

"Well, Phil, I've been dabbling with commodities lately and have done quite well. It's a matter of being patient, placing your stops properly, and acting at the right moment. But of course you have to understand leverage." Dion's confident attitude, his fluent silky tone and refined demeanor had not fooled her father for a moment, Melissa could see that clearly.

Her father looked at her directly, easily, as though his eyes were happy to have a break from everything else. He took a mouthful of food and chewed it without taking his glance off her. Finally, he swallowed and asked, "When are you coming back to the world you belong to? When are you going to stop befriending the bottom of the gene pool?"

Melissa shook her head, wanting to lash out at her father. She looked at John who was smiling while he continued to eat. *What would John say to that question? I know he's thinking something. I wish I was as quick-witted* ... She turned to her father. "I don't know. In order to have a better understanding of the universe, I was told in school that it's important to study the flaws of nature."

Philippe's brow furrowed and he truly seemed to have nothing to say, although it was evident that he wasn't pleased with her little joke or attitude. Melissa could feel her cheeks rise, but tried not to let her smile show victory.

Camille barely touched her food as she sat, waiting anxiously. Everybody had finished except her father. He ate slowly, chewing each bite numerous times. He would dab both sides of his mouth after each bite. Everybody sat patiently until he placed his cutlery parallel over his plate. Before the sound of the silver hitting the plate had faded, the door swung open and three servants came rushing to clear the table.

"Thank you, you've all done an excellent job," John said as a woman cleared his area.

"They're paid to do that." Philippe's eyes narrowed.

A man came around after the woman and filled John's glass with water.

John leaned back in his chair to give the man room. "An incredible job. I've never seen anybody as efficient as you. Keep up the good work." He patted the man on the back. He looked over to Philippe and grinned.

A woman rolled in a cart of dessert. Melissa looked at John and smiled, knowing what a sweet tooth he had. The tray was decorated with a kaleidoscope of patterns and colors. There was chocolate shaped as wrapped birthday gifts with candy bows; ice cream swirling in green, white, and blue cake; musical instruments made from mousse. They offered Philippe first pick, then his wife. John was last.

John smiled. "Did you make all these yourself?" He looked at the tray then up to the woman serving him. She did not respond. "They're wonderful. You're very talented." He took a dish off the tray.

They all ate their dessert without a word. Philippe again was the last to finish.

Camille clapped her hands together and her eyes lit up. "Is it time for me to open my presents?"

"Yes, sweetheart, you may open your presents." Philippe snapped his fingers. "Clifford, roll in the presents."

Melissa shook her head at the large array of presents that Clifford brought in. Camille tore into the wrappings and unveiled diamonds, gold jewelry, and priceless figurines. She began opening the present Melissa had brought. She excitedly unwrapped it. Her head shifted and she put her hand over her mouth. Her eyes thinned as if studying it. "Friedrich," Camille called.

The door swung open. "Yes, ma'am?"

"Hold this up so everybody can see." She handed him the painting.

Melissa sat, her back straight, looking at her piece of art. This light really emphasized the hues and tones. She was proud of her work.

Camille looked over the picture. It showed a sailboat sitting on a calm, star-speckled ocean with two whales swimming side by side in front of the boat. The waves flowed gently away from the mammals as they swam. A fine mist from their spouts reflected the moon over them, a symbol of freedom and love. "It's so … nice. Thank you, Melissa." Camille gave a sympathetic nod like she really wanted to be excited, but wasn't. "Just put it over there." She waved the back of her hand to Friedrich. He put it down and left the room. Snapping on her new gold bracelet, she held it out and moved it so that the diamonds shone in the light from the chandelier above.

John looked at his watch, then at Melissa. "Well, it's getting late, we should go."

Melissa let out a fake yawn. "Yes, I'm beat." Good call.

"So soon! It's still early." Melissa's mother looked at her watch. "It's only nine o'clock."

"I start work very early in the morning, Mrs. Belmont." John stood.

Philippe snapped his fingers.

Friedrich rushed into the room. "Yes, sir."

"Melissa and John are leaving."

"Yes, sir." Friedrich left the room.

They all got up from the table and made their way to the foyer along the gleaming oak plank flooring.

"You should come by more often. We hardly get a chance to see you." Philippe looked at Melissa.

Melissa leaned over and gave her father a kiss. Angeline walked over and hugged her. She held her tightly. "Yes, please come by more often. You look thin. Are you eating enough?" She smoothed Melissa's hair.

Friedrich entered from an adjacent room with their jackets.

"Yes mother, I'm eating fine." Melissa allowed Friedrich to slide her jacket onto her arms and over her shoulders.

"Why can't you come back and live here? There's lots of room. You could even use the guest house if you need your privacy."

"Mother, we've been through this before. I don't want to get into it again." Melissa looked over at her sister. "Happy Birthday."

Camille was holding Dion. "Thanks, Sis. See you later."

Friedrich opened the front door. Melissa waited for a moment, looking at John and then at her family. "Bye, we'll see you."

John paused for a moment as if waiting for her parents to say goodbye. Her mother rushed over and gave him a quick hug. "It's nice to see you, John." She returned to Philippe's side.

John turned and left the house. Melissa followed.

"Bye, sweetheart," Philippe said just as the door closed behind them.

John and Melissa made their way down the front walkway to where John's car was parked. He opened the passenger side door and waited for Melissa to get in. He walked around and got in himself.

"I don't know why you go through so much trouble to give your sister anything. She doesn't appreciate it." John looked toward Melissa while he started the car.

"Yeah, I know. I thought she'd really like this one. The last time I was there all she talked about was whales and sail boats." She shook her head. She could feel her voice quiver a little. "Camille doesn't mean to be hurtful ... and you must admit I had a lot of competition."

"Yeah, your father probably had Brinks deliver her presents to the house." John reached out and grabbed her hand tenderly. He pulled out of the driveway and started down the road. He looked over at her and smiled.

"What?" Melissa asked still feeling a little insecure.

"Flaws of nature. That was a good one."

Melissa laughed and could feel her confidence returning. "It's scaring me, I'm becoming more like you all the time."

"You can run and you can try to fight it, but once the seed is planted you can't stop the growth."

Melissa placed her hand on the inside of his leg, leaned over and kissed him on the cheek. "I don't want to fight it."

# Chapter 6

Melissa stared at the front page of the Toronto Daily newspaper. Beneath a picture of the Olympic symbols there was a caption: "World will have its eyes on Toronto." She read the article. It confirmed that there was a parade planned in April to demonstrate that Toronto was the best place to hold the 2008 Summer Olympic Games. The Olympic committee would be scrutinizing the plausibility closely. "Even the President of the United States would be watching this event," the journalist predicted in her article.

Melissa took a sip of tea while reading the newspaper in a soup kitchen. It was the first time she had been in any hostel or kitchen in over two weeks. No, not two weeks, it was longer. This was the time of year to paint. Actually, other than Camille's birthday party, and of course the funeral, she could not remember setting foot outside the apartment building. It had been so cold lately … She turned through the pages quickly when struck by the headline, "Bread Not Circuses" in which the article reproached Toronto for wasting money on the Olympic bid while people were starving in the streets.

"Hey, Melissa," a man yelled across the square room lined with bench tables. "How about sketching me today? I could use the five bucks."

Melissa looked up. "What do you need the five bucks for, Henry?"

Henry looked in both directions derisively and pulled out a poster from his jacket. "We're having our own little wake for Joanne," he whispered as he unrolled the poster, "and I need a little something to drink."

"That's Joanne?" Melissa shot up and hurried toward Henry.

Henry shook his head. "That's Joanne, all right. Look how beautiful she was." A tear welled in Henry's eye.

"Where'd you get that poster?"

"They were posted in many shelters the day before she died, then the day after, they were all gone."

"Gone where?"

"I dunno, one day they were there, the next they weren't," Henry replied shrugging his shoulders. "Except for the few I took." Henry looked fearfully around the room, like he had just robbed a bank, and pulled another poster out of his jacket and gave it to Melissa. "Here, Melissa, maybe you can draw her, or something."

She grabbed the poster. "Did you know her at all, Henry?" Melissa hoped maybe he could shed some light on her situation.

"No! You don't gotta know someone to have a drink for 'em when they die, ya know."

"Thanks, Henry." Melissa waved the poster and started out the door.

"Hey how about some money, Melissa?"

Melissa looked back and lifted her arms. "Never for booze, you know that, Henry."

Melissa opened the door of her apartment and immediately went to her easel. She smoothed out the poster of Joanne, seeing the unblemished, smiling face of a grade nine student, her lustrous, ash blonde hair pulled back into a French braid. Her mouth curled into a cupid's bow, drawing up her round firm chin, reflecting light off her prominent cheekbones. Her nose had a high, distinctive bridge tapering down to a button at the nostrils. Melissa looked sadly at Joanne. Beyond the picturesque, harmonious proportion of her facial features, that showed the innocent purity of an unspent youth, there was a look of isolation in Joanne's wide, circular eyes. Clearly, there was something deeply disturbing her. Was it only her father's death? She threw off her coat, thumb tacked the picture into the dry wall in front of her easel, and went to work on her painting. This one would require many renderings to evoke strong feeling.

Melissa was always eminently conscious of the form her ideas took. Shape, color, characters, even the presence of a seemingly unimportant fixture, everything had profound meaning and played an integral part of the whole.

She swept her brush across the canvas with diligent, fluent, strokes bringing out the wretched life of Joanne and the life that could have been. She felt a surge through her body. She looked up and smiled. "Of course!" she shouted to the empty room. "Yes, yes, yes, the parade. It's perfect!"

\* \* \*

Melissa was on a mission. Up University toward Queen's Park, she walked. Although nothing was confirmed, word had it that the parade would finish at Queens Park where a ceremony was being planned. She stopped at the two towers that mirrored each other just south of Pearl Street. Looking up, Melissa thought that these buildings must be fifty stories or more. She marveled at how clean they looked in design. They were cut in irregular shapes to break the boring straight-up-and-down look. It was almost as if cubes had been taken out, like an artist in the process of removing unnecessary material to expose the masterpiece that dwelled within. Lines cut through the buildings at odd levels; every second floor seemed to be higher than the one below. But it was the negative space between the mirrored buildings that created an interesting shape. It was always the negative space ... She walked north.

Stopping again, a building caught her interest. It was set on the northwest corner of Adelaide and University, a seven-story high abandoned apartment building. The brown-bricked structure showed, near the top in between two windows, a year engraved in cement: 1926.

It seemed odd that this building had survived so long in a place that had almost been completely refurbished with new structures that shot toward the sky. What a great city, Melissa thought. This building before her had character and strength, and was not dwarfed by these other buildings, but stood as the foundation of skills and knowledge necessary before they could be built.

The front door was open. Strange. She looked around and walked inside; the staircase in front of her was abnormally wide. It was the only way to get furniture up to the higher levels, she concluded, no elevators and small windows. The hardwood floors creaked as she trotted up the steps. From the seventh floor she looked out the window and thought, *this is perfect. I wonder who owns it ...*

A voice resonated behind her. "Who are you and what are you doing here?"

She swung around. "My name is ... Melissa." She could hardly speak.

The large dust-covered man came from a room across the hall. Melissa noticed that it was being stripped clean. "This is private property and you're trespassing."

"I just came to see if I could ..." She could feel her heart beating quickly. "I would like to know who owns this building."

"Why?" the man asked in a cool severity.

"I was just interested in finding out some history about it. I'm an artist and I'm doing some research." Melissa drew a deep breath and exhaled slowly. "What's your name?"

"My name is Steve, and you're still trespassing."

"Can you please tell me who owns this building?" Melissa kept her voice soft.

The man looked down with a slight squint. "The company is called Plains. It's based out of Mississauga."

She smiled. "And the owner ... ?"

"Matthew Sylvan."

"Thank you. I won't bother you anymore, you look very busy."

"Good," he said seriously, "I wouldn't want to have to get rough with you." His face was stoic, but a smile broke through his eyes.

She hurried back down the stairs.

Melissa found the address in the phone book at a booth just outside the building.

She made her way to John's apartment, borrowed his car and drove to the office building in Mississauga. She walked in to see people busy at work. The staff did not dawdle; they moved swiftly and surely. It was strange and exhilarating, she was not sure why. These people moved with calculated steps, their faces serenely intent, their backs straight and eyes confident.

Melissa stood there feeling energized and clear headed.

"Can I help you?" A woman lifted her head from the work in front of her.

"Yes," Melissa opened a piece of paper, "I'm looking for Matthew Sylvan."

She looked up at Melissa over the top of her glasses. "Do you have an appointment?"

"No."

"Well, Mr. Sylvan is a very busy man. I'm not sure he will be able to see you today. What's it about?"

"I'm an artist and I was hoping to get permission to use one of his buildings for a project I'm working on."

"He's up on the fifth floor." The woman pointed to the elevators. "You'll have to talk to his secretary, Suzanne, to make an appointment."

Melissa made her way to the fifth floor still strangely exhilarated from the mood in this building. Her energy was high and she felt like she could do anything. She was determined to see Matthew even if she had to wait all day. The elevator doors opened and she saw the same buzz of activity that she had noticed on the first floor.

"Yes, can I help you?" a young woman, maybe Suzanne, asked with a smile.

"I would like to speak with Matthew Sylvan, please." Melissa cast her glance upon the small brass nameplate on the desk: Suzanne Benton. Above, in a thin metal frame, were Suzanne and her young family, smiling, happy.

"I'm sorry, he's not seeing anybody today. What's it pertaining to?"

Melissa looked back into Suzanne's eyes. "It's about the building he owns on University Avenue in Toronto. I'd like to get permission to use it for a painting."

"I'm sorry, but he—"

An office door opened and a man walked out. He lifted the lid of a photocopier machine.

Suzanne leaned toward Melissa. "There he is now. If you're lucky, he's got something for me. I'll introduce you and then you're on your own." She paused. "You have no more than thirty seconds to grab his attention."

Matthew made a photocopy, slid the piece of paper in an envelope and made his way over to the desk.

"Good luck," Suzanne said.

Matthew was in front of Suzanne. "Out by four, please." He said nothing else and started to turn away as though he didn't even notice Melissa there.

"Matthew," Suzanne said. "Melissa here would like a minute of your time."

Matthew looked at his watch. "No, I don't—"

"This won't take long, Mr. Sylvan," Melissa cut in.

Matthew scanned her up and down. He stopped at her eyes, paused for a moment, then said, "Come in to my office." Suzanne nodded her head and smiled.

Melissa was impressed with his office. The big oak desk was clean, but looked well used. Renderings of buildings hung from the walls, some in the construction phase and some completed. Melissa felt that she could paint a picture of Matthew's building on University Avenue. It held such character. He needed an older building on the wall here. There was a spot where it would fit perfectly. She looked around the room.

"What can I do for you?" With a gestured of his hand, Matthew offered Melissa a seat.

Melissa sat. "I'm impressed with the way your employees seem so happy and confident. It's very rare. Not that I have that much experience in the workplace, being self-employed and all, but most people ..."

Melissa felt uneasy. Matthew's stony face looked right through her. "Anyway, I have a proposal for you."

Melissa waited for Matthew to ask what it was. He remained quiet, without expression. His penetrating gaze shot through her. She sat paralyzed looking into his midnight dark pupils. A great wall flashed before her mind's eye, then a young boy reaching out for warmth, affection and love. His face seemed made of concrete; concrete that had not quite set. There was a pale scar above his right eye.

"I'm an artist who needs to portray an idea." Melissa cast her glance downward. "What I want to do is paint a picture of Joanne, the girl who froze to death on the street ... Did you hear about that?"

Matthew nodded yes and said nothing.

"I do a lot of work with the homeless and hope this will be a way to raise awareness of their situation. Then I want to take the painting and drop it in front of the world while the Olympic-bid parade passes by. After it's done and this painting has been seen, which I think will lead to something positive, I will paint a portrait of any building you want for your wall here as payment." She gestured with her open hand at the wall. "I would recommend the one I saw today at Adelaide and University. It's a wonderful building, full of character." She paused, waiting for some kind of response. Nothing. He looked right through her without expression. She stopped speaking, her shoulders rolled forward, she curled her toes in and balled her hands together into fists. She was determined not to say another word until he spoke.

Matthew turned his head and looked out the window. His eyes squinted slightly. The silence made Melissa anxious. Her thoughts were racing.

"How large will the painting be?" He continued to look out the window.

"I'm thinking sixty by forty feet."

"With paint, material, and other supplies that will be a big project. Can you finance it?" He turned back toward her.

"Yes," she replied confidently. His voice made her feel more comfortable.

"How? Do you get government support for your work with the homeless?"

"No. I finance a hot line for people in distress." She eased back into the seat. "I've set up a soup kitchen, and I'm going to have flyers made up and distributed everywhere. I do this with the money I make from my paintings." Her back straightened and her chin rose. "I have an account that I plan to use for this project. I have more than enough money. I wouldn't need any help."

Matthew looked at Melissa directly. "I'm not sure—"

"I would take full responsibility," Melissa cut in. "It would be as if you didn't even know what I was doing. I'm not doing it to upset anybody, although I know it will ruffle some feathers. This is not to hurt anybody, it's to help."

Matthew's lips curled gracefully, compressing the shallow vale under his nose as two creases slanted out like wings around his mouth. His smile was like a cool breeze for the couple of seconds it lasted. "I have no problem sharing the responsibility." Matthew looked out the window again. He rubbed the bottom of his chin.

"So it would be okay?" She was surprised.

"Let me see some sketches and I'll let you know. Have you planned how to drop this painting? Have you got the proper mechanisms for it to work?"

"No not yet, but I'm sure I'll be able to get help there. My boyfriend is a gas fitter and knows all about mechanical things. He'll help." Melissa got up and extended her hand. "I would love to talk more with you, but I know you have more important things to do than to sit with me."

Matthew said nothing. Melissa felt uneasy again at the lack of emotion in his face. She left his office and smiled at Suzanne. "Thank you."

Suzanne smiled back and nodded her head.

Melissa felt a surge of emotions rush through her blood. *This is for you, Joanne.*

\* \* \*

The alley was dark and cold, with only the fixture from a building overhead casting diffuse light over Charlie. He wondered if he would ever sleep peacefully again; a thought that had plagued him many years ago when his beautiful visions turned into terrible realities. There was only one place he could live without contradiction.

Here on the streets his mental prowess would kill no one. With nothing to do but take care of his basic survival, Charlie found himself penetrating deeply into self-analysis. At first, minutes passed like hours, hours like days, and days like years. Every second week he would clean up into someone respectable and sit in the library from open to close, reading books on history, psychology, philosophy—everything but physics. He already fully understood the premise of physics and would not let those poorly written books obscure his clear thinking. Although, over the last few years, he did keep updated, via the Internet in the library, on the sorry state of a misguided science, to which only death and destruction could logically follow.

In all the cities he had lived, he liked London the best. Many more street people knew how to read. And the reading level in some! Charlie loved Russian literature. It brought him closer to his heritage. He discussed, at length, *Dead Souls* by Nilolai Gogol with a man who could barely find food. Then there was Dostoevski's *Crime and Punishment* debate. Charlie looked up at the building that seemed to narrow where it met the sky. The building was old and beginning to fade, like Charlie, but held a subtle power. It had stood the test of time. Charlie could feel time catching up with him.

His head sank and his body could hold off sleep no longer. His eyes closed and he began to breathe slowly and deeply. He was about to doze off, but shook his head and woke himself. He ran his hands over his tangled hair as a vision of the world being blown to oblivion flashed before his eyes.

# Chapter 7

"I have another test next week." John looked at Melissa who was studying some sketches. "I'm thinking that I really don't want to take it." He paused. "Actually, I've decided to quit my job and live on the street."

"That's interesting …" Melissa did not look up from her work.

*Only three weeks until this is over. I can hardly wait,* John thought.

They had both been so busy over the last two months, she with her painting and John striving for his next license. There had been little time left for their personal lives. The truth being, John felt Melissa was not taking into account all factors with this painting of Joanne. He had let her know his thoughts on the whole issue before she started. They didn't seem to matter. He could not remember the last time they were intimate together. Actually, yes he could. It wasn't long after Joanne died. Almost two months. It came back to him vividly.

John smiled in reflection. "I think I'm going home to finish my homework."

Melissa did not look up right away. It was as if John's statement took a moment to sink in. She looked at him. "Sorry, I haven't been very good company lately." Her face lengthened and her mouth and eyes sagged. "I'm just running out of time and I really need to complete this project. When this is done, I want to spend a full day with you and treat you like a king. Yeah, 'King For a Day', that's what you'll be!" Melissa smiled as though looking forward to that day. "You've been so understanding."

That was enough for John, the thought of Melissa treating him like a king set his thoughts overflowing. "It's a deal." He walked over to her and opened his arms.

She bolted up from her sitting position and embraced him affectionately. She shifted her head upwards, her mouth open slightly. Slowly, John pressed his lips against hers. He paused for a moment to take pleasure in the touch of her mouth. Her warm, moist lips were exquisite torment for the deep pleasure he so badly needed. He pressed harder and ravenously kissed her, his lips, tongue, and hands exploring the outer and inner depth of her beauty until the critical point where blood turns to fire. He pulled back. Holding her in his arms he felt her body loosen and melt. If he were to let her go, she would surely fall to the ground. She opened her eyes and exhaled.

"King for a day. I like that." John looked deeply into her eyes.

"Anything you want." She firmed her grip and embraced him. Her head rested gently against his chest.

"Okay, I'm going to leave before this gets out of hand and neither of us gets any work done." John gently broke her embrace. "I'll call you before I go to bed," he said as he opened the door.

"I love you." Melissa touched her mouth with the tips of her fingers as though something special remained.

"I love you, too." John left the apartment.

Melissa sat and picked up one of her sketches. It took a moment for her to remember what she had been doing. John's touch was powerful and she missed his compassion and affection. She had been so busy over the last couple of months that their relationship had seemed nonexistent. John was so wonderful, never trying to thwart her plight, but concerned, and expressive of those concerns. He just couldn't understand what she had to do. Melissa looked out over the lake and reflected on what had been accomplished in just over two months.

Matthew had sent a team to come and clean out the basement of the very same building her painting was to drop from. She was surprised that he let her work there. He also had a mechanism placed on the roof from which the painting would fall. That was done by the third week. By week five, Melissa had the canvas stretched, sewn in ten-foot squares, and ready to prime. Three passes of triple stitching, bar tacked at all stress points, with seam sealant applied to ensure integrity to the image being painted on its surface. It was expensive but Melissa would not allow shoddy prep work to distort this image. She washed a base of acrylic, a mix of black and white, over the finely woven linen material to seal and protect it. Weights were anchored to the base so the painting would descend dramatically.

Fifteen-hour days had turned into eighteen-hour days over the past three weeks. Outlining one-foot squares on the sixty by forty foot canvas, to mirror and enlarge the one-inch squares on her painting, was painfully time consuming.

Melissa stared at the sketch in her right hand and could not determine what was wrong with it. With her left hand strapped across her mouth, she massaged her cheeks as though the solution could be caressed to the surface. She shook her head and looked up. Shadowed images of the sketch clouded her vision as she looked around the room.

Her major concerns were subject, selecting a scene that would make the world think and feel, and style, how would she present this? She started with this premise, but continued to struggle with the overall theme keeping in mind that this was to be a work of art that heightened and emphasized Joanne's reality. It had to be clear, driving perceptions to the conceptual level. Awareness was the key, and if Melissa could put a vision into the heads of people with the power to make changes, then maybe it would start the ball rolling in the right direction. Change was not only possible it was necessary.

The phone rang. She could not believe it had been three hours since John had left. She had accomplished practically nothing.

She spoke to him briefly, then decided to go to bed. The softness of her pillow and the comfort of her bed eased her off to sleep. After four hours, her body bolted upright and her eyes shot open. She looked at her clock radio: 3 a.m. She rushed out of bed, ran down to her work area, picked up the sketch and said, "Yes, that's it!"

She marked up and erased images on the piece of paper. Her focus was strong and her intent clear. There was a strong foundation of skills beneath her and she felt she could only get better. Initially, it had been difficult learning her trade, as she remembered. The teachers, and even other artists, her father had hired when she was young had done little more than try to control her creativity. Yes, she agreed, it needed to be harnessed, but it also needed to breathe, to flourish.

By the age of eleven, Melissa had fired them all and told her father not to bother with any more, but she knew she needed more training. As important as it was for her to be original, in style and form, she had to go back to learn.

For five years, Melissa studied widely and intensively the work of the masters, and made familiar their modes of expression: Michelangelo, Leonardo da Vinci, Rubens, Van Gogh … Her father pulled her out of school and took her to museums in London, Paris, Glasgow, and many other cities, to sit and paint in front of the authentic pieces of art. Her portfolio had grown to well over fifty completed paintings. She was offered money for them, which she outright refused. And then, a "position" was offered, at age sixteen, to reproduce some more great works for commercial purposes. Without hesitation, she destroyed all of her copied work, save one, "Wheatfield with Crows." There was a connection, deeper than with the others, she got while working in Van Gogh's style. It was almost as if his energy was breathing through her paintbrush. All the others had to be destroyed because it was never her intention just to copy, but to acquire skills from the great ones themselves, through their medium, their vision. After attaining an intimate sense of their principals, she had found her own unique expression and a strong foundation had been set. There was only one more painting she had copied: "Potato Eaters," by Van Gogh. It was shortly after her friend Stephanie had died. Melissa looked over at that painting. It rested slightly above "Wheatfield with Crows" on the wall beside the bathroom door under the kitchen railing that separated the two rooms. Stephanie's face rose clearly in her mind. Why had she run?

On identifying that her mind was wandering and strong emotions were starting to surface, Melissa corralled her thoughts together and focused on the task at hand. There were three weeks left and that was plenty of time.

The painting of the canvas was about to begin. She was almost there. Melissa was happy with the work done in just over two months. She had hired three stagehands to help with the labor of the painting and pulled three styles from her foundation of skills to work from.

Rubens would help in areas that needed to be rich in glowing colors and vibrantly alive. That part of the painting would be fused through the hard lines of force and speed of futurism into the gray morbidity of Goya. Bringing all these styles together harmoniously was the key to turning this painting into the concept it would become.

An extraneous line projected out from the paper and stood before her like a cold sore on the Mona Lisa. The eraser met the impurity with three hard strokes. The back of her hand took away the rubber and her focus was again on the page.

Melissa had seen a completed product in her head before she started. She had made the necessary adjustments, and now sat on the edge of it becoming a reality. It was as if a force beyond her own had taken over and she became the means to carry out this project, the physical manifestation of an idea.

\* \* \*

*Got to get to the Plex before the parade tomorrow.* Charlie yawned, barely able to keep his eyes open. He felt he had been awake for days. *Just an hour or two, then I'll leave.* He sat between two tall buildings on University Avenue. Warm rain washed over his body as he thought about where he would spend the next week or so. Having all eyes on the city was unnerving. *Stay as far away from a centralized government as possible …*

The Plex was a place in Mississauga Charlie had gone when the driving force of inspiration could no longer be contained within his body. It was an out-of-the-way abandoned complex that gave him the privacy to work on his theories without being detected. In the eyes of the homeless he was a craftsman, in the eyes of the government a scientist. In his mind's eye he was both. He had found the art of science and the science of art and could deny neither.

His head fell forward into the palms of his hands. His eyes closed and he fell over onto the hard pavement. Pain radiated through his body as shock waves. A distant sound of metal striking metal echoed from somewhere. The sound became louder and the pain more intense as Charlie drifted through a mass of gray tissue, reaching the thalamus and then the pain spiraled down his spine. He could see the back of a girl. She was striking, with a long shiny metal object, the base of his tailbone. Dark mocking faces radiated as electrical impulses, immobilizing Charlie with excruciating pain.

The blonde-haired girl plucked the cords, creating a rhapsody of agonizing sensations. He screamed but made no sound. Just beyond his grasp, the girl remained.

She turned around. Charlie's heart stopped: Joanne.

"Why did you let me freeze? I trusted you …" Joanne's lips did not move, but her voice was unmistakable.

Everything faded to gray and then to black. "Jo, Jo, don't leave. I'm sorry I couldn't find you …"

Charlie could hear a muffling noise. He felt a poking sensation on his left side. This time it was external, traveling slowly, and was not painful.

"Come on you. It's time to go."

Charlie opened his eyes. His body twitched, his hands shook, and he was drenched in rain and sweat. A police officer was gently tapping him on the side with his baton.

"We have to get you out of the area for a while." The officer leaned over and helped Charlie to his feet. "You'll have a nice comfortable place to stay for the next thirty-six hours. It'll give you a chance to dry out a little."

"No, I can't go to jail, they'll find me." Charlie began to panic. He felt like he was still dreaming.

"I'm sorry, but I have to clear the area. You should have gone to a church or shelter where everybody else is. Well, mostly everybody else." He looked Charlie in the eyes. "You'll have some company. Some of your companions passed out too close to the parade route as well, you won't be alone."

"I promise to clear the area." Charlie pleaded. "Don't put me in jail."

"You'll be just fine. It will only be for a short time, and, hey, we'll even feed ya and get you some medical attention. It's for your own good." The officer escorted Charlie over to a wagon, opened the back door, and helped him inside. "Don't worry, we'll take good care of you. You'll have a soft place to sleep on and some warm food."

"Damn." Charlie sat on the bench beside three other homeless men. The place smelled like a distillery. He lowered his head into his palms.

# Chapter 8

April 13, 6 a.m.

The sun broke through the clouds. It could not have worked out more perfectly for the people assigned to clean the street for the big parade as the overnight rain had swept away the remaining winter crud. Melissa had walked along University Avenue yesterday to see swarms of people cleaning windows, replacing old garbage cans, and covering parking meters. The police were readying themselves to block off intersections and new lines were being painted on the road.

The exhilarating feeling of spring had arrived. Flowers filled the concrete barriers that divided the boulevard, and fresh scents of April filled the air. Melissa now looked at the building that her painting would fall from. She felt the warm breeze cut through her thin green shirt and she was one with nature, her spirit growing, extending. She closed her eyes, took slow deep breaths, and allowed the scents and sunrays to bathe her. The air entering her nose tingled, sensual, as if these beautiful plants were thanking the floriculturists for nurturing their growth. Mists of fragrance sprayed by the petals danced on the back of her tongue, subtle, fleeting. Upon opening her eyes, a mirage was waiting. The blue flowers seemed to be vanishing up between the clouds and into the pastel sky while the red ones tunneled toward her, past her sight and into her, causing a warming sensation to spread through her body. Her lips curled into a natural smile as everything came back into perspective.

She walked over to the building and made her way to the roof. It was important to get here early, before the police were out in full force. Seven stories over the city, Melissa felt powerful. The soft, turquoise and blue sky was broken by the hard lines of skyscrapers, and white billowy clouds drifted slowly across the horizon as images flashed through her mind. Photographs turned into moving pictures of chained homeless people evolving into confident value producers. A vivid evolutionary scene flashed open in her mind's eye and remained for her to analyze. Frightened faces on weathered bodies rose out of trenches of filth and garbage, and frame-by-frame, the people gradually stood upright, their faces smoothed, and their bodies strengthened. The momentum of their evolution, like a high-speed train pulling them in by its force, pulled other less fortunate people off the streets.

Melissa checked the mechanism that would release her painting and determined that everything was fine. She sat on the roof waiting patiently. It would be at least 6 hours before the entourage passed through. She thought about her friend in University, her only friend.

Melissa had met Stephanie in her first year. She was quiet, withdrawn, and difficult to get to know. Stephanie went about her work without a word, and had an easy, natural demeanor. Being an expensive university, about an hour out of the city, most of the students were concerned with outward appearances. The girls wore the latest fashions and the boys showed their wealth and muscle through fast colorful sports cars. Stephanie did not mingle with anybody and dressed down, almost slovenly. This intrigued Melissa, and she felt a bond growing with Stephanie right away. The school would have suited her sister Camille perfectly, had she chosen to pursue an education. Most students were imbued with superficial superiority.

After much verbal prodding, Melissa began to establish a relationship with Stephanie. She found her to be bright, fun, and showing the kind of caring and love she could not get from family. They spent all their time together, working mostly. Stephanie took Melissa's art to new levels. Before she had even thought about working with the homeless, Stephanie had created scenes, incredible scenes, of life on the street. The compassion and caring of her work had touched Melissa deeply.

As a credit course, they studied philosophy. They would sit up all night discussing politics, ethics, the depth of their souls. Melissa learned more in those discussions than throughout all of her schooling. Going back to school was not Melissa's first choice. She had all but given up on any type of formal education by then, but thought to give it another chance. It hadn't taken long to figure that she wasn't meant for that form of thought control and stayed only because of Stephanie. But as close as they had become, Melissa had always seen a distant look in Stephanie's eyes, a place she had not let her into.

Melissa and Stephanie became an object of ridicule throughout the University. They were unwilling to join any of the clubs, did not go to any parties, and generally avoided extracurricular activities. They didn't care, since they would change the world with their art. It had indeed been a long time since anybody pushed the envelope of society with breakthrough work. Even the professors gave them poor marks for not abiding by guidelines. Melissa remembered saying after a project, "My passion is not fueled by your opinion ... what great accomplishment have you achieved that gives you the right to judge me, anyway?" From that day on her work became deeper, richer.

She and Stephanie ate lunch together, went to movies, even double dated on a few occasions. They found the school a poor place to meet their match. There was nobody to look up to, no *one* to admire. They often spoke of their ideal man over wine and laughed at finding a needle in a haystack. Melissa never really understood friendship before she met Stephanie. Then one day in their second year, Stephanie stopped coming to school. No notice, no goodbye, nothing.

Melissa went to her residence and found that the few things Stephanie had, were gone. After all this time she didn't know where her family lived even though Stephanie had been to her place many times. She had never spoken of her family. It surprised Melissa to learn that Stephanie had won a scholarship to be at this school and came from a poor part of Toronto. Why hadn't she been honest? It all made sense to her then. The worn clothes, her not wanting to do things that required much money ... it didn't matter to Melissa, she could help. She looked up Stephanie's parents' address and went to tell her that their friendship was greater than any financial burden she might be facing.

On approaching Stephanie's home, she could hear screaming. Cautiously, she peered through the front window and saw a man and a woman fighting. Melissa ran to the pay phone across the street and called the police. She watched as an officer took away a scratched-up man in handcuffs.

"Stephanie ran away," her mother said while reproaching Melissa for meddling in something that was clearly none of her business. "She'll be back, she always comes back."

This disturbed Melissa deeply. Two months had passed and she was depressed. Then while walking in the downtown core one day, she saw Stephanie asking for money at the corner of Yonge and Queen.

"Stephanie?" Melissa asked, knowing it was her, but unwilling to believe it.

In slow motion, she saw Stephanie lift her head. All the noise of the city disappeared for Melissa. There was a connection so strong that it eclipsed all of her senses. In that moment, Melissa knew that there was a light so bright beneath that disheveled look, something so important. In a flash, the force was severed, the noise of the street returned, and Melissa's feelings broke the surface as a tear rolled over her cheek. Stephanie turned and ran the other way. Melissa ran and ran, even after she lost sight of her friend. Why did she run? Couldn't she see how important she was?

Immediately Melissa went to the police for help to track her friend down. Three days later an officer then, Terese Bolino, had notified her that her friend had been found in an alley off of Sherbourne Street. She had been stabbed twice in the stomach and bled to death. *You could have trusted me Steph, I would've understood. I was your friend ... I didn't mean to scare you even further into the darkness of the street.* Melissa sat hunched over her legs, her hands cupped under her chin. A single tear, holding a world of sadness, rolled across her cheek and over her lips, the salt stinging her tongue with guilt.

\* \* \*

Charlie was put into a holding cell with eleven other men. It was a good size room. Benches bolted to the bars, lined with thin cushioned seats, were positioned two feet off the ground. An officer brought the men some sandwiches, soup, and drinks. They had all been fingerprinted before being placed here. Just routine, an officer had said as he rolled Charlie's fingers over the thick black ink. He was given a physical, had blood drawn, and told he would have to wait here until the results came back in case medication was needed. Tuberculosis among the homeless was of imminent concern these days, the officer had said. Charlie felt repugnance toward the "for-your-own-good" lies as he sat in a jail cell. It was nothing more than a legal infringement of human rights because he and the rest of the people in this cell had no means to defend themselves. Initially, the smell of sweat, alcohol, and urine overwhelmed Charlie, but he soon became used to it.

The men gobbled their food as though they hadn't eaten in days. Charlie ate nothing. He sat on top of a bench staring fixedly at the door, waiting for the inevitable time when they would come and take him back. He looked around the room after lunch and noticed that all but one man had fallen asleep under the benches on the floor. Charlie's eyes became heavy, his head fell into his chest, and he drifted off into sleep.

\* \* \*

In a parallel I formation, 12 decorated motorcycle police officers rounded the corner at University and Front, their uniforms cleanly pressed, the polished bikes shining brilliantly. Melissa could see the sheen on their boots even from seven stories up. 3 p.m. *This is it,* she thought.

At a snail's pace, the motorcycles passed by. They were in front of a long float holding waving athletes and colorful Olympic symbols. Four police Trans Am cruisers maintained a close distance behind, demonstrating that security was strong, able, and plentiful. The media were out in full force. From where Melissa stood, she could see at least fifteen cameramen, some snapping pictures, others rolling film. Windows in the buildings across the street were filled with a cluster of people, all struggling to get a glimpse and holding up signs, welcoming the 2008 Olympics. There were a few protesters around that Melissa could barely hear, Anton's group, no doubt.

A wave of exhilaration rushed through her veins. Not yet, not yet. She held her hand on the switch to release the painting. Everything seemed to be in slow motion. She welled with pride at her accomplishment. This was her biggest moment yet. All the praise, adulation, and money made from her other work meant nothing now. This was what she had worked so hard for all this time.

Melissa looked intently at a line she had mentally marked as the point when she would release her work. It felt like years until the float hit the line, then it happened. She knocked the lever. It would not budge. "Ah, oh no!" With both hands, she pushed harder. It was jammed. She shook it repeatedly imploring it to fall, "Come on … come on!" The rain must have seized it. She smacked the back of her fist on it. Nothing. She turned and began kicking at the switch. Still, it would not dislodge. She stood up, trying to get more leverage, and kicked furiously as though fending off a vicious dog. The sound of the motorcycles was fading now. The float inched by in front of the building. Melissa scanned the roof to see if there was something, a rock, a bar, a piece of wood—anything! to knock the lever free. Nothing. Her heart raced and she could feel a spasm in her stomach. She took a deep breath, narrowed her eyes and raised her right leg up high, touching her breast. It was her last chance. With all her focus and energy, she came down hard. Her heel hit the lever and continued past as her left leg buckled at the knee. The momentum of her body followed the right leg and she could see the ground racing toward her. Out of pure reaction, her hands flew out in front of her chest. She crashed to the ledge and held tightly. Pain rippled outward from the vertical center of her body. The painting was falling.

The chain rattled like the anchor of a ship descending and the snap of the canvas when it stopped ripped like a sail caught in the cross wind of an ocean squall. Melissa pushed herself up.

Time stopped. There was no motion, no wind, no noise, and not one camera snapped.

The painting was breathtaking. Melissa knew exactly what they were seeing. The upper right section showed Joanne, bright eyes, rosy cheeks joyfully walking to school with a handful of books, her demeanor was radiant, one ballet slipper raised on a pointed toe. It took up the top quarter: ten by fifteen feet. The float, the main attraction of this parade, was directly in front of this painting, no more than fifty feet away. Joanne's pointed foot was suspended over a precipice, her head was held high, drawn toward a brilliant, shining star on the north corner. The shadowed image of Joanne escaping gravity and pirouetting toward the star was overpowered by the dark inevitable future. The brightness of the corner was drawn in by a dismal area, which spanned down the left side and took up the whole bottom except for ten feet. The darkness of that part took away none of the detail. Joanne fell over the edge and her image slowly twisted and turned down in a spiraling motion as though being sucked into a vortex. Pieces of her school uniform changed slowly to rags and brilliant colors changed to dull grays. She landed in a bus shelter where a suffocating cloud swirled in around it. The deep blue and purple cloud funneled behind the shelter, as though it had sprung from the center of the earth. Joanne was backed against the corner with her hands crossed in front of her body. Her head was tilted up and her expression exuded terror. The colors were deep and rich, the forms were perfectly scaled, and the image heart wrenching. The bottom ten feet showed an assortment of homeless people standing reverently, a silent salute to a fellow human being.

Pictures snapped, a quiet rumbling from the street below steadily became louder. Melissa stood with pride and elation. There was no pain now from falling into the building. She felt weightless, as though a gust of air had swept under her feet and lifted her from the roof. The float slowly passed. *The world could not so easily turn its head from this, she thought.*

Melissa took a deep breath. She was starved for oxygen. A murmur from the city below echoed between the buildings. She felt as though she had just reached the Summit of Mount Everest. All the noise seemed to come from a different world; a distant place Melissa had left behind as she transcended to a new dimension. Time cracked open, and she could see the way to the future as the energy of the universe swept through her body. Benevolence and love filled the planet.

From a distance, she could hear a door open and then shut. Gravity, a power she felt weakly in her elated state, became strong, forceful, grounding. Her arms were forced behind her back and handcuffs clasped around her wrists.

"Melissa Belmont, you're under arrest for public mischief and inciting a riot …"

The officer kept reading Melissa her rights. She could not hear anything clearly, only a muffling sound that seemed to come from somewhere else. She was in a daze as she, at that very moment, discovered and realized her greatest fear.

# Chapter 9

The rigid metal handcuffs around Melissa's wrists made her hands throb as she stood outside an unmarked door at the police station. She could not remember the ride there or her walk through the building. She was in a state of shock as she stood beside the uniformed police officer. He said nothing and looked angry. Thoughts flew through her mind one after another so quickly they were all a blur. She felt like she had just gotten off a dizzying ride at an amusement park. All that was left was the empty, queasy feeling in her stomach. She could not remember the last time she had eaten.

Terese Bolino took over for the arresting officer.

"Could you please take these handcuffs off me?" She was relieved to see Terese, her friend.

Terese turned Melissa around gently by her shoulders, and put the key in the handcuff lock.

A door flew open and Gerald stuck his head out. "Leave them on!"

Melissa looked at Terese. "Oh, no." She could feel the blood drain from her face at the unexpected sight of Gerald. This was not his office.

Terese directed Melissa into the office and stood off to the side. The phone rang. Gerald did not pick it up. He just stared at it. It continued to ring.

"Yes." He finally answered it. "No, sir." He rubbed his temple with his free hand. "But I couldn't … Yes, sir. No, my force is not to blame."

Gerald looked up at Melissa. He was furious. She had seen him angry before, she had made him angry before, but this was different. His eyes were on fire.

"Yes, sir, I will do that right away." He placed the receiver gently into its spot.

He stood there not saying anything for a moment, not moving, breathing deeply. There was a storm brewing, and Melissa was afraid.

He picked up the phone and threw it against the wall. It bounced and hit the floor. "Who the hell do you think you are?" He raised his finger and pointed it at Melissa. "What exactly were you thinking? You've done some stupid things in the past, but this one …"

"I just thought—"

"Quiet." His voice resonated through the office. Melissa felt that the people outside could surely hear him. "Do you know what you've done with this little stunt here?" His eyes flashed as his heavy fist came down on the desk, jostling its contents. Melissa felt for sure it would collapse from the force. He took a deep breath. "Did you ever stop to think why the story of Joanne did not make front page to begin with?"

Melissa's knees fell together, her head sank. It was everything she could do to maintain composure. This wasn't really happening. She wouldn't cry.

Gerald took another deep breath, and again Melissa felt the tempest brewing. He lifted his head, walked to the window, and kicked the phone against the wall. "Not only have you jeopardized my job and the jobs of people below me, you've made a mockery of my station. My people worked night and day to get that area ready and give this city a fighting chance at this bid. They did a superb job, but that will not be noticed now. They worked hard only to be undermined by a naïve, selfish girl who showed zero respect for their livelihoods and safety. Was it your intention to start a riot? Are you teamed up with Anton Strand now?"

He stopped speaking for a moment, looking intensely at Melissa.

"No! I wouldn't—"

"Quiet! You will not speak, you will listen!" Gerald paced back and forth, becoming visibly more upset. He went to kick the phone again, but stopped himself. His anger seemed to hit the threshold of restraint and intractability. He turned and pointed his finger at her. She felt a surge of energy pass through her heart, and she stood unable to move. Her body was numb.

"You realize that you'll probably be sued for this stunt. Do you think the Woodrows are going to take this lying down? You've plastered their little girl's face all over the world. They went to great lengths for the media not to release her picture, do you think they'll be happy about this?" Gerald shook his head. "I've let you get away with a lot around this city, mostly because your intentions are good. Damn you for disrespecting me that way! I've always been fair with you." He balled his hands into fists. "For once I thought you were going to stay silent. I thought, wow, what a nice surprise, she must see the magnitude of this event and what it means to everybody involved. Boy, was I wrong about that, and you. My people deserve acknowledgment for the incredible job they'd done." He dragged both of his hands across his face as though he was trying to pull the skin away. "You know, in any other country you'd have been shot off the roof before the painting finished dropping." Gerald shook his head. "The way that thing snapped ... Jesus Christ, Melissa! What if one of my officers had shot you, thinking it was an attack?"

Melissa felt as though she was going to fall over. There were a million things going on in her mind and she felt terrible. It was true, he had always been supportive of her. Had she really incited a riot? It never crossed her mind that she could spark the fuel of violence.

"From now on this station and my officers are off limits. If I catch anybody even thinking about helping you in any way, he or she will be suspended immediately. Providing I'm still in charge." He looked at Terese, paused to make sure she got that last message, and said, "Take her down and lock her up."

"But, sir—"

His face turned a deeper shade of red.

Terese tried to continue. "Do you really think we need to—?"

"Are you disobeying an order?"

"No, sir." Terese took Melissa outside the office.

They walked down to the corridor, out of sight of the officers that were working at their desks. They stopped in the hallway.

"Could you please take off the handcuffs?" Melissa asked in a stern voice, as if she was still strong.

Terese moved around to the back of Melissa and took off the cuffs.

"Am I going to jail?" Melissa lifted her chin high.

"Everything is going to be okay. Wait here for a moment."

Terese made her way back to the office. Everything was silent when suddenly the door flung open. Gerald came rushing out toward Melissa and grabbed her by the arm.

His strong hand was squeezing tightly and she felt a surge of pain down the bone to the tips of her fingers as he ushered her into the open elevator. She could feel tears well in her eyes, but not one fell. "So now I have to reprimand Terese, for not following orders." He pushed a button in the elevator and it began to descend. The doors opened and he shoved her out.

He took her down a corridor of holding cells. He stopped in front of one.

Looking down at Melissa he said, "You have so much sympathy for your homeless friends, why don't you socialize with them tonight? I'm sure they'll be happy to see you." He slid a pass card through a scanning machine and a door opened to a cell lined with bars, directly beside one filled with men. He shoved her inside.

\* \* \*

Melissa could not stop trembling. Watching the door close, she began to feel lightheaded, as though she needed oxygen. With a deep breath in, she turned around and was immediately hit by the most noisome smell she had ever experienced, her eyes watered and her stomach turned. The noxious stench of alcohol and body odor seemed to permeate her whole body, as if it had found a home in her senses. She tried to breathe through her mouth but the taste of the air was worse than the smell.

Melissa looked around and felt confined, empty, a lonely spirit trapped. The padded benches were uncomfortable and the bars surrounding her seemed to be closing in. The men in the next cell sleeping under the benches snored. Taking a couple of deep breaths of air might stop the shaking, but would surely induce vomiting. Her heart slowed a little and she scanned the next cell with dismay.

There was one man lying on top of the bench, asleep but twisting and turning. One man was sleeping upright with his head tucked into his chest. He was motionless. The rest were fast asleep under the benches. The only signal that they were still alive was the motion of their bodies taking in air and the snoring.

Maybe her father was right she did not belong with these types of people. It was all too clear now. What had she done? Who was she saving? *I should have listened to John.* She looked around. *I would give anything just to smell Camille's perfume and to feel the smoothness of a satin blouse.* She took a breath and almost choked. As she looked down at a man who was sleeping on a bench directly beside her cell, she noticed a big cockroach crawl out from his jacket, across his face, and scurry along the floor. The man flicked at his face, but did not wake up. The roach ran into her cell, across the floor by her feet, and into the next cell.

Melissa jumped, and her whole body tightened. She wiped down her legs, across her stomach, breasts, face, and hair. She felt like a million insects were roaming her body. Her skin crawled. She could hardly breathe as she backed her way against the opposite bench. Without thinking, she turned to run. Her hands flew up to stop her from walking into the barred door. She clutched the cold metal and one thought, the core of her insecurity, hung in front of her clearly. It was the root of her fear.

A Sumatran tiger stood in her mind's eye, majestic, agile, powerful. Ever since she was young, she had loved tigers. They stood for everything she was: solitary but never alone, independent, strong, sleek. They hunted their prey, killed and ate with guiltless ambition. Hunger was the fuel that drove them steadfast toward their goal. It was an innate ambition independent of feeling. Desire was Melissa's fuel. Desire to succeed, desire to be the best, desire to pull people up in her wake so that they, too, might experience the best within themselves.

The sign was as clear in her mind today as it had been in grade seven: "Sumatrans." It had been her first and last visit to the zoo. Her heart raced at the memory. She had wondered if she would be able to contain her feelings as she looked into the eyes of her most revered counterpart.

On first sighting, he was lying down facing the other way. His body muscle-bound, his paws like huge thick mitts meant for a giant ... He rose and paced the enclosure with strong, lithe strides. The movement gave Melissa goose bumps, her shoulders automatically mimicking the easy cautious flow of the animal. She felt light, powerful. She opened her hands into claws, stretching them wide, moving them in large circular patterns, and then tapering down to the tiniest of orbits. An enemy would be extinguished on contact with the life force around her axis. She narrowed her eyes and looked through the tiger's eyes, the brightest of all: the blaze of awe-inspiring intensity. She willed it to turn around so that she may see his face, and him hers. It took five minutes, then he turned showing his large head, the distinct lines on his face and the unique markings above his eyes, like fingerprints showing individuality, character, strength; whiskers that showed this killer animal had the sensual response of keenness, of awareness, of Melissa.

Her heart palpitated as she looked in his eyes. She did not see the magnanimous glare of the most beautiful animal alive as she had expected, she did not see any life at all. She could not determine the look at first.

The animal roamed around the enclosure, sniffing quickly at a hunk of animal flesh that lay on the ground as food. He pawed it, moving the piece of carcass about a foot, then looked at it without interest and fell onto his side. He looked up at Melissa with sad eyes, as though someone had cut him open, took out his heart, and left him to live. The basic instinct of survival was not there. Melissa felt that it was a tragedy and a horrible dereliction of duty to extinguish the magical fire in any great spirit.

With her hands gripping tightly to the iron that enclosed her, she was open to the same fate as the Sumatran. Her freedom was lost. She turned at a noise from the next cell. The old man sitting upright began to move.

His body shook and sweat poured down his face. He remained asleep. Melissa had had the same ominous feeling before Gerald blew up at her.

The old man's eyes flew open. "No! Stop, please stop!" He looked around the room, halting abruptly when he saw Melissa in the next cell.

His wild green eyes were filled with violent fervor, surrounded by orbs of white flames that made Melissa's heart skip a beat. She tried to back up, but realized she was already against the back of her cell. His heavy, gaunt face and sharp features held power. An unkempt gray beard surrounded the lines of his mouth.

"What are you doing here, Child?" His voice was venomous.

Melissa bowed her head. "I've ... I," She looked up, "met you not long ago. I don't know if you remember. My name is Melissa."

"Of course I remember. You think that because I'm a street person that I drink, or is it just that you think I'm stupid?"

"No, I didn't mean anything by—"

"You know nothing, Child." He looked at her with piercing eyes.

"Stop calling me child, I'm an adult." She felt uneasy saying that, but it just came out. "What's your name?" He flinched. "Well?"

"Charlie." His head sunk and his eyes became distant.

Melissa moved slightly away from the wall and felt a strange curiosity building within her. He drew inward, and this pulled Melissa closer.

"How long have you been living on the streets?" Melissa tried to keep her voice from shaking.

"A long time," he replied, his head still sunken.

Melissa looked around at the other people. They were still sleeping. She did not notice the smell as strongly anymore and felt a strange magnetic pull toward this wretched man.

Charlie looked up. "You must have done something terrible to be in here with us, Child."

Melissa backed up. "Yes, I dislodged a painting while the parade was traveling along University Avenue. My vision did not encompass this, though." She looked around the room.

"A painting of what?" Charlie lifted his head.

"I had a vision ..." Melissa's eyes lowered and her mouth crimped. "I get visions, I see things already put together like ... you wouldn't understand. It's like I work backwards with information." She looked at

Charlie expecting some kind of reaction. His eyes creased knowingly. They were deep, and arrested Melissa's thoughts. She momentarily forgot what she was saying. "Uhm ... oh yes, anyway, I thought it would be a good opportunity to help the homeless by exposing the streets, not the clean streets that they had worked so hard to impress with, but the real streets with real people who need help."

"What do you know about helping the homeless?" Charlie shot back.

"I do a lot of work helping ... I thought you would know of me." She felt upset that he would ask such a question. He should be thankful for people like her.

Charlie pointed his finger at her. "I know of you, and you are no better than the government who throws us scraps to feed on while feeding off the rest of society."

Melissa did not know what to say. He could not be further from the truth. She really had made a difference, and did it without public money. "That's not true. I've helped many people. I sell my paintings to fund a hotline and soup kitchen—"

"When you're done patting yourself on the back, look at yourself." He studied her reaction with a critical squint.

Melissa looked down. "What?"

Charlie shook his head. "You've backed yourself against a wall, you're shaking like a leaf, and you would never touch a dirty, smelly homeless person with a ten-foot pole. Even with a wall of bars between us you feel endangered." He pointed to the people under the benches. "You keep us away at arms length, or pencil length, never touching because you belong to a different class. You're high society, and think you're doing some great service by bestowing your insights upon the world," There was a brief pause, "showing them how clearly you see the bottom of the food chain!"

She remembered what her father had said, "Bottom of the gene pool." *No, that's not how I think.* She tried to firm her stance and look self-assured in her surroundings.

Charlie shook his head and said insolently, "You're only fooling yourself."

"Have you ever seen my paintings?" she replied, meekly.

His mouth contorted in annoyance. "See, that's exactly what I mean. No, I haven't. The street people, you may be aware, don't socialize with the high society people who buy your paintings. I've not met anyone who's seen any of your work other than rough sketches." He stopped. "Why isn't any of your work in kitchens or shelters? Even today, that painting wasn't meant for the homeless."

"Most of my work is extremely valuable and …" She noticed a disbelieving smirk cross Charlie's face and could not finish her statement.

"And there's the double standard. We're good enough to portray, but not good enough to see ourselves. You should be asking permission to paint these people. You exploit the homeless because most are not educated enough to know that the ones portrayed deserve more consideration than an extra bowl of soup." His tone was even, cutting. "You're worse than the government. Did you get permission to paint the people you portrayed today in front of the whole world?" He paused for a moment. "I didn't think so. Who was it? Stan, Jake, Fred?"

This hurt her deeply, too much for one day. She felt weak, the foundation of her emotional structure about to collapse. Everything was wrong all of a sudden. "No, it was Joanne, a girl who—"

Charlie's back straightened and his fist slammed against the bench. "Who the hell do you think you are? It was not for you to expose her—"

"I know, I know! I don't need to be told again. I'm sorry." Her posture firmed and she could feel the rage burning through her body. "I can't take anymore today!" she yelled. "It wasn't malicious! Please show me some compassion. Have you never made a mistake?"

Charlie's head fell into his hands and he began to weep.

Melissa did not know what to do. This was completely unexpected. Slowly, she walked closer to Charlie's cell. He continued to cry as his body convulsed.

"I'm sorry, Jo Jo." Charlie's face lifted toward the roof and he let out a sound like nothing Melissa had ever heard, as if there was somebody else inside of him yelling to get out.

"What, who … ?" One of the men under the bench woke. He looked at Melissa. "An angel, the Lord has sent an angel." He smiled, rolled over and went back to sleep. Some of the other men stirred but did not wake up.

"It's okay, Charlie, it's okay." Melissa tried to keep her voice soft, reassuring.

"I don't need your consolation, Child."

"I'm sorry for your friend. I was trying to show the world the tragic death of a young girl with my painting."

"How would you know that tragedy?" He dried his eyes with his hands.

"I don't, but not so long ago I had a friend who died on the street that I had no idea was being forced to the street. Had I known, I could have helped. She had run from an abusive home. I want to raise awareness so that people who care, can help." Melissa stood in front of Charlie, feeling more secure with herself. "I didn't know Joanne or exactly what had happened to her, but—"

"That's right, you didn't," he said, his tone low, deep. "And her beauty had already been exploited enough. You had no right to that because of some kind of philanthropic need you have to salve your conscience." He stopped.

She looked into his eyes and a feeling of realization ran through her veins. "Exploited, how? You know what happened to her, why she ran, don't you? It wasn't because of her father dying, was it?"

Charlie continued to look at her, and in those eyes was information. He did not combat, deny, or acknowledge Melissa's questions. But he knew. She was sure of it. "You have to come forward and tell what you know," she implored.

Melissa's cell door opened and Terese walked in. Charlie froze. His body did not flinch but he looked frightened.

"Let's go, Melissa, you've been sprung." Terese gestured toward the door.

"You have to tell, for Joanne." Melissa opened her hands beseechingly.

"I can't, I ..." Charlie's head fell into his hands almost as though he was trying to hide his face.

"Come on, Melissa, let's go." Terese grabbed her gently by the elbow and escorted her out of the cell.

"I have to see him again. When are they being released?" Melissa asked.

"Melissa." Terese looked seriously into her eyes. "No more today."

Melissa bowed her head and crossed her arms in front of herself. "I really am sorry to cause so much trouble." She looked up at Terese. "What's going to happen to me now?"

"I don't know yet. I'm to tell you not to go far, charges are pending. Don't worry, he'll get over it, just stay low for a while."

"Thank you for staying in Gerald's office with me. Oh, why am I being released so soon? I expected to be there for longer than I was. Was it my father?"

"No, actually, the Chief had second thoughts about leaving you there. Once he had cooled down a little he realized he'd made a mistake."

"It was my fault, not his," Melissa acknowledged.

Before leaving the station, Melissa took a deep breath, ready for the flood of reporters. She raised her confidence, held her head high and walked out the door: nothing. Strange, but she knew they would be waiting for her at her apartment. She flagged a cab and made her way home, going over in her mind what she was going to say.

As she got out of the cab, reporters and cameras swarmed her. She smiled. Most would be clamoring for a sensational story. Melissa knew to be direct, not say too much because long statements could be spliced to say something totally different from what she meant. There would also be manipulators there who would try to elicit a response that would be harmful to her cause. She was totally surrounded, microphones shoved close to her face. She took a deep breath and relaxed. They would not be able to rile her, and she would make this short. A vision of her bathtub, some relaxing classical music, and candles rose to life in her mind. That was her goal.

"Melissa, is it true that you were arrested and locked-up with homeless men?" a reporter Melissa liked asked.

"No, George, that's not true." It was beside them, she thought.

"Melissa." A small weasel faced man barged through the sea of reporters and inched his way closer. "I have it from a reliable source that you were locked up with other men and sexually assaulted."

Melissa looked down at this man and laughed. "Stop mixing your fantasies with my life."

"Oh, very good, Melissa. Is it safe to say that you dropped that painting in response to something that had happened to you? A form of vigilantism?"

Melissa was calm, but serious. "Listen, unless you have some relevant questions, step aside." She wanted to say more but would not add fuel to this potential fire.

"What were you trying to say with your painting?" a man asked, Melissa could not tell where from.

"I wasn't trying to say anything. I just wanted the world to see the whole of our great city. This is a wonderful caring city, but there's a problem, and it's as much our responsibility as citizens to help, as it is the politicians. This painting was meant for everybody. It was nothing more than a magnified view of the way some people live and die in Toronto. In my experience with the homeless, I've discovered an array of issues, and feel that any one of us is potentially only one step away from that fate. Life can take cruel turns. Awareness and understanding are important." Melissa wanted to continue but that was already too long for one breath.

"Are you saying you weren't arrested?" A voice echoed through the crowd.

"I went down to the police station of my own accord and was treated with due respect," Melissa answered.

"Are you a part of the Coalition Against Poverty group headed by Anton Strand?" a reported shouted out.

"Absolutely not! I am not at war with anybody, and the painting was strictly of my own doing. I do not condone or support initiated force by any group, against anybody. Okay, one more question, I'm very tired."

Wally barged through, but another reporter headed him off and asked, "What's your real motivation behind this homeless crusade of yours, Melissa?"

Melissa placed her hand to her face and thought for a moment. "I think there are great spirits living on the streets that don't know how to rise above that environment. In a lot of ways it's like falling into a deep well and nobody noticing you're there. With the technology and information available, not one person in this whole world should die because basic human needs weren't met. There are many problems in the world, but none more important than saving human lives." Melissa smiled. That was a good message. She parted the reporters with her hands. "Excuse me, everybody, I'm very tired." She opened the front door.

The door closed and Melissa was out of the chaos. The sight of her apartment as she walked in held a healing comfort. She looked up at the kitchen landing. Through the black metal railing, the yellow on the cupboards sparked a creative desire in her, but rest was paramount, and the Japanese design on the rice paper partition above the cupboards seemed to be saying, "Your bed is here waiting for you." What a great place to live, she thought. It would now be her oasis for the next few days. She entered the bathroom that was under the kitchen and started a bath. She checked her messages: twenty-three. The first three were from talk shows or reporters. The next twenty she deleted.

# Chapter 10

Heat radiated through the front window of the van, warming John's face. The van was parked at a strip plaza on the east side of Toronto. John and his helper were waiting for their next assignment. They had just finished doing a service call on a gas pool heater. John's helper, Brent, was seventeen years old and had quit school last year. John was teaching him the business. School had been difficult for Brent, but here in the gas trade he did well. It seemed he had a ready facility for mechanical things and he was strong, ambitious, but most importantly, excited to learn.

John's beeper went off. He pulled it from his belt and read the message. His eyes narrowed. "Looks like we're going to Mississauga." He looked at his watch.

"Mississauga, why are we going there?" Brent asked.

"I don't know, exactly." John clipped his pager back onto his belt and shrugged his shoulders. "But we go wherever they send us." John started the van and looked at his watch. "Well, it's at least a thirty minute drive. We have time to study."

Brent pulled out a book from under the seat and opened it. He asked John questions along the way, but John was not paying much attention. He hadn't seen Melissa in over a week and she hadn't returned any of his calls. Maybe she had gone to her parent's after dropping the painting. Still, she should have let him know that she's okay.

The address they were assigned was not far off the highway on a dead end street. John pulled the truck into an apartment building and waited. A pickup truck pulled in. A man got out and walked toward them. John stepped out of the truck to meet him.

"Hello, my name is Hayden. I take it you're John." The man extended his arm.

John shook his hand. "Yes. This is my partner, Brent." John called Brent his partner because he knew it made him feel important.

Brent was just making his way around the front of the van. "Hi," he said confidently.

"This is what we need done." Hayden pointed past the apartment building to two older five-story buildings enclosed in a chain link fence. His tone was quick and businesslike. "We need all the gas piping and heating equipment removed. So have a look and give us a quote. The gas company has already been and disconnected the service." Hayden reached into his pocket and pulled out a set of keys. "This master key will get you into all units except one: 15. You won't need to go in there, just yet, anyway."

John did not take the keys right away. "I have a question before we go any further. Why did you call me? There are plenty of good companies in Mississauga that are closer. Travel time would've been cheaper if you had called one of them." John raised his eyebrows.

Hayden smiled. "I know, that's what I said, but my boss wanted you. So I got you here. Your dispatcher said the same thing." He shrugged his shoulders. "When you have an estimated price, you're to set up an appointment." He reached into his pocket, pulled out a card, and handed it to John. "I have to go now. See you later."

John was curious about this whole situation. He looked at the two older housing units set in behind this new ten story red-bricked apartment building. A metal sign had fallen sideways and was swinging, holding precariously to a gate. It said: The Plex.

"Whatever." John opened his hands and smiled at Brent. "Never turn down work."

He opened the side door to the van, pulled out a tape measure and a note pad from the wooden shelves he had built inside. John had organized his truck in a way that tools and supplies could be easily found and time would not be wasted on looking for things. He locked the door and signaled Bent to follow him. He looked at the card Hayden had given him. It was a plain white card with simple block letters: the name Matthew Sylvan was in the center, a phone number in a slightly smaller font sat in the bottom right corner.

\* \* \*

Melissa stared out her window. It had been three days since her arrest. Her body was sore and her emotions drained. Looking out the window over the lake, with its waves rolling over onto each other, rising and sinking, Melissa rested, allowing the tranquility of the apartment to rejuvenate her.

She had called the police station and confirmed that Charlie had been released. There was something uniquely different about him for a street person, no, not only for a street person, just something different. He spoke well and was obviously educated. So why was he on the street? She thought of Stephanie and how she, too, was incredibly bright, and Joanne ...

Melissa's thoughts returned to Charlie, his face illuminated clearly in her mind. Worn, weathered, and full of dark clouds; his eyes piercing, sunken deep behind his high cheekbones; his mouth a sheath to hold his sharp tongue. Melissa threw her jacket on and started out the door. The phone rang and, for the first time in three days, she answered.

It was John. She had not spoken to him since ... she could not remember exactly. It was at least two, maybe three, days before she had dropped the painting.

"Is everything all right? I heard—"

"Yes, I'm fine, John. Just tired, that's all," Melissa cut in, trying to shorten the conversation.

"I saw your painting. It was incredible. I tried calling you. I even left you a couple of messages. Were you at your parents'? I would have called there but—"

"No, John, I was home. I just needed a couple of days alone to think."

"I'd love to see you. I was hoping to come over," John said. "I really miss you."

"Actually, I'm just on my way out. Maybe tomorrow we can get together."

There was a long pause before John replied, "Call me when you're free."

She said goodbye, hung up the phone, and walked out the door.

The East Street shelter looked different to her this afternoon. It was as if she understood things more clearly. She could not determine what it was, but she had more appreciation for it somehow.

"Hey, Melissa, how's 'bout sketching me today?" Jake asked, breaking her train of thought.

Melissa looked over and smiled. He would be perfect for a painting. His socks were mismatched, one pulled up straight, the other one a different color and hanging loosely around his ankle. His clothes were baggy and dirty, his face covered with a scraggly beard. But he had a distant majestic look in his eyes as though at one time in his life he had commanded a platoon of soldiers into a battle field, no, he had sailed a ship, an ancient ship, a Viking ship ... Melissa shook her head. "Not today,

Jake." She opened her purse, took out a five-dollar bill, and waved it in the air.

Jake quickly made his way over and snatched it out of Melissa's hand before she had a chance to change her mind. He looked at her inquisitively. "That's it? I don't gotta to promise I ain't gonna buy no booze?"

Melissa restrained herself. "You know what, Jake, you're a grown man. You decide what you want to do with it. I hope you don't buy booze, but it's your decision."

Jake left the shelter. As he was walking out the door he turned back and looked at Melissa with a blank stare. She maintained her smile and waved.

Melissa did not feel like being here. She needed a nice place to go, a place where coffee was extremely overpriced.

As she made her way to Swaltzers her mind was preoccupied with finding Charlie. There were so many questions that plagued her. He had information about Joanne, why had he not come forward? What was stopping him? He obviously had cared for her a great deal. Why would he not want to do anything he could to help clear up why Joanne had run to the street? The warm breeze felt good against her skin as she walked, and she could feel her nostrils automatically expanding with the different scents of spring. There was still a sensation where the handcuffs had restrained her wrist. She waved her hands to feel the freedom of her arms.

Melissa opened the door to the cafe and walked in. She was immediately bombarded with an array of bittersweet coffee aromas that made her mouth water. Digitally synthesized African music played, filling in the space around her. The walls were splashed with bright colors, three foot stools lined a thin mahogany counter, which looked out onto Yonge Street, private booths for two were set along the closed-in wall, and teas and coffees from around the world were served in oversized cups. She ordered a green tea and took a seat in front of the window.

Her thoughts drifted without order or conscious effort. The rhythmic beating of the drums mixed with tribe-like chanting channeled a path directly to her subconscious. It felt good to have no deadlines. People gathered around in front of the window. It did not strike her as strange at first. She was comfortable and relaxed, drifting between thoughts that rose to life in her mind. Subtle abstractions appeared frequently. It was unnecessary to pull them down and make them concrete, she was happy in just a relaxed state. Somehow, her true self was in-between those thoughts ... She snapped out of her trance and realized something extremely disconcerting was going on outside. Quickly, she made her way out the door and past the onlookers.

A man of no more than thirty-five stood on the street corner, his hands moving frantically, as though a swarm of bees had clustered around his head. He fell to the ground recoiling in horror. His hair was shoulder length and fell in front of his eyes, his body rocking back and forth as though movement would save him. He had nothing on except an old ragged pair of underwear, which hung around his hips by a thread. He was speaking poetically to himself. Reciting scriptures, Melissa thought.

The man leaped to his feet and pointed to the crowd. "Stay away, or they'll get you, too." He swiped around his head. He turned to Melissa. "You! Stay back." His head shifted up, down, sideways, in sporadic whips. His eyelids were open wide showing panic, as though he was being terrorized by some inner demon.

Melissa backed up a little but remained focused on this man. She was only ten feet away, but ready to bolt in the other direction if he decided to lunge at her. The sun broke over the top of a building and cast its rays on the corner, creating a quartz prismatic field around the man. Melissa looked into his eyes. *He does not see the world the same as* ... her thought trailed off.

Again, he fell to his knees. He put his hands together, held them over his head, and looked into the sun. "Oh righteous sun, cast your long drawn out filaments of energy through me and cleanse my body, I will obey you." He bowed to the ground. He looked up, opened his arms, and tilted his head back as far as it could go. "I melt from your rays and my body is falling apart, it is only my skin that holds me together. I am disappearing and exist no longer. Where am I going? Stop ... don't leave ..." He fell backwards and lay motionless on the ground, as if all the bones in his body had turned to fluid.

Two police officers approached. One stood over him, with his baton holding the man by the chest, while the other carefully placed handcuffs on him.

"All right everybody, let's clear the corner. The show's over." The taller of the two shouted into the crowd.

Melissa took a deep breath as she watched the man being placed into the back of a police car. She had never witnessed anything quite like that before. A sense of sorrow ran through her for the man, but also a strong connection to him. She felt he was losing, or maybe even had lost, the very thing in herself that she had struggled to protect all these years. It was strange. She could almost see the man's visions, could almost feel his pain. She turned around to walk away, and noticed Charlie watching this scene from the other side of Yonge Street. Her heart raced. She ran across the street, never releasing him from her sight.

The squeal of tires and the sound of a horn made Melissa turn back.

"What the hell are you doing? Cross at the lights." A man stuck his arm out the window and made an obscene gesture with his hand.

Charlie looked over and noticed her coming. He turned and started walking the other way.

"Charlie, Charlie," Melissa yelled as she approached him.

He turned back. "Stay away from me, Child."

She ran in front of him stopping his forward progress. "I need to speak to you."

"I have nothing to say to you."

"Why won't you come forward and tell what you know of Joanne?" She gently placed her hands on his shoulders. "I feel you know."

He looked down to the ground. "I can't. Who would believe me, anyway?"

Melissa thought for a moment. She wanted to tell him what she thought of him, the visions she had when looking into his eyes. His Slavic face was worn, his skin pale and weathered, the lines around his eyes curving down his cheeks like dried up rivers. It was as though he had thrown himself into a galling storm, using his body as a shield to protect something very fragile. "You owe it to Joanne to come forward."

"What do you know?" He knocked her hands off his shoulders. "And what business is it of yours? You didn't even know Joanne."

Melissa's head sank. "I know. When I dropped my painting, it seems I messed everything up." She looked up at Charlie. "I know you're not a stupid man and have your reasons for not wanting to come forward, but if there's something to tell …" She looked directly into his eyes and waited. "I guess there isn't." She turned, and slowly started to walk away.

"What do you want from me?"

Melissa stopped and turned around. "Just to know why she was really on the streets." As she said that, curiosity was building as to why Charlie was on the street.

"You have no idea what this could mean for me." Charlie's eyes creased lengthening and deepening the creases down the sides. "What do you want to know?"

"Let's go somewhere else." Melissa looked down the street and tried to think of a place to go. She looked in the other direction and scratched the back of her head.

Charlie pointed to a bench. "We'll just sit there for now."

Melissa did not know what to ask first or how to ask. "What really made her run?"

Charlie's face winced with pain. "Her stepfather, Edward."

Edward's eyes roaming over Melissa body and the lustful look he gave her at Joanne's funeral, sent a shiver through her body. "The bastard! What did he do?"

He looked at Melissa with rage in his eyes. "He pierced her spirit!" He slammed his hand against the bench. "He also impregnated her which was the breaking point that made her run."

"What? She was pregnant?" She could feel adrenaline course through her veins.

He shook his head. "I begged her to see a doctor. I knew she wanted to have an abort—"

"Why didn't you … ," Melissa began, treading lightly, "have a doctor come to her?"

Charlie's mouth crimped with disdain. "For somebody who thinks they are the savior of the homeless, you know little."

"I'm sorry, I just meant that you seem to be a smart and caring man. Surely, you could have …" She stopped as his eyes narrowed even further.

"If I had broken her trust in such a way she would have run from me and never returned." He looked toward the road, opened his arms, and said, "These streets are so vast." He turned back to Melissa. "I told her that I would make sure it was a walk in clinic and we would use a false name. She was not to have an abortion without me making sure it was safe!"

"She had an abortion?"

"I'm not sure. She was adamant about not wanting his child, but was conflicted about her beliefs." Charlie's head shook slightly. "She knew her religion well and followed the rules, she was pure at heart even toward the end … I tried to help her come to terms with what she had to do."

Melissa thought of how she had looked all over for Stephanie before she'd been killed. "Why did she run from you?"

"Her stepfather put up those posters. I looked all over for her. I wouldn't have turned her in. She trusted me, but she was so scared." He ran his hand across his face. "I would have taken her to a different country if she wanted, and made sure she got off the street. This world needed her!"

Melissa looked at him and rubbed her forehead. It seemed incongruous to listen to this man and look at him at the same time. She could not determine if it was because he was dirty and unkempt that he looked ignorant, or because he spoke so well that he must be ignorant to let himself become this way. "What did she tell you about him?"

"Not much, initially, but as she came to trust me she told me everything. Information came slowly. I knew she needed to talk about it, to release it. I listened empathically and she let out more and more each time. I didn't judge or give my opinion." Melissa noticed that he had clenched his fist and he was becoming physically agitated. "She was so young, so innocent." His eyes glowed with reflection. "She longed to feel wholesome again, a feeling she had taken for granted when her father was alive. An angel, that's what she was, and she didn't even know it. I tried so hard to give her some comfort, to take away some of her pain, but I was useless."

Melissa inched closer to him and hesitantly put her arm over his shoulder remembering what he had said about her keeping homeless people at pencil length.

He flung it away with a violent thrust and looked venomously into her eyes. His nostrils flared. "Don't you even think about consoling me, there is nothing you can do for me, you are not Joanne!"

Melissa backed away. She felt scared. Not physically scared, but something deeper, like he was able to see right through her. She could not comprehend the power of his glare, there was no mark from which to compare it, no standard. "I know," she began softly, her lip quivering. "I would like you to tell the police and the Crown Attorney what you know."

Charlie's body slouched as he exhaled. "Yes, I guess I have to. What happens to me is unimportant now. We have to stop him from doing this to Joanne's sister."

Melissa looked Charlie up and down. Her back straightened, her confidence returned. "First, we'll have to clean you up. Why don't you come over to my place and you can shower while I buy you some clothes?" She felt the need to take control. It came naturally and for some reason she needed him to see her apartment, her paintings.

He shook his head. "I will take care of that myself. I will meet you at the police station on Queen Street tomorrow morning at nine."

Melissa reached into her purse and pulled out her wallet. "Here, then, let me give you some money for clothes and whatever you need."

He pushed her arm back. "I said, I'll take care of that myself." He spoke firmly. He turned and walked away.

Melissa was worried about the state Charlie would show up in, if at all. Would they take him seriously? Could he really convince the Crown Attorney to prosecute? He seemed to know so much about what had happened to Joanne. He was intelligent and well spoken, unlike most homeless people Melissa knew. Why was he on the street? Damn, it was her stepfather! She should have known it the moment she met him. Melissa watched until Charlie's legs, body, and head disappeared into a sea of people.

# Chapter 11

Melissa stood in front of the police station, waiting. She had not slept well last night. The air was warm, and a slight breeze brushed across her face. People rushed by in front of her on their way to work. Some were dressed well and smelled of sweet perfume, others smelled of cheap cologne. She wondered for a moment what it would be like to have a nine-to-five job, actually, any job. The collective sounds from the street made her feel lonely, she did not know why. She shook it off and continued to survey the area.

A young man dressed in a blue suit stopped beside her and lit a cigarette. He took a puff and then hurried on his way. The smoke drifted across her face, distorting her vision. She scanned the street. An older man approached. He had short gray hair, wore new running shoes, blue jeans, and a thin nylon jacket. Could it be? His hair was groomed, his face shaved, and his clothes were clean, but yes, it was Charlie. He looked no different from the rest of the people who hurried by, he did not stand out at all. As he got closer, she looked into his haunting green eyes and there was the difference. They showed a kind of pain and suffering she had seen many times in the street people, but also a depth of compassion, struggle, and power she had seen nowhere else. This mixed together look gave Melissa an ominous foreboding, of what shape or form she didn't know. She would like to paint those eyes. He stopped right in front of her. She did not say a word, and continued to study his eyes, unafraid but at a loss for the ability to project them onto a physical surface with accuracy.

"Are you ready, Child?"

He broke her trance. "You look great."

He looked toward the station, the two lines between his eyes shaping into capital J's, one backward and slightly higher. His forehead was deeply corrugated. He took a slow breath. "Let's get this over with."

Melissa realized that he was nervous. She tried to keep her voice soft and reassuring. "You're going to be fine. I'll be there with you."

A subtle contempt crossed Charlie's face.

They walked up the ten steps and in the front doors. A uniformed officer sat behind a long high counter, working on something in front of him.

"Hi. We're here to see Detective Terese Bolino," Melissa said.

The officer lifted his head. He looked directly into her eyes and waited a moment before responding. "Is she expecting you?"

"Yes, my name is—"

"I know who you are, Melissa," he cut in. "Are you sure she's expecting you?" His eyes narrowed speculatively.

"Yes, she's expecting me," Melissa said with a cold stare.

He looked at her for a moment without expression, the slight indignant downward curl of his mouth showed Melissa that he was not impressed with her. He looked at Charlie. "Have a seat over there." He pointed to a seating area. "I'll call her."

They sat, and had waited for ten minutes when a door opened and the detective approached. They stood up.

"Hi, I'm Detective Bolino."

"Hello." Charlie shook her hand.

"Come this way." The detective looked toward a door on the east side of the building. "There's a room where we can talk privately." She looked at her watch. "Alban Bruner, from the Attorney General's office, will be joining us shortly."

Approaching the door, Charlie had the feeling he was walking into a cage. For fifty-five years he had successfully dodged the most astute tracking people of the world. He had lived in Europe, England, Vancouver, and Toronto slipping into vagrancy where nobody gave him a second look. He was the elusive electron free from detection, but a box surrounded him now and the sides were crushing in to pinpoint his position. An electron, he thought, would become frantic bouncing off the walls with frenzied, unpredictable speed, because microscopic particles become increasingly wild when confined to ever-smaller regions of space. Not unlike people, Charlie mused, feeling claustrophobic.

The detective swiped a key card and opened the door. Charlie knew this would be dangerous, but he had to speak for Joanne. Her story must be told. They entered a room with a table surrounded by six chairs and a large mirror on the wall.

"Please have a seat." The detective held the door for Charlie and

Melissa, and sat down after them. She faced Charlie. "So how did you know Joanne?" Her voice was even and direct.

Charlie thought for a moment of what Joanne had meant to him, how he had met her, and what he was going to have to say here today. "I met her on a cold windy night in late November. She was shivering and crying. I sat beside her and gave her my blanket." Charlie rubbed his arms. "I remember it being so cold that night because of that. I didn't mind." He took a deep breath thinking he had barely known her at that time, but shortly thereafter, he had been affected like he never thought possible again.

Detective Bolino looked at Melissa, who was watching Charlie intensely. "Go on," she said. An open notepad sat on the table in front of her.

"I looked out for her through the night as she slept. I learned later that she hadn't slept in days because she was so scared of the dark." A tear welled in his eye as Joanne stood, clearly defined, in his mind. "The dirty face, torn clothes ... her eyes showed a different picture. She had a magnanimous spirit, an intense inner light still burned within her soul!" He pounded his fist against the table. "She held such guilt, guilt for what had happened to her, and guilt for leaving her sister home alone. She blamed herself mostly. That night, she curled up close and held onto me tightly as she slept. When she woke in the morning, she looked into my eyes and said, 'Thank you for protecting me, I've not felt this safe for a long time.' I was speechless." Charlie could not figure out why she had felt so safe with him. Most people, he had frightened, but not Joanne ... Beyond the faded brown tattered shawl, that Charlie could have sworn he had seen in the Salvation Army the previous day, beyond the sagging dirt smeared face, beyond those sad eyes that showed the mournful air of and old woman was veiled a beautiful spirit with all the pure and honest love of a child. "Her voice was soft and endearing. I can remember it as though it were yesterday." He looked at Melissa and then to the detective. They sat silently. "I told her that she could count on me anytime. Then she just got up and walked way.

"I kept my eye on her, though. I would give her food and money. One day we ate lunch together, and she just kind of stayed close to me after that. I must say it was easier than me following her around. It took some time but I finally found out why she was on the street." Charlie lowered his head, then drew it up slowly. "She'd been sexually abused by her stepfather, and not just once."

"How do you know that?" Detective Bolino asked, her tone formal.

A door opened and a man in a plain gray suit entered the room. He took a seat across from Melissa, opened his black brief case, pulled out a file in a thin manila folder and introduced himself as Alban Bruner, Crown Attorney.

"Charlie, as I was telling you on the phone," Detective Bolino began, looking toward Alban, "was Joanne's friend and may have information on her abuse. He was just about to tell us about it. Please continue, Charlie."

Charlie looked at Alban for a moment. *So begins the Ordalia* ... "She told me of the abuses, how often they had happened, and exactly what he had done. She told me he came to her when her mother was intoxicated, an occasion that had happened frequently after her father had died. Sometimes three nights a week, he would enter her room late at night and force her to submit. She said it burned when ... he had become the torch of white heat cremating her innocence!" Charlie could feel the thorn of anger pierce his heart.

Melissa's eyes were fixed on him. She did not say a word. Charlie held her glance and had a strange feeling. He had only seen Melissa as pompous, self-righteous, even arrogant, but now she was frozen. He felt, for the first time, that she needed protection from this story as a child does from the first exposure to death.

"Her stepfather noticed that she was getting sick every morning and began to worry that he had made her pregnant, so he told her to take a home test."

Detective Bolino made some notes on her pad and sat silently. Alban's index finger and thumb made a checkmark across his jaw. Every now and again he would tap his cheek twice successively, then stop.

Charlie looked at the detective. "Yes, you know she was pregnant from the autopsy. Did she have the abortion?"

The detective said nothing, but Charlie knew by the flinch of her face and troubled look in her eyes that Joanne had.

"Probably a bad one. Damn." Charlie needed to be sheltered now. He wasn't sure he could handle this. "When she told me she was pregnant and was considering an abortion, I begged her to see a doctor. Not without me, though, I had to be there." Charlie brushed his hand across his face. "Edward was a 'very important man' Joanne said, 'very powerful'. She was important, not him!" Charlie relaxed a little and felt a deep pain. Joanne must have been very lonely in her lasts moments. A tear dropped from his eye. With all the power his mind could create, he felt impotent for not being able to save Joanne.

"She ran to the street. It was difficult for the few weeks before I came along, but she survived. Fifteen years old." He lowered his head and said nothing more. There was a long pause.

Alban removed his hand from his face and gestured that he would like to help. "Do you have any solid proof, something written by Joanne, maybe? Did she tell anybody else this?"

Charlie shook his head no.

Alban sighed. "I'm sorry, but that's just not enough."

Melissa stood up quickly, knocking the chair to the ground behind her. "Not enough! He's telling us what happened. Don't you believe him?" Her eyes narrowed.

Alban raised his eyebrows, obviously not impressed with Melissa's outburst. "I'm not saying his testimony isn't true. You have to look at it through the jury's eyes. We have one witness, Charlie, a homeless man. The defense will tear his life apart and make him out to be a drunken louse." He turned toward Charlie. "No offense."

Charlie's natural reaction would be to take offence, to say something against the establishment, but why? It was all so much bigger than that.

"Even if we do convince them that his story is accurate from his point of view, it is uncorroborated and therefore hearsay. Not a strong foundation to take into court, especially with Edward Woodrow. As it is, he and Joanne's mother are filing a suit against the city for harassment; they're not happy with Children's Aid, either." Alban looked at the detective. "Detective Bolino, it hasn't helped our case any that you've had Children's Aid badger Mr. Woodrow. I know you think it will protect Joanne's sister, but this man is not happy and we don't have enough to lock him up yet." Alban closed his briefcase. "He has many lawyers on his team and the full support of Joanne's mother. The case is just not strong enough. If you have other ideas, I'm all ears." The room was silent. Alban looked around the table pausing at everyone for a second or two as though open to any suggestions. There were no comments. He snapped the tabs on his briefcase closed, got up and made his way to the door.

"That's it! You're leaving? So if Woodrow was poor, we would have a case?" Melissa was still standing.

"Sit down, Melissa." Detective Bolino motioned with her hand. "I'll be in touch," she said to Alban as he walked out the door. "Melissa, he's not the bad guy. He's doing his job. Also, he's on our side and it is best not to make enemies of the people you need help from. There are rules of conduct you must learn if you're to advance to your goal and get things done."

Melissa stood up again. "I can't believe it. This monster is going to walk, and nobody gives a damn." She paced the floor, becoming visibly more upset.

Charlie looked at the detective, then got up and stood in Melissa's path. She stopped pacing. "Now look. Do you think there's anybody in this room who cares more about retribution for this man than I do?"

"No, but—"

"Then come to your senses. Nobody is saying that this is over, for him. There has to be a way, and I know the detective will do whatever she can to make it happen. She knows now for sure what she's always suspected." He held Melissa by the shoulders as he looked at the detective. "You were almost positive that he had abused her, before I came here today. Correct?"

"Yes," she answered.

"And now you know for sure?"

"Yes." She nodded her head.

He turned and looked Melissa in the eyes. "You have to stop going off half-cocked. I see that you're deeply concerned for Joanne and her sister, but there's no point going to court and losing. That helps nobody." Charlie could see that Melissa was about to break down.

She threw her arms around his neck. "How can this be? How can we let him go? What's wrong with this world?"

Charlie felt his heart open. He wanted to embrace her tightly to take away her pain, but he could not. It was something he had to fight. There was pain down his spine from her grip. Charlie broke her embrace. "Now let's have a seat."

"I'm sorry, I just feel so helpless."

Detective Bolino was making notes as Charlie and Melissa sat down. She raised her head. "Okay, I have an idea. Edward already knows he's a suspect." She looked over at Melissa.

Melissa looked up, her eyes almost hopeful.

"Charlie, can you come down here again in the next couple of days?"

He let out a deep breath. "Whatever it takes," he said resignedly.

The detective pulled a card out of her pocket and handed it to Charlie. "Call me tomorrow morning."

"What about me, do you need me to come?" Melissa looked nervously at Charlie, hoping for some kind of response, that he needed her to be there.

"No, I don't think that's a good idea," the detective said.

"But what about Charlie?" she asked.

He shook his head. "I can take care of myself."

"Listen, Melissa, I appreciate you bringing Charlie here and sitting with us for the first visit, but there's a very real tension throughout the station still at the mention of your name. When I tell the chief you were here, he's going to have a fit. So I think it best that you just stay away for a while until things cool down." She spoke clearly, making sure Melissa understood that she was not to come back unless specifically asked.

Melissa bowed her head with acknowledgment.

Detective Bolino stood up. "That's it for today. Call me tomorrow, Charlie."

Charlie agreed, and he and Melissa left the station.

"Can I buy you a coffee?" Melissa asked.

"No," Charlie said abruptly, "I have things to do."

"Oh, I'm sorr—"

"Listen, Melissa, there are things about me you don't know. Please leave it at that. I don't have room for a friend, nothing personal. I know you're a caring person, but we're worlds apart." Charlie turned and walked away.

*He called me Melissa! At least he acknowledges I have a name.* She looked in both directions, not sure what to do or where to go.

\* \* \*

"... and, as we discussed two weeks ago, Jesus had taken God from 'out there', and forged a path, through the vehicle of metaphors, to show that it wasn't only Him who had access to the great spirit of God, it was everybody, no exception!"

Will stood behind the altar, giving service to a church that had not seen this many people for well over a decade. In fact, it was the only Church in the city where attendance rose for Sunday service so dramatically. There were at least two hundred and eighty people here. Just recently he had been promoted from one service a month to two. His goal was to do weekly services. The Mahogany door swung open and Charlie walked in. He slid into a seat near the back. Will could detect Charlie in any crowd, even though he was cleaned up.

Will wore a simple black suit with a collar. His back was straight, his head tilted upward slightly. "This spirit we have come to call God must find a new space in our minds and in our hearts. The dogma and old creeds of the past must be broken open and exposed for what they are.

They give us incredible insight to the true nature of God, but the search should not end there. God must be rediscovered!

"The valuable lessons from Abraham to Moses to David to the Prophets to Jesus have been lost in a politicized world that have appropriated control of these teachings in order to control the masses by the very same words that were intended to set them free. Language has been the problem and the solution. When God shone Himself through Jesus, the people described Him in the only way they knew how: through theisms and symbols of the past. In that time the educated Pharisees sat on 'Moses' seat' and were able to manipulate the uneducated peasants into oppression. Their words were righteous, but they did not practice what they preached. It is obvious to us now that Moses' teachings were meant to give everybody choices, tools for self-responsibility, but those simple peasants were helpless to the great forces that used those powerful words. In much the same way, we are subjected to the same oppressive methods used by political and religious leaders who have righteous words but do not practice what they preach. But a man came to help us take back that power—" Will stopped to engage the congregation.

"Jesus Christ," many people said at the same time.

"Amen," others said while crossing themselves.

"He preached against false authority and we must honor Him by rejecting false authority! This Spirit is not above or below, nor has He given a 'chosen few' a special connection to Him, He's given it to every-single-one-of-us! We must take the responsibility to think for ourselves, and look within for His light, only then can we experience a oneness with God, like Jesus had, and fill our lives with meaning and promise."

Will's glance brushed across the many faces before him. Some were focused intensely as though in deep thought, others nodding in agreement with the occasional "Amen" quietly escaping from inside them, but in the front row was a young girl that most attracted him. She had black shinny hair pulled back into a ponytail, maybe ten years old, dark skin and eyes that showed unwavering faith and innocence. She held a rolled up paper in her hand and sat in between a woman and man, probably in their mid to late thirty's. The young girl's hand waved to Will and her face broke into a huge smile at his watching her.

Will nodded, smiled back, and continued, "I am happy to see more and more people coming to my sermons, but especially the young. The interactive assignments I have given out over the last two months have brought me a world of wisdom. It's truly in the young that we can see the essence of Jesus." Will could feel strong emotions rising within him. "In my next service two weeks from today, we will reanalyze the words of Jesus and come to see his message in a new light. And remember, your input is valuable. There are more work sheets on the back tables and reading suggestions. Again I say, those works sheets are for everybody. It seems I've inspired the young with a greater interest to participate, but I need input from everybody. You can write me a note, a letter, a book, on how you feel about religion and its direction. It is only through you that I can see what we need to guide each other in wisdom, in knowledge, and how we can open each other up to the nature of God. It's my goal to expose ignorance and prejudice in all areas, even in the Catholic Church. I want to remove barriers that hinder the development of creativity so we as people can live side by side in peaceful harmony." Will smiled, clenched his fist and finished with, "I want to see you all back here in two weeks to remove all claims that the Church, in its quest for power, has heaped onto the back of Jesus, so we can redefine him as the doorway to this Spirit that lives in all of us. Until then, I want you to think about what Jesus told the Pharisees. 'Woe to you, teachers of the law and Pharisees, you hypocrites! You are like the whitewashed tombs, which look beautiful on the outside but on the inside are full of dead man's bones and everything unclean. In the same way, on the outside you appear to people as righteous but on the inside you are full of hypocrisy and wickedness.' Will held his forefinger up straight and allowed enthusiasm to burst forth through his controlled passionate words. "You tell me if Jesus, a symbol of enormous strength and courage, a man who without fear preached for the protection of life with the essence of pure love!" Will clenched his fist and held it high. "… You tell me, would He be proud of the way our churches and societies developed after all He had sacrificed so that we might live in a better world? We'll speak more on that next time. Mercy, peace and love be in your abundance." Will crossed himself and stepped down. He could see that the young girl in the front row wanted to speak with him. Will motioned for her to come over.

"What can I do for you?" Will crouched to the girl's level. What wonderful honest brown eyes she had.

"My name is Lisa, and I wanted to give you this." She held out the rolled up paper she had in her hand. "Mama thinks you'll really like it."

"Well let's have a look, Lisa." Will unrolled the paper and saw a picture underneath a title, 'A Friend With Friends'. This is very nice, Lisa, what does it mean?" There was a star in the top left-hand corner and two faces shaded lightly. The images were from a clear-thinking vision; she was incredibly talented. Below was a scene with two black girls with short hair standing on one side of a lake. Beside them a tall red haired man with wide shoulders was smiling, his hand resting easily against a boat named "Mayflower."

"It doesn't really mean anything. I started drawing it while reading *Underground to Canada.* There's Jullily and Liza comforting each other. Liza was whipped and hurt badly, that's why she's hunched over like that. And that's Mr. Ross. He was the nice man who helped them escape from the Riley Plantation. There were lots of nice people in the book who helped."

"Who's this?" Will pointed beside the star, knowing exactly who He was.

"That's Jesus. He said to Liza, 'You ain't meant to be beaten. You is a woman same as Missy Riley'. I think when Jesus talks he says it in a language that the person understands because I'm sure he can speak properly." Her big brown eyes were full of life.

"I think you're right, Lisa." Will could barely contain the feelings rising in him. "Who is this then?" He pointed to the other shaded face.

"That's Adam." A tear welled in Lisa's eye. "He died 'cause when they were running to Canada, the bad men caught him and they chained his legs too tight and he got blood poisoning." She sniffled. "It was sad so I put him with Jesus and now they both smile on Canada. They came here because Queen Victoria didn't allow people to have slaves. She made a law declaring that all people were free and equal."

"This is a really meaningful picture, Lisa." Will looked up at the man and woman watching them. Many people were still in the church standing and socializing. "Are those your parents?"

"Yeah," she said in an honest sigh, as though really proud.

"I'd like to meet them."

"Great! They'd love to meet you. We come all the way from Mississauga on the Sunday's that you're here. Mama says you're the best!"

"Thank you, Lisa." Will smiled.

Will stood and walked over to the man and woman. "Hi," Will outstretched his hand, "you have quite a talented daughter here."

Eagerly the man shook Will's hand. "Thank you, my name is Russell and this is my wife Emma." Russell had on a brown corduroy blazer matching his pants and an orange tie. His wife wore an orange dress with a light brown shawl over her shoulders. It was evident that they were dressed in their best clothes.

"It's a pleasure to meet you." Will turned again to Lisa. "Lisa, I would like to hang your picture near front doors, if that's fine with you."

"Yeah, that would be great!" She turned to her mother. "Mama, can we give the work sheet to Father Bower now?"

"No, honey, we should drop it where we're supposed—"

"Oh I would be happy to take it now," Will said. "I'm glad to see that you do them."

"I always do them, they're so much fun!" The gleam in Lisa's eyes filled Will with pride.

Emma pulled out a sheet from her purse and handed it to Will. She turned to Lisa. "Okay, Baby Girl, we should go, I'm sure Father Bower is very busy."

"It's been very nice meeting you and your parents, Lisa. I hope to see you in two weeks."

"Oh yes, we always come early to get a good seat," Lisa said.

They said goodbye and made their way out of the church. Will could see Charlie waiting for him. He looked at the picture again and decided that it would have to be framed before being displayed, to protect it. He quickly browsed over Lisa's worksheet. There were colorful drawings around the corners, and every time Jesus was mentioned there were hearts surrounding the area. Will's heart had just grown stronger, and his goals more determined.

\* \* \*

"He's gone too far this time!" a priest with narrow lips and squinty eyes muttered as he hurried toward the back of the Church. "Nobody gave him the authority to speak like that!"

Charlie smiled. It was the first time since Joanne's death that his face had been able to form any upward movement. Gravity pulled his jowls back down to match the heaviness of his heart. He sat patiently as the Church cleared. The quiet mumbling dissipated as a magnificent white silence permeated the cool air and settled over him. Will approached, his feet gliding across the floor, purposeful, direct, soft.

He slid in and had a seat beside Charlie pushing a subtle breeze across his bare arm. "Well, what did you think?"

"I think you'll be looking for a new occupation soon." He looked into

Will's eyes. "The world is not ready for you." Charlie felt Will exuded too much optimism.

Will's eyes showed deep reflection as he stared in front of himself. "Oh, I don't know. I can feel the world taking part in a spiritual quest, and with a little direction we can all find and exude His love."

"I have to go testify on Joanne's behalf tomorrow," Charlie said with apprehension. His heart sank as a warm breath escaped over his lips.

"It's the right thing to do."

Charlie said nothing.

"Since meeting you, Charlie, I've searched for a way to help you but I'm not sure I've been successful in—"

"Will," Charlie cut in. There was a long pause. "It may not be apparent, but you have helped me." Charlie liked Will, even though on every occasion their talks ended in heated debates. Well, Charlie became heated. Will was always passionate yet composed, resolute yet open to new ideas, and always concerned for Charlie's well being.

Will let out an easy breath. "It's nice to hear you say that."

Charlie's face turned cold and hard. "You shouldn't need me to say it! You should know by my returning that I appreciate you." His face eased and a deep pain released through the green in his eyes. "My interpersonal skills have never been my strong point," he said as an apology.

Faint, broken streams of air released from Will's nose that showed he was laughing. "Maybe so, but you do have way with words. I think it's mostly the way you say things that scares people."

"How could she have ever loved me? She was so beautiful, precious in every way, and me ... well, look at me."

Will sat quietly for a moment. "Would you let me tell you a story?" Will asked as he inched closer to him, their arms now pressed firmly together. Charlie thought to pull away. Why had he always wanted to pull away?

"Yes," Charlie replied, without capacity to fight or challenge anything.

"There was a boy named Tommy, he was fourteen years old and had few friends, actually he had no friends. He did poorly in school. His awkward appearance and lack of coordination had also prompted verbal abuse from his peers. His home life was not much better. His father worked hard but made little money and was angry a lot of the time, yelling and screaming mostly. There was only one place to go, a tiny space, his private domain and shield from the world.

"In his bedroom there was a small window. Its curtain was an old thick blanket. It made the room dim even during the daytime. He had only a lamp that didn't give off much light, but Tommy preferred the dark, anyway.

"One night, with a wintry cool air cutting through the seams along the window, Tommy took the blanket down to warm himself." Will pressed himself more tightly against Charlie. "He was awestruck at all the stars in the sky. He'd never noticed the view he had from his room, he had never moved the blanket to look outside before. In fact, he didn't look up much at all. His visual field consisted of the ground beneath his feet and a few yards ahead of him, and every now and again a quick look up into the eyes of his peers, teachers, and parents. The stars were so beautiful that night, twinkling in the sky, as if waiting for Tommy to see them. Somehow, by him watching, they became brighter, more luminous."

The sidewalks of Toronto appeared before Charlie. He knew every line, crack, and bump along his regular path. His head straightened up slightly, but it wasn't the buildings and streets of Toronto he was seeing, or even the church before him, his imagination showed him the stars and planets as the universe unfolded in magnificent colors, shapes, wonder.

"The very next day while walking to school he noticed a ball. Tommy paid little attention to it as he hurried along the sidewalk, the wind pushing at his back. After a while he turned back, he did not know why. And there it was right at his feet. The ball seemed to be following him; somehow his energy was attracting it. He bent down, picked it up, and cradled it in his hand. It was an unusual ball about the size of a grapefruit. It was a perfect sphere and not made of plastic or glass, but it was crystal clear to look through. Not magnified in anyway, just more transparent than he had ever seen, like a filter of distortion, and fragile, like a Christmas tree ornament."

A vision of Joanne appeared before Charlie, beautiful, delicate, and in those eyes an innocence that was so pure.

Will continued, "It seemed to have no weight as he held it in his hand, but there was a power emanating from it."

Joanne's image became bigger consuming all of Charlie's thoughts. He looked down and traced the lifeline on his hand with his finger.

"At school that day he kept the ball close to him. He wasn't afraid now of looking into the eyes of his peers to warn them to stay away, or else. In his feelings for the ball was a building confidence. He would do what he had to do to protect this newfound love. After a long day, he brought it home and hid it under his bed, safe from the world."

Charlie could almost feel Joanne, his arm draped over her body pulling her close.

"That night, Tommy held the ball gently in his hand. He lifted the corner of the blanket, which was now pinned back to the window, and looked out into the night. The ball was warm in his hand and sent energy throughout his body. He rolled it across his face lightly. He liked the warm feeling. He closed one eye, placed the ball in front of the other one, between him and the stars, and something incredible happened. Light from the stars curved with the ball and the whole universe seemed to be trapped in the ball. The beauty in his hand, in his vision made him feel important, like he finally had purpose. He had control of the universe. What power he held!

"He studied the stars and picked one out that he called Tommy. He watched it for a moment, twinkling, happy, and right beside it another star flickered through the darkness. It wasn't long before these stars fused. It was then that he knew he had a soul-mate. He wasn't alone, as he had always thought."

Charlie envisioned light running from one side of a subatomic particle to the other. He did not know for how long he was imagining this, or why.

Will continued, his voice a little faster and higher in pitch. "The white light shone into his eyes like a warm liquid and filtered through his whole body reassuring Tommy that he was worthy. He placed the ball back under the bed and curled up in his blanket and slept more soundly than he could ever remember. Then he woke. It was quiet, and Tommy could hear heavy footsteps approaching his door.

"The door swung open and in walked his father. The pressure created by the door opening quickly created a vacuum and sucked the weightless ball out from under the bed to the middle of the floor. Tommy's father walked in, stepped directly on the ball without even noticing, and sat on the side of Tommy's bed. Tommy couldn't move as he lay pretending to be asleep, watching the hallway light flicker off the crushed ball in the middle of his floor. A single tear ran down the side of his face and onto his pillow."

The bus shelter rose to life in Charlie's mind in vivid colors, Joanne in the corner, alone. Tears rushed out of his eyes.

Will put his arm around Charlie and continued. "His father told him how much he loved Tommy and how he was sorry to be so angry all the time. It was a speech he had heard often. Then his father left the room, not noticing the crushed dream beneath his feet."

Why even bother? Charlie thought. It's out of anybody's control. He felt cold inside. There was a long pause, and it seemed Will had nothing more to say. Charlie waited even longer. Still, silence. His mind raced to a solution, a happy ending ... "You can't just end the story there!" he snapped.

Without hesitation, Will continued, "Tommy went to the ball that lay flat on the floor and picked it up. He held it up to the window and could see nothing more than a fragmented sky, a shattered vision. He threw the ball back down on the floor and curled up into the bed." Will stopped, took his arm from around Charlie and placed his hand firmly on his knee. "Now that's the end of me telling the story. You must finish it yourself. All I ask is that you take the story out of Tommy's viewpoint and put it into the ball's viewpoint." Will turned his head and smiled at Charlie, then turned back and stared at the statue of Jesus on the cross.

Charlie accepted this because he knew he had to find some kind of happy ending, some purpose for it all. It was difficult to change points of view. Charlie was the boy who held the universe in his hand, in his vision; he was the boy pained by a cruel world. That was Will's connecting strategy in his little metaphor. But now he had to become Joanne. No, he couldn't. He wasn't worthy of that. What would Joanne do? It seemed like a long time before he thought about anything else until the ball reformed into a perfect image of Joanne, alive and vibrant. The vision sent a warm sensation through Charlie's heart. His body made a subtle twitch and a new universe broke open before Charlie that was the essence of Joanne. A universe filled with peace, love, growth in every area. Charlie looked at Will through the distorted vision of his tears.

"Joanne is still alive within you. Let her guide you. If you listen, she'll tell you what to do." Will smiled confidently and turned toward the front. Charlie did the same.

They sat for a few minutes, both staring toward the altar.

Charlie got up and started to leave. He turned back to Will, who was watching, smiling. "Thank you, Will. I'll come to see you after it's over, then I'll have to leave the city."

"You know where to find me. I look forward to it. Please, don't leave without saying goodbye. I'd like to finish our discussion on evolution. Think, Cambrian Explosion: Intelligent Design?" Will stood and out stretched his hand and smiled derisively.

Charlie grabbed it and shook it with as much respect as he could show through a handshake. He knew he had to go, but he wanted to shed some light on this so-called Evolutionary Big Bang. Fact was, he knew Will was trying to provide a distraction from all he had to do. "I look forward to it as well. You're a good man, Will."

The walk down the aisle toward the church doors was unnerving. Outside the sky was covered with streaked white clouds and the shadow they cast over the city wove like a blanket over Charlie's heart. Will had helped him realize that Joanne would never have bestowed painful punishment on anybody. She had done nothing to inspire fear in Charlie, and her memory was better served in warm, peaceful feelings. Will was right she deserved at least that from him.

People passed by in front of Charlie, some walking quickly, in a hurry to rush through their life, others slowly because they had no direction. Maybe it was just his own pessimism, but no one really seemed happy. Charlie did not belong here. Why had he lived so long? His life, a flash of fire, would exhaust soon and his black box of treasures would remain hidden. The only motivation left was to protect Joanne's sister. His head bowed, and he could feel Joanne's warm, gentle presence within him. He would not resist anymore.

# Chapter 12

Standing outside the interrogation room, Charlie felt as though he was walking into the past. His insides were churning. He tried to maintain an upright posture. All he could think of was the schizophrenic man on the corner. The shining floors, polished desks, and clean-cut officers reminded him of the laboratories ...

Detective Bolino and Alban approached.

"Hi, Charlie." The detective seemed to force a smile; her face was pensive. "You remember, Alban Bruner, Crown Attorney."

Alban extended his hand. "Nice to see you again, Charlie. Thank you for coming down." He turned to Detective Bolino. "Edward, his wife Julie, and his lawyers will be here shortly. It will not be easy to get a DNA sample from him."

"Yes, I know that," the detective said as her chin raised and her eyes took on a searching look. "What other choice do we have?"

Alban shrugged his shoulders and gave her a long sideways glance. Charlie said nothing and thought about Joanne. Would he be able to remain composed while looking her tormentor in the face? Joanne's brilliant light had formed a shield within him, but would it be strong enough?

Detective Bolino looked past Alban with probing eyes. "Here comes our ace in the hole now. Joe Nilsson is the coroner who did the autopsy on Joanne."

Charlie noticed that this tall thin insipid man had let a trace of concern pass over his pale face.

"What is it, Joe?" the detective asked.

"We have a problem." Joe smoothed his face with his hand bringing to the surface a trace of crimson.

"What problem?" Alban asked.

"The DNA records from the part of the fetus that still remained in Joanne have gone missing."

"Missing! What do you mean missing?" Detective Bolino was beginning to lose composure. Her face paled and was not much darker than the coroner's now.

Alban closed his eyes and rubbed in between them with his forefinger and thumb.

"The computer files developed some kind of virus and wiped out a whole program," Joe replied.

"Was there no hard copy, no paper work? What about the actual sample?" Alban's anger showed through the muscle twitching at his jaw.

"Misplaced, apparently." Joe raised one eyebrow in a questioning slant.

"Do you think somebody has taken it on purpose?" the detective asked.

Both of Joe's eyebrows raised as he replied, "It's not my job to determine that."

"Damn." Detective Bolino peered over Joe's shoulder. "Here they come now." She took a deep breath.

Charlie's mind tracked every moment he had spent with Joanne. The openness in which she had confided in him, the way her spirit danced through her eyes, a light that could not be shadowed. In what way could he help today? A cold shiver ran through him and he felt like running.

\* \* \*

A long narrow pressboard table separated eight chairs. On one side were Charlie, Terese, and Alban; on the side facing the mirror, sat Edward, Julie, and two lawyers, Oliver and Walter.

Terese began the discussion. "Mr. Woodrow, you have become a suspect in a police investigation."

"I know that, I'm been maligned and you will pay if my good reputation is mired in any way. Mark my words, detective," He wagged a finger at Terese, "you will pay dearly for this!"

Terese caught Julie's glance. She looked insecure and scared. Terese knew that if this worked out the way it was supposed to, it would be Julie who would suffer the most here. By acknowledging what really happened, she would have to face a great deal.

Alban spoke up. "Mr. Woodrow, are you telling us that you never had sexual relations with your stepdaughter?"

"Of course not! I've spoken with my wife about this and we cannot figure out why this is being done to us. Don't you think we've been through enough?" Edward put his arm around Julie. "It seems I have the justice system rallying to accuse me. The Children's Aid Society has sent social workers from four different offices and found nothing. They've spoken to the whole family, including Joanne's sister. And all of our neighbors have been interviewed. We've had enough!" He looked at Alban. "Not enough cleared cases in your file? Now you have to go after honest people to make your quota!"

Alban responded, "Well, Mr. Woodrow, there's mounting evidence that your stepdaughter was sexually abused—"

"Am I being charged with something here?" Edward shouted as he stood up.

"No, at least not yet," Alban replied in a cool tone, seemingly not at all impressed with his outburst.

"Then I'm not going to sit here and listen to this crap!" He grabbed Julie's arm. "Come on, let's go."

"Why can't you just leave us alone?" Julie cried.

"Sit down for a moment." Walter gently pulled Edward down into a sitting position. "Mr. Bruner, what evidence do you have?"

Alban opened a file in front of him. "Well, from the coroners report we know that Joanne was pregnant and had had an abortion. From a discussion with Mr. Woodrow we know that she was probably pregnant before she ran away from home. We've spoken to her schoolmates and found out that she didn't have a boyfriend that anybody knew about." Alban flipped through some pages while Oliver took notes. "And just recently, we found a friend of Joanne's, Charlie." He looked at Charlie.

Terese was studying Charlie. His face was calm and grave, but a feeling, energy, radiated outward from him as he sat motionless. She felt comfortable but somewhat nervous. She wasn't sure why.

"And how did," Walter paused and raised one eye questioningly, "Charlie?" He waited for affirmation before continuing. Alban nodded and Walter wrote something on his notepad. He placed his pen on the table. "So how does this older man know so much about what went on between Edward and his stepdaughter?" Walter leaned back in his chair and crossed his arms in front of him, looking genuinely interested in the answer.

"May I?" Terese looked at Alban.

He nodded yes.

"Charlie lives on the street. When he met Joanne and saw the condition she was in, he took her under his wing. He tried to protect her from the elements and—"

Edward broke in, "Oh isn't that wonderful. He tried to protect her from the elements. What happened the night she died? Was he too drunk to be concerned about her?" His voice rose with the last accusation.

Terese thought to herself: what a shameless, egotistical bastard. He knew he had abused Joanne and impregnated her. She shook her head.

"First of all, I don't drink, sir." Charlie spoke for the first time. He looked directly into Edward's eyes and studied him momentarily. "And I know exactly what you did to her, every detail." He spoke softly, evenly, it did not match his intense expression.

Terese could see that Edward was taken aback by Charlie. She knew why. His face looked old and worn, but his eyes showed a deep understanding, honesty, and intelligence.

Oliver had been taking notes since the first word was spoken. He placed his pen on the table, and smiled. "So, Charlie, you took Joanne under your wing. And what exactly was the cost of that, sir?"

As though a tag team, when Oliver stopped taking notes, Walter began.

"I don't know how to gauge it in dollars and cents, but her impact on me was far greater than mine was on her, that I can guarantee. I am the debtor." Charlie's eyes took on a deep reflective look as he looked toward Julie. "Your daughter was a beautiful girl. She had a heart of gold and a pure kind of innocence that is truly rare to find these days. He did not take that away from her. Her spirit is alive and well. I know you find this difficult to believe, Mrs. Woodrow, but your husband needs help." Charlie words filled the air with a temperate but crisp tone.

The wounded look in Julie's eyes and her fallen features showed that she had been tormented from the inside out. She seemed to be on her last thread of strength. Her head fell between her shoulders and she looked down at the table.

"These allegations are unfounded," Walter cut in. "Any more of this without any proof and you'll all be sued for slander. Now let's have some proof, or we're out of here. We came down here to clear this good man's name." He turned to Edward. "He doesn't want to proceed with the harassment charges, but you're leaving us very little choice."

Alban turned toward Terese. "Read them what we have."

Terese opened her file. "First of all, the coroner's report shows that Joanne had had an abortion, performed within thirty-six hours of her death, which complicated into an acute case of peritonitis. Part of the fetus still remained." Terese looked at Edward. He had a clean face with a rounded chin, a perfectly constructed nose, brown eyes, and an arrogant 'you can't touch me' smirk. "We have DNA samples and if the obligate paternal DNA matches Edward's, beyond ninety-nine point nine percent—"

Oliver placed his palms on his thighs and leaned forward. "First of all, young lady, to match DNA samples there must be something to match them with. I've advised my client not to submit to any form of test." Oliver looked at Alban. "Mr. Bruner here will tell you that he does not have to unless there is some other kind of evidence to support these allegations. You can't just go around taking samples from people against their will. There is a Charter of Rights in Canada you know, and I assure you it will work in our favor. The truth is more likely that Joanne became pregnant at school and ran because she was afraid to tell her mother."

"We've arranged this meeting as a courtesy, sir," Alban began, looking at Edward, and seemingly not put off by the alternate story. "You have a chance to come clean now. If you maintain your stand of innocence then we have no choice but to go for a maximum sentence on Sexual Assault and I will air your depraved indifference to human life through whatever court I have to. When we match your DNA there will be no turning back. If you wait, there will be no deals. Now is the time to come forward." Alban shrugged his shoulders. "If you're innocent this is a perfect way to prove it. It only makes sense. Why would you not want to clear your name? I will have to assume you're guilty if you maintain your stand without a test. It's not like we're asking for a vital organ."

Terese dutifully wrote in her notebook. Alban had done it, he was trying to illicit some kind of response from Edward and his team. She quickly looked up at his lawyers. They didn't seem angry or concerned and both had ceased writing, as though it wasn't necessary to take more notes. The bottom was falling out. Insecurity overtook her. She looked at Julie. Her eyes were red and puffy, her body twitched occasionally. It looked like she hadn't slept in days. Julie's chest heaved as she breathed in. When she exhaled Terese could smell stale alcohol.

Oliver's lips twisted into a sneer. "Listen here, Alban, if you think you can scare us with hollow threats ... We know that you've lost the samples from the fetus." He paused for effect.

Terese felt her heart palpitate. She looked at Alban, his mouth dropped open, Charlie's eyes creased, his lips were pursed together, and he looked as though he was in deep thought.

"And how exactly did you get that information?" Alban asked, his face showing suspicious bewilderment.

"We've done our homework. And let's stick to the case at hand. If you want to waste more of the taxpayers' dollars on a case against my office, then by all means." Oliver waved a dismissive hand. "It would not matter about the DNA anyway. There's no way you can get my client to submit to a test. And because you believe my client is guilty does not constitute proof. As far as your witness, Charlie, goes, I'll tear so many holes in his story that he'll wonder what he believes. You have nothing. Now, my client and his family have been through enough. They came down here of their own accord and unless these accusations and harassment stop right now you'll all be facing charges. Can I assume that this little charade is over with?" Oliver flashed a superior look Alban's way.

Terese's shoulders sagged as she waited for the inevitable response. It was all over. Alban lowered his head conceding the loss.

"Mrs. Woodrow." The room became deathly quiet as Charlie addressed Julie. "Do you want to know, before you leave, how your daughter felt about you and her younger sister in her last month?" His eyes showed a sympathetic and ineffable compassion.

Julie looked up at Charlie inquisitively. "What did she say about—"

"Okay, that's enough!" Edward grabbed Julie by the arm as he stood up. "Let's go."

Julie slapped Edward's arm away. "I want to hear what he has to say. You said there was nothing to worry about. I want to know how my daughter was before she—" Her eyes filled with tears. She wiped her cheek.

Edward sat down with a look of disdain on his face. He loosened his tie.

Charlie's eyes illuminated as though a great inner light needed to escape. "She spoke of her younger days when her life was simple and filled with love. She really loved you and her father, her sister, too. I can see in your eyes, Mrs. Woodrow, that you are a caring person. Joanne always said that. She was deeply concerned about her sister. You have to ensure that no harm comes to her, no matter what happens here."

Terese noticed that Charlie was studying Edward while talking directly to Julie. Edward kept looking away, but always turned back quickly to see if Charlie was still watching. Edward loosened his tie even more, undid the top button of his shirt and ran a nervous finger along the thick silver chain that hung around his neck. Charlie watched this for a moment. The top corner of his lip curled up, his head angled slightly as though he had just discovered something, and his eyes narrowed. He turned to Julie.

"I failed my family. She ran because of me. She felt that I didn't care for her father because of what I was doing. That was before Edward came along and gave me a sense of purpose again. How could she have loved me? I was in great pain and," Julie let out a deep breath, "I didn't realize that she, too, could be in so much pain. Then, Edward came along, but it was because of me that she ran, not him." She embraced his arm with hers. "He was so caring. Joanne didn't understand that I'm the kind of person who needs to be with somebody. I'm too weak to make it on my own. I loved her and her father." She bowed her head, covered her face with her hands and wept.

"She came to realize that. She did forgive you, Mrs. Woodrow. This is not your fault," Charlie reassured.

Julie lifted her head. "Then why didn't she come home?" Her body shook violently.

"It wasn't you she was afraid of—"

"No, you don't understand. None of you understand." Her head moved around the room looking at everybody in turn, stopping at Edward. "Edward is a caring man, he would never do what you're suggesting. There's no way. He's been so supportive." She looked at Charlie. "Listen, you seem to be an honest man, but I'm afraid Joanne was telling you stories. She told many after her father died. Her imagination was always overactive, even as a child. She must have become pregnant from some boy at school. She was trying to get back at me for being promiscuous. I was such a bad mother after—"

Edward draped his arm over her shoulder. "We don't have to continue this anymore if you don't want to." He spoke to Julie then looked around the room with an ashen face that showed that he knew exactly what expression to wear at any given time.

Julie began to stand up. Edward followed.

Charlie massaged his temples and squeezed his eyes closed tightly. When they opened, his faced winced with pain as though something was tearing him apart inside.

"Mrs. Woodrow, just one thing before you leave. Joanne told me many things over the short time that I knew her. I am reminded of one now." He took a deep breath. "When he came to her late at night, always on a night that you had had too much to drink, he would undress in front of her with the light on. It aroused him for her to see him naked, he told her that."

Julie looked inquisitively at Edward. Terese could see that Charlie had piqued her interest.

"Come on, let's go," Edward said nervously.

Julie held her hand up into a stopping motion, saying nothing.

"When sufficiently aroused he would mount her and proceed with the rape." Charlie eyes, dark and powerful, looked at Edward. "He would let his heavy silver chain brush against her and say, 'I can see that this feel nice across your breasts and that it enlivens you'. She felt so guilty because she could not control the way her body reacted." Charlie breathed deeply as though at any time he could collapse.

Julie stepped away from Edward. Oliver and Walter stood up.

Walter said, "That's enough, we're through here. Come on, let's go."

Julie looked at Edward and his lawyers. She turned back to Charlie. "Go on."

"He would then he press his lips over her breast at the same time that he tore through her flesh. He moved slowly at first whispering in her ear that she was a beautiful woman, and that he felt more like a man with her than anyone else." Charlie took a deep breath as though it would be his last. "He would then caress her breasts until the final moment when his body shook without control. At that moment, he clenched painfully hard ... always leaving a bruise ... every time it was the same. You see, Mrs. Woodrow, she couldn't tell you. She thought it was her fault. He instilled that guilt. She didn't feel comfortable at school, she felt the whole world could see her and what had happened—" Charlie's voice cracked and he did not continue.

Julie's hand rose and slightly brushed across her breasts. Her body let out an uncontrolled shiver. Terese could not move. She felt an ache, she could not determine the source or area. Julie stood as if in a reflective trance. In a wave, realization overspread her face. Then it hardened as venom filled her eyes. Her breathing became erratic.

She turned to Edward, who looked somewhat sheepish, a genuine emotion that showed for the first time this morning. "You bastard!" She lunged at Edward, catching him off guard and knocking him to the ground from the momentum of her pounce. Her feeble demeanor solidified to the strength and power of rage. She began to thrash him with all her might. "Feel more like a man now?" She tried to strangle him with his thick silver chain. It snapped off and fell to the floor.

Terese dove in to break it up. Julie was not easy to separate from Edward. Terese wedged her way in between them as Alban and Oliver tried to pull Julie away. Julie continued to aimlessly throw strikes at Edward. He opened his hands, which were protecting his face, and breathed a sigh of relief to see Terese on top of him deflecting her strikes.

Alban and Oliver finally pried Julie away and restrained her. Terese stood and helped Edward up. She shook her head, walked around behind him, and handcuffed him. "Edward Woodrow, you are under arrest for the …" This was it, she longed for the day that she could read him his rights. "… you are not bound to say anything, but anything you do say will be taken down in writing and may be used as evidence. Do you understand?"

"I understand," Edward replied, after getting a nod from Walter.

Alban moved forward and looked at Walter who was now standing beside his client. "Sexual Assault and Willful Disregard for human life. We'll ask for leniency if Mr. Woodrow agrees to a psychological examination and undergoes therapy."

"Willful Disregard! How exactly do you get that?" Walter opened his arms.

"Mr. Woodrow chose the coldest two days of the year to place posters in all the shelters. It's clear to me that he knew, after what he'd done to her, that she would be too scared to go to any of them, and therefore have to take to the streets for refuge. That's why she died the way she did. That's Willful Disregard." Alban showed no emotion, just a stern look showing he would not haggle.

Walter took his client into a corner of the room, away from Alban and Terese. Oliver released Julie's arm and made his way over to Edward and Walter. They whispered to each other. Alban made sure he stood between Edward and Julie, who looked like she was ready to lash out again. Her face still housed the look of anger and disbelief.

Oliver turned to Alban. "We will settle for—"

A look of disdain crossed Alban's face. "No settlement, no deals. You've heard the offer, that's it." He held up his watch. "You have 10 seconds to decide, then the deal comes off the table and we go to court, and I can guarantee it will be a high profile case."

Oliver turned back to his client and began to whisper again.

"5 seconds left. 4, 3, 2—"

Edward stood out from behind his lawyers. "I need help."

*Five minutes ago he was fine, now that he's caught he needs help?* Terese grabbed Edward's arm and led him to the door. She felt no sympathy for his plea because it was something his lawyers had told him to say, something that would evoke leniency from the crown.

Edward bowed his head as Terese escorted him out of the room and passed him off to a uniformed officer. His two lawyers followed him out. Terese returned with a woman.

The woman went straight to Julie. "Mrs. Woodrow—"

"Don't call me Woodrow!" Julie backed herself up against the wall and slid down to a sitting position, cradling her knees in front of herself. "It's all my fault. Oh my God, what have I let happen?" She let out a mournful cry.

The woman sat down beside Julie and put her arm around her. "Listen, Julie, it's not your fault." Julie did not look up. "My name is Sonya and I'm from the Women in Crisis center. We're going to help you get through this." She held her tightly.

"Come on, let's leave them alone." Terese stood at the door looking at Alban and Charlie. They left the room.

Charlie kept walking, making his way out of the station.

"Charlie," Terese called. "Where're you going?"

Charlie turned around. His eyes were sharp and filled with silent grief. "You don't need me any longer. I have to go. Tell Melissa that I thank her for persuading me to come forward. She made this happen."

"But …" Terese did not know what to say. Charlie continued down the hall and out of sight.

"Interesting man," Alban said.

"Yes, he is." Terese felt a strange attraction to Charlie. Maybe it was because he knew exactly what to say to make Julie turn against her husband, or was it the way he said it? He spoke articulately and his voice resonated on a different level. She felt mentally paralyzed as he spoke. She shook her head and looked at Alban. "We got the bastard."

# Chapter 13

John was massaging Melissa's shoulders. "I'm not sure how to say this, but I'm getting the feeling that I'm second, maybe even third priority in your life." He continued rubbing. The last three months had been difficult. Melissa had kept her distance and seemed completely uninterested in his life. The softness of the freshly laundered sweater over her bare shoulders emboldened his desire to run his hands across her breast and down—

"I have a lot on my mind." Melissa's voice cut through the air, freezing his zeal.

He stopped the downward movement of his hands, stood, and went up to the kitchen. He poured himself some water. "I've barely seen you since you started that painting. Now you're done with the painting, and I still can't get one day when we are just together." *Remember your promise to me.*

"Can't you see that I'm worried about what happened today with Edward Woodrow? This is important, more important than us right now." Melissa looked out the window over Lake Ontario.

"I'm trying to be patient, here. You're not making it easy." John sat at the kitchen table looking at a painting on the wall and began to feel the huge space between them. Had there always been that space or were they growing in different directions?

"Easy," Melissa looked scornfully at John, "do you think it was easy for Joanne? Why do you think everything should be easy?"

"Melissa, those are two different things. My patience has nothing to do with how much I care. And I didn't say I thought everything should be easy. Do you think I don't care? Why, because my contribution is less than yours?"

"I didn't say that."

"But you feel it." John's heart sank, Melissa didn't answer back. She did feel superior to him. "What am I to you?" John waited for a moment, hoping she would cut in with something, but it seemed she had nothing to say. "What is it you want from me?"

Melissa shook her head. "You just don't understand. There are things I have to do."

"I think I understand."

Melissa sat silently as though she didn't know what to say. Maybe she was right, there were more important things for her to do than to be worried about him and his feelings.

The phone rang.

Melissa jumped up and quickly answered it. "Terese, what happened?"

She listened quietly and John watched the face that held a depth of beauty that was always new and ever changing. It was not that she was exceptional looking, physically anyway. John looked over her body. She was actually disproportioned. She stood 5" 5', her arms and legs were thin and seemed too long for her torso, her breasts were not large, but seemed too big for her thin frame, they were firm but sat low on her chest, and her forehead seemed too high compared to the rest of her face. But there was power in the way she held herself, the way her hair hung naturally over her shoulders. She looked directly at John as she listened. He knew she didn't see him.

Her eyes remained still and her body filled with tension, her face broke into a smile and she cheered, "Yes!" She threw one arm up with the pronouncement of victory and jumped from the ground.

John's heart raced as he felt the excitement of her moment. It was her movement that captured him, alluring, energized. Her body rippled electricity, sending a wave of passion through him. He felt selfish now for what he had said. Adrenaline ran through him and he wanted to take her and explore her love, to be with her alone in body and thought.

In a flash her face changed from elated to somber. Her chin and shoulders lowered. "He just left?" She paused. "That sounds like he won't be around. I need to speak to him." She looked at John, her shifty eyes showed her agitation. "How long ago?" There was a pause. "Okay, thanks for calling." She flipped the receiver closed, ending the call.

"Sounds like they got him." John clenched his fist. "That's great!"

Melissa scratched the back of her head with the phone's antenna. "Yeah, it's … good." She looked down over her body and shook her head. She ran up two flights of stairs to her dresser and stripped off her house clothes.

Heat radiated through John's body as he watched her look through her dresser in just her bra and panties. The silhouette of her body showed from behind the thin rice paper partition. His adoration for her grew and he felt humbled by the feelings she inspired in him. He wanted to seduce her, to take her away to a remote place to have her all to himself; he wanted to know that he inspired the same feelings in her.

She put on a pair of jeans and a T-shirt. She ran down the stairs and grabbed her keys. "I have to go."

"Hold on. Where are you going? What's happening?" John placed his hand on her shoulder and turned her towards him.

Her eyes were a million miles away. "I'm sorry, I have to go and find Charlie before he leaves."

"What? Where's he going?" John asked, but really wanted to know, *what about me?*

"I don't know, but I have to find out." She opened the front door to leave.

"Just a second. When will I see you next? We need to talk," he said firmly.

Melissa threw her arms up in despair. "I don't know, John," she said, as if he was becoming a nuisance.

"I'm going up to visit my mother in Caledon next week. I would like you to come."

"For the whole week?"

"Yes, for five days. I thought it might be a good get-away. You have nothing pressing and I thought you could relax around the pool, maybe do some sketching or painting, while I took care of the chores. I've taken a week off from work. The kitchen and phone service can run themselves for a few days. I was hoping …"

Melissa looked at her watch. "I have to go now. I can't promise to go with you. There is too much I have to settle here." She hurried out the door without even a kiss goodbye.

"Was hoping that we could do that king for a day thing you promised," John said despairingly to the empty room.

\* \* \*

*Maybe back to England,* Charlie thought as he looked down University Avenue. He had five thousand dollars hidden away in a lock box, emergency escape money, *money that could have helped Joanne.* He would have to get another forged passport, but that was easy enough. He looked up at the cloud-streaked sky. He loved looking at the sky. It was always different. A new day had broken and he felt good about himself. Tears welled in his eyes, *thank you for the peace of mind, Joanne.* He thought of Will with affection for bringing a healthy memory of Joanne back for him.

Charlie watched a uniformed police officer heading in his direction. His body froze. He felt a thin bead of sweat form over his brow. He wiped it away. His heart quickened as the officer came closer. He could not move. As he stood there motionless the officer approached and walked right by him. *I have to get out of here.*

\* \* \*

Becoming weary and discouraged, Melissa walked into the Main Street Mission. It was her last hope of finding Charlie tonight. She had been everywhere else she could think of. On entering, she could see a group of homeless people sitting around eating soup and drinking coffee. An attractive young man, with short raven black hair framed over a pleasing but plain face, sat holding a young girl's hand. They were laughing.

The young girl wore a tattered earth brown shawl, her hair was matted, eyes dusky, and face pale and drawn. It looked unnatural for her to smile. It was strange the way they were sitting. One of the girl's shoulders was high, almost abnormal, while the other rested low. The young man mirrored the girl's appearance tucking his chin into his chest, his left shoulder high. He stood up, rubbed her shoulder, which seemed to automatically relax from his touch, and sat down beside an old man with tarnished-penny skin and shifty paranoid eyes that made him seem shell-shocked. The man's face twitched nervously as he sat huddled in the corner.

Melissa watched with great interest, as again this good-looking young man seemed to take on the shape of the man, his shoulders rolled forward and his head sunken. They sat for a moment conversing. Completely intrigued, Melissa watched as they spoke. When the old man scratched his chin, so did the young man, they seemed to shift position at the same time, nod in tandem, and even … no. Melissa's imagination was running now, but yes, they seemed to breathe at the same time. Suddenly, like a wave, a calm tranquility passed over the old man's demeanor. His face stopped twitching, his back straightened, and he did not appear to be frightened anymore. The young man lifted the old man's hand, placed his other hand over top, and said something. The old man looked at him as though struck by realization, his face lightened, then he leaned over and kissed the young man on the side of the cheek. Melissa stood in awe of the transformation in the old man's appearance. Who was this guy?

The young man stood up and walked over to Melissa. He extended his arm. "It's a pleasure to formally meet you, Melissa." He had remarkably beautiful, gentle brown eyes. True windows. He looked at Melissa with infinite serenity.

Melissa hesitantly extended her arm to shake his hand. "How do you know who I am?"

"Your reputation precedes you." He smiled.

"Who are you?"

"Ah, the eternal question." He paused for an unusually long time. "I'm Father Will Bower."

Melissa looked him up and down. "Father?"

"Yes, I'm an ordained minister of the Roman Catholic Church where Joanne had her service."

Melissa looked him over again. He wore blue jeans and a tan button-down, long sleeve shirt, pressed, clean, and simple.

He smiled. "I don't wear my collar when I help out in the shelters. It makes some of these people feel uncomfortable. Now, what puts that troubled look in your eyes?"

"I'm looking for a man I met. I must find him." Melissa looked around the room.

"What makes you think he might be here?"

"I've looked everywhere else I can think of," she said despairingly.

"Am I to assume he is a homeless man?" Father Bower asked.

"Yes. His name is Charlie and I convinced him to testify against Joanne's ... why did you refer to your church as the one that gave Joanne's service?"

"Because I saw you there. In fact, I escorted you to your seat."

Melissa remembered not being able to see when she first got into the church, but his gentle presence had made her feel at ease.

"I also saw you speaking with Mr. Woodrow," Father Bower said.

"He won't be speaking to anybody over the next while." Melissa spoke spitefully. "I hope he gets what's coming to him in jail. May do him good to have a little of what he did to Joanne, done to him."

Father Bower held his hands together. "Don't carry hatred in your heart, Melissa. It's poison and will eat away at you."

"Don't give me that forgiveness garbage." She looked directly into his understanding eyes. A warm sensation softened through her body. "How old are you?" she asked. His face was young and vibrant, but his eyes held the wisdom of an old man.

"Twenty-seven."

She did not know what to say. It seemed impossible for him to be so young.

"I can see by the disbelieving look in your eyes that you think it improbable. True, it's unlikely to become a priest by the age of twenty-seven, but that's only because most men of such a young age don't feel the need to search their soul." He paused with a humble look in his eyes. "I think it's important for the younger generation to have somebody to identify with. In this day and age fewer and fewer people are inspired spiritually."

"It's not that you're a priest that surprises me, and no offence, but I think all religion is brainwashing, spiritual nonsense, and very prejudicial."

"No offence taken. I find it intriguing that you feel that way. I've seen some of your work and see ascending visions, similar to the great artists of the Renaissance. The one you dropped from the building last week was very powerful." Father Bower creased his eyes inquisitively. He opened his hand offering Melissa to sit down.

"I can't stay long." Melissa took a seat on a bench in front of a long wooden table. She looked at her watch. "I have to find Charlie, I think he's leaving town. And I don't paint like the artists of the Renaissance. It's true that they were fantastic visionaries, and is where I obtained my foundation of skills ..." Melissa shook her head. "If they had been free to create without limits, who knows what marvelous works of art might have come from them?"

"Do you think that they would have created any differently had they the freedom of today in this part of the world?" Father Bower looked at Melissa with a truly accepting look in his eyes.

"Don't ask me questions if you can't accept my answers. I respect your position, but won't change mine to suit you." Melissa raised her eyebrows.

"I never ask that of anybody."

"Yes, I think some of them would have created other pieces had they not been forced to paint for the church. Religion, especially Christianity, has been built on persecution and propaganda. The Catholics slaughtered anybody who didn't believe, they treated women as second class citizens, they've instilled guilt into the recesses of the mind about natural human needs."

"You look at the negative aspects of a message that became distorted over the years. You've missed its true meaning." Father Bower spoke casually, but with deep conviction. "That was many years ago. Our religion, like everything else important, is evolving into a higher understanding."

Melissa placed both hands on her thighs and raised her chest. "Okay, I can accept that. Let me ask you this: if Edward Woodrow comes for salvation, repents, and asks for forgiveness—and he will—will you give it to him?"

"Yes, of course," Father Bower said confidently.

Anger began to build within Melissa. She could feel her cheeks flush and that warm feeling was turning cold. Melissa remembered his church turning away the homeless people at Joanne's funeral. "Well there we have it. I watched as your church turned away people who cared for Joanne, righteous people, religious people, and now you would prostrate yourself before a rapist and murderer. I'm sorry, but I can't subscribe to that." She stood.

Father Bower gently placed his hand on her arm. "I hope one day you will find forgiveness in your heart, for when you do, you will know the hidden source of understanding and power it inspires." He held her arm briefly. "Hating something strongly, even something you feel to be vile and cruel, does not diminish evil, it actually increases it." He released her. "Don't become a spiteful person and let the darkness win."

She could feel a warm sensation spread up her arm and through her body washing away the ice that had begun to form. "I have to go," she said softly.

"I hope to speak to you again." Father Bower stood up.

Melissa turned and walked toward the door, stopping as she pulled the handle. She looked back and noticed that Father Bower was sitting down beside a young homeless man. He smiled radiantly, which inspired a hesitant smile from the young man. She paused for a moment, then walked out the door confident that this would not be their last meeting.

\* \* \*

It was Friday morning and John sat outside Matthew's office. Suzanne had asked him to have a seat. He could not figure out why he was here. John watched as people worked. The area was clean and bustling with activity, everybody was busy. A man in an electric wheelchair rolled by in front of him. The man's upper body was strong but his legs hung loosely in front of the chair. There was a basket on the back of the chair filled with documents and one open in his left hand. He was reading the document while motoring by. John could feel the breeze as he passed. Then, without looking up from the document, his right hand flicked a switch and he halted abruptly. A woman coming from an adjacent hallway walked right in front of his path with a stack of files in her hands that rose so high that her chin had to stretch to rise over top. She seemed not to see the man in the wheelchair at all. Then without looking up from his document, he flicked the switch and began to roll forward again.

John laughed to himself. *Yes I saw the whole thing, officer.* John envisioned the accident actually happening. *The guy in the wheelchair ran right through the intersection without even looking, hitting the woman and de-filing her.* John shook his head in an attempt to become more serious.

Matthew's door opened. He looked at John, lifted his hand and waved him to come over. John got up and walked past Matthew into the office. Matthew closed the door, offered John a seat, and sat down behind his desk.

"Well, let's get to it, John. I've checked your quote on removing the piping and equipment from my buildings and have adjusted it accordingly."

"Actually, Mr. Sylvan, I've been told to give this priority, but I have some personal things to take care of over the next five days. If you wish, I can recommend another fitter who's been in the business a long time. His work is probably the best in the company," John said. He felt relaxed speaking to Matthew; there was a strong connection right away.

"No, next week is fine. I want you to work for me." Matthew paused, swiveled his chair sideways, and looked out the window. "How long have you been a gas fitter?"

"Well," John reflected, "I became an apprentice right out of high school, worked for a year and a half, and wrote my Fitter's 2 exam. Then I moved from Caledon into Toronto because there was more opportunity there. Now I'm going to night school to get my Fitters 1. Four and a half years, I guess now. Wow, time flies." John shook his head.

Matthew looked back toward John. "What are your goals?"

John smiled and started speaking right away. "I want to run my own business someday, have a team of the best trained fitters in the market beneath me, and teach people who were not so fortunate in school to become productive people who make a decent living. And of course I want to prosper from my efforts." John was happy he could recite his goals so readily. It was Melissa who had instilled that confidence in him.

Matthew looked seriously at John. "Those are ambitious goals, how do you propose to make that a reality?"

"Just by working hard and never quitting, I guess." John shrugged his shoulders. He could feel his face widen into a smile as he thought of Melissa. Her face stood in his mind as a dream that could not be broken.

"Good, you have to have your Fitters 1 ticket to have people work for you as a company."

"Yes, and there are others I'll get. Right now I'm a contractor for Metro Mechanical, so I'm kind of on my own. I do piece work and have a full time helper who I have to pay, and my own truck and tools. The next step is starting my own business and hiring contractors," John said, his words filled with pride.

"Concentrate on getting your Fitters 1 and everything else will follow." Matthew stood up. "That's it for now. Set up an appointment with me after the work is done on my buildings. I'll have other work by then for you." Matthew gestured toward the door, indicating to John that the interview was over.

John stood up. "If you don't mind me asking, Mr. Sylvan, why me?"

Matthew looked inquisitively at John. "I've done a background check on you and your work, and was impressed with what I saw. My company is filled with top-notch people. You'll find I settle for nothing less. I'm always on the lookout for young ambitious people. You fit that description."

"Thank you," said John as he walked out, still wondering why him specifically? What was it that made Matthew do a background check?

John left the building feeling good about the meeting. It was as if he had been given a surge of energy. He wanted to rush home and tell Melissa. His heart sank at that thought. He would not make the call. It was up to her to call him. The relationship could not grow unless she could show him that he meant as much to her as she did to him.

\* \* \*

"In New York. When did he leave?" Charlie asked.

"Two weeks ago." A man with long hair and a three-day beard replied.

"Damn. There's nobody else you know?" Charlie rubbed his temples.

"Not like Jim. You can take your chances with—"

"No, no, it has to be perfect." *Especially now*, he thought. Charlie turned around and walked up a set of concrete stairs leading into an alley lined with garbage. Urine was the predominate smell, although, there was another odor beneath that seemed to be struggling for top stench. *So much for going back to England right away*, Charlie thought. Too bad, he had been looking forward to more literature debates. He heard rustling beneath some boxes right beside him and remembered why he left England to begin with: too many rats!

Back to Vancouver seemed a better thought. Rain he could handle, and he wouldn't need a passport. He would leave soon, but now, a few nights of solid sleep were necessary in order to make the journey. Traveling alone with five thousand dollars cash across the country would require keen awareness. A few nights at the Plex, Charlie's hiding spot in Mississauga, would give him a peaceful place to rest and regain his strength for the journey.

He made his way to Union Station, purchased a train ticket, and waited patiently on the platform for the Go Train. He smiled as he thought of Melissa. The white and green train pulled up and Charlie got on. An overwhelming sense of loneliness cut through him and he felt like he was moving away from something positive, something healing. He pushed that feeling down as he had done many times before. He was forced back against the cushion seat as the train pulled out of the station.

# Chapter 14

Staring out the window of her kitchen, Danielle watched her son cut the three acres of grass surrounding her Cape Cod home. It was built at the turn of the twentieth century and had soaring rooflines, wrap-around porches, and six bedrooms, each with a balcony and view. At the front door was a hand carved sign that said, "Home Of The Westons." Inside the door was an antique table with a vase that held fresh cut flowers from the garden. Four rooms branched off the main hallway. All were outfitted with a mix of Victorian, colonial, and some modern furniture, accented by intricate details in the molding. It was a 3000 square foot, two-story house on forty acres. Most of the land was forest growing out of swampy mire. About ten acres were suitable for farming, of which two housed a flower garden flanking a spring-fed pool. The rooms of the house were large with high ceilings. The furniture was restored or made by John's father, Harold. He had continued to make ornaments and trim for the house until his dying day. As an expert carpenter, Harold had refurbished and made many additions to the house that had been in the family since it had been built. He had died at the age of sixty-two of a massive heart attack. That was three years ago.

Danielle smiled and thought of how much John was like his father. He was caring, thoughtful, and strong. She missed Harold dearly, though she had only to look around the house to feel his presence. His spirit was in everything.

John made his last round of the field and parked the riding mower in the large shed beside the house. Danielle set out fresh squeezed lemonade, biscuits just out of the oven, and cookies she had baked earlier in the day. It was wonderful to have him here for the week. The screen door creaked open, then slammed shut.

"Come to the kitchen, John, I'm in here," Danielle shouted.

John entered the kitchen and sat at the long farmer's table. He poured himself some lemonade. "Thank you." He took a cookie from the tray.

Danielle watched as John sipped his lemonade and ate his cookie. *His eyes look so sad.* "Is everything all right?"

John's posture straightened slightly. "Yes, fine."

Danielle knew he was hurting and did not want to burden her with his problems. He had been so strong after his father passed away and had never really emotionally let himself go. She remembered all the times she had needed to talk to him and release her pain. He was a rock through the whole ordeal. Every weekend he would come up and stay with her. Now it was her turn to be his pillar of strength. It would not be easy to get him to talk.

"Dinner will be in an hour," Danielle said as she got up and opened the oven door. "Maybe an hour and a half."

"That's fine." John looked around the room. "Aren't you lonely here in this big house all by yourself? Have you ever thought of selling it and moving somewhere easier to manage?"

"Oh no, I still really like it here. The neighbors help me with everything and you come up and help out. Your father's spirit is everywhere here. It brings back wonderful memories of you growing up and of your father and of your grandparents. Don't you feel it?" Danielle was happy here, but even if she wasn't, she wouldn't deprive her grandchildren of this place, their history. John would be a great father and she was looking forward to being a grandmother. Hopefully.

John looked around as sadness filled his eyes. "Yes, I suppose," His agitation returned, "but the place is too much for you! If you really want to keep it, maybe I should move back to help out."

"Everything is fine, dear, follow your dreams." She reached out and held his wrist. "Ever since you were a young boy, you wanted to live in the city. Your father was so proud when you moved down and got a job."

"Sure, that was okay when he was … alive, but now the place needs work. The grass around the northeast corner is almost as tall as I am. The pool needs a good cleaning and the garden is overgrown with weeds. And what about the house? It needs a ton of work." John looked up and around the room. "It needs paint, the floors need repair, the windows—"

Danielle cut in, "John, the place is fine. It's my place now and I don't mind if a few things are in need of repair or overgrown."

"Dad would roll over in his grave if he saw the state of this place."

"Do you think of your father often?"

"All the time." John looked up to the roof and let out a deep breath. "I miss talking with him."

Danielle smiled. She looked into John's eyes. "Maybe I can help you now."

"What do you mean? With what?" His posture firmed.

"I can see that something is troubling you. Sometimes it helps to talk about it." Danielle held more tightly to his hands.

"I think I have to let Melissa go."

"Oh?"

"We're growing apart and I feel like I'm holding her back from something." His eyes narrowed and his face grew dark with pain.

"Why do you say that?"

"She doesn't seem to look at me in the same light I do her and ..." John stopped. "We'd probably both be better off in the long run."

Danielle looked at the painting hanging over the country-scene motif wallpaper, and she released John's hand. "She's an amazing girl. I look at her painting often, sometimes for hours at a time. She's captured the true essence of our land. It's an exact expression of how I feel about this place and a constant reminder of how fortunate I am. Look," She pointed to an area of the painting, "see how she's incorporated the strength and power of the willow tree with a loose easy flow, and in that power is the presence of ... I want to say God, but I know she doesn't believe in that. At least she doesn't think she does." She looked reverently at the painting. "And there," She pointed to the other end of the painting, "the shadowed image of your father overseeing the land. You can barely see him, but his presence illuminates and protects my heart." Lightness moved through her body, lifting her mouth into a smile. "I've never seen him like that, but always seen him like that. I know, it sounds crazy. Out of all the pictures she worked from, in not one does he have that exact expression; it seems to be the sum of them all. I feel him as closely as ever."

John looked at his mother incredulously. "So what are you saying?"

"I'm just saying that Melissa has shown a heartfelt understanding of our family, to produce such a perfect piece of work. She must love you very much to see so deeply."

"I don't know, it seems to come so naturally for her, as if it's no more effort than me buying her flowers or rubbing her shoulders."

"Yes, maybe, but if it's for the same reasons, the act is an expression of something deeper," Danielle replied.

John looked up at the painting. "I don't know if she could ever respect me in the way I need her to ..."

Danielle could feel her eyes narrow and wished she could help more.

She said, "You're proud like your father. Your feelings are deep and strong. It's not always easy to measure up to that, even for Melissa. Try to show some patience and understanding, and do what's in your heart."

"That might mean letting her go," John replied. "I know that would disappoint you."

Danielle smiled, thinking he could never disappoint her. She had helped raise, from a baby, this wonderful grown man before her. A tear of pride filled each eye. "Yes, I do like Melissa, but it's your well-being that I'm most concerned with. You do what you have to do."

They both stared at the painting in silence. John went to the family room to lie down on the couch to have a pre-dinner rest. Danielle continued to prepare dinner, looking out the window, watching the willow sway from the breeze. "Thank you, Harold, for giving me such a wonderful son. Please show him his strength," she whispered with a smile as she crossed herself. *Thank you, Jesus.*

* * *

Melissa watched out the east window facing the city. The Romantic Piano of Frederic Chopin seemed to close in around her. She turned and looked out the south window. There was no moon and the lake looked dark and cold. A strong sense of loneliness set in. She wondered why John had had to go see his mother. He could've taken care of the chores on any weekend. Could he not see the painful predicament she was in? She needed his soothing presence. And there was the distance in his eyes lately. She looked across the city, past the buildings, past the lights, and along the streets, mentally scanning the alleys where she thought Charlie might be. Had he left the city? There was something unfinished in her; it was deeper than a feeling and not as simple as a thought. She hated when things were unfinished. Fragmented visions taunted her as the piano keys resonated through her apartment.

She couldn't figure Charlie out. What was he running from? Was it her? She was too pushy and self-righteous, she knew, but surely he could handle that. How could he leave? He would need some money. *He's got to be down there somewhere, I have to believe that,* she thought as she continued to look down over the city. She shook her head and stood up.

There was one light shining down, like a stream of consciousness, on a blank piece of paper taped to her easel. She sat, sharpened a pencil, and began transferring, with rigid and forced lines, the image she held of Charlie in her mind, onto the paper.

"Damn!" she said as she threw her pencil against the picture. She picked up an eraser and removed all she had done so far. She brushed the shredded rubber off the page and began to draw again. Her mood became agitated as anger constricted around her heart. "I can't believe he just went away on me! I need him. And Charlie, just leaving without even saying goodbye." She worked quickly, shading, illuminating, until she pressed her pencil so hard on the paper that the end broke off. She clenched her fists, then threw the pencil up toward the kitchen. It bounced off the table and landed in the sink. She ripped the paper off the easel, crumpled it up, and threw it at the window.

*I have to go for a walk.* She put her shoes on and left the apartment.

\* \* \*

Charlie sat in the shadow of a balcony with his back to the wall at a corner of the Plex. It was a warm night with a slight breeze, but he was cold in thought, emotion, and body. Two young men wearing baggy clothes meant to conceal things passed around a smoking pipe in the middle of the area. The Plex was two abandoned buildings facing each other. They were five stories high, and from the decrepit metal pipes sinking into the ground, Charlie figured that it had been at one time a playground for the inhabitants. Now the rotting metal acted as leaning posts and foot rests for young people who came here to "party," as they would say. He always felt safe here for reasons he could not determine. Some of the worst sorts used this place for selling and doing illicit drugs. But there was a strange positive power that emanated from this area, even more potent than the dank septic smell.

Charlie's head sank into his shoulders. He did not want to run again, he was getting too old for this. Why did his heart continue to beat for so long? What purpose could this painful existence have? In his consternation, he thought about how much he had looked forward, as a child, to growing up and unleashing himself on the world. New knowledge would surely bring about peace and understanding. Once illuminated, how could anybody not be humbled by the fantastic and ingenious ways of the universe? Why had he had to witness the horrible destruction? Charlie looked up towards the pitch, dark sky with a heavy heart.

\* \* \*

## Washington, D.C.

Eric Becket sat in front of a computer terminal. Periodically, he would key in commands, engage in a computer generated chess match when his eyes felt heavy, and wait. Shaking his head, he tried to clear his eyes and focus on his screen. He hit the enter tab and read the list of names he had already been over four times today. There was nothing new to be concerned with. Suddenly, his screen turned green. An hourglass symbol turned in the center. The message "Scan for access" appeared. Erin placed his thumb on a scanner mounted on the monitor, a Loading File message appeared. He sat back, staring intently at his screen, hoping for something exciting to break the monotony.

After a minute and a half, a picture of a young man appeared on the screen. There was a name beside it: Mihaly Kolazar located. He opened the file.

Mihaly Kolazar had been sought-after by the CIA and FBI for over fifty-five years. Now a query fingerprint check placed him in Toronto, Canada. Eric read, and reread the file, then rushed the information to his superior, Special Agent Peters. Eric knocked on Peter's door.

"Come in."

He opened the door. "Excuse me, sir, I have something you'll want to see."

Behind a large oak desk was a man planted like a fixture. He was well into his fifties with a stubble hair cut, a mammoth face centered with a boxer's nose, and wearing clothes so starched they might have maintained the sharp, pressed form had there not been a body in them. "What is it?" Nothing moved on his face but his mouth as the question shot out with sharp indignation, as though he had better things to do than talk to Eric.

"I've found a man we've been searching for," Eric said. "His name is Mihaly Kolazar, of Carpathian heritage from Bohdan. He would now be seventy-five years old and we've been looking for him for fifty-five years. We brought him onto the Manhattan project when he was nineteen years old—"

"Nineteen?" Peters questioned, his eyes narrowing only slightly.

"He was transferred out of the mountains to Poland when he was fourteen. He was hidden underground as the Hungarians moved in to reclaim the area they had lost in 1918. He was taken into Berlin, and quickly moved to the U.S."

"Is this man still alive?"

"I assume so. Either that, or somebody has found his dead body and is running his prints for identification."

"Go on."

"He had inspired a great deal of interest from scientists in that era." Erin looked over his file and pointed to a section. "He was immediately placed into school here, where he finished a degree in physics and medicine within three years, top of his class in all areas." Eric laughed as he read the next part. "Says here that he had upset some the professors for correcting the physics books they had been using. Along with achieving the highest marks, he started developing theories that nobody understood, but had piqued the interest of the establishment. Doesn't say here exactly what it was that piqued their interest so much, but he was made an American citizen and placed right in the heart of the A-Bomb Development team, mixing chemicals and watching for radioactivity."

"What possible value could he have had at nineteen?"

"Well, it says here that he was quite a prodigy. Although it also says that the development of the bomb was almost complete by the time he made the team. He had started on a cell generative theory in school, which showed great hope. He got almost all the way through before disappearing on August 30, 1945. He hasn't been seen since. Apparently, he left behind half-done theories on working with the atom for both commercial and medicinal uses. It seems that everything he left had some hole or needed a bridge to complete. It was like he took the most pertinent pieces of the puzzle with him."

"So why is his file still open? Why have we been notified of his existence?" Agent Peters asked.

"He's sought after by the Department of Defense, that's why we have his case still active in our files. To bring him back would mean great points for us. After all these years, finding a man who has eluded the most astute tracking people we have. That could mean major funds for this office," Eric said.

Agent Peters scratched his forehead. "The people doing the query would not be privileged to know his true identity, would they?"

"Not unless he told them himself."

"All right, send a team of two to investigate. If he's still alive, bring him back; if he's dead, we can close the file."

"Yes, sir." Eric went back to his desk and sent out an e-mail to two agents he wanted to send on this mission. *If this works out it will mean a hefty raise and maybe even an office with a window.*

* * *

John walked into his apartment.

"Please call me when you get home." Was the message from Melissa. She had been on John's mind every waking moment. Everything reminded him of her—the scent of the flowers on his land, the way the trees moved with the wind, the free flowing stream passing over rocks smoothing them, the sense of purpose when working the land and the pride it inspired. Over his heart a bleak, wintry feeling set in.

No matter how hard he worked to improve himself, he would always be on a lower level looking up, alone in admiration. It didn't seem to be an issue in the initial stages of the relationship, too much bliss to notice the space maybe. Because of her he had accelerated his goals and deep within the soul of his conviction he knew that he would have a fleet of men working for him. Nobody could change that now. But he knew it would never be enough to lift Melissa to higher levels, she would soon get bored with him.

He picked up the phone.

With his shoulders pulled back he tried to sound confident as he said, "Hi, Melissa." There was a short pause before she responded, he was not sure whether it was because she didn't know what to say, or whether he had interrupted her in "creative mode." Her voice was solace and distant at the same time. The coolness of her tone as she asked him to come to see her sent a shiver through his body. He agreed, hung up the phone, and looked up at her painting hanging over his computer table. It was incredible, depicting perfectly his feelings about moving to the city from a country home. She captured the essence of his spirit stuck halfway between the comfort of a small town and the hustle and bustle of the big city. This painting used to lift him beyond preconceived barriers, now it was the lid closing down on him, taking away the light. In stern defiance of his insecurity, he grabbed his keys and left the apartment.

* * *

Melissa used charcoal to bring to surface an emotion that needed to be pried from her imagination and made physical. This was her fourteenth attempt at rendering Charlie's image onto a piece of paper. Pencil was not working, paint frustrating, and ink impossible. Charcoal gave her the medium to represent Charlie as she remembered him. She shaded areas of his face to shape the light that was trapped beneath the surface.

Her focus on the paper and her energy were more direct and intense than the stream of light cast down from the ceiling. A key rattled in the lock and the door opened. Melissa looked up and felt torn between a warm sensation that spread through her body at the sight of John, and the deserted feeling she felt when he left to go to his mother's.

"Hi, Melissa." John didn't rush over to kiss her. He closed the door.

"Hi." She remained seated at her easel. If this was a game to see who showed the first emotion, she could surely win. "How's your mom?" she asked, making conversation. She could feel his uneasiness tonight.

"She's good and sends her love. She was disappointed that you didn't come with me." His voice was low and monotone, obviously making no attempt to win her favor.

*Was I even invited?* Melissa scanned her memory. She remembered something about him asking her, but that was at a bad time. She had had to find Charlie. Her heart sank at the thought of never seeing him again. She looked at her drawing.

John moved around behind Melissa and looked over her shoulder. "Charlie, I take it. I've seen him around."

She turned barely able to see him in her peripheral vision. "Where and when?" she blurted out.

"He comes into your kitchen most Wednesdays." John moved away and sat on the couch. He looked out the window, seemingly uninterested.

"He wasn't there when I went on Wednesday, when did you see him last?" She turned around, looking directly at John.

"It's been at least two weeks, maybe longer, since I've seen him." He didn't take his eyes from the window.

"Oh," she sighed.

There was an uncomfortable silence. John's face did not show his normal contagious, alluring roundness; it seemed sharp and withdrawn. It stirred feelings of reproach in Melissa. "Is there something bothering you?" she asked sharply.

"No, I'm fine." His tone was unresponsive.

"Well, there is something bothering me." She paused, waiting for him to say something.

"I'm sure you'll let me know what it is."

Her anger built and her stomach knotted. "You haven't even asked me how I'm doing. You left me when I needed you to be with me and now

I need you and you're still not here. What have I done to deserve this treatment?"

"It's not what you've done, it's what you haven't done."

"What are you talking about?"

"What about me, Melissa? You haven't asked how I am tonight, either. I've needed you many times over the last few months, but you always seemed to be busy with something. You didn't seem to notice that I, too … never mind." John's voice rose only slightly.

"But I was busy with the painting. Couldn't you see how important that was?" Her posture firmed. "I know it seemed like a mistake at the time, but as it turns out, if I hadn't been arrested and put in the cell next to Charlie, Edward Woodrow might still be free."

"Yes, Melissa, what you do is very important, but you seem to have no room for me. You don't listen to me, like I'm unworthy of your attention, and you make promises you can't keep."

"What promises? What are you talking about?"

"Forget it, it wouldn't be the same now." John scratched the back of his neck.

*What's he talking about? What promise?* She could not remember promising him anything. She could feel her lips tighten. "Well, if I've been distant that's because you don't seem to care what I've been through over the last three months. Talking to you has been like talking to a wall."

"That may be so, but you've shown no interest in what I've been doing, either. I've landed a huge contract. I'm not sure why I got it, but I was sought after by a well-established builder who wants to give me work. You've been so busy that when I need support, you're not there. I gave you my opinion of the painting, I tried not to be forceful, but I openly discussed my concerns. You brushed me off. Then you never really spoke about the painting to me. All of a sudden, you didn't need me to hook-up the mechanism to drop it." John's face tightened. "I wanted to know more while it was in process, but you had no time, as though talking to me was wasted time. You were distant from me before I was distant from you."

Melissa listened to what he said and felt that he could not understand her visions. "You don't—"

"Understand, right?" He tilted his head, his brow knitted.

"It's very complicated, it's not that I don't love you, but—"

"I could never relate to you in the way that you relate to the world. We see things differently and I should understand that."

"Yes, that's right." She let out a long breath and felt emotionally drained. Her shoulders sank and there was nothing she would like more than for John to come over and massage her, seduce her, and let her fall asleep in his arms.

John got up, pulled his keys out of his pocket, and walked past Melissa.

She could feel the breeze brush over her arm. He opened the door and left. *He couldn't even touch me ...* She looked back at the picture of Charlie.

# Chapter 15

The air was mild and the sunshine flooded through the windshield of the van as John and Brent pulled up to the Plex. John stripped the sunglasses from his face, jumped out of the truck, and strapped his leather tool pouch on. He opened the sliding side door of the van. It was 7:30 a.m.

Thoughts had raced through his mind throughout the night, and still now as he felt wide-awake. It was difficult to be cold to Melissa, but he needed reaffirmation of love and commitment from her.

"Are you okay?" Brent asked as he buckled his tool pouch around his waist.

John looked over. "Yes, I'm fine. Why?"

"Oh, I don't know, you just don't seem to be yourself. You've been very quiet." Brent slid two pipe wrenches into the loops on the side of the pouch. "I thought we were going to study on our way here."

"Just some personal things on my mind. We'll study on the way back home, I promise."

"Anything you want to talk about?" Brent turned to John, raising his dark bushy eyebrows.

"No, not right now anyway. We have work to do." John firmed his lips and closed the door of the van. They walked to the gate and opened the lock with his key. There was a hole in the fence big enough to walk through, but he would need a clear path to bring tools in. He stopped in between the two buildings. "Okay, we need a plan. Each building has four boilers that need to be removed as well as all the piping, and the radiators in each unit. Let's start in that one." John pointed to the brown-bricked building on the west side.

They walked over to the building and let themselves in though a rusty metal door, dented and scratched around the lock. Inside, to one side, was a set of concrete stairs that lead down to the basement. Descending,

John's flashlight illuminated dimensions of space that spiders had trapped in webs of darkness. He brushed away the silky spun fabric and opened the less secured boiler room door. There were two grimy windows, which gave him a little light, but not enough to work in. The room was damp and musty. Mildew and another undetermined noisome stench crept up and around John clinging to his body making his eyes water. Carefully, he made his way to the window and, with a flick of the lock and a strong tug from both hands, he broke the caked on seal that had formed around it, and slid it open. Fresh air poured into the room.

He shone the flashlight around the area. The shadow of four huge boilers sat in series beside each other. The heavy metal shells and the dulled silver pipes shooting out from the sides and tops of the boilers, mixed with the dark musty atmosphere, made the units appear ominously ready to rumble to life again. The decaying galvanized piping told John to be wary of this job site.

He flashed the light towards Brent, lower than face level. "Well, let's go get our generator, we're going to need electricity here."

Brent agreed and they both went back to the truck and lifted the generator onto a large four-wheel cart. They loaded more tools and rolled it back to the building. On the way back, John noticed a person sleeping in the corner of the opposite building. He thought it strange, being this far out of the city, to see a homeless man, but paid little attention.

Before returning to the boiler room, John handed Brent a mask.

"You're *not* to go in there again without it on. These boilers are likely insulated with asbestos." John spoke directly, making sure he was understood.

"Got it, boss man." Brent smiled.

John laughed and slapped Brent on the back.

Having a full week's work was good for John. He did not have to call the office or travel around to different sites, and the removal work required little thought. Mechanically, John went about his work. He felt comfortable that Brent was able to carry on without supervision. His methodical step-by-step duties organized his mind in such a way that he was able to weigh the pros and cons of his dilemma.

He thought about his conversation with his mother. She was right. Melissa had looked deeply into his soul and presented his life to him in a way he could never have known otherwise. He loved her in response to everything she was and stood for. The physical relationship was intense and served as more than affection; it was a gateway to an ever-deepening range of inner emotions. Even his thoughts were deeper, more intelligent for being with her, he mused. A warm feeling overspread his senses as he thought about Melissa and the morning slipped away into early afternoon.

He was exalted by his feelings for her, until his thoughts moved from emotion to logic. Intellectually, what value could she draw from him? He still felt many rungs below her. John was only a tradesman, a guy with a good mechanical skill that could direct energy into heat or cold; but Melissa was a transmitter of ideas, holding a power to rearrange the world and bring it, newly perceived, into the cultural mainstream via the breadth of her imagination. At least that's what she claimed to do. How would he even know? Her paintings were breathtaking and moved him deeply, but he didn't understand them completely. Melissa's love might be of the heart, but how could it be of the mind? For her to accept him and spend her life with him would mean her sacrificing part of her own happiness, that need she seemed to have to find an intellectual equal. She had always talked about Stephanie being so smart. He could not remember her ever referring to him in that way. Every piece of piping removed seemed to nick slivers from his self-confidence.

John's confusion, his conflicting feelings toward Melissa, left him bewildered about what to do. He came to the conclusion that he was over-analyzing and as a result was not reading the situation objectively. The best thing to do would be to talk to Melissa about how he was feeling. She always encouraged openness and even though she had not been receptive of late, it was up to him to let her know his thoughts. He admitted to himself that he, too, had not been totally fair or understanding throughout her recent ordeal.

From the window, John could see that the sun was getting ready to set behind the five-story building.

"Well, let's call it a day," John said to Brent.

Brent was struggling. "They tighten this with a vice?" He was planted firmly on a four-foot ladder, reaching up with his wrench secured to the black pipe hanging from the roof. His muscles showed strain as he reefed. "Malleable, my ass!" he exclaimed.

John laughed and asked, "Can you get a larger wrench around it?"

"No, I already tried." Brent reefed even harder. "There's not enough room."

John tapped him on the leg. "Hold on, then." Brent stopped and looked down. John could see that his face was wet and red with strain, even through the white mask that covered his nose and mouth. He stepped down off the ladder. "Well, what are our options?"

Brent thought for a moment. "We could heat the pipe to loosen it." He looked over to John to see if he was correct.

"Yes, we could, here, but let's pretend that there's still gas in the building. Would we be able to heat it then?"

"No, I suppose not." Brent scratched his chin and looked around the work area. His face lit up as his glance stopped at a piece of pipe he had removed earlier. "Can I try something?"

"Of course."

Brent secured the wrench to the pipe. He picked up the three by one and a half foot length from the floor and slid it over the top of the wrench, elongating the handle. He looked at John.

John smiled. "There you go, you've just increased your leverage. Now all you have to do is make sure, when you're loosening it that you don't pull everything else down. Control the torque and make the pipe do what you want it to."

Brent took a deep breath and applied pressure. A puff of dried sealant exploded from the seam and it began to turn. "Yes! I got it." He pulled off the wrench, climbed up on the ladder, and removed the eleven-foot long piece of pipe.

"Good job." John patted him on the shoulder. "You're really starting to think like a gas fitter. But only use that if you really need to, you'll warp the wrench if you do it too often."

"And we wouldn't want that." Brent laughed as he started to pack up the tools. "Maybe we could buy a proper wrench for the job," he jested.

"Can't afford one with high priced labor like you."

John was happy that Brent was excited about his discovery. He knew it gave him ambition and pride. John wanted more than anything to tell Melissa of Brent's accomplishment today, and how he was training him to become a self-reliant and successful gas fitter. It would be a good way to get the ball rolling, a way to break the ice, in his attempt to clear the air. John went back to the office to finish up his paper work.

\* \* \*

Thoughts of getting together with Melissa inspired all kinds of wonderful images in his head about how the night could go, wine, quiet music, deep conversation. The more he thought about a romantic evening, the more excited he got. He was sure he could clear up the tension between them and create some positive energy. Lightly, he made his way out of the office and out the front door as the weight of the day drifted away.

He noticed a black Jaguar idling, blocking the path to his car. Where had he seen that car? The dark tinted window opened as he approached.

"John, have you got a minute?" A voice resonated from within.

Curiously, John looked in the window. *Great*, he thought, *Melissa's father*. "I guess so." This, he was not looking forward to. He had just built up his confidence where Melissa was concerned.

"Jump in, let's go for a ride."

They drove down Yonge Street toward the Gardner Expressway. Not a word was spoken until they cut onto the highway, heading west.

"I know you think I don't like you, John," Philippe started, "but that's not true. In fact, I have a great deal of respect for you."

John said nothing and felt uneasy about receiving praise from this man.

"My daughter is quite a girl. A lady, I suppose I should say, but she'll always be my little girl." Philippe dropped a gear, forcing John forward in his seat, signaled, tromped on the gas, and swerved out from behind a slower moving car. He shifted up a gear, evening the pressure of motion. "You may think I'm not being fully honest with you, John, but I assure you anybody who can make Melissa fall in love with them, is deserving of my highest respect. You're her first love, did you know that?" He looked over at John. "She never had time for a boyfriend before, or never wanted one I suppose is more accurate. She said it was because there was nobody she liked enough to let into her life. I was relieved in a way, but also concerned. It's not natural …"

Philippe's voice drifted to monotone as a thread of thought unwound in John. He and Melissa had never spoken of previous partners. For him it was because there was no reason to discuss prior relationships. In fact, when Melissa came along he had dismissed them as necessary experience, but meaningless by comparison. She was so much more in every way. It never crossed his mind that the reason she didn't speak of prior relationships was because there were no others. It made sense to him now, the first time they made love … her expression … what she said. It all rose in his mind like an awakening.

"… She's so strong, so independent. Even as a little girl she demanded to do things for herself. She was filled with questions and tired me out with her inquisitive mind. I always tried to enlighten her when I could, but by the age of ten she had grown past the answers I could give. She was always reading, I think it was an escape for her." Philippe shook his head and smiled. "That and her art."

The vision of Melissa as a little girl sent tingles through John's body. He would have loved to have known her then. She probably hadn't changed much, he thought.

"She grew so fast, her mental prowess gave her many ambitious dreams. She was out to save the world. I planted the seed in her early that if she ran my business she would be able to do anything she wanted. I gave her a future she could look forward to, but there was one thing I couldn't give her: Love. It's not that I didn't love her. I did, in a way more deeply than anything. I just didn't know how to show it to her in the way she needed—"

"Why are you telling me this?" John asked, feeling a fog surround him.

Philippe cut off at the 427 and headed north. "This road is great for speed when it's free flowing like this." He shifted up a gear and stepped on the gas, pushing John deeper into the soft leather seat. "Because, John, if you really love Melissa, you'll have to let her go."

"For you?" The fog in John's mind was turning into a black cloud, thick and dark.

"No, John. For her." He paused for a moment as if to collect his thoughts. The car was now traveling at one hundred and seventy kilometers per hour as he cut off to the 401East. "Damn!" Philippe geared the car down quickly as he noticed the traffic backing up. The 401 resembled more of a parking lot than a highway. "You may look at Melissa and think, wow, what an incredible girl. She's vibrant, smart, sensitive, but what you didn't see was the fantastic growth prior to her working with the homeless and how that's been stunted as a result. You know why she became involved with the homeless." Philippe said as more of a statement than a question.

"Stephanie."

"Right. She was so hurt when Stephanie died and held such guilt. Melissa felt responsible because she thought she should have known about Stephanie's situation. She puts a lot of pressure on herself because of her gift. Melissa thinks she's everybody's savior."

*No kidding,* John thought.

"So to ease her guilt she started on her campaign with the homeless. She gave up her life, her dreams, to a cause she thinks is hers now. But it's not, John. I think you can feel that. She's destined to do great things in this world and she doesn't realize she's selling herself short. She could do so much more, and she'll come to realize that. Her pain is deep and the wound still fresh, even after three years, but you know what?" Philippe paused briefly. "She'll heal, and when she does she'll be ready to fly again. But there'll be a problem."

John looked over at Philippe. "Me."

"You may think that I'm out to get you, that I'm vengeful for you taking my daughter away from me. Actually, I lost her long before you came around. But I let her go because I knew I had to; which is why I've kept my distance from her crusade with the homeless. My feeling was that she would make her way through this and be ready to take on the world again. Don't you see, can't you feel that she's doing something beneath her? Her potential's stagnating. It won't be long until she gets the itch and is ready to take off."

"Don't tell me, you're here to protect my feelings when she dumps me." John was still lost in a cloud. What was he getting at?

Philippe cut off at Islington Avenue and headed south. "No, John, she won't dump you. Your affection and love have been a big part of her healing. You've affected her emotions deeply in a positive manner. She'll never forget that, she's very loyal; to a fault I'd say. You know that."

"Yes, I do." The cloud was dissipating and light was beginning to break through.

"If she had any indication that you still loved her, even though she didn't love you any longer, she would never release you, on principal alone. When her spirit again cries out to pursue life with the vigor and energy that's her birthright, she'll look back at you and be torn. She'll repress her dreams because of the way you've helped her. She won't show it, but the seed of ambition will die within her and she'll stay with you."

*... ambition will die within her and she'll stay with you*, burned in John as if a magnifying glass had been placed between the sun and his feelings. Not another word was spoken. Philippe pulled onto the Q.E.W. east and went back to John's work address.

John went to open the door and get out, but he turned back to Philippe. "You know, I thought you were going to offer me money to stay away from your daughter."

"Whatever you may think of me, I don't think that lowly of you. Actually, I'm intrigued by the way you've stolen Melissa's heart. Others have tried. I, in fact, feel a little more secure knowing that you're watching out for her within the environment she's chosen. She won't be happy there always, but she'll stay for your sake." Philippe narrowed his eyes. "Don't get me wrong, I'm not above paying for my daughter's happiness, I just figured that you were too noble to accept such a bribe. You're not a stupid guy, John, and I know you love Melissa, but can you be happy knowing that she'll love you for some gesture of the past, and not fully in the present or future?" Philippe turned and faced forward, his chin thrust upward, leaving a triumphant silence between them.

John opened the door and got out. His first reaction was to tell Melissa about his conversation with her father. Honesty had always played an important role in their relationship. The more he thought about it, though, the more he knew he couldn't tell her. She would be resentful toward her father and that would give her one more reason to stay with John when she shouldn't. John wanted what was best for both him and Melissa. On his way home, he reflected over the last few months and could now see clearly that Melissa was moving on, her healing where Stephanie was concerned in its completion stages. The painting of Joanne had repaired her somehow. Her father was right, she'd be moving on soon.

It was becoming obvious to him that he had to sever the relationship before it became impossible to do. He weighed the pros and cons of breaking up and staying with Melissa. His thoughts went into a wild battle between intellect and emotion. The dark inner conflicts faded as he came to a conclusion. It would not be fair to either of them to stay together. Pain was the only forecast, either way. He would write her a note tonight telling her that it was over. This would be best for both of them in the long run. It was time to be strong again.

# Chapter 16

Melissa had not been sleeping well. Why had John been so distant the other night? She wanted to call him, but felt it was he who should make amends. Maybe she had been distant lately, but he was always in her heart. It wasn't as if she had given herself to another person, there was nobody else. She could not control her need to create. John didn't really understand that, but he didn't have to, either. She could love him for what he was. A gas fitter was a respected career. He played an important role. She would talk to him later and straighten things out. Right now, though, her mission was to find Charlie.

The last time she had looked for him, he was out in front of the cafe with the African music. Maybe he would be there again. It was 6 a.m. She grabbed her keys and left her apartment.

Her mind was preoccupied as she walked along the faded concrete sidewalk. She felt for sure that she would see Charlie again, that he had not left the city. There were so many things to ask him. She shook her head, stopped, and turned back. She focused on the tail end of a van. *Was that John's van?* she wondered. Looking down the alleys and under stairwells, she continued toward the cafe.

This time, in the cafe, it was not synthetic African music they were playing, it was soothing classical. After getting a cup of tea, she took a seat on the same stool as last time and watched out the window. She was really beginning to like this place. It held a quiet comfort. Her thoughts drifted as the steam curled up under her chin and tingled peppermint through her nostrils. She reflected on her childhood. Things had seemed easier back then, playing in the garden, reading great stories, freely working on her paintings … the world had not yet weighed in on her with contradictions. Now there were many things to be concerned with. Stephanie had showed her the way. Couldn't John understand that? She thought of her family and how she had not seen them since before dropping the painting.

She was putting it off, not looking forward to the occasion. Today she would go and get it over with. She finished her tea, called her mother to tell her she was coming, and hailed a cab. She would look for Charlie later. During meal times would be the best time to search, anyway.

Upon opening the front door of the house she was greeted by Francis, who announced her presence. Her mother came running.

"Oh, it's so good to see you!" She hugged and kissed Melissa numerous times. "Your father was wondering when you were coming to visit." She ran her hand over Melissa's hair and her eyes became serious. "He wants to speak with you right away. He's upstairs in his office."

It was a long lonely walk up the circular stairs-case to her father's office. She knocked on the heavy oak door.

"Come in, Melissa." She heard from behind the door.

She walked in. He indicated one of the chairs opposite him with a straight finger and a serious look. She sat down. He continued his paper work. She looked around and remembered as a child that she had never been allowed in this room. Then one day on her tenth birthday, he had brought her in here alone and let her sit in his soft leather chair. Her feet had shot straight out over the edge because the bend at her knees was only about half way across the seat. She would work at this desk and do what he did. He told her that she was a very unique person and that with her creative abilities and his guidance, she would amass great wealth. She had felt so proud to be there. It was no different now. She was a good person because of his positive influence.

He looked up and put his pen aside. "I was hoping you would come and see me sooner than this, but I am happy to see you. Now, I want you to know that I have spoken to the Mayor and smoothed things out. Initially, he was taken aback by the graphic nature of the painting, but after some analysis he came to see the power it portrayed. There will be no action taken against you, in fact he's expressed an interest in meeting with you." Philippe rubbed his forehead. "I heard that you had been arrested and locked up with other people. Is that true?"

Melissa thought for a moment, she wouldn't cause any more trouble. "No, that's not true, I went to the police station of my own free will and they treated me with the utmost respect. They were just a little upset that I rained on their parade. I don't blame them."

"Good, they should know better than to put a daughter of mine in jail. And about your little stunt, you cannot go around and do whatever you feel. It's fortunate for me that I'm in a position lately where the Mayor is in need of my support. If things were changed, as often happens during the course of a term, I don't know what he would have done. You must understand my position requires me to work with whatever political party holds office whether city, provincial, or national. I need them and they need me. For me to negotiate effectively, I need my family to be in place. I can't have you running around the city creating disturbances. Do you understand that?"

"Yes, I'm sorry. I know I didn't take all factors into account."

"I do understand your compassion for the Woodrow girl. I never did trust Edward." Philippe looked directly at Melissa. "He was an awfully good trader, though. Anyway, what I wanted to say is that sometimes the end justifies the means. Maybe this is one of those times. I must admit, you have the courage of a Belmont. You're a go-getter." Philippe let out a laugh. "You're like me taking chances and afraid of nothing. I'm amazed that you were able to drop that thing without anybody noticing. You're surreptitious, and that's why you will be perfect for the position I have to offer you."

*No, the end doesn't justify the means, ever.* Melissa realized that she just understood something important.

"It's time we had a talk. You're twenty-three years old and should be doing something with your life. I understand your sympathy for the homeless, but this associating with them is unacceptable. There are better ways to help them than paintings. I want you to start working for me, learning what it is I do. You'll find it very rewarding and it will give you the flexibility to help the homeless and many other worthy causes. You'll be of far greater service than you are now." He paused, as if waiting for an answer.

"What about Camille? Don't you want her to take over?" Melissa asked.

Philippe took a deep breath. "Don't get me wrong, I love your sister, but she doesn't have what it takes to do what I do. You, on the other hand, are more than capable of taking control of this business. You'll meet interesting people, people you couldn't hope to meet on the streets. I know how you feel about politicians. I feel the same way, but sometimes you have to associate with governing bodies to get what you want." He frowned. "I also want to talk about your relationship with John." He paused.

*Oh no, here we go …*

"I know you have very strong feelings for him, but you're not using your head. By the look on your face I can tell that this is not easy for you. But I must tell you. It's my responsibility as a parent. I know you think I don't like him, but that's not true. I have a great deal of respect for blue-collar workers. They're the fabric of society. Without them nothing would get done. But without people like us, there would be nothing to do. We control the way society interacts and forms. We have the insight to mold society into a productive working entity. You're a visionary. You must not let that ability be wasted on menial things. With some training on how money works, how to move it, make it grow or shrink when required, you could unleash your creative abilities onto the world. You'll have the power to change things! Do you know how liberating that is? You couldn't yet know that feeling. Anyway, it's my concern for you and for John, that he would only clip your wings. He deserves to be with somebody that he could inspire. He'll not be able to do that for you. Can't you feel the difference between you and the people you associate with? You must." Philippe looked directly into Melissa's eyes.

"Yes, I suppose, but I'm no better. I've met many wonderful people and I do love John, I could not see living without him." There it was, out in the open. She had never told her father that she loved John. Why could she never tell him?

"I know that, Melissa, but you're thinking with your heart. You've got to think with your head. You're a grown woman and I cannot choose for you. I don't need a decision right away about my offer. I want you to think about it. If you accept, I want you to move back home. It will be a better training ground for you. Once you have a good feel for the business then you can live anywhere you want. With the incredible communications equipment available today, you could live in Australia if you wished and still run the business. You will become the executor of the estate. You should think about it, Melissa, it's a wonderful opportunity." He waited momentarily, apparently looking for some kind of response. She said nothing and lowered her head. "Listen my dear, I want you to be happy and I don't wish to control your life, but I don't think you'll be able to find the kind of happiness you deserve with John. I also think that you could not give him what he needs. It wouldn't be fair to either of you. You belong in a different environment. You have no idea how limitless your future can be. You would be in a position to move the world from the top. If a benevolent society is your goal, there can be no decision." Philippe stood up. "As far as your art work goes, you'll have more than enough time to pursue that part of you. Take me, for example. I chair many associations, I run charity drives, make time to study sociopolitical reform and am deeply involved with international trade policy. Fact is, I couldn't have done any of those things had I not learned how money works. I want to pass that knowledge on to you, because I think you could become a great benefactor to this world."

Melissa stood up and said nothing. He was very persuasive and she took what he said to heart. Could he be right about her relationship with John? She started to leave the room.

"Will you stay for lunch?" Philippe asked.

"No, I have a lot to think about, and besides, I'm not very hungry. I think I'm just going home," Melissa replied in a thoughtful tone.

She went downstairs and said goodbye to her mother and made her way home.

Her apartment seemed lonely. Melissa had always felt comfortable there, but now it was different. It didn't feel like home. She thought about moving back in with her parents. The idea did not make her feel uneasy as it usually did, it was almost comforting; she could not leave John though, he needed her. She knew that, no matter what he said, or didn't say for that matter.

In the kitchen, Melissa took notice of her painting, "A Vision of Hope." It was strange how it struck her today. Looking deeply into the concept, she felt as though she was floating on a luminous cloud. A sense of joy ran through her body. Then, as if coming back to reality, she turned to see an envelope on the table. On the front of it was her name in John's handwriting. Without conscious thought she ripped it open and read it. She could not believe her eyes:

Dear Melissa,

I am writing you this letter because it's the only way I could convey the totality of my thoughts. If I were to do this in person it would not be organized and, surely, I wouldn't get my true feelings across accurately. You have a way of making me forget things that seem important.

I feel our relationship has hit a crossroad and we are moving in different directions. You have inspired my life like no one else, and I thank you for that. I have grown in ways I never thought possible. But I can't and don't wish to grow more in the way you want me to. I have other aspirations. For this reason I think we should end the relationship and make our ways down the paths in life that

most suit us. I believe them to be different. Because of you I have gained a great deal of confidence. If I inspired you a tenth as much as you've inspired me, then I am happy. This does not mean that I don't love you. It's just that I don't think I could be happy with you as a lifelong partner. We are different people. I wish for you all the freedom you need to aspire and do great things and I hope you find your true soul-mate. If it pains you to read this letter, try to remember that time has a way of mending wounds, and in the future when you look back at our relationship, I hope you can do so with warm sentimentality.
Sincerely, John

Melissa read the letter five times before any emotions surfaced. First it was anger. How dare he be the one to make the break? She stood up, opened the drawer by the sink, and threw the letter inside. With a crashing slam, she thrust the drawer closed. Sadness overfilled her and she felt depressed. Maybe if she had paid more attention to him. Even though she had been wrestling with the idea of leaving him, she could not think of living without him.

Her relationship with John flashed through her mind and she realized that he was the thing she valued above all else. Her father was wrong. John was her inspiration and always would be. He was the foundation she sprang from, the platform sustaining her love; without him down was the only way to go.

\* \* \*

John felt badly about yesterday. Thoughts and emotions had consumed the day and he hadn't stopped for lunch or even taken a break. Brent must have been very hungry. He had worked so hard.

"Let's have lunch," John shouted over to Brent, who was cutting a piece of galvanized pipe.

"Sounds good to me, I'm starved." He placed the hacksaw down and rubbed his hands together.

"I want you to know, Brent, that you're allowed to take breaks when you're ready. I'm sorry we didn't have lunch yesterday. Why didn't you ask if you could eat?"

"I don't know, I thought maybe you wanted to get things done quickly to impress our new client."

John smiled. "Yes, I want to impress him, but you have to eat. You start taking responsibility for your own breaks, okay? Of course, if we're working together we will have to come to an agreement, but when we're working separately you're on your own. You really kicked ass yesterday. We're already ahead of schedule." John patted him on the shoulder. "Let's eat outside, it's a nice day."

They grabbed their lunch and went out to the common area.

"I wonder what Matthew is going to do with this place," Brent commented as he pulled from his lunch bag two apples, a loaded sandwich on a long Italian bun, some kind of cake in a clear plastic wrapping, and a bottle of orange juice.

"Probably some high-rise or something." John took a bite of his comparatively tiny sandwich. "When I was in his office he had pictures of all kinds of tall buildings." He stopped chewing his food. The man was still there from yesterday. This time he was awake and sat motionless. John looked at him, and although he was a fair distance away, he could make out his face. He was familiar. Obviously, he was homeless, maybe he had served him in the soup kitchen. He took another bite of his sandwich and continued to look at this man. It was bothering him that the more he looked, the more familiar he became. Then it struck him. The last time he had seen him was at Melissa's apartment on a piece of paper. It was Charlie.

John lost his appetite immediately. Should he inform Melissa? She would want to know, but he felt that if Charlie wanted to see her then he would not have left the city. He was torn about what to do. Melissa was meddling in something that was clearly none of her business. He shook his head and realized it was none of his business now. As he and Brent worked throughout the day, he came to the conclusion that he should tell Melissa. If Charlie really wanted her out of his life, it might be best that he told her himself.

They finished up for the day and started back toward Toronto. Brent studied from his book quietly and John thought about how lonely he was, but he would not shackle Melissa's ascent with his need for her. He dropped Brent off and went home. On three occasions he went to pick up the phone and stopped himself. Finally he took a deep breath and punched in her number.

"Hello," answered a solemn voice on the other end.

"Hi, Melissa, it's me." John's heart raced.

"Oh, hi, I was hoping you would call, I really need to talk to you." Her voice rose slightly, trying hopelessly to sound upbeat.

"Actually, I just called to tell you that I've seen Charlie."

"When? Where?" Her voice was genuinely up now.

John sighed as he now realized for sure that he had made the right decision.

"At the complex where I'm working. He's been there two days in a row now."

"Two days! Why didn't you tell me yesterday?"

"I didn't know it was him yesterday and I had other things on my mind." He tried to sound sarcastic.

"Oh, yes, your letter ... we have to talk about that—"

John tried to keep a stiff upper lip as he cut in with directions to where he was working. He informed her that the letter was genuine and that she should not hope for any type of reconciliation. She didn't fight it very hard, and that just reinforced his decision. She sounded hurt, but that would pass and she would find herself someone with whom she would be better suited. John also tried to convince himself, without any luck, that he, too, would find somebody better suited for him. He sat in the darkness of his apartment and contemplated his decision.

\* \* \*

Melissa immediately went downstairs and hailed a cab. When John mentioned he had seen Charlie, she lost sight of all other concerns. What was it about him? Why did she need to see him so badly that she again blew off the most important thing in her life? This is what a drug must feel like, she thought. She had things to say to John, but when he had mentioned Charlie her mind drew a blank and nothing came out. Charlie's face appeared like some kind of mystical force. What would she say if he was still there?

The cab dropped her off in an apartment building parking lot in front of where Charlie was supposed to be and she asked him to wait. It looked as if the newer apartment before her was put up to replace the older buildings behind. Melissa looked at the hole in the rusted chain-link fence she would have to climb through. The sun was setting and she was apprehensive about going into an abandoned complex as it was getting dark. Slowly, she made her way through and cautiously walked between the two buildings into the common area. It seemed empty.

She looked around and wondered whom this place was meant for. It was old now, but held some kind of strength in its design. The common area gave Melissa a protected womb-like feeling. She looked up at the five stories and felt a kind of comfort, as though a protective eye was watching her. She looked over the area, with all the rusting metal sinking into the ground, and again felt nervous. She'd let her cautiousness slip; this was not the place to be daydreaming. The grayness of the day was quickly turning darker, and the buildings were now only black silhouettes in front of a pale sky.

"What are you doing here, Melissa?"

Her heart raced. She spun around to see a man standing behind her shaking his head. "Charlie, I'm so glad to see you! I need to speak with you."

"You should not have come here."

She heard the fence rattle where she had entered the complex. Charlie pulled her aside and quickly ushered her into the shadows thrown by a second floor balcony.

"Shhh." He pulled her face close to his and kept her still. There was a strange ebbing power being so close to Charlie. She felt like a little girl in her father's arms.

"Yes, sir, it's time to party." Three men made their way into the common area laughing and joking. Melissa could not see them clearly but felt this was not a good place to be.

"Who's got the pipe?" Another voice resonated.

Charlie motioned for Melissa to stay still as he went to the corner of the building and looked out. He waved her over with his hand. Silently, she obeyed. Charlie took her out of the common area and back through the fence. They were now out of the complex and in front of the newer apartment building. Cones of light were splashed across the parking lot by towering pod-shaped fixtures.

Charlie scornfully looked at her. "What the hell do you think you're doing?"

"I came here to find you, to talk to you," she said with apprehension.

He let out a long breath and shook his head. "I knew when I saw your boyfriend here that you would come, I just knew it. What is it you want from me?"

"I don't know, I have so many questions I don't know where to begin."

"Child—"

"Why did you leave so suddenly? Where are you going?"

"You could not understand. I have to leave, I have no choice after testifying."

"I would understand, please tell me," Melissa implored.

Just then another group of young men walked through the parking lot. In a slow animated rhythm they strolled, staring Melissa and Charlie down, sublimating movement into a lurid expression.

"You cannot stay here, it's not safe." Charlie watched as the men crawled through the fence.

"I'm not leaving until you give me some answers," Melissa said haughtily.

"Don't you ever threaten me that way!" He pointed his finger at her. "You will not use your safety as a crutch. If anything, that kind of attitude will only push me away. That's unfair and cruel!"

Melissa felt a surge of shock pass through her when he pointed at her. "I'm sorry." Her voice cracked. "I've made so many mistakes lately, I feel so desperate. My life is slipping away before my eyes, and I know I have no right to you or your feelings but there is something between us, like for some reason we were meant to meet. And I don't even believe in fate. I just can't help this overwhelming feeling that … I don't know, maybe it's just me. I don't see the world the way most do …" She looked up at Charlie. "I sense that you understand. Aren't you at all interested in me?"

"Yes, Melissa, but I can't stay. I need some rest and then I must go."

*He is interested in me.* She could feel her heart race. "Why don't you come and stay at my place, rest for a few days, and then go?" She paused. "You can't be getting much sleep here." She looked over at the complex and then at Charlie. The pale light across his face showed his fatigue and look of unrest.

"No, I couldn't—"

"Even if it's just for one night, please, I wouldn't be able to sleep now knowing that you're here. Please show me the same consideration you want me to show you."

"I can't go back to the city, it's too dangerous for me."

"Nobody will know you're there. You'd be in my apartment and wouldn't have to leave until you were ready. I could run around and do things that you need done before you go. I could be of great help to you." Melissa felt for sure she had said the right thing, as Charlie did not say a word. He stood there in deep contemplation. "I will not press you to tell me anything you don't want. I will leave you completely alone if that's what you wish. You can trust me."

Charlie looked her straight in the eyes. There was a long pause. "Very well, I'll come. You could be helpful."

Melissa smiled. "Anything you need."

Melissa flagged the cab that was waiting by the ten-story apartment building. They rode back to Melissa's in silence. She was trying to figure out what to ask him first. There were so many questions.

# Chapter 17

On entering Melissa's apartment Charlie felt a strange surge of exhilaration. It scared him. He thought about why he had accepted Melissa's proposal. What did he need from her?

The high ceiling of her studio rose across three levels, starting at about twelve feet in the living room, expanding to over twenty feet by the back wall. On a raised platform, the small kitchen bridged the lower room, which he entered, and bed area, which was raised even higher than the kitchen. Because of the high ceiling and expansive view, the place looked quite large, although the actual living area was compact. A ceiling fan circled on low, deflecting little bits of light around the apartment from the metal bands around the blades. Three plants hung from the ceiling and two sat on the floor in front of the window. The apartment looked exactly the way he had pictured it, paintings on the wall, books on shelves, and a work area for her to produce her art. Even though it was dark, he was taken aback by the view out over Lake Ontario. He stared out for over a minute. He turned and scanned the room, taking a brief inventory. His gaze brushed across two paintings that appeared to be authentic Van Goghs. He would look at them in more depth later. He walked up to her easel and saw his portrait.

"It's not very good," she started. "I did it rather quickly and ..."

"Don't apologize, it's fine." He turned away.

"Are you hungry?" She ran up to the kitchen and looked in the refrigerator. "I have." She pulled out a bag and looked at it inquisitively. She squinted her eyes and ruffled her nose. "Phew, that's no good. Uhm ... I have ... nothing. Would you like some water?" Smiling, she held up a water jug.

"Water will be fine." Charlie sat down and looked out the other side of the window and could see the SkyDome opening. He mused at the separating womb-like pod, then looked up at the CN Tower standing proudly beside it: A symbol of virility. There was a positive energy here, looking out over the lake and city.

Melissa ran down the stairs with a large glass filled with water. "I'll go out and get some groceries. What do you like to eat?"

"Don't go to any trouble."

"We have to eat," she said insistently.

Charlie just looked at her without a word.

"I'm sorry for my tone, I just want to get something I know you'll eat. You need strength for your trip." Her voice was soft, caring.

Charlie thought for a moment. She was right. He would need some nourishment. "I eat raw vegetables, sun flower or buckwheat spouts, cantaloupe, apples, pears, chicken two nights a week ... organic if possible." He took a small drink from his glass.

"Really?"

"Yes, I know it might seem expensive, but I don't drink or do drugs, have no bills, and when you eat properly, it is actually cheaper than filling your body with empty calories." He watched Melissa for a moment and could not help but say, "When the metabolism of the body is perfectly balanced, it is not susceptible to disease."

Melissa thought for a moment as if validating the last statement. "I know a great fruit market down the street that has organic foods." She grabbed her keys. Her sprightly manner returned. "When I get back we'll eat and I'll fix my bed so you can sleep there, and I'll sleep down here on the futon." She was smiling from ear to ear and was almost too perky. It gave Charlie a rush to see such life, such youth. It made him feel sad.

"Listen, I won't be here long. You will not give up your bed for me. I'll sleep down here. I want you to carry on with your life as though I'm not here. I won't ask too much of you, don't ask too much of me."

"Fair enough." She raised her head high. "Then I want you to make yourself comfortable. If you're hungry fix yourself something to eat and if you're tired I will respect that and work quietly. If you want to talk, I'm always ready, and if I get too annoying with questions, just tell me to leave you alone. For now, I want you to look around the apartment and get comfortable, there's nothing off limits to you." She jingled her keys. "I'll be back in about an hour."

"Very well, then." He turned and looked out the window. The lake gave him a calm serenity. This would be a good place to rest and rejuvenate.

Melissa left the apartment and locked the door behind her. He stared out at the lake for ten minutes and then stood up. He was curious about her living quarters. Again, he looked at his portrait and marveled at how closely she had depicted a feeling in him, a state of mind. She was talented. He moved up to the kitchen and opened the refrigerator. It was next to empty, only some water and condiments. Did she not eat? Not much, he determined, reflecting on her thin frame. A painting on the east wall captured his attention. His eyes narrowed and shifted from side to side, top to bottom. He pulled out a chair and sat down. He rested his elbow on the small kitchen table, held his face up with his hand, and looked deeply into the painting. The title, which was etched discreetly on a silver plaque on the bottom boarder of the frame, read, "A Vision of Hope."

The name did not seem to reflect the painting. It portrayed a young boy dressed in ragged clothes sitting up against a corner of a building with his hand out. His small hand amazed Charlie. He focused solely on it for a few moments. The detail was incredible. It was the focal point of the picture, although most would not notice that. The boy was almost obscured by the people passing by. It was apparent that they were in a hurry and that most did not even notice him there. His hand was cupped out in front of him as though holding a ball. His dirty face was sad and bruised. A handprint could almost be detected on his cheek, but not clearly. It was an awkward face; there was no chin that could be seen, a nose that looked too small for his high cheekbones, a thin-lipped mouth that crimped sarcastically, and large droopy eyes. Each part looked odd, almost ugly on their own, but when integrated together appeared harmoniously beautiful. It was incredible. His hair was oily and unevenly cut. But it was his hand that showed everything somehow. Charlie looked up to the roof. A tear welled in his eye from a feeling he could neither describe nor justify. He brushed it away and was immediately drawn back to the painting. On his palm Charlie could, on careful scrutiny, see the lifeline on the boy's hand. It branched off into two directions, one aimlessly, hopelessly short. The other bridged the other lines of his hand and discretely ran around, seemingly without end. Charlie's equation, ten-to-the-power-of-ten depicting the extended longevity in seconds, stamped on the hand in his vision flashed before his eyes.

Anger overtook him and he stood up; his thoughts were not to go that way. Happiness was not an option! He stormed down the stairs, walked around the living room in circles and felt like smashing something. Enraged, he shouted at his vision to stop. Claustrophobia set in as a tightening rope around his neck. His breathing became erratic; he had to get out of there. After pacing for a few moments, he stopped to regain his breath. The room opened up as he looked out over the lake. A calming force spread through him. He breathed deeply and vowed not to look at the painting again, but he could not stay away for long. He could look at it without emotion, be purely objective. Slowly, he was drawn back up to the kitchen, his curiosity thin strands of hair attracted by the electric pull of a creative mind. Gravity planted him firmly into the chair and he looked into the painting again.

The people passing by the boy had very expressive looks on their faces. A woman's eyes shifted down at the boy, her face showing contempt. It wasn't her fault the boy was there, why should she feel guilty? It was the perfect depiction of a look Charlie had seen many times. In front of her a man walked without noticing the boy at all. It was apparent that he had many things on his mind. Charlie moved on to the next person, the person that intrigued him the most.

He was a well-dressed man in his late thirties, maybe early forties, good looking with a confident smile. He also looked in a hurry, but there was something different about him. The whole demeanor of this man was peaceful, as though he had found serenity and inner prosperity. His clothes, gold watch, and shining shoes showed that he had achieved prosperity of a monetary kind. As Charlie looked at his shoes, that reflected a clear blue sky, he noticed neither of the man's feet touched the ground. He was in a normal walking position but his right hand held a fist and was ear level. His thumb escaped the clench and seemed to have flicked something. Charlie followed the trajectory of the object that would have been flung. There it was. He had mistaken it for a mark on the building, but it wasn't, it was a gold coin en route to the boy's open hand. It would have landed squarely in his palm on the lifeline.

He looked at the boy again and saw a different picture. It wasn't a sarcastic smirk, it was a defiant smile, as though he was about to hold the world in the palm of his hand. He now noticed that the coin, on close examination, did not house the image of the Queen, it was the image of a key. *Truly fascinating*, he thought, as he looked even closer. The boy's eyes were deeper than before, somehow, and now seemed incongruous with the rest of his unkempt appearance, eyes that seemed familiar, but from whom? Where had he seen them before? Then it struck him. Could it be? He was almost afraid to look. The man who tossed the coin showed only one eye because of the way he was walking, and the profile of his chin, and that nose … Charlie slapped his knee as it all came together for him. It was him, the man and the boy were one and the same, separated by only a few years and some good fortune, no, not good fortune, something else.

It was impossible, but his disbelief had been suspended: The coin was given to him by himself. The coin symbolized motivation, thought, and freedom from a chained existence. How had he done it? How did the key work? Not only had he succeeded in pulling himself out off the street, he had transcended past everybody else in a quantum leap. Now he walked on air. He had found a gate.

Charlie now noticed that the well-to-do looking people had a subtle mist around them that seemed to be closing in. The man defying gravity radiated a transparent colorful mist, emanating away from him, as though giving back to the universe more energy than he used. It was the way Melissa painted, it was so clear. Charlie turned away and looked out over the lake from the kitchen. His eyes had been straining so he gave them a break by bathing them in the darkness of the night. Something was opening up inside him, something that had been buried years ago.

The water was a cold black, giving way to white caps on the tips of the waves. They rolled inland, licking the shore clean.

As a symphony could not be heard, this painting could not be seen. It had to be felt. It had been a long time since he had seen work produced with the clear essence of the senses in mind. With a deep breath in, Charlie went downstairs and sat on the futon.

His eyes became heavy and his body fell over onto the soft cushion. He could feel himself falling and, unlike the entrance to his recent dreams, he was not afraid. He fell through eleven dimensions, taking inventory and extracting all the information he needed. He landed in Sick Children's Hospital. Electronically charged, he drifted through the halls until reaching a room with CRITICAL written in big bold letters on the door. As he entered he saw five young girls and five young boys of no more than ten years apiece looking at him with wide trusting eyes, waiting for him. All were sitting in wheelchairs, their souls chained to the decrepit tomb of their bodies. Charlie smiled as the molecular form of his body changed into a controlled stream of conscious energy.

He entered the first child and directed himself through muscle tissue, the spine, the nervous system, all organs, then finally through the brain, repairing all damage. He entered the next child in the same fashion, then the next, and the next until all were healed. They stood up, smiled, and gave Charlie a silent thank you. Their faces grew strong and their eyes majestic, a look that showed Charlie that they would become the productive seeds of a benevolent universe.

Charlie's eyes opened and he could see a pale, yellow line reaching over the dark horizon of the lake. Morning was breaking. A warm healing sensation spread through his body, and for the first time in a long while, he closed his eyes and freely allowed sleep to embrace and carry him away ...

\* \* \*

*Try not to think about it,* John thought as he flipped though his Natural Gas codebook. He read through the manual, taking in nothing. Realizing he could not concentrate, he closed his book and stared at the painting on the wall. After a moment, he looked around the room. He lived on the fifth floor of a seventeen-story apartment building. It was spacious, with two bedrooms and a large kitchen. The living room and dining room fed into each other, creating an open concept and making the place appear larger than it actually was. There was a three-seat leather couch with a pine coffee table in front of it. A reclining chair sat off to the side, a cabinet holding a television and stereo system was centered on the wall separating the kitchen and living room. Melissa's painting was hung on the dining room wall over his computer table.

The place was spotless, but John got out the vacuum and pushed it over a four by eight rug in front of the couch. For fifteen minutes he unconsciously, neurotically, made imprints on the carpet as though he was trying to pull the fibers from their seams. The whining hum of the machine numbed his thoughts and he was free, momentarily, from his loneliness.

He turned it off and slowly, methodically, wrapped the cord around its housing. Frantically he tore it apart because it was not put away neatly enough. It took four tries until he was satisfied with the way it was. He stood looking around the living room. "Yes, that's it." He went to the dining room, took the painting off the wall, pulled out his tool box, grabbed a hammer and a nail, and moved the painting to the adjacent wall. Happy with the move, he looked around the room and went about switching everything around. With high energy, he unhooked his stereo, unplugged his lamps, and rearranged his furniture to other parts of the room. It took well over two hours and the room had completely changed. Not one item stayed in the place it was. Sweat rolled off his forehead and he took a deep breath. Proudly, he sat on the reclining chair and looked at his creation. The apartment was now his and his alone.

He picked up his book and tried to study again. Every few minutes he excitedly looked up at his new surroundings. Confidence overfilled him and he realized that he could make it on his own, he did not need Melissa's input anymore. He was self-sufficient. He continued to study, he did not look up for quite some time, but when he did something didn't seem right. As quickly as his confidence had come, it disappeared. The apartment wasn't right and he was only fooling himself thinking that he had any creative abilities. Slowly, resolutely, he moved everything back to exactly where it had been, the only evidence showing that something had been changed was the hole in the wall where he had moved the painting.

\* \* \*

Charlie could not remember the last time he had slept this well. When Melissa got home from shopping last night, she hadn't waked him. "A Vision of Hope" remained in his mind's eye throughout the night and protected him. He felt safe in Melissa's apartment and comforted by the way it was set up. He looked out over the lake and thought about the man who walked on air in Melissa's painting. It was as if he had been floating on a cushion of air while sleeping on the soft futon. He felt younger than his seventy-five years.

He watched Melissa move around the kitchen on the next level. She opened a closet on the wall just above the stairs, grabbed something, and ran down, being light on her feet.

"Good morning, Charlie. Did you sleep well?" Her smile was infectious.

He let out a half smile, but his face was heavy and pulled the muscles back down. "Yes, fine, thank you."

"Here's a towel." She pointed to the bathroom just under the kitchen beside her bookshelf. "If you want to shower you can …" She paused and her smile turned into a concerned look.

He grabbed the towel. "Yes, I think I will have a shower."

Her smile returned. "There's soap and shampoo on the rack. Please make yourself at home—" Again her face turned distressed.

Charlie placed his hand on her right shoulder. "Melissa, you're trying too hard. Stop being afraid of saying the wrong thing."

She relaxed her shoulders and tilted her head. His hand was large, heavy on her shoulder and emanated warmth down her arm. It made her feel good that he touched her. "I can make some tea if you want, I don't drink coffee, but I can go and get some," she said softly.

"No, tea is fine." Charlie went into the bathroom and closed the door.

When he finished showering he made his way to the kitchen where Melissa was sitting at the table. A steaming cup of tea awaited him. They sat in silence for a few minutes. Charlie looked at "A Vision of Hope" for a moment, then turned and looked out over the lake.

"Where are you from?" Melissa asked.

This was it, the beginning of their getting to know each other. Charlie had not looked into his past for a long time. Somehow it was safer that way. It was time. He had loved his childhood. In Melissa's eyes could be seen a soul that had not created any boundaries, a soul that had allowed the world to come in and release itself in an honest way, a soul that was close to the surface, too close. He was scared for her, it was not safe to be so open.

Charlie drew a deep breath and exhaled slowly. He was ready to let her into his world, at least partly. It took a moment to recall the images of his childhood, but then it all came flooding back to him in vivid colors. A feeling of euphoria overspread his body.

"I'm from No Man's Land." He paused for a moment. "It was called No Man's Land because the mountains bordered many countries. Immigrants built their own ethic communities." Melissa sat wide-eyed. "Bohdan, one of the highest, most remote places in the Carpathian Mountains. What a place!

"Our humble home overlooked the small village. We could see everything, as we were 200 feet above the rest. The only way to get to where we lived was from a suspension bridge over a rushing cascading mountain river. We were very isolated. I was the youngest of three brothers and a sister. My father was semi-literate, as were many people in the area, but he was a brilliant farmer and craftsman. He helped many people fix their dilapidated homes, not only for function, but also for style." Charlie could envision his father's large hands churning wood into unique living spaces that made people proud to live in small quarters. "He garnered a great deal of respect among the townspeople. Growing conditions weren't as good as in the lower regions, but my whole family tilled the land and brought forth a decent harvest, everybody but me. You see, I was considered different, special. My father would never let me touch anything with my hands. I was not to be taught to do menial work. I was supposed to read and educate myself." Charlie could feel his eyes narrow, visually impaired by the blinding thoughts of his youth. His memory, the invisible chamber of secrecy, would now open to Melissa and the theater of life would be exposed. "At the age of eight I was introduced to the spiritual leader in our community, a priest with a huge heart and a big stick. He reminds me of a young priest in the city here, minus the stick. He gave me the Bible to read. I read the whole thing in under a summer and remembered everything vividly. We spoke on many occasions about interpretations and meanings. I think he learned more from me than I from him.

"As interested as I was in the Bible, math was my true calling. Whenever my brothers and sister wondered why I was not helping out on the farm, my father would ask me to dazzle them with some math equation or thought they could not understand." Charlie smiled. "He would say to the rest of the family, 'He was not put here to work the land, the Lord put him here for a special purpose, I will not waste his talents on hard labor!' So I had the freedom to do what I wanted, which was mostly read and study. When I wasn't reading, I watched the sky. What mysterious beauty those mountains held. They were a panorama of color, depth, and majesty." A vista cracked open in his mind's eye showing him the rich spruce forest below the rocky tops, steep slopes, deep valleys, sharp edged glacial features ... It was safe to look now.

Charlie paused for more than a minute. Melissa sat silently. "I would sit and watch the sunsets. In the summer, the early evening sun would illuminate sparse areas of sky not blocked by clouds, adding more to my depth perception. It would cast bright yellows, deep reds and oranges over the tips of the rocks that shot thousands of feet out of the ground. They reached for the sky, cutting it open and turning everything blood red as though they had pierced the skin of the atmosphere. The scene was truly breathtaking. The sun would then sink in between the peaks, turning the sky yet other colors, this time softer, easier to look at yellows, purples, and oranges. The sun was the giver of life, warmth, energy and it was then I understood that light was the most important part of discovery. And it can be harnessed!" Charlie shook his head; he would not get into that now. "The mountains seemed less than spectacular in front of this color until they were able to draw the sun down behind them, leaving only the blackness of night. But not before, as though it would be the last time, all the colors melded together and shone, with all their force, and clutched onto the tips of the mountains to prevent the sun from sinking, dying. The thin line of fire red gave the impression that the sun had crashed into the other side of the earth, setting it ablaze." Charlie let out a long breath. He could feel sweat escaping from his pores. He remembered the vision perfectly and his voice grew animated as he carried on. It was as if his whole childhood had risen before him. He was breathing now as he had breathed then, a nine-year-old boy. He could almost smell the fresh bread baking in the wood stove through the mountain air as his senses sprung to life at the memory. He did not resist. "It was as if I could figure out how things were, how the universe worked, just by watching the sky." Charlie sighed. "One day, as I looked up, I asked my father, 'What makes the sky so beautiful, so blue?' He looked around and smiled a smile so content, so inspired, and replied, 'It's all part of the grand design of our creator. Look at all that God has given us.' His arms opened wide. 'The magnificent sky and the transparent air that gives us life, the singing birds, the flowing tender grass in the breeze. Look, my boy!' he blurted in a fit of passion. 'At the beauty of immaculate and sinless nature! We should be humbled by this grand design because we as humans are filled with vices and sins. Life is heaven, should we choose to live up to it.' He patted me on the back and went back to his chores. It was then that I made an important discovery about myself. I was different. His response did not answer my question. I needed some kind of proof or theory, some way for my senses to validate the cause.

"At the age of nine, armed with what little knowledge I had accrued from some hopelessly outdated books, I set out to watch the sky and to figure it out. Then there it was, clear as the mountain water rushing over the stones. On the third day, when the mountains began to swallow the sun, I felt the lump in my throat move, and I figured it out. The sun sank quickly, and then at the transition from light to dark, just as it was about to vanish, a flash momentarily lit up the tips of the mountains, which opened a channel in my mind. I knew why the sky was blue and what caused the spectacular sunsets I had before me." Charlie felt a surge of energy radiating within him. His recollection opened areas in his mind that he had not willfully gone to for a long time, and all the boundaries he had created over the years had now fallen. He remembered being different, independent and unbound by common ideas and conventions. A healing sensation spread through his body and he felt excitement well within him as he continued, a little more animated than before. He described in detail how the sun's white light meets the earth and how it's scattered across the atmosphere ... Melissa sat attentive. "I explained it all to my father and he said, 'That's God's creation and he's given you the vision to see it clearly, my son'. Then out of nowhere popped into my mind numbers and equations that put together some of the most beautiful visions I had never seen before. And that's when I figured out who I was.

"It was a connection I had with the vast capabilities of my mind. On that day when darkness spread through the valley, a light illuminated my soul. I realized that the sun, which had betrayed me so often removing its warmth and color from me everyday, was only a beacon of blinding light taking from me the star-coated universe that was mine to discover.

"The endless black wove itself between the stars as our planet propelled through space. I was in awe of the magnificent symmetry of our galaxy. I was a part of the overall method of things, an integral pulse of energy, hearing, feeling ... I was a spectator, an active spectator! It was my job to bring forth my visions for mankind to use in the spirit of life. My father was correct in a way, I was not born to turn the soil I was born to look out into all of life's creations to perceive that which is!" Charlie stopped there, still deep in reflection. He was that boy of nine years old and he didn't want to leave for a while. He held on tightly to this memory as he turned and looked across the living room, out the window, casting his glance onto the lake.

Melissa waited for a few moments and then said, "I don't understand." Her face turned crimson. "How did you go from there to ... here?" She opened her arms in despair.

"Not now, Melissa, we'll discuss that on another occasion." Charlie's head tilted up slightly as he let out a contented sigh. How wonderful it was to feel like that again.

Melissa got up and went down to her easel. The phone rang and she jumped up to answer it. It was John, and Charlie could see that there was something deeply disturbing her as she slowly placed the phone into its cradle.

"I have to go out for a little while. Are you okay? Do you need anything?"

"No, I'm fine."

She looked solemn and the light in her eyes defused. "Please tell me that you'll be here when I get back." Her voice was diffident.

"I'll be here."

She grabbed her keys and left the apartment.

# Chapter 18

Splitting up with Melissa was not going to be easy. There were many things to deal with. As talented as she was with her art, there were many other things to consider when running a soup kitchen and hotline for distressed people. It was a hundred thousand dollar a year expenditure. Not only were there employees and volunteers to deal with, there were all the bills: rent, electricity, heat, food, and on and on and on. Melissa had dealt with none of those things. John took it upon himself to make sure things ran smoothly in these areas. Everybody liked him. He recruited people he knew from other shelters to work for Melissa. He trusted them all implicitly and treated them as friends. Dealing with people was not Melissa's strong point, so he happily took on the operational responsibilities of the business. It was good experience for when he would start his own company. John decided he would still help out, but didn't feel right about dealing with the finances now. He called her and set up an appointment to meet. Donna's Deli was the chosen meeting place. Their apartments were not options, too much could happen being alone together.

When Melissa arrived, John was already sitting at a table. He had in front of him a file folder, a coffee for himself, and a tea for Melissa. She sat down without a word and looked at John. His face was sharp and emotionless. He showed her what bills to pay and when. The accounts had to be kept at a certain amount because some bills came out automatically every month. He wrote everything down and highlighted important dates, she listened but took very little in. Everything seemed unreal. Her mind drifted and touched upon many things: times they spent together, feelings they shared, the day they met.

John was serving soup and she was sketching. He was an attractive tall youthful man, with thick brown hair, and compassionate eyes. Melissa had watched John, although he would not have known she was watching because of her ability to be inconspicuous; in fact, she had even sketched him on a couple of occasions. His profile was round and soft displaying a gentle demeanor without obscuring his strong physiognomy. She was wearing comfortable, loose fitting clothes, had her hair pulled back, and although had found his presence pleasing, was not interested in "getting to know him better" as others had asked. But he approached and tried to make conversation. She was her normal cold and callous self. He persisted, being funny and charming even by her standards, and at some point while looking into his eyes something inside her had completely opened up. A place she had always kept closed and safe.

"... and this is the account you use for paying the gas bills. Don't mix it up, because you get a considerable rebate from the government at the end of the year, and we want to make it as easy as possible for them to see where it's coming from. Melissa ... Melissa?"

"Oh yes, I'm sorry. From this account. I understand." Her chest tightened. "Why do we have to do this? What is so difficult that we can't—?"

"Melissa, let's not go there now, let's stick to the business at hand." His face tightened a little. "This is not easy for me, either, but I think it is best for both of us."

"Is that it?" Melissa let her anger free. "So after all we've been through together, you're willing to just call it quits?"

"Listen, if you need me to help with these things," He directed his attention to the files in front of him, "or something around your apartment, I'll be there for you, but only on a friendship level."

"I know we'll see each other at the kitchen, but can we still go for coffee or dinner together, you know just to talk or ...?" Melissa eased her tone.

"Let's just see how it goes and deal with things as they come."

"Okay," said Melissa resignedly.

They discussed the rest of the things pertaining to the finances. Melissa told John that she had found Charlie and that he was staying with her. She didn't go into too much detail other than to say that there was something very special about him. She noticed that John wanted to say something, maybe ask something while she was speaking of Charlie, but he remained silent. He was so strong. She wanted to know what he was thinking, to give his opinion, to make her laugh. They parted without a kiss, a hug, or even a handshake.

* * *

As Melissa entered her apartment she noticed Charlie was sitting at the kitchen table scribbling something on a piece of paper. She went up to have a look. He had taken a post-it note from the refrigerator and was writing equations so small, she wondered how he could see them. The paper was filled except a tiny corner he was now working with.

"Do you need some paper?" Melissa asked.

Charlie looked up at her and said nothing. His eyes showed deep concentration, his body was relaxed save the deep wrinkles on his brow that seemed to hold all his stress, pressing together as though being pinched by fingers. He scratched his head, messing up his hair so that a clump stuck out to the side. "Yes, some paper. That would be good."

"Why didn't you take a sheet from my sketch book?"

"It's not my place to do that." Charlie's brow relaxed.

"I told you to feel free to do what you wanted." Melissa shook her head and ran down the stairs. She opened a box beside her easel and pulled out a fresh pad of heavyweight drawing paper. She ran back up the stairs.

"Don't you ever walk, Child?"

Melissa furrowed her brow. "What do you prefer to work with? Pencil? Pen?"

"A light pencil first, then a thin black marker for permanence." Charlie looked Melissa up and down, seemingly taking inventory of her tension.

She opened a drawer where cutlery would normally be. "In here," she began sharply, thrusting numerous objects out in front of her, "is everything you'll need, pencils, erasers, sharpeners, thin markers, thick markers …"

"Close the drawer and sit down." Charlie's voice was low, but his tone held the authority of a father with a stern disposition.

Melissa automatically sat down and had the strange feeling that she was about to get a lecture. She crossed her arms in front of herself.

"What's troubling you?" His voice softened.

"John doesn't want to be with me anymore." Her voice turned angry. "I gave him the best of me and now he's willing to just end it. What gives him the right to do that to me?"

Charlie did not say anything.

"He doesn't understand how I am and what I have to do, how could he? You understand that, don't you?"

"Understand what?" Charlie's eyebrows rose slowly.

"You know, having a special capacity. Being able to see things others don't. Because of that, I am obligated to act in a certain way. I couldn't just let these visions lie dormant in my mind. If I didn't let them out, I don't know what would happen to me. There's a strange connection I have with something inside me, something powerful, I can't pretend it doesn't exist." Melissa looked at Charlie and noticed a sad expression pass over his eyes. Then, as if he had noticed Melissa watching him, his eyes became strong, reassuring.

"What was the reason he gave for breaking up the relationship?"

Melissa shot up from her sitting position, opened the drawer below the one with pencils, and pulled out John's note. She handed it to Charlie and sat silently while he read it.

He folded the note back up and placed it on the table. "Has he ever tried to stop or hinder your visions in any way?"

"No, actually, he's been very supportive."

"Then it's very simple, what he needs from you, that is."

"What do you mean?"

"It's all in the letter. Maybe it's because I'm a man that I understand so clearly."

"What? What's in the letter?" She quickly picked up the note and read and reread it. She didn't know what he was talking about.

"Let's start from the beginning. Things between the two of you were good and strong at one point, correct?"

"Oh yes, the passion, friendship, love." Melissa felt her body warm.

"When did things start falling apart?"

"When I began the painting of Joanne, I suppose."

"A big moment."

"Yes, when I was standing on top of that building and the painting fell," her body tingled at the memory, "I was connected with … I don't know, it was like I was some kind of transformer of universal energy, like I had a direct line to something great … something I don't fully understand yet. And now that I've made the connection, I know that I can make it again." Melissa studied Charlie's reaction for a moment. "I can see you know exactly what I mean."

"I do, Melissa, but I also know that you will suffer the same fate I've suffered if you don't change a few fundamental things. This world can be a lonely place for people like us."

"Change!"

"Relax, I am not suggesting that you change anything about your nature. It's not possible, believe me I've tried. I'm saying that you have to mature into yourself."

Melissa placed her hand over her mouth and thought deeply.

"Let me ask you a few very important questions. Do you love John?"

"More than anything, more than I think possible for most."

"Do you look up to him?"

"He is my highest ideal, I respect him immeasurably. I used to think that I would never find somebody that could lift me the way he does."

"Do you have questions about him being worthy of you as you discover new areas within yourself?"

Melissa could not answer that right away. She thought about what her father had told her. How she would leave John behind and that it wouldn't be fair to him; if she really loved him, she would have to let him go so that he may find his true soul-mate. "My father doesn't think so, he says I have to let John go for his own good. I questioned that for a while, but came to the conclusion that there's nobody that could fill his position with me."

"And what is that position?"

Melissa thought for a moment and a light went on in her mind. Her eyes lit up and she picked up the note and read it again. "Oh, my," she said.

Charlie smiled and opened his hands. "You seem to have found the answer."

"John is not doing this *to* me, he's doing it *for* me. He thinks he's holding me back, like my father said."

"He's worried that he won't measure up to you in the future. My guess is that you were so wrapped up in the painting of Joanne that you looked down on John as less important. He seems to be a proud man, you have to validate that pride, and you have to value him." Charlie paused. "Only if you believe that inside, though. It is not something that you can fake. Especially you."

Melissa smiled. "I never have to fake my feelings with John." She thought about the times that they had spent together in the past. How stupid she felt! Mostly for treating him improperly, but also for abstaining from the love that had always been available for her. A warm glow burned within her heart. In a flash it turned cold and her whole body seized with regret. "King for a day."

"Pardon."

"I've just remembered a promise that I didn't keep. It's no wonder he dumped me. How could I have treated him so poorly? He doesn't know how much I need him. How could he?" Her head sank.

"Tell him."

"Why would he come back to me now?"

"Because he loves you," Charlie replied.

"How do I get him back?"

"By understanding what he needs as a man. You have to understand that a man needs to be looked up to. You must love him for your own interest, but value him above all else. He needs to know that you're inspired by him."

Melissa sat, attentive. She was looking at herself in a new way. Her thought process was engaged by his words. It was the way his voice resonated that opened channels, she thought. She could feel it in the pit of her stomach.

"Love is the greatest reward you can achieve as a human being. And for you, my child, it will not be easy to find again. With your special abilities, you won't have many people you'll be able to look up to. Whether it's John's honesty, his sense of life, his generosity, or something else that you have come to adore, does not matter. What matters is that you are willing to give yourself to him, surrender that part of you that you've been protecting. Trust him with it."

*It's his sense of life* ... "I've been above him in my mind." Melissa looked down across the living room and out the window. What a sense of life John had inspired. "I'm not sure I deserve him now." The lake was unusually calm.

"No, Melissa, you deserve him. Your love must be an integration of mind and body, of rational self-interest reflecting back to him all that you value of life and of him. You can not dichotomize any of these things, because even the most minute issue will expand and sabotage the whole relationship."

"Yes, I can see that." Melissa got up and walked down the stairs and sat in front of her easel. She looked up at Charlie who had watched her walk down. The clump of hair was still vertical on the side of his head. She smiled, that this brilliant man looked so child-like. He opened up the sketchpad, looked reverently at his pencil, and continued making impressions on the paper. Melissa looked at her easel with the picture of Charlie still on it and contemplated his words.

*  *  *

Charlie filled ten sheets of the drawing paper that Melissa had given him. On top of the first page was a note written so tiny that it was barely legible. It read: A metaphor for society. Identify pathogenic organisms through quartz-type illumination and dispose of to let the natural healthy state grow and flourish. It was written in Greek. The rest of the ten sheets were filled with symbols, circles, oblongs, figure eights, and a few other obscure shapes that only Charlie would be able to decipher without a map. Similar to the work he had left behind so many years ago. There was little white left on either side of the pages.

He stared intensely at page five. When Charlie possessed a thought, it had always found a way to express itself. It would start precariously clinging to the seedling of the possible, searching to find its full expression and grandeur in the flowering tree of reality. There was something disturbing him, something that did not fit. The whole of his attention was directed at that series of equations.

"Mind if I put on some music?" Melissa asked from the lower level.

Charlie heard her speak, but her question did not sink in for a moment. He lifted his head and the whole world seemed to change. Numbers flashed in the corner of his eyes transparent, then disappeared.

"Yes, if you wish, you don't need to ask me to put on music in your own home." Charlie felt the sharpness of his voice.

Melissa smiled. She fumbled around for a moment with the plastic case and dropped the compact disc into the player. She tapped the button directly and the music began.

A piano key struck a low cord ...

The sound rippled through Charlie, trapping all his thoughts in a sensation. *Why do I have to always feel so deeply?*

Mozart's Fantasy in C Minor thrust him into a captivated state. The incessant crashes of mortality thundered through his body. His heart was an anchovy stunned by the blasting sound of a Sperm Whale. But the music was not loud, it was the magnification of what it meant that left him paralyzed. The crashing keys were followed by a series of rapturous, serene sounds that elongated his spirit, bringing him to higher planes of feeling only to be snapped back with grounding recollections of violence. His blood pressure rose and his fate seemed imminent; he would surely not make it to the end of this piece of music.

Charlie's eyes were frozen to Melissa's work of art. There was a connection, and his mind struggled through the internal conflict brought on by the music. Her art and the music seemed to fuse together into a single concept, but what was it? It posed a challenge to Charlie's mind, a challenge as difficult as he ever had. All was soothing now in the notes, but he knew it wouldn't last long. Part of the equation was in the notes and part in the painting. It hung just out of his grasp, somewhere in the vast resources of his mind begging to be brought into the forefront and demanding resolution. The keys pounded ferociously, pushing the equation back into the depth of his mind. Again Charlie felt as if his heart would burst. He needed control, Bach's control; this piece was too erratic for an equation to free itself.

Just as the final curtain was drawing to a close in front of his eyes, the music turned heroically defiant, pulling him back from the abyss. Resonant chambers of his imagination opened and pictures flooded his consciousness. The music moved and imploded in his heart, like the crushing density of matter in his central core power then opened up with relative force; a nuclear furnace set off by the majesty of sound, changing the slow burning candle in his soul into a blazing flare. Exhausting in minutes, years from his time in this space. All turned silent now, except the last note, which hung in the air and echoed through his mind. It faded out and he could hear the thumping of his heart as sweat escaped from his pores. Melissa hit the stop button.

Charlie breathed deeply, looked down out the window and over the lake. He wiped a tear from his eye. In the span of twelve minutes he had climbed unsurpassable mountains, dove the depth of the sea, and reached out to distant stars only to be metaphorically slapped in the face and told, 'You're only human' as though that were insignificant. To feel the spectrum of ugliness and beauty, power and weakness, prosperity and poverty all within the exchange of a few breaths! A profound sense of wholeness filled his soul as he confirmed that being human was the highest order. The depth of all his senses and introspection made him feel strong, deserving.

"Isn't that a wonderful piece of music?" Melissa looked up at Charlie. "It really fuels my imagination."

Charlie looked into her eyes, thinking that she could not fully experience the depth of that piece. Grooves were still being formed in her mind, and deep rich connections were yet to be made. He rested his hand under his chin to stop his head from crashing onto the table. His body was old and could not handle many more moments like that.

"Yes," was all he could say as he wiped the sweat from his brow.

Melissa's face turned crimson. "Are you sure you don't drink?"

"Yes, I'm sure."

Melissa ran up the stairs and sat across from Charlie. She looked down at his notes. Charlie turned to her painting and stared. There was a minute of silence. He tried to regain composure.

"What do you think?"

Charlie did not say anything right away. He turned away from the painting and toward Melissa. "Is this typical of the ones you sell?"

"Similar. It's one of my favorites so I kept it, something unfinished in my mind about it. I did get offered twenty thousand dollars for it, though."

"I'm surprised." Charlie looked back at it.

Melissa's eyes narrowed and her back straightened. "Why are you surprised?"

"I thought as a painter that you would have grown a thick skin by now. You seem offended."

Her shoulders relaxed. "Usually it doesn't bother me, I get all kinds of bad reviews on my work, and I am paid well for my efforts. It's just you saying … ." She fell silent

"I would like to meet the people that buy your work." She had a natural appearance, an easy but strong energy. He was really starting to like her.

"That's what I used to think. I used to go to the openings and the parties to meet people who bought my work. It's not the kind of appreciation I was looking for. Nobody really understood me. But that didn't matter as much as giving back to those I … ," Her eyes met his, "… exploit, I think was the word you used."

Charlie's heart opened. Her eyes were brilliant, innocent. "I was wrong to say that. I was angry and scared, and you were a perfect place to vent."

"That's okay. You were right in a lot of ways. I know I have growing to do. I feel like I'm making a lot of mistakes."

"No, Melissa, you're making just enough."

She placed her hands between her knees, stretched her arms fully, and rubbed her face against her shoulder. She waited a moment and took a deep breath. "Why are you surprised that I was offered twenty thousand dollars for that painting?"

Charlie turned his head and looked at the painting. It was so deep and accurate. He got a little more out of it each time he looked.

"You can tell me honestly what you think, I'm strong. I can take it." She straightened her posture.

"You're still so young." Charlie paused and organized what he wanted to tell her. He had wanted to talk about her painting. "You know so much and so little at the same time. Look at what you've done here." He pointed toward her painting. "You've accentuated this young boy with intricate clarity. His eyes, when seen with the whole of his body, show the totality of the human spirit, from the hearth of the streets to heights of the tallest skyscraper and all the soul is capable of. You have shown it all in the eyes of the boy." Charlie studied the painting. "The people passing by depict clearly how little they have discovered about their own true nature. They are automatons being dragged around by a force they deem their own, but it's not. They fancy themselves independent, but they're trapped by torpid minds that never put forth the effort needed to view reality honestly. They look down on the boy with the key to life in his eyes and stick up their noses in protection of that which scares them the most: the light part of their soul. They are above him; a trick the ego plays to protect them from stepping out of their comfort zone, a zone that shrinks as they grow old until they are barely able to stretch their arms. That key!" Charlie was becoming riled as his fist came down on the table. Melissa's eyes were wide and her expression blank. He lifted his finger to the coin. "Is the answer to their life, a symbol which if turned, could connect them to reality and juxtapose them with the energy of the universe so that they might walk effortlessly, freely, as the boy does later in life." He pointed to the man who flicked the coin. "They don't know that they are actually following the wretched boy with his hand out. He's not begging for money, he's summoning the energy of the universe. He's willing to look at reality and garner its power for his own use and turn it into gold. This is not a painting of the homeless, it's a metaphor for all the people that waste their lives never seeking out that which is their birthright: to live side by side with nature and each other in happiness, prosperity, and benevolence."

Charlie's heart raced. His head fell towards his chest and he took slow deep breaths, thinking his heart would burst if he continued to look at the painting. His heart slowed and he looked up at Melissa.

Her mouth was frozen open as she looked at him. Her unblinking eyes showed Charlie that she did not know what to say. Then, in a split second, she jumped up from her chair and embraced him with unfettered emotion, as only a woman is capable, as Melissa was capable. Her affection stirred in him emotions he had hidden for so long. Feelings he thought he would never experience again after Joanne's death. He gently broke the embrace.

She moved as slowly as he had ever seen her move and sat down. "Thank you. Nobody has come close to interpreting my painting like you have. You've even helped me see it more clearly." She paused and looked at her work. "With all you said, why do you find it surprising that people would pay large sums of money to have this?"

Charlie could not look at the painting for fear of seeing more. He had been through enough this evening. "For the same reason Van Gogh lived his life in poverty."

She had a deep look in her eyes. Charlie liked that look on her. As impulsive as she was, she did think about things deeply and would, in time, understand him. When he spoke she listened with reverence. He watched her for a moment then snapped his fingers. "Yes! That's it." The sought after equation took root and broke to the surface of his mind.

Melissa was startled from her trance-like state. She smiled knowingly.

Charlie cupped his hand over his chin. Looking down at his work, he flipped to page five and began making notes. He could feel Melissa watching him as he made lines and amendments. He looked up at her.

She stood up with her normal perkiness. "Sorry, I'll leave you alone now." Her eyes danced and her smile spanned the width of her face. "I can't believe you figured out that the boy is actually the man. Now if you could let me know how the key works, I would be happy. I have this strong sense that I will find out, maybe even from you."

Charlie continued to look at Melissa. He would not look at the painting again tonight. And no more music!

Melissa flew down the stairs and continued working at her easel.

* * *

The plane descended toward the runway. The tires hit the ground at Toronto's Pearson Airport with a screech. It bounced once, then abruptly slowed down, jolting Special Agent Edwards in his seat.

He turned to his partner. "Let's get this trip over with quickly, Ken. I still can't believe we were sent here to find a seventy-five year old man that they're not even sure is still alive." Mark undid his seat belt as the plane docked.

"Yeah, I know. They didn't want to alert anybody by calling ahead. Must be something special about this guy."

"They give us this assignment like there's nothing else for us to do. I can't believe all the crap they're putting on our plate these days," Mark scorned.

"Cut, cut, cut, pretty soon we'll be looking for lost dogs." Ken laughed. "Oh well, no questions, remember."

"What a line of crap. Our last three missions were so open that even the customs agents knew what we were doing there." Mark shook his head. "I have to get a new job."

The plane began to empty. The two agents got off, cleared customs, and rented a car.

# Chapter 19

Melissa opened her art box and looked for some sketches she wanted to work with. It struck her that there was a sketchbook at John's apartment. The idea of calling him to bring it over thrilled her.

She called and left a message on his service to ask him to bring it by. At 5:30 she ran up the stairs, past Charlie, who did not lift his head from his work, and up to her bedroom. She picked out some clothes, ran down the stairs into the bathroom, and changed into a skirt that hung just above the knees. It was John's favorite. She came out, ran back up to the kitchen, and stood in front of Charlie.

He did not look up, as though she wasn't in the room. She tapped her foot on the floor. Still, he was deeply enthralled in his work. She coughed.

Finally his head raised and he faced her. His eyes narrowed. "Is there something you want?"

"Well?"

"Well what?" Charlie seemed upset at this game.

"Aren't you going to ask why I'm looking so sexy?" She smiled radiantly.

"Because John's coming over," he replied.

"You heard me on the phone. I'm hoping he comes over, anyway. I was thinking of asking him out to dinner. What do you think?"

"Good idea." Charlie dropped his head and continued with his work.

Melissa ran down the stairs and stood in front of the window and looked out over the city.

Six o'clock on the nose and a knock came on the door. Melissa looked up at Charlie and smiled. "He has a key, you know. I don't think he's ever knocked to get in," she said.

Charlie just nodded his head.

She answered the door. "Hi, John. Thanks for coming."

"Hi." He held out the pad, trying not to enter her apartment.

She pulled him in by the arm. "Come in, I want you to meet Charlie."

Reluctantly, he entered. She introduced them. John shook Charlie's hand and they exchanged pleasantries, acknowledging that they had seen each other before in the shelters and at the Plex. Melissa beamed at her two most favorite people in the world meeting. When John shifted his glance her way, she pulled her shoulders back and took a deep breath in. She felt like a peacock spreading its tail.

"Well, I have to get going." John shook Charlie's hand again.

"It was nice meeting you, John." Charlie embraced his hand a little longer than normal for a handshake.

Melissa ran down the stairs before John. She turned around. "Do want to have dinner with me tonight?"

"No, I don't think it would be—"

"It would be just as friends," Melissa cut in. "And I ... need to ask you some questions about running the shelter."

"Melissa, I don't think we should."

She touched his shoulder. "Please have dinner with me?"

He held his forefinger up straight, firm. "All right, but just as friends."

"Absolutely, let me grab my purse." She ran up the stairs to her bedroom, her movement hindered only slightly by her dress.

Charlie looked at John. "She's creates a good breeze."

"Yeah, I know, she has to learn how to slow down a little."

She flew down the stairs past Charlie, down the next flight of stairs, and straight to John. She slipped on some shoes.

John waved his hand to Charlie and walked out the door. Melissa grabbed under his arm and let him guide her to the elevator.

* * *

They decided on San Pedro's for Mexican food. As they walked in a dark-skinned man with a heavy Mexican accent greeted them. He sat them in a booth in the corner, obviously assuming they wanted privacy, and gave them menus.

They scanned them. Another man approached and asked if they wanted something to drink. When he mentioned wine, John abruptly cut in with a firm "No!" knowing what had happened in the past over a bottle of wine. He could not afford that right now. Especially the way Melissa's hair hung around her face like a waterfall, and her skirt clinging close to the subtle lines of her body. The look in her eyes, the ever-so-slight perfumed scent, and the soothing Spanish guitar in the background caressed his senses. He found himself letting go when he noticed Melissa looking at him, smiling. She was trying to seduce him. He took a deep breath and detached himself.

He lifted his eyebrows. "Have you decided what you want to eat?"

She pointed to an item on the menu. "Yes, I think I'll have this."

They ordered their food and made light conversation. It wasn't long before dinner came. John ate, Melissa talked. She spoke of Charlie and how brilliant he was. She told him of his home and how much more there was to him than met the eye. John was truly fascinated by the way Melissa described Charlie. Her face glowed and her body was animated as she spoke. It was difficult to control his feelings. He thought it was a mistake coming here with her, but he was enjoying the moment. Her presence lifted him. John finished his meal. Melissa pushed her untouched plate away and the waiter hesitantly cleared it.

"I have a confession." Melissa looked John in the eyes.

"Oh?" John had a strange feeling, a foreboding of some deep discussion. He wasn't sure he was ready to go there yet.

"I don't have any questions about the running of the shelters."

"Well, there's a big surprise."

"Okay, there's no need to be that sarcastic. I know I'm not a very good liar." Her face took on a serious look. "I need to talk to you. I have to get this off my chest. I know you're resolute in your decision that we should go our separate ways and I respect that, but I want to let you know that I assume full responsibility for this." Her elated and bright appearance had all of a sudden turned dark.

"Melissa, it's not a matter of responsibility." John thought for a moment. He could not say what he really felt, that he would only stunt her growth. He would have to hurt her. It was the only way to make a clean break. "It's just that you're traveling in a direction in life that I don't want to travel in. I have ideas of how I want my life to be, and I'm sorry, but you're just not a part of it."

"Yes, I know, I realize that now looking into your eyes, but for me to carry on with my life in the direction I'm going, I have to clear my conscience where you're concerned. When I started the painting of Joanne, I became totally absorbed with it. I was so caught up in doing this wonderful thing for society that I forgot about everything else that was important to me. Your opinion, which I respected above all else until then, I couldn't even hear because my need for justice had consumed me. The most important things seemed unimportant and all that mattered was that painting. As I look back, I realize everything I missed with you during that time. You never once tried to stop me; you only, rightly I might add, tried to dissuade me from doing it. I never thought about the people that could be hurt by such a stunt. It was like I was doing this marvelous thing for humanity, not fully taking into account how it affected individuals like Gerald, his officers, you.

"You knew that, though, but I wouldn't listen." She paused for a moment and studied John. Her face took on a concerned look and a diffused sadness spread out across it.

John didn't know what to say and was concerned about this sudden change in her.

She continued, "You know, John, some people look back on their lives when they are old and wonder where they went wrong. What was it that made their lives mediocre, humdrum? Most would not be able to pinpoint a single time as they struggle with their memory. They live their lives, their one and only life, reinforcing self-doubt, always putting off until some later date getting started on that big dream, then settle comfortably in helplessness until the spark of life that burned so strong in youth, fades into, 'If only I was ten years younger …'

"That won't be me, though. Nope. I'll know exactly where I screwed my life up and where I failed. It will be the painting of Joanne, a venture I took on without prudence. It didn't have to be done that way. I will reflect back in my golden years, and look at the only love I could have had. I already know now that there will be nobody else who will inspire me the way you have; nobody else I could look up to the same as I do you. I will look back with sadness, but also with joy, for even though I can't hold onto you, I still have a kind of admiration that most could not comprehend … You know the thing I will regret most as I look back on my life?"

All John could do was shrug his shoulders.

"The opportunity I missed to treat you like a king. One day is like an eternity to me now. How great that would have been. You did everything but slap me in the face and say, 'Don't you remember your promise to me!' But it's not you who suffers most from my thoughtlessness, it's me. In your life and on your path, you will find many women who will treat you like a king, not only for a day or a year, but always. It will be easy for a man like you to find someone strong and independent to grow with. You deserve that. She'll be fascinated with the woman you loved. 'How did she let you get away?' she'll ask as she revels in having you then." Melissa stopped, shifted her head sideways, and held her chin high.

"Thank you for all you've done for me, how you've inspired me, and I hope you, too, can look back on our relationship with affection, and not only think of me as a self-absorbed person who didn't know what was good for her."

Melissa stood up. "I'm going to make my own way home. I need to walk alone, to think awhile." She opened her purse and placed fifty dollars on the table.

John stood up, not knowing what to say. He could feel his mouth open and hoped that the right words might magically appear.

Melissa placed her forefinger over John's lips. "Please let me walk out without another word, I need to digest what I just said. It wasn't really what I intended to say, but looking at you now, I know you're right to leave me. You can do better. I'll see you around." She turned and walked out of the restaurant.

John sat there for over an hour. He stared straight ahead, and at one point, forgot where he was. He went over everything he could recall from her admission. It was not all her fault! After all, he could have been more understanding. He felt horrible that she was so upset with herself. He had never seen her so down before. He didn't like it. Her confidence had always inspired him. Did he inspire her in that way, too? Her finger had been firm while touching his lips, leaving the area she had touched all he could feel and bringing up vivid pictures of the two of them together.

* * *

Gerald looked at Terese as though to say, "What's going on here?" He faced the taller of the two men. "Charlie Smith is what we have in the file here." He opened his hand to some paper on his desk.

"What's his address?" The taller of the two men stood with a pad and pen making notes as he asked questions. The other looked around Gerald's office.

"What's this all about? Has he broken some law?" Terese did not like the looks of these men. They were hiding something.

"Oh no, it's nothing like that. Ken and I are private investigators from the States hired by a distant family member. Actually, the estate of Joyce Hampton hired us. She has recently passed away and left a considerable fortune to her next of kin. We did a search and found out, through some tedious legwork, that he was here in Toronto. We discovered that he had just recently been fingerprinted and a query had been done by this precinct. That's why we'd like his address, so that he can claim his inheritance and we our fee." Mark closed his note pad and put his pen away.

Terese narrowed her eyes and shifted her glance toward Gerald. She hadn't gotten to be a detective by being naïve. There was something wrong here, something unscrupulous about these two men, although she couldn't quite pinpoint it.

Gerald smiled. "The man is homeless. He was picked up off the street and given medical treatment. While he was here, we discovered that he had information on a young homeless girl who died on the street. He told us what he knew and we released him. Of course we could get no address because he has none."

"You mean he just went back to the street?" Ken asked abruptly.

Gerald opened his arms. "I don't know. With no fixed address it's hard to say."

"We heard that a young painter actually brought him to the station. What was her name?" He flipped through his notepad. "Melissa Belmont?"

"No, he was brought into the station by one of my officers," Gerald replied. It was, in fact, his officer who brought him in the first time to clear the streets for the parade.

"Well, thank you very much for your time," Mark said as he pulled out a business card. "If you find him and he's interested in claiming his inheritance, please give us a call."

Mark and Ken left the room.

"Private investigators, do you believe that?" Terese questioned.

Gerald shook his head no. "They look like government agents of some sort."

\* \* \*

Melissa stopped at her soup kitchen, said hello to the volunteers, and had a seat at a table. Her legs burned as she had walked for what seemed like miles. She stared blankly at the bare wall. She had not expected to say what she had said in the Mexican restaurant, and she could not figure out why she had had to say it. The moment her lips opened, she could not stop herself. There was a knot forming in her stomach. It was the first time she had felt that the best part of her life was behind her, the first feeling of getting older.

"Is this seat taken?"

"What? No, I guess ..." Melissa looked up to see Father Bower standing beside her.

He sat down and smiled. "How are you, Melissa?"

She shrugged her shoulders.

"Anything you want to talk about, I've been told I'm a good listener."

"Part of the job, isn't it?"

"Yes, I guess it is, at that." He smiled easily. "Well?"

His voice soothed her. She softened her tone. "No offence, Father, but it's a matter you could know nothing about."

"You may call me by my first name, Will, and I assure you that I am well versed in matters of the heart. In fact, you might call it my specialty."

"What makes you think it's love?"

"People are open books, Melissa, if you take the time to read. I can tell much about a person by the way they walk, how their faces distort when sad or elated, by looking without bias into the eyes to see the condition of their soul. You do the same every time you paint. You look and feel deeper than most."

"How would you know about what I put into my artwork and what I feel?"

"I've gone to some of your art shows. I was so moved the first time I saw anything of yours that I stared at it, losing myself to time, until I was told the gallery was closing for the day. I went back the very next day to look again without knowing that it had been sold. Again, you had released another painting. This time I was smart and went to the show early so that I might have longer to look. The piece was called 'A Life Cycle'." He paused, staring directly into Melissa's eyes. "And of course there was the painting you dropped on the day of the parade."

She could not explain the feeling, but it was recharging. "A Life Cycle" had been her second favorite piece, and later she had reproached herself for parting with it. The fifteen thousand dollars it brought was the most she had sold a painting for at the time, and she had become caught up with what she could do with the money, not realizing how much she would miss it.

"It didn't take long to realize that I wanted that painting, so I made my bid high and won out over many other interested parties.

"You have my painting?" Melissa felt a surge of jealousy.

"Yes," he said proudly.

"Aren't you supposed to give up all worldly possessions? Where did you get the money?"

"That's not entirely correct. Technically, though, my parents own the painting and it is, in fact, at their home. They mortgaged their house so that I could look at it when I wish. Which is often. I went to other shows and auctions of yours, but you were never there."

Melissa bowed her head. "No, I couldn't bear it any longer."

"Yes, I guessed that. You could never find anybody who appreciated you and your work. Even the buyers." Will stopped for a moment and studied Melissa. "Don't be so hard on them though, they are not yet capable of identifying with the type of beauty your soul possesses."

"What do you know about my soul?" Melissa shot back defiantly.

"I know the beauty you allow through your work. But now looking into your eyes, it appears you've lost something important." His voice was soft, confident.

He reached out his hand and took hers. She tried to fight it internally, to show him that she was independent and could get through this without help. But his hand was soft and strong and housed an energy she could not describe. She could not pull away now if she tried.

"Maybe I can be of help, if only an ear to listen."

"John, my boyfriend—ex-boyfriend—has decided to leave me. I never once thought that he could leave me. But when I looked at him across the dinner table, I saw a man who could have anybody he wants. He's handsome, honest, and cares more deeply than anyone I could expect to meet. I looked into his eyes and saw a man that deserves better than me."

"Ah, so it is, with the good." Will smiled.

"Pardon?"

"Melissa, you're good in ways that you're totally unaware of. It's as natural to you as walking or even breathing."

"What are you talking about?"

"He dwells within you."

Melissa pulled her hand away from his. "You had to bring God into it. Everything was going fine until now. I don't believe in—" She eased her tone. "I don't really want to go there right now."

"Oh but, Melissa, it's hard for me not to see God in you from your work. It's so deeply spiritual. The transcendental faces you depict, and your response to human nature, are of the deepest forms of meditation. So deep, in fact, that the only conclusion I can come to is that you are well versed with some of the most enlightened ways of praying. Your soul, although in need of some repair, is of a level so rarely seen these days. You have a profound connection with the Divine. Open your heart and let yourself experience it."

"Your God was created by man, not the other way around. And I don't pray." Melissa paused to gather her thoughts. Will had been kind to her and she did not want to insult him or his beliefs. "I think we should stop this conversation."

"No, please continue. I'm interested in what you have to say."

"Your religion has done nothing but suppress society. The man you revere as a saint, Augustine, set the foundation that dragged all of humanity into a thousand years of darkness. The premise of his writing is still accepted today, instilling guilt into the mind of man in order to control him. We are presumed guilty before we can even speak. Your religion traffics in guilt. You tell me what a child, an innocent being, is guilty of?"

Melissa paused. She could feel a surge of emotion pass through her body. "God, in your religion, has been a weapon of oppression against pagans, Jews ... and women are considered far beneath men in your religion. Actually, weren't women an afterthought? Wasn't woman only a companion for man extracted from his rib? Why was it, in the Dark Ages, condoned that a woman could be beaten, killed, even raped within the Church?"

"There's nothing in the Bible condoning any of those things." There was a pause. "Both man and woman are created by the force of the Holy Spirit and reflect that image through their individuality," Father Bower said patiently.

"Yes, but your religion believes that a woman is only a possession of the man, filling the role of servant, or slave is probably more accurate." Melissa paused, trying to control her anger. She took a deep breath and felt a pang of guilt, she did not know why, and continued, "Women are not considered quite worthy in your God's eyes. It was Eve who persuaded Adam to eat the forbidden fruit. After all the literature, the sermons, the beatings, rapes, even killings women believe, innately, that they are inferior. You know what it is, Father? It's the strong emanating sexual presence women hold naturally, beautifully, that leaves men feeling inferior and out of control. And when a man can no longer control the empty lust within him, he has been allowed to use his overpowering physical strength to take that which he did not earn. You sit with your high morals behind a philosophy that condones the most vile form of treachery."

"I don't condone any form of violence against another human being, except in defense of the self. Also, two thousand years ago there was limited information about human nature—"

Melissa cut in. "Yes, but the prejudice stands today. Don't get me wrong, Father, I don't advocate or support any women's movements, but I strongly support individual rights. I know of the many differences between the sexes and know that equality, in no uncertain terms, cannot be achieved. But, Father, I'm a strong willed person whose soul is as worthy as yours or any other man." Her back straightened. She could feel goose bumps forming on her arms.

Will chuckled. "More worthy, I'd say."

Melissa narrowed her eyes. She had said exactly what she felt. She was willing to look at life honestly and ... That was it! The guilt she felt. That was the conflict within her. How could she preach so adamantly against a system that puts men on a higher level than women, when she had put herself on a higher level than John, the person she loved and respected most? She became completely empty inside.

"You're very intelligent and I have learned more about you today, Melissa." Will rubbed his chin.

"I assure you, Father, that my beliefs do not stem from ignorance." Melissa stood up, getting ready to leave. She thought of Charlie and needed to find out more about him.

"Neither do my beliefs." Will stood up. "It seems there is a great deal I can learn from you."

"Well, I have to go now." Melissa extended her hand. It felt strange that Will did not try to combat her. She had driven close to the heart of his religion and he did not try to give excuses or even try to persuade her that she was wrong. He was truly a different kind of person. *I'd sure love to look at my painting again ...*

"I hope we can sit and talk again sometime. Maybe you can learn a little more about me next time." Will shook her hand.

"I'd like that." Melissa left the shelter and made her way home.

# Chapter 20

Agents Edwards and Tracey entered a shelter, hoping maybe it was here that they would find Charlie. This was their tenth stop on a seemingly endless list. They couldn't believe that they had been sent to find a homeless man. They went to the serving section of the shelter and asked the man behind the counter if he had seen the man in the photograph, a picture they had obtained from the police headquarters. He shrugged his shoulders as though it was possible that the man had been there.

"Maybe I can help you." A voice spoke from behind Agents Edwards. "I'm Father Bower."

He turned and said, "Yes, maybe you can. This man." He gave the Father the picture. "We are looking for this man. I believe his name is Charlie."

"Yes it is. I haven't seen him for two maybe three weeks now. Has he done something wrong?"

"No, why do you ask?" It was becoming tiresome, people asking that question. The fact was, he didn't' know exactly why this man was wanted, only that it was a defense issue.

"Professional men from the States looking for a homeless man. At least the accent leads me to believe you're from the states." Father Bower raised his eyebrows.

Agent Tracey cut in. "Actually, we're here to find Charlie because he was left a great deal of money by a distant relative who has just recently passed away. It's imperative that he be notified, as the estate will be in probate unless he comes and claims his fortune."

"Oh, he'll be very excited to hear that he's rich." Father Bower smiled.

"Do you know where he might be?" Agent Tracey pulled out his notepad.

"The last time I saw him was down at the East Street Mission. We spoke at length about the state of affairs of the world and how to change them so that we could all live in peace. Of course, I take a more spiritual view on that issue, Charlie is more secular."

"Hm," Mark began, "drinker, huh?"

The Father shrugged his shoulders and smiled.

"Well, Father, if you see him please call this number." He handed him a card.

He nodded and put the card in his pocket. "Good luck and God bless you."

Agent Edwards scratched a name off his note pad. "Well, only 16 more places to check today."

Ken shook his head and they walked out of the shelter.

* * *

Melissa opened the door, marched up the stairs, and sat across from Charlie and stared at him. He did not look up from his work and continued scribbling notes. Charlie knew she was waiting to talk and felt it could be a long discussion. He wasn't going to lift his head until she said something. Ten seconds was no different than a hundred thousand years when integrated with the space now open in his mind. It was enough time for his subconscious to crunch out one more of the many equations and bring it into conceptual terms; implicit symbols beating against each other in order to find a concept, a word, an anchor ...

"Charlie."

The pattern broke. He looked up and placed his pencil down on the table. "How are you, Child?"

"I need to know what happened to you. I know of your youth, but I have to know why you live on the street. It doesn't make sense to me." She looked impatient.

Charlie searched deeply into Melissa's eyes. What life. It would be difficult to go back to those days where his life had changed forever, but she had a right to hear it from him. "Very well, I will tell you everything.

"Before moving up to Bohdan, my family lived just outside of Kiev, the capital of Ukraine. My father owned sixty acres of farmland in a small, overpopulated town. He was well off. In 1928, to the total befuddlement of my family, he moved us up into the mountains, leaving everything behind. Of course, I was only three at the time so I have no recollection of that. In fact I wasn't even speaking yet. I was pegged as slow, dumb. My father never thought so, though. He told me later that he saw the brilliance in my eyes even at that young age. 'You wait and see,' he would say to everybody."

Charlie thought of his home: A simple design, plastered with clay and thatched with straw, a large rectangular room for eating and sleeping, a storeroom, and a barn extension for the animals. Hand woven colorful rugs hanging over the silvery gray walls; his father's intricate carving deeply imbedded into the window frames, supporting beams and posts, and the large multi-function ornamented ceramic oven was vivid in Charlie's memory … The portly, round, smiling face of his mother came to life in his mind and a tear to his eye.

"It wasn't until a year later that my family understood the decision by my father. In 1929 the rumors began. By the end of the year the policy of compulsory collectivization was upon the Ukrainian farmers, issued by Stalin. The farmers fiercely resisted, clinging to their land and possessions." Charlie shook his head. "They were crushed. They killed millions of people. Was it a premeditated plan with the sole purpose of destroying the Ukrainian people as a nation? Personally, Melissa, I think it was a genocidal famine. There was nothing natural about the famine of 1932-33. But my father saw it coming, as he could see my capabilities before I even started speaking, the way he knew to smuggle me out of the country to the U.S. …

"October 11, 1938, Transcarpathia received its first Government. My father was so upset. The reason he had moved in among the Hutsuls was to get as far away from Stalin as possible. Now there was a formal Government right next door. It wasn't long before the Carpathian Sich organized an army. Five thousand men, 'Brave but stupid,' were his words. Now there was reason for the Russians, Hungarians, and Germans to come and take it over. My father believed that if the Carpathians remained without a governing body or any worldly ideas, they would be left alone to live in peace. 'So what,' he said, 'if they change the borders every couple of years.' And although the Hutsul territory was quite beautiful the climate was extremely trying, and he felt there was no real advantage to them taking over the area. 'Nobody wages war at the top of a mountain unless they organize an army to protect it.'

"As an intuitive man he was somewhat naïve. The rugged conditions of the Carpatho-Ukraine turned out to be an ideal site for extensive guerilla operations. There was a movement by the Russians to convert Greek Catholics to Orthodox. And of course there were the Germans. All that pressure, and my father still got me out of that place."

The tear from his eye fell. "I remember a man coming to our home late one night and my father coming to wake me. 'You're not a soul to be sacrificed. God did not put you on this earth to serve a tyranny.' Then he embraced me, strange, for affection wasn't his strong point, and said that I had to leave. I cried no, I couldn't leave my family, my home. He said, 'This isn't your home anymore.' The man took me and smuggled me out of the mountains. Never again would I see the fantastic vistas, wondrous sunsets, my family, friends …"

The next few months were a blur in his memory. He knew he had been taken through Poland, then to Germany, then to the U.S. The journey had been long and dark. Weeks, maybe even months had passed before he saw the light of day. He remembered his excitement, and it even welled within him now, as he thought of how he had been in those days: alive, free, a vibrating collection of molecules with a natural rhythm of creativity running through him; a constant oscillation between disciplined thought and relaxed concentration, between outward and inward attention. Then he met those brilliant men … His heart raced.

"The energy from around the world was truly inspiring. I was immediately admitted to the highest level of school. I flew through science with honors. I had already put together the information I needed to pass all their exams. My interests then moved to medicine. It wasn't long before I knew that information as well." When Charlie thought of medicine, needles of hatred stung through him. All the pain, premature deaths, diseases that could have been fixed, so easily and inexpensively … He forced his thoughts back to physics and a time when he was still happy.

Charlie remembered no longer being interested in memorizing rules from a book, he wanted to develop new rules, discover new laws. Expand the known! That was his purpose. The validation he got from those men, even when they refuted his work … it was undeniably the best time in his life. The way they looked at him, inquisitive, as though he had created new thought for them, too. How wonderful those days were.

"But, how?" Melissa's hand crossed her mouth, which was slightly open. "Why? Who made you …?"

Charlie continued speaking, not acknowledging Melissa. "I was excited to be in the States. Intelligent men from all areas of thought flocked to America at that time. And there I was among them. My loneliness for my family vanished. I got along fine, because the men who kept me company were brilliant, men of intellectual vigor. They were studying the atom. But more than that, they were one step closer to seeing the true nature of the universe.

"I showed my mental prowess by discussing ongoing theories. I was there while the atomic bomb was being assembled. I really loved some of the people I met there. They became my family and showed me that the discoveries in science don't come from analytical and logical thinking alone. It's the subconscious that operates the creative process on which science is based. Of course, new information begets new information, but there is a space vaster than any universe in your mind, where truly creative ideas are born, and it's accessible only through disciplined thought followed by a period of incubation. But when that idea appears, it does not come from any defined place. You understand that, don't you?" He watched as Melissa nodded.

"These men were the leading scientists, scientists who expanded barriers in their field, scientists who went beyond the domains of existing knowledge, some training no fewer than ten Nobel Prize winners. I was allowed to roam freely among the group. I was in my glory. I'd never been in a world that understood me, or more importantly, that I could relate to. I knew so much about what was going on, but was appalled when I found out that they were training me to become a weapon of science."

Charlie took a breath. He felt starved for oxygen. Melissa looked as though she had a million questions. He knew this was a lot to put on her at once, but he didn't have much time. Through all the countries where he had lived and all the people he had met, Melissa was the only one he trusted implicitly with his story and all his work. An aroused understanding of Atomic energy and its implications was necessary to show that the nature of the universe would not constrict itself into the arbitrary idiocy of nationalism. Maybe, just maybe, Melissa could show that to humanity through her art, open new space to create new worlds by tearing down boarders. Then his equations, a magnifying glass into the nature of reality, could fertilize life, not facilitate violence, destruction, and death.

"The energy in the room was incredible." Charlie continued. "It was like I floated on air as I made my way to different stations. Everyone had a puzzle piece to perfect. The others could immediately watch for the next step that became possible as a result of one area coming together. Everybody was working to further the entire group's achievement, working independently together, toward a climax. I learned as much there as I had at any other point in my life. Not only about physics, but also about team effort and comradeship; the power of combined intelligence.

"You see, I was still excited to see Little Boy and Fat Man completed. It was an unexplainable feeling of wanting to make it work because it was possible. Where the mind goes, energy flows and if the mind had to be there, then it should complete with all available resources the focus on which it was set. I was well aware of the destructive capabilities of such a weapon, but never once conceived of using it on people, innocent people! I believed that America had the ability to end the war without more bloodshed. I was wrong to think they wanted to …

"Melissa, all the good information that came from that era is overshadowed by those two days. Such disrespect for the earth and its inhabitants is inconceivable. In letters, some of the men wrote to the president that they were appalled by such a thought, that they could not know what kind of destruction they were talking about. But no, 'Air power alone is not sufficient to put the Japanese out of the war,' the high ranking officials had said." Charlie could feel his heart quicken and his temples throb, as though his brain was swelling. He took a deep breath, lifted his fist, and said, "The willful refusal to utilize the large brain they were given, puts those politicians in the category of prehistoric savages. I would rather be burned to death, one match at a time, than to engage in so base an action as murder under the guise of war!" Charlie's fist came down on the table. He breathed deeply to calm himself. After a moment he continued:

"I became more and more depressed the closer the time came to drop these horrible bombs. There were rumors going around that the Japanese were about to surrender." Charlie shook his head and breathed deeply. "But no, it had to be unconditional or nothing. Murder is the worst of human actions. We all seem to agree on that. But as a means to an end, with the backing of the people, they used weapons of mass destruction on civilians in undefended cities. How barbaric …

"I was in a daze for weeks after they dropped those bombs. I didn't work or think about work. It was like somebody had taken a pin and burst my self-contained delusion of grandeur. The world would be a better place for me being alive, I had always thought, until then. All the life-expanding theories I was working on, struggling with, changed in my mind and I could only see my discoveries being used as tools of death. It became all too clear to me that every equation, every sentence I wrote would be turned into killing fields.

"'Science is to blame,' they said, but nuclear fission was not invented, it was discovered. You *cannot* evade reality by pretending it doesn't exist. I have discovered over the last fifty years things that could annihilate the world with one action of stupidity, things that could also fix so many problems. You see, it's what you use the forces of nature for. It's philosophy that guides people's lives and it has not evolved as quickly as information. In fact, the despots have deliberately misrepresented it to usurp unearned power.

"I could not be a part of that any longer, so I ran. It was actually quite easy. Still in the aftershock of the bomb, they didn't even notice that I was gone for over a month. Every one of them thought the other was taking care of me. By that time I was in England living on the street. I took my father's advice. I never really understood how smart he was. Stay as far away from a centralized government as possible. What wonderful advice. While I was being so brilliant and self absorbed as a child, my family was living well. They produced life. Growing vegetables, plants, and flowers is of the highest order. Treat life with respect and it will flourish. My family always had the best food and received praise from the community, a community often ravished by hunger.

"That's why I took to the street. There is no place farther from the government. I was right under their noses all this time, in front of their face asking for handouts. It was the perfect hiding place. I lived and worked from there. Some of those brilliant men spent the better part of their careers attempting to dismantle the era of terror they had helped create. They heroically tried to mix rationality with an irrational system. All that brainpower wasted, fighting a battle they could not win. What great things could have come from those minds had they moved forward with the intensity that was their birthright. I would not give my mind to them and I knew I couldn't shut it down either. My nightmares were a signal of that."

Charlie paused, pursed his lips, and narrowed his eyes. "There are things you will have to do for me because it will not be long until they find me now that I have come forward as a witness. I'm going to trust you with my work. Much of it will be foreign to you. You will not understand the content of my work and you need not understand it, you are an artist, not a scientist. And that's why you'll know when the world is ready to move to the next step. You have that awareness and the ability to take it there. All the instructions will be in the first box I send you. I have outlined a philosophy that must be in place before my work is brought forward. I trust you with seeing to that."

Charlie stopped speaking. He was done for now. It would take a few minutes until Melissa could ask any questions. Her mind would have to assimilate what he had just said. He sat patiently staring at her painting. He felt a kind of healing, healing he thought Joanne must have felt when she had poured out her soul to him. All these years and he had never told anybody his story. It was like the cage surrounding his heart had opened, allowing it to beat with unobstructed freedom.

# Chapter 21

Caught between the urge to run over and console Charlie and her preoccupation with the unexplainable emotions that welled up within, Melissa felt paralyzed. Thoughts raced through her mind so quickly that she could not clutch onto one to explain her overwhelming state of confusion. It was as though her rib cage had been pulled apart and a finger pressed firmly on her heart. Ripples of emotion coursed through her veins, no single feeling stood out clearly. Just as one began to overpower the others, it would be displaced by yet another feeling, then another, all in a subtle sort of way as though her senses were waves rolling onto a beach. She noticed that her vision had been blurred when it came back into focus. She breathed in deeply and asked, "Charlie, why are we here?" Her thoughts, which were normally unhindered, voyaging carelessly through vast seas, were tangled as fish caught in a net. It was the only question that could break free.

His face broke into a smile and he laughed.

Melissa had never heard him laugh like that before. It was a deep resonating laugh. His face curled up and the smile looked natural on him, even though his heavy sagging jowls and the way the lines curled around his cheeks, showed he did not smile often.

"I don't know what I said that was so funny." She felt her heart beating again.

"You ask that question as easily as you would a mathematics problem."

"I have this unexplainable urge to know your thoughts and feelings. I wanted to ask a priest I know, Father Bower, when I saw him earlier, but knew he would give me some godly reason."

"You should have asked him." Charlie's mouth crimped derisively.

"You know him?" Melissa thought for a moment. "Of course you do. He's the one that reminds you of the priest back home."

"He's quite intelligent." Charlie laughed, his eyes in reflection. "He's one of the few people who can speak to me in terms I understand. He's like a sponge for information. Sometimes when I speak to him I don't think he understands, and he probably doesn't to begin with, but he studies and the next time he knows. I think I've turned him on to physics." Charlie laughed again. "He knows the Bible almost as well as I do."

"You don't believe in all that stuff, do you?"

Charlie smiled. "I don't wish to influence your belief system with what I believe right now. You will find out soon enough what I think and come to terms with your beliefs in your own time. I'll say only that these are the basic questions: does the universe just exist without prior cause and has it always existed? Or: is there some consciousness that we don't understand fully that created the universe and us?"

"The universe just exists. I don't believe in a higher consciousness and think religion has been just a way to make people feel guilty enough to give their own power over to somebody else." Melissa could feel her body tightening. Why had she always felt this way when speaking of religion? It was like she was fighting some internal battle, a battle of wills an unidentified battle.

Charlie smiled. "Hm, that's what Will might have said."

"What?"

"Actually, both are likely true." Ocher lines, like branches of thought, seemed to be thickening through the intense green in Charlie's eyes. "There's a great deal for you to learn. Will can help you with that. Let's be more secular for now. Do you think there's something wrong with this world?"

Charlie really seemed eager to listen to Melissa. It was like he was setting up a debate. Melissa replied confidently, "Yes, of course. I'm afraid because I don't think the world can continue in this direction much longer without ... I can't even think about it. I've been struggling to find an answer for—"

"Yes! Melissa. That's why I trust you. You're an intellectual and not afraid to say I don't know, but yes there is an answer: The universe is intelligible." Charlie spoke quickly.

"I don't understand." Melissa was becoming more confused.

Charlie smiled. "Our intellectual leaders, the people who shape society, acknowledge that a problem exists, but give way to meaningless generalities and encourage the real problem: a mass of dependant people who can't think for themselves."

"I'm sorry, Charlie, but I still don't understand," Melissa replied.

Charlie squinted his eyes and thought for a moment. "What's the state of art today?"

"Soul murder," Melissa blurted without thought.

"Ah yes, now we're getting somewhere. But it's not really soul murder." Charlie looked into Melissa's eyes.

Melissa hated the way art was being praised these days. People paid hundreds of thousands of dollars, even millions, for an oversized canvas that had paint sprayed on it by the force of an airplane's propeller, or animals walking through paint then over the canvas, or paint hurled from across the room. Abstract artists who needed others to give meaning to their work because there was none to begin with. Talented, hard working artists never got recognized. She and Stephanie were going to change that …

"You see, Melissa, genius is not praised, encouraged, or rewarded these days, it's exploited." Charlie looked at Melissa's painting and shook his head. "That's why you're an outsider. You protect with your paintings the very thing the establishment works so hard to diminish. You have an active mind with the fantastic ability to take perceptions and change them into concepts. Our minds are endowed with the ability to use the universe and manipulate it for our advantage, our growth. Of course destroying it senselessly, or even pieces of it, is detrimental to that goal. Persuasion of nature in that way is as impractical as persuading man by force. But even worse, they have found a way to stunt the growth of the conceptual faculty so that force is no longer necessary. It's your identity that you've been protecting through your artwork, Melissa, your ability to form concepts that identify reality. You understand that reality cannot be created, it is waiting patiently to be illuminated." Charlie smiled and looked at her painting again.

"What's our purpose?" she asked again, understanding, but still confused.

Charlie stared at her as if he knew she was facing a crisis. "I've always felt that we evolved into conceptually-introspective beings so that the universe could experience itself." He paused for a moment as if letting that sink in. "Consciousness, an inevitable end of cause and effect. The cause being the bringing together of elements that support chemicals in such a way as to create the effect: us." He opened his arms. "There is just too much beauty in the universe to go unnoticed. They, the people who choose to use the powers of the universe for destructive purposes, don't realize that we are here to garner its power for …" He paused. "To bask in the glory of beauty, awe inspiring magnanimous beauty! We're all individuals capable of wielding the infinite power of the universe. You know that we are at a critical turning point of history. The world is on the verge of annihilation. Joanne had the kind of pure love and compassion that has kept people from destroying themselves, she had that essence. It's a powerful force, but there is a lack of that kind of understanding, compassion, and tolerance in the world today. Will can explain that part better than I." Charlie scratched his chin and pursed his lips. "You will understand more in time." He looked at Melissa, the brownish-yellow lines in his irises, still thick.

She said, "Sometimes I get flashes of the man in the underwear on Yonge Street like there is some kind of deep connection. When he spoke of sun and its filaments of light I, too, could see the photons of light." Melissa remembered as a child seeing and hearing things. It never scared her, in fact the voices and visions were comforting.

"That man we saw, in my view, lost his consciousness. Not in the way that people mean when they say they lose conscious, I mean he lost the ability to think for himself and gave his mind over to a higher power. He flipped the switch in his mind and allowed himself to be directed by voices that are probably saner to him than the external voices. Let me ask you this. Who would be most threatened if people took responsibility for their own lives?"

Melissa thought for a moment. "Politicians." The word just automatically released from her mind.

"Ah ha! And they control every aspect of your life. It is not in their best interest for you to take responsibility for yourself and they reinforce that you can't survive without their system. They need you to need them. Under those circumstances, how can change happen?" Charlie looked deeply into Melissa's eyes and let out a half smile. "You still hold an innocence of life that should be protected. Contrary to popular belief it is not natural to lose it, and in fact it is stolen from you." Charlie lifted his hand to his face, cupped his chin with his palm, and tapped his nose. "Let me explain it this way. Tell me, what is the most unimaginable horror the world has experienced?" He took his hand away from his face and held his fore finger up. "Let's stay in the past century to keep it simple."

Without thought Melissa replied, "The holocaust! I ..." She had just listened to him speak of the bombs and she chose the holocaust. He must think she was unsympathetic, or stupid. "I mean—"

"No, that's okay, I thought you might choose the bombs, but the holocaust was no less horrific, and actually might demonstrate my meaning more clearly." He took a deep breath in and said nothing for well over a minute. He was in a deep reflective mode as though trying to gather his thoughts. "Germany's greatest claim was its superior intellectual and cultural prowess; it was the land of poets and philosophers, not a place of ignorance. In the pre-war days the German ideology was flaunted openly. Through Nazi propaganda, the essence of the up-and-coming political system was clear. In fact, in 1933 when the totalitarian state was established, people were still allowed to flee the country if they wanted.

"People stayed, Melissa, most of the people stayed. It was a place where the state had absolute power over every realm of human activity. No individual rights existed. So how could an educated group of people allow such hate and destruction? A planned systematic slaughter of people, a slaughter of unimaginable proportion, unparalleled in history; educated people willingly allowing themselves to be treated as cattle, to be sacrificed for no other reason than that the state decided it. No explanation was necessary. This is the disease I'm referring to. You may think that it's over, that that was then, this is now, and nothing of that sort could ever happen again. You're wrong if you think that. The United States, a country so far removed from the ideals of the total state, is only masking its true identity. The constitution of life, liberty, and the pursuit of happiness has been deformed by people educated in a malevolent philosophy where honesty in dealing with natural law has become trivial and arbitrary. As if people are expendable in the name of 'Higher Realities'. An ideal sweeping through the nation, not so unlike Nazism, has enslaved America by disabling the mind through machine education. The weapon of choice now is not amethyst-blue-crystals of hydrogen cyanide, it has evolved, so much in fact that it is not necessary to kill the body anymore. They have become expert at stealing the spirit, leaving behind confusion, acceptance, indifference, allowing you to live, but far beneath your potential."

"The tiger! That's what he lost!" Melissa blurted out as she struggled to understand more fully.

There seemed to be more for him to say. She could tell that there was information in that body of senses and she needed to know more. If Melissa was not so saturated now she would ask more questions, but she couldn't, she could only sit there with the weight of the world on her shoulders. She let out a breath of air, almost in a sigh.

"That's enough for now." Charlie's voice was strong, resolute.

Melissa could not fight it. She nodded and stood up. "I'll let you get back to work." She went down and sat in front of her easel.

She stared blankly at her canvas, still unable to grab a hold of any one feeling. After a few moments she looked up at Charlie. He was looking at her with concern, the way a father would his daughter. He held her glance for more than a few seconds, picked up his pencil, and buried himself in his work again.

* * *

It took all morning, but he was finished. John had written his test. It was his finest moment with regard to work. He had reached for and achieved his goal. Now the real work was about to begin. Every step of the way he had set goals and attained all of them. The seemingly insurmountable goal, set four years ago, had been achieved. Breaking it down into small steps was the key, he thought. Little awards along the way to show forward progress and keep motivation strong; one eye always looking at the distance, never losing sight of the big prize, the other focused firmly on the necessary steps to get where he wanted to go. He stood up from his desk and handed his paper in. He was confident he had passed, knowing fully ninety-five percent of the answers. Three other men and one woman were still writing as he left the room. He was hungry, not only for food, but for somebody to share in his accomplishment. He called Melissa. After all, she had helped him to get this far. And he did owe her lunch.

They met at a small Greek restaurant. The place was bright and the tables were close together. It was two o'clock and the lunch crowd had mostly cleared. There were only five other people in the restaurant when John entered. Melissa sat alone at the end of the room. She let out a half smile as John sat down.

"Hi, John." Her voice was soft, almost meek.

John sat down and smiled, which lengthened Melissa's immediately. "I'm done, I can't believe it but I'm here!" He could see Melissa's melancholic expression lighten and her eyes glisten.

She went to jump up, as if wanting to run over and hug John. She stopped herself and instead grabbed his hand and squeezed tightly. "Congratulations, I knew you would make it. You're so good." Her back straightened and her lips tightened. "Now you can get started on that business of yours."

The thought overwhelmed John as Melissa said that. It had always seemed so far away, but now it was right in front of him. He would need a business plan, capital, there were legal issues to deal with. He had focused single-mindedly on obtaining his license so that everything else had taken a back seat. Now he felt again like his dream was out of reach. What did he know about business? He ran the kitchen, but that was only a matter of paying bills and making sure the place ran smoothly. He was a contractor, but that was more like a wage. There was more to running a business for profit. He let out a long breath of air in almost a sigh. His head and shoulders sank slightly as the image of his business faded in his mind.

Melissa laughed. It was as though it were unintentional, a quick release of a thought she could not control.

John was feeling insecure. She could always see through him. "Sure, laugh at me now!" John looked into her eyes.

It seemed as though she was trying to stop as she held her hand over her mouth, forcing air out her nose. "I'm sorry," she said finally. "I'm only laughing because this is the same look you had shortly after we met. You were so worried about making it down here in the 'Big City'. You tried to understand everything too quickly. You wanted to be good at everything right away. You're so adorable. Just remember what your father told you, make a plan and work the plan, one step at a time. You're more than capable of achieving all your aspirations. You know why?" Melissa paused for a moment. The smile left her face and a look of clear confidence overspread it. She leaned over the table and touched his chest. "Because there is a deep and rich connection between your heart and your mind." Her hand moved slowly up to his temple. "You are caring and smart, a combination that can't be beat."

When she moved her hand, it was as if he could feel the connection Melissa was talking about. "You always could inspire confidence in me. Thank you," John said naturally.

The waiter came to the table and took their order. John's feelings were close to the surface. There was somebody out there better for Melissa than he. On his own, he could almost rationalize the choice he had made to leave her. When they were together, it was impossible. To change the subject, he asked about Charlie.

Melissa went into much detail about her talk with him and how she was confused. John was fascinated with Charlie and he almost understood what Melissa was saying, although not completely. She hesitated a few times, as though trying not to put too much focus on her on John's big day. John picked up on this right away, and asked questions to keep conversation going. Her eyes showed that she needed to talk about this. Fact was, he wanted to know everything. Melissa paused as the waiter served their food and walked away.

"I'm sorry, I've only spoken of me and I know you wanted to celebrate your big day," Melissa said. "I felt so heavy with emotion before coming here. You've helped me to feel lighter."

"Don't be sorry, your life is very exciting. You know, Melissa, you'll meet all kinds of extraordinary people in your travels."

"That may be true, but I lost the one person ..." Melissa stopped as the waiter came around to see if everything was okay.

John did not acknowledge what she was about to say, but he knew. "So what is it that Charlie wants you to take care of?" He stabbed at a piece of chicken on his plate and drew it into his mouth.

Melissa threw her hands up in the air. "His work, I guess. He said I would find out what I needed to know after I opened the first box. He said they were coming to take him away."

"Who?" John swallowed the food he was chewing.

"I guess Americans: CIA, FBI, INS, I don't know, maybe it's the military."

"You're not in any danger, are you?"

"I don't think so. I'm certainly not going to turn him in," she said with and air of defiance. John finished eating. Melissa had moved the food around on her plate, but had eaten nothing. The waiter came and cleared the table.

"No, I suspect you won't. Is there anything I can do for you?"

"I don't think so." She shrugged. "Anyway, I should get back."

"I should go as well. I promised Brent that I would help him study this afternoon." John stood up and grabbed the bill. He went to the counter and paid. Melissa walked to the door and waited.

She opened the door as John approached.

As they stepped outside, John asked, "Can I give you a lift somewhere?"

"No, thanks. I have some things to do before I go home. Thank you for lunch. I would like to ..." She stopped. "I mean, maybe we could get together next week or sooner."

"I'd like that. Let's not wait too long, or I might forget that it's your turn to buy." John smiled.

Melissa laughed an easy laugh.

She looked up at John with childlike imploring eyes. "Can I have a hug?"

Even if he had wanted to he would not have been able to resist. He never could. It was as though she needed to protect something sacred within her. He was the shield, the only armor strong and noble enough to do the job. No, he thought, he wasn't, and never would be. He opened his arms as he walked closer to her. Embracing her was rejuvenating. First his heart sank to the pit of his stomach and then got caught up around his Adam's apple. Her body fit nicely in his, her head resting firmly under his chin and over his heart. She was the one to break the hug. An overwhelming sadness, heavier than led, filled his soul as the void of space between their bodies increased. They were worlds apart and he could never be a full citizen of the one she inhabited.

"Thank you," she said, her eyes dreamlike.

John did not say anything.

"I'll give you a call." Melissa smiled, then turned and walked away.

John watched her until he could no longer see her.

\* \* \*

Melissa walked into her apartment. Immediately, she noticed that Charlie was not there. She didn't know what to think. Did he go out on his own? Was he found and taken away? He could not leave, there were still things to know. A note written in pencil was sitting on the kitchen table. "Back soon" was all it said. She breathed a sigh of relief as she noticed the spare keys had been taken from the rack. She picked up the phone and realized she had a message. It was from her father, wondering if she had come to a decision on his offer. She had not even thought about that, in fact the whole issue had escaped her mind completely. She would call him back later. Right now she had the urge to produce something. Somehow, someway she would make clear all the new information that lay waiting to find expression in her mind. She knew it would become coherent through her paintings. It would enrich the images as she found places to anchor the floating abstractions that taunted her now. A sense of keenness sharpened within her. She knew that each and every one would find a home in her mind, body, or spirit either as a painting, a concept, or maybe even just a word that would corral them all together. Melissa felt like a child struggling to make sense of the world around her. She stopped to put a CD in the player. Back in her chair, Mozart's

Piano Concerto Number 21 in C major rose to life, filling her apartment with wondrous sounds.

She could not determine how long she had been working when a completely unexpected feeling stabbed through her. Her body burned in a quick flash, her shoulders fell, and her vision blurred. She held on to the easel for fear of losing her balance and falling off the chair. She stood up and her vision cleared, but she did not have her usual energy. She thought for a moment and could not determine the last time she had eaten. At lunch with John she had not touched a morsel. It must have been some time ago, she concluded as she could almost feel her body feeding off itself. She went to the kitchen and opened the refrigerator. Nothing.

She reproached herself for being a bad host. Charlie probably couldn't take it any longer and had gone for something to eat. She scribbled on the pad Charlie had left out. *Gone shopping for food!* was all she wrote. The paradox of a homeless person starving to death in her apartment scared her. She shook her head and hurried out the door.

# Chapter 22

"Yes, two men in suits were here a couple of days ago looking for you." Will sat beside Charlie in the church.

"I knew they would come."

"What are you going to do?" Will's eyes showed concern.

"I'll let them take me back if they want to. I'm too old to run. I've found somebody to take care of all my things, my *work*." Charlie said work with emphasis trying to let Will in a little more about his true identity. But Will knew and would not be surprised at who he really was. Charlie was comfortable with his decision to let Melissa care for his work, and happy that he didn't have to run. The sense of freedom he had experienced as a young boy, moved through his body.

"Oh, who?"

"Melissa, I can trust her. Her work is incredible. I thought the world had rid itself of that kind of creative energy."

"I like her, she reminds me a lot of you, not in any way I can describe, but there's a strong energy there. I think we'll have many discussions together." Will smiled and looked up at the statue of Jesus. "She has many reservations, but she will come to realize the light He had."

Charlie looked up at the statue then back towards Will. "Yes, I know," he replied. "She will come to see your light, that's why I can trust her. I want you to look out for her," Charlie dug into the pocket of his trousers, "and also to give her this after I'm gone … this world, that is." He handed Will a pocket sized note pad filled with instructions and a set of keys.

The look on Will's face showed that he understood. He held it tightly in his hand, and said, "I'll look out for her." He said nothing else.

Charlie got up and left the pew. He looked back. "Tell her whatever she wants to know about me." He walked out of the church knowing that that information was safe in Will's hands. He was confident that he wouldn't look into the pad before giving it to Melissa, even if he wanted to. Somehow Charlie wished he would.

For more than five minutes, Charlie stood on the street corner, periodically raising his arms as if to say, "Come and get me, I'm ready to go back." The sense of freedom enveloped him and he felt light.

* * *

It was there. Somewhere between the moment Charlie lifted his arms for the fifth time and the moment he decided to make his way back to Melissa's; the answer to the riddle that had plagued him since … he could not remember when. Was it a week, a year, ten years, fifty years? Was this the answer he had been seeking?

He opened the door to Melissa's apartment and noticed the kitchen light was on. Outside was becoming dark. He sat down in his regular seat at the table and began to make notes. It was a sudden realization that made everything else possible. His work was scattered in eleven lock boxes throughout the city and the world, and he had to go over all of it in his mind. He began making notes, crystallizing the work of his life. The key on the coin in Melissa's painting stood before him as a beacon.

Rain began to fall outside and dark ominous clouds rolled in over the lake. He looked up as his mind processed information. A bolt of lightning shot down onto the lake illuminating the room, creating a flash of internal light. He looked up at Melissa's painting and his heart began to race. That was it, the painting. It gave him the mind space to realize the quantum leap that needed to be made. His heart pounded with great fury, too fast he thought, he was beginning to lose control. It was as though his heart was trying to catch up to the speed of his thoughts. It couldn't do it much longer. He tried to breathe deeply to slow it a little. Another flash of lightning shot down from the sky. This time closer, brighter than the last. He could not determine where he was anymore as all thoughts and feelings seemed to gel together with glorious triumph in a way he could not name, nor needed to. A crash, like metal striking metal, resonated through his mind, then a pop. In his euphoric state, he could no longer feel his body and he was weightless as darkness spread out around him.

* * *

Melissa opened the door to her apartment and walked in. She could feel her hair clinging to her shoulders and her clothes were soaked. She felt ugly and agitated, like a wet rat. The room was completely dark. She thought that strange as she was sure she had left the kitchen light on. She flicked the switch just inside the door. Nothing.

"The power went out." Charlie's voice startled her.

She jumped back and dropped the groceries. By the sound, she could tell he was sitting up at the kitchen table. She left the bags on the floor and cautiously made her way up the stairs. She felt around for a handle and opened a cupboard with the fuse panel in it and flicked a switch. "It's just the breaker." Her heart slowed a little. It was still dark as she felt for the switch to turn the kitchen light on. Nothing. Cautiously, she walked down the stairs and flicked the living room switch and the light came on.

"That's better. Now I'll have to change the kitchen bulb." She looked at the silhouette of Charlie, then up to the florescent tube that hung on the ceiling where the kitchen dropped off to the main floor. She made her way up the stairs, looked again at the light, then toward Charlie.

He stared at the fixture. Then as if realizing that Melissa was staring at him he said, "Don't look at me, I've never changed a light in my life."

She cupped her hand over her mouth. "That would be dangerous for me to try." She looked down at the landing below.

"Why don't you call the landlord to come up and change it?" Charlie suggested.

"Yes, I suppose I could do that." She could feel excitement well within her. "With that storm out there, I'm sure he's busy." She could feel her face expand into a smile.

"That's fine, I don't need this light." Charlie held up his pad to his face. "I can see with the light coming from downstairs."

Melissa ran to the phone, feeling all her energy coming back. "No, it's not fine. You need proper light to work with." She called John to come over.

Charlie smiled and shook his head as she picked up her groceries and started to put them away. After she was done she pulled out some strawberries and cut up a cantaloupe. She put the fruit in the middle of the table and sat down across from Charlie.

"I'm sorry, I haven't been a very good host."

"You've done well." Charlie paused for a moment. He took a strawberry off the plate and ate it. "Melissa, I need to talk to you. It won't be long now until I have to go."

"Where? You don't have to go anywhere. You can stay here, or if this place isn't good, I can find you a place of your own, somewhere they would never find you. I—"

"Melissa, listen to me." He cut her off. "I'm not going to run anymore, I'm too old. I'm sorry to put so much responsibility on your shoulders. You won't have to do anything but study and nurture it. The world is not ready for what it contains, so I want it kept hidden until they are. But I want you to find like-minded individuals to help you. Teamwork, Melissa. You're young and may see a day when it can be used to help people, not destroy them. I sense a movement throughout the world that's fighting for that day, but I won't see it. Do you see, Melissa, why I ran, why I had to escape the death trap of society? It would have been impossible to carry on with my work not knowing what it was going to be used for. We're at a time in history where information and technology have accumulated to a point where one malevolent action could annihilate the world. I have that information. But now each bit of knowledge turned over to mankind must hold within it the ability to erode irrationality and genocidal ignorance! That's what I've been struggling for, an implicit seed within every equation.

"You may encounter people who think that I have given you that information. I assure you that I will do everything in my power to make them believe that I shut my mind down after I escaped their ugly world. But they will come looking at first for any scraps they can lay their hands on. The power structure usurps that information from creative people primarily for enslavement purposes, not protection purposes. The United States is, in a way, less free than any other country in the world." Charlie studied Melissa for a moment. "You will find out things that you don't want to know, but you know what, Melissa, whether I had come along or not, you would have discovered the ugliness. Great spirits, my child, and I include you in that, have always been met with violent opposition from those who wish to exploit them. Don't let them take your soul, guard it for all it's worth." He stopped speaking. His voice was calm and sincere. It had an element of caring that she had not heard from him before.

A knock at the door startled her and took her from her thoughts. "John," she said excitedly. "He has a key you know."

"Yes, I know." Charlie smiled.

She stood up and felt her hair. "Oh no, I forgot to change and fix my hair. I must look terrible."

Charlie laughed.

"Thanks for the encouragement."

As she started past him to go open the door he grabbed her arm. "If you want him back, Melissa, I have a piece of advice for you."

Melissa could feel her eyes widen.

"Before he leaves here today, listen to what your heart tells you to do.

The message will be clear if you give it your full attention." Charlie paused and smiled. "There is no time in life to play around with feelings. You must let him know how you feel. I get the impression that the two of you are thinking that neither of you is good enough for the other."

The door resonated with another knock. "I'm good enough." Melissa squeezed his hand. "Thank you."

Charlie released her arm and she went down and let John in.

She laughed because he, too, was drenched and looked not pleased to have come out in the rain.

"Oh, it's funny that I'm soaked. Just from my truck to the front door and this is how wet I got." He shook off his hands and looked up to the light.

Melissa opened the cupboard and took out a towel. She dried his hair, face, and hands slowly because she liked the feel of his strong body underneath the towel. He tried to remain obstinate about the reason for his coming over and went about changing the light. Opening the door where the fuse panel was, he pulled out a two-foot cylindrical light.

"Hi, Charlie," he said as he stepped on a chair.

"John." Charlie smiled and nodded.

John rested one foot on the railing between the kitchen and living room and one on the chair. "I'm nice and dry, sitting with my night clothes on, and I have to get dressed and come here in the pouring rain and change a light." John grumbled to nobody in particular. He pulled the old bulb out and handed it to Melissa. She handed him a new one and smiled. "You, a talented painter," he said taking the bulb from her hand. "A girl with the ability to transfer brilliant visions onto paper, a skill most would die for." His voice was sarcastic. "And Charlie," He stepped down off the chair after replacing the bulb, "who can split an atom." He flipped the switch on the wall, illuminating the room. "But neither of you can change a bulb. Unbelievable!"

The room was silent for a moment when Charlie's face broke into a huge smile and he laughed, almost uncontrollably. "He's right you know, what helpless fools we are. Can you imagine a world filled with people like me and you, Melissa? We'd die of starvation." Charlie said as he broke into laughter again.

Melissa's heart opened when she saw Charlie laugh.

"Anything else before I go?" John looked around the room.

"I think that's it." Melissa hurried down in front of John to block his exit.

"Okay then, I think I'm going to go and get into some dry clothes." He looked down at his shirt.

Melissa stopped just in front of the door. John opened his arms as if to say, "Can I go now?" He made his way closer and looked down into her eyes. His look changed from discomfort to inquisitiveness. He did not say anything. Melissa lifted her shoulders in an attempt to kiss him. She could not go through with it. It was like the opposite polarity of a magnet forcing her back away from him. Minutes seemed to pass as she stood there awkwardly building up the courage to reach up and embrace him. She felt a spasm in her heart and she could think of nothing but tasting his salty mouth. Then, as though breaking a law of nature, her heels left the ground, her hands swung around the back of his neck, and she pulled his face to hers. He offered no resistance. His lips were soft and responsive. Her hands held tightly to his neck, her lips pressed firmly, and her breasts barely brushing against his lower chest sent a vibrant shiver through her body. His restless lips hungered for more, as now whatever resistance he had tried to manufacture could not manifest in any way. All that remained was his primordial longing for that which he could deny himself no longer. His weakness stood as her greatest triumph and his noblest gesture. He showed her the deepest part of his soul and she protected it with her compliance. The world seemed oblivious and unimportant. Now the magnet changed polarities and she could not remove her mouth from his. His hand glided purposefully down her side and onto her waist, warming her sexual energy. She pushed herself closer. The heat was intense between their bodies and his arousal was imminent.

Then, as though his mind came back to the present, he pushed her away with a violent thrust. "Melissa!"

She looked up at him as a confident calmness overspread her body. "I want you, I need you, I would do anything to have you spend your life with me. Please reconsider, without you I am only half a person."

John pulled back and looked at her with contempt. Not contempt for her, but for himself and what he had allowed to show her of his most sacred feelings. He said nothing and hurried out the door.

Melissa looked up at Charlie who was busy scribbling notes on a piece of paper. He was enthralled with his work and she felt he did not even notice her presence in the apartment. She sat down in front of her easel and stared at a blank piece of paper.

\* \* \*

Melissa felt confident and resolute in her decision, even though her future was uncertain. The large oak desk weighed just shy of a thousand pounds, but it did not look heavy. A six-inch thick piece of solid wood seemed to float over the top of the legs that bowed downward, as though shouldering the weight, only to sweep up before meeting the floor, as if in defiance of gravity. On the ends, four pads met the ground, like it was resting on the paws of a tiger. The piece had been carved out of one solid piece of wood. It was six feet long, four feet wide and sat two and a half feet high. The design lightened its mammoth presence. The curves flowed naturally into each other with smooth brilliance as the intricate design showed the creative energy of the mind that had formed it. All the forces of nature could not have put together such beauty, save the forces that created the artist whose vision turned out exquisite lines from the lifeblood of his imagination.

Melissa's father continued to speak. "I just want to make clear the window of opportunity I've presented to you. If you dare to soar with eagles, consider excellence your motivating force, and wish beyond all else to make this world a better place for you and your children, then your choice is clear. You have strength and courage, the world needs you at the helm. You see, Melissa, we are the movers of the world, we create the capital necessary for everything else to function. As traders we have the power to create life where there is none, to put people to work, to put money to work in the arts, in the sciences, in the medical field … And you, you have a special gift, which can only help if you allow it to. You see, most people can only see a small percentage of the world and what is possible, but you have a greater scope to see beyond what is known and visible to the eyes. Don't you want to look at every new day as important? Don't you want to look at the end of every day and know that you have left something to symbolize that you, Melissa Belmont, have been here and have changed people's lives for the better? It's the most exciting thing in the world to tear apart outdated thinking and to explore the realm of the unknown. I give you that opportunity right now." Her father sat back in his chair. His thick graying hair was cut just above his ears and his face held an air of superiority. Not over Melissa, but over life. She knew he had taken the little money his father left after the market crash and turned it into a fortune, little by little. He studied and understood the way money worked and had spent countless hours watching the markets and studying industry. Now sitting behind his desk with most of his life behind him, he wished to pass that knowledge on to her to keep the family name on the top moneymakers list in the world.

"I know you want what's best for me and I appreciate your concern, but I can't promise to uphold my end of the bargain if I were to try this endeavor." Melissa felt a little surprised at her confidence. Her father had always made her feel a little insecure. He was so powerful, strong. Now he was just a man who happened to be her father. She did not feel reliant on him in any way.

"I don't understand. What conditions can't you keep? I haven't been unreasonable." His voice sounded agitated.

"You offer me the world and tell me what wonderful things I'll be able to do for society. But it's myself first that I must think of because if I can't take care of myself and meet my needs, how will I be able to understand and meet the needs of others?" Melissa spoke quickly and the words came out naturally.

"What is it that I'm asking you to do that you are unable to do?" He leaned forward and tried to intimidate her by looking directly in her eyes.

She did not flinch or even blink. "You want me to leave John, and I won't."

"I thought you two had already split up." His eyes narrowed.

"How do you know that?" Melissa clenched her fists.

"You should know by now that there is not much that gets by me." He sat tenacious, smug.

Melissa stood up. "I don't appreciate you spying on me. I can take care of myself and you know what? If John wants to marry me, I'll marry him." She began to walk away.

"Melissa, if you do this I cannot support you any longer. I've told you before that you can't, as part of this family, keep running around with the people you feel have become your friends. I've worked too hard to restore this family's name. I didn't want it to come to this, but if you walk out that door you are not welcome back," he said, with a resolution that sounded like it hurt him to say it.

"What do you mean, support me?" Melissa stood firm, anchored to her confidence.

Her father did not answer.

"You may not have noticed, but I've been taking care of myself for over three years now." Still, her father said nothing. Melissa stormed out of the room. On the way out she turned to her mother who was standing at he bottom of the stairs. "Your husband just disowned me." She turned and walked out the front door.

Melissa walked down the long driveway and made her way to the bus stop. It was a long walk. She was sad that her father had snubbed her like that, but if that's the way it had to be, then so be it. It was liberating and took away none of her confidence. After all, she had established herself as an artist and her work would only get better.

# Chapter 23

She knew he would be working tonight. Melissa sat on the creaky wooden bench as John cleaned the floor around her feet. Ten minutes passed and he had not said hello. She was troubled, her shoulders sagging, her head heavy as though it were about to pull her body to the floor. He went about his work occasionally glancing at her, then quickly turning away without any acknowledgment that he had seen her.

She enjoyed watching him work. His body carried out tasks with fluent precision, even small things like sweeping the floor he made seem the highest of deeds. He cleared a table beside her and came back to wipe it clean.

"I've been trying to build up the courage to talk to you and I want you to know that I think you're beautiful and—"

Melissa cut him off. "Listen, I came here to see how things were going and to have a cup of soup." She looked down at herself. "Does it look like I want to be hit on by the likes of you?"

"I just thought that maybe you might want to go out with me sometime. If you got to know me, you would find that I'm smart, funny, and deeply passionate."

Melissa looked him up and down. "You don't look like much." She casually sipped from her cup of soup. She lifted her head and looked at him over the top of her nose. "Are you some kind of janitor or something?"

He sat down beside her and straddled the bench. She turned away and faced the table. His heavy gaze fell over her increasing her heart rate and lightening her sluggishness. She tried not to look and succeeded for a few moments. She could take it no longer and turned to give him an icy stare, a stare that would freeze his heart. She still had it in her and wanted to use it, to test it. John needed to see it, to break it. As her face turned, his lips met hers. She did not see his face coming and there they were embraced in a kiss. It was a quick warm kiss. A sense of relief shot through her; he made the move this time.

He broke the kiss and stood. "Yeah, we're probably not compatible."

She pulled his arm and he sat. "Are we back?"

John placed his hand over his mouth. She turned her body and inched closer to him until she could rest her head against his chest. She could hear his heart quicken as he wrapped his arms over her.

"I don't think I could live happily without you," John ran his hand through her hair, "and that scares me a little."

"I'm scared, too. I used to think I was so independent until you left me." She grabbed hold of his arm and squeezed. The strong muscle in her hand and the increasing speed at which his heart beat made her feel comfortable and secure. "Promise me something."

There was a momentary pause.

John cleared his throat. "Anything."

"Promise me that you'll never leave me again, and that no matter what you'll tell me how you're really feeling." She could feel her voice crack, and between the moments she asked and when he responded, felt like a million years.

"I promise." John rubbed her back.

They sat in silence for over five minutes, absorbed in each other's presence. Melissa took pleasure in the musky smell of his clothes with a hint of cedar from his aftershave, the feel of his hard body pressing against hers, and the passionate bloom of youth flowered inside her. The best part of her life was again before her.

"We have to talk." Melissa pushed herself just far enough so she could look him in the eyes. John gave her a smile that was neither happy nor controlled. "I don't know how to tell you this exactly."

"You can tell me anything."

"Well, my father offered me a position with his company. Actually, he offered me his position." She looked for some kind of reaction from John. There was none. "It's quite a position and would allow me to do many things and grow in many different ways. But he's put stipulations on the agreement."

"He wants you to stop seeing me." John squinted his eyes.

"Yes."

"What did you tell him?"

"I told him that I loved you and that I couldn't." She tried to remain without emotion but knew she was not doing a good job. "He told me that it wasn't acceptable and if I was to maintain my stand, he would not support me any longer. I'm not sure what he meant, but it was clear that I wasn't a part of the family any more." Her head sank.

John placed his hand under her chin and raised her head. "I'm sorry, Melissa, but I think he might be right. You have so much potential. Will you be happy with me? I need to know that you can grow with me as your partner. If I were to hold you back in any way—"

"No, John, you don't understand. There is a part of me that would never have been discovered had you not come along. I know that I haven't been fair with you but I promise it will never happen again. There are so many things I have to do now. I need your help. John, you're the only one, you've always been … there's been nobody before—"

"Let's talk about the future, not the past." John placed his hand on Melissa's cheek and looked deeply into her eyes. "Melissa, will you marry me?"

It took all of her restraint, a task more difficult than anything she had ever done to not blurt out yes, yes, yes, yes. She breathed deeply. Her response was slow, elegant. She raised her hand to his face, and looked sincerely into his eyes. "Yes, John, I love you."

It seemed like a long time that they just sat there when a startling realization ran through Melissa like a jolt of lightning. "John, about the wedding."

John sat silently, as if he knew what was coming.

"You can decide on the honeymoon, where we go, you can decide where we live, how many children you want, I would even walk three steps behind you for the rest of our lives, but—"

John leaned forward and kissed her on the lips. "No church wedding."

"Yes." She pulled back, not sure what to expect. They had never spoken of this before. She felt it strange at this moment that she could not clearly define where he stood on this issue. Definitely, he was aware of her thoughts, everybody was well aware of her thoughts on this subject, but now after all this time she was not sure of his.

"That's fine with me," he said nonchalantly.

"I don't even know how you feel about that. You've never told me." Melissa looked imploringly into his eyes.

"It's actually quite simple for me. My father told me when I was young, that God gave me the ability to choose between right and wrong, and that if I listened to my internal guiding system, then I would live a happy productive life. After church every Sunday he would ask me what message I had gotten from the service. I would tell him and he would smile a proud smile and pat me on the back. He told me that I should not place anybody over me and that the message from the preacher was only an interpretation and that not all interpretations are right. One day he placed his hand over my chest and said, 'You have the Lord within you. You don't need to go any farther than your heart to feel Him. Blessed are the pure at heart for they will see God'." John smiled. "My father was a good man.

"Now, I don't know if I believe in 'God' per se, but I know that there are good messages to be learned from the Bible and I use what applies to me and try to live my life the best way I know how. And for me, that means producing values by working hard and do my part in raising the standard of life for those I touch. Personally, I think you make things more difficult than they need to be. But then again, I'm simple and not endowed with the incredible talents you possess. Maybe I'm fortunate that way." John stopped there and looked at Melissa.

She was lost for words. He was as intelligent as anybody she had ever known, no, more intelligent. "Why have you never expressed that to me before?"

"Do you believe it to be true, for me I mean?" John smiled easily.

"Yes."

"Do I express those thoughts in the way I act and live my life?"

"Absolutely."

"Then what's there to say? Words would only be redundant."

Melissa said nothing and lowered her head. She was in deep thought that was more a feeling than anything her mind had put together. It was clear to her now that she was looking everywhere for answers that were right in front of her. The simplicity of life that John held was the key to understanding. She had let so many things cloud her vision and she wondered how she could have overlooked the brilliance and light he had to offer. How could she have looked at him as being lower than her in any way? She understood now that high intelligence was more a way of *acting* than of *being*. Her father was wrong, she thought, John would lift her to new heights. The worn, white, linoleum tile floor under her feet was filled with dark scratches that looked like the deepening lines on an aging hand.

John lifted her chin again and made eye contact. "Now about how I choose to live our lives." He laughed and stretched his arms fully. "Ah, I love the control." He brought his arms back around Melissa and embraced her. "You can have everything you want except where we go on our honeymoon."

The way he said that made her feel somewhat uncomfortable. "Okay," she said, not sure what to expect.

"A five night, six day canoe trip in Algonquin Park. It's my favorite part of Ontario and I would like to experience it with you."

"That's like camping, outside, in the wilderness?"

"Yep, just me, you, and nature." He emphasized the nature.

"Not Hawaii, the Cayman Islands, Greece, Italy, Mexico, how about a cottage up north?"

"Nope, Algonquin in a canoe."

She breathed deeply and conceded, "I would love to go with you to Algonquin."

"Great, when do you want this to happen?" John asked.

"Tonight," she replied impetuously.

John smiled. "Well I would like my mother to be there. She would be upset to miss it, I'm sure."

"Oh, yes, will she come if it is not a church service?" Melissa wondered. Now that her family had disowned her it was important that John's mother welcome her. Melissa loved her dearly.

"Of course she'll come. If it isn't a church service, who else will bless us?" John chuckled. "She wouldn't miss it for the world. Where do you think we should we live?"

"Well I think my apartment would be too small," Melissa replied and thought of her view and how much she loved her apartment. But it was only an apartment and change would be good. "Yours would be fine until we buy something. I'd love to buy a house with you." She thought about Charlie and what he had told her about his family. "I want to learn how to work a garden and grow flowers, maybe have a little pond ..."

"Yeah, that would be great, but we might have to wait for a little while until we can save for a proper down payment. With me starting a business, it might not be the best time to go into debt with a mortgage." John thought for a moment. "Maybe we can set up the spare room at my place, *our* place," he corrected, "give the sixty days notice at your place when we return from our honeymoon, and we would be saving a twelve hundred dollars a month in rent right there."

Melissa cuddled up closer to John. "Yeah, that would be good. I could work from your, *our*, place. I'll miss my apartment, though." She felt a pang of sadness as she thought about her life changing. She had always thought her family, especially her father, would be there on important days like her wedding. Who would give her away now? She thought of Charlie, but no. John's words rang in her mind, *who else will bless us?* Then it came to her. It would be perfect, someone his mother would love.

\* \* \*

Charlie always loved the soup here on Wednesday nights. He could taste the love the cook put into every meal. She was a fifty-five year old woman whose husband had passed away and left her with little money. She had a room in the building next door with rent geared towards government checks. Even when he was avoiding Melissa, he would come here. The soup was too good to pass up, even though it broke his stringent diet, a discipline he more or less abandoned when Joanne died. The place was always full on Wednesdays. A feeling of comfort spread over Charlie as he had been touched deeply by Melissa, and this shelter held more depth now. And as he watched the cheerful round Slavic face of the cook dishing out her food, his mother's face fell before him. He wondered if Melissa had ever painted or sketched the cook. His glance moved around the room and the scuffed white walls had only some pamphlets and magazines in clear plastic holders. He was right about one thing, he mused: her work should be on these walls if she wanted to lift these spirits. A quiet mumbling and the tinkling sound of spoons hitting bowls made Charlie smile, he was not sure why. Life was so simple sometimes.

Charlie did not even look toward the door and he realized this was it. A man he knew vaguely, Collin, shifted his head to Charlie and then to the door, a number of times. Charlie bowed his head as Collin's expression turned rigid and nervous.

*Go tell them who I am, Collin, and collect your reward,* Charlie thought. He noticed Collin get up and nervously walk by him, furtively looking at Charlie through the corner of his eye.

A minute or so passed. "Excuse me, sir, are you Mihaly Kolazar?" A voice resonated from behind him.

Charlie turned his head and looked up at the two men in suits. He nodded yes.

"Would you please come with us, sir?"

Charlie smiled and indicated his bowl. "Give me two minutes to finish my soup." He dipped his spoon into the bowl and lifted it to his mouth. The warm, chunky liquid smoothed down his throat.

He ate slowly, savoring the moment. He was going to miss it here. The two men stood behind him without movement or emotion. Charlie could feel the energy vacuum they created with their presence. Without even speaking to them, he knew that they had sold their souls a long time ago for a life of destroying people's livelihoods for harmful organizations.

Charlie finished his soup and stood up. "Very well, let's go." He stretched his arms and smiled. He walked out the door and the two men followed.

\* \* \*

Melissa and John entered her apartment. Immediately realizing that Charlie wasn't there, she ran up the stairs to the kitchen table. There was a note. She picked it up and looked at John, afraid to read it. He walked up the stairs and held Melissa from behind. They read the letter together:

Dear Melissa,

Thank you for all that you have done for me. You could not understand fully the resolution and peace of mind you have inspired. I know I have left you with a great responsibility, but you, my child, have the power and strength to carry out that responsibility. You have shown nothing but a deep seeded desire to see the world as it is and change it for the better. All of your questions about me will be answered on your journey. I feel a wave of goodness spreading through the world and hope that you will see a day when the world will live in peace and can use my work for the benefit of all. I have entrusted you with my belief system. The story is in the numbers where when seen by an irrational-free mind, one simple thought, chicken scratch on a piece of paper, is worth a thousand pictures. It's interesting that one piece of new knowledge, one simple equation can change the course of human affairs. You, Melissa, have the right kind of mind to create the proper pictures, and it's through your art that you can help. I've set a good foundation, but there is still work to do. Find people who will take it in the direction it is already going. Live your life with love and happiness, it is your purpose.

You are truly a child of the universe, don't let anybody take that from you. Open yourself up to Will, there is nobody who knows more about the soul than he. I will miss your presence but will always keep you close to my heart. We will not see each other again. Please destroy this letter for your own protection and I will do my best to dissuade them that I had dealings with you other than regarding Joanne.

Rise up and be great!

Mihaly Kolazar, aka Charlie

Melissa stood in front of John and unlike her recent flux of emotions, she was able to pull down a singular feeling and allow it to run through her body: Pain. It was not a localized sensory infliction, it was all over, and affected all of her body with a tingling, prickly sensation. She was an open wound in need of outside help for recovery. She hungered for a universal endorphin, some kind of energy that would heal her mind, body, and soul.

She bowed her head as John wrapped his hands around her waist and rested his head easily on her shoulder. It was comforting. It hadn't been a year since she had met Charlie on the street, but their souls were kindred. It would be difficult not to be near him, to never see him again. The thought made her shiver. John's hold tightened, but he said nothing.

Melissa turned and looked up at him. She pulled his hand away from her waist and led him down the stairs. John sat down on the futon and Melissa cuddled in close. They both watched out over the lake for the whole evening. Not one word was spoken as the white caps on the waves rolled endlessly over each other.

# Chapter 24

John's mother was ecstatic about the news. She spoke to Melissa over the phone and welcomed her to the family. After reading Charlie's note, Melissa thought of how important it would be to have Will at her wedding. The next morning she went directly to the church and asked that he attend. His eyes gleamed and his response was immediate: "I'd love to marry the two of you. I can set up a time in the church here and have a good ole Christian wedding." He laughed then said, "Don't worry, I know you do not want to get married in a church by a priest and I would love to attend as your friend."

\* \* \*

Melissa didn't wear make-up often. She could rarely justify the time it took to apply. Today was special. Her goal, as she sat in her underwear at her dressing table, would be to take the vibrant colors of her innermost self and transpose their beauty along the physical plane of her body.

No foundation was necessary and only sparsely applied cream blush was enough to emphasize her cheekbones. She pulled out her lip liner and followed the contours and straight lines of her mouth with the precision of an architect. She filled the sensitive flesh of her lips with a brownish pink color, which showed that her blood was hot and close to the surface. The hard cool stick was a pleasurable contrast to the warm soft feeling that ran through her body. Her hair was silky and hung down around her shoulders with long layers in the back and face-framing layers in front. Her mouth widened, exposing her brilliant white teeth as she applied smooth, dark, shimmering eye shadow over the eyelid. Over the purple, a covering of pale lavender shadow dulled slightly the glimmer and gleam as not to draw attention away from her eyes. Her eyes danced and glistened as though her dark round pupils were exploding universes sending stars out along her cheeks in all directions, her face a sunburst unable to contain the brightness of love and exquisite joy emanating from within her.

Methodically she stroked her eyelashes with the ease and flow she used while painting. The mascara thickened and blackened her lashes giving them the appearance of sharpness, like a fortress able to take away the treasure with the ease of a blink. She batted her eyes seductively toward the mirror. She smiled, imagining the reflection was through John. Her eyes opened wide and her pupils dilated, he would be allowed to enter her soul any time.

She was pleased with her make-up and began to dress. Like a gentle gust of cool wind, the amethyst-silk-fabric slid sensually over her breasts, across her hips, stopping just below her knees. The dress was simple, supporting no design other than the curves of Melissa's body. Her bare shoulders and the exposed part of her bosom tingled as she strapped on the cool necklace.

It was a necklace given to her by her father on her eighteenth birthday. She had worn it only once, at a showing of her first piece of commercial art. Disappointed with the event and people she had met, she put the necklace away, comfortable in the knowledge that it might never see the light of day again. There had not since been an event worth wearing it to.

The roundness of the double-rowed diamond necklace was contrasted sharply by the central rectangular pierced panel with a diamond border. On the panel were two black emerald dancers flanking the central pointed oval diamond. This piece was one by two inches. A sapphire sky, a lunette diamond sun, and a black onyx heart lay as a back-drop on this panel and would be spectacular on its own, but humbled in comparison with the whole necklace. It was heavy and cold across her chest and around her neck as she pinned in her earrings. Matching the necklace, they fell in a cupola tassel from her re-pierced earlobes, suspended from a rectangular black emerald and diamond mounts. Melissa shook her head easily to feel the stream of diamonds brush gently against her face. She looked at her image in the mirror and felt more radiant and happy than ever.

\* \* \*

The Justice of the Peace stood facing John and Melissa. Will was on John's right and his mother was on Melissa's left. Behind the Justice of the Peace a park spread open with lush green grass lined by tall evergreen trees that were shaped by the now silent northern winds. Above them an empty sky, save one cloud neither streaked nor puffy, only a delicate sweep of gray across a light blue canvas. A spout of water shot up thirty feet from the middle of a pond forming to an umbrella top, over which hovered a hawk that had found an updraft of air and spiraled in tight circles looking toward the ground for its next meal. Bullfrogs' resonations from the lily pads floating on the pond and the strident song of the crickets was the musical background that nature had provided for this special day. Sweet smelling flowers filled the air with their amber fragrance. A bird chirped from a near by tree and Melissa was ready to say her vows.

She took a deep breath and suddenly felt as if her legs would collapse from beneath her. Her body shook and her mind went blank. She was frozen. John grabbed her gently by the hand. Her confidence slowly came back. She lifted her head and looked deeply into his eyes. There was no mistake, no reason to feel worried or scared. She loved him and he her. Her mind started to fill with the thoughts she had organized and wanted to express.

Her mouth separated like a parting sea of affection. "John," her voice cracked. She took a deep breath. "In my youth, I ran through the garden with my sister, the warmth of the sun on my skin and the taste of salt on my lips ... The only problem we had had been what game we would play next. Laughing until our stomachs hurt was a daily occurrence. Days would slowly fade to dusk and we went running to the call 'Dinner's ready' knowing that after dinner we would laugh some more. The summers seemed to last forever ...

"In those days I lived and dreamed. I didn't know exactly what I would be when I grew up, but it would be fantastic! Life was exciting and great and I would do something good in the world, something incredible. But as I grew up, life became increasingly more difficult. Running until out of breath, jumping on the bed, and pillow fights changed, seemingly overnight, to deep philosophical questions that illuminated into perpetual seriousness. Then you came along, John, and it all came back, the fun, the laughter, the joy ... Every time I look into your eyes, the spring of youth returns to my heart. Your love is a melody to which I surrender. Life bursts forth with everything you touch and you have touched me deeply, inspiring in me all that I am and could be. You are my universe, a soul turned outward giving without measure. I'm the caterpillar that's been set free by the openness of your heart and the strength of your forgiveness. You have shown me my wings and taught me how to fly. With the ground below me and above me only sky, I look up to see you, to feel you. The dancing energy that surrounds my heart was given generously and selflessly. Your love fertilizes the seeds of light in my spirit. It is in you that I meet my potential. I love you with all my heart and wish not to grow old with you, but to grow young together. Here and now, I surrender myself to you for the rest of my days and promise to give to you all I have. Accept my commitment to you, not as an outside gift, but as an inside piece that completes the fabric of your being. It was always meant to be this way. I will always rest in your heart listening to the music of your spirit as you rest in mine. I'm yours now and forever."

Melissa stopped speaking, feeling energized by her vow. She could see by the look on John's face that it was perfect. He stood motionless, resting his eyes easily over her face. She had touched him as she had intended.

Melissa watched as John looked at his mother, who appeared ready to explode with emotion, then to Will who had his head bowed with a slight smile that he struggled to keep from expanding the width of his face.

John shook his head as he turned back toward Melissa. "I knew I should've gone first." His eyes were deep and reflective. He pulled his shoulders back with confidence. "I really tried hard to come up with the perfect thing to say today. I wrote many verses that now lie shredded in the garbage. I became so frustrated because this is as important a day for me as I've ever had, and I wanted it to be perfect." John stopped and shook his head. "Look at how beautiful you are … I would have walked to the end of the earth to write something to make you feel like I do now. But words were never my strong point. I don't know how to phrase what I want to say, how to make words match my feelings. I could go to school for a thousand years, learn all of the languages of the earth, but I know now that there would be no way to convey my true feelings accurately other than to say I love you. How inadequate that phrase is sometimes. I could think of no better life than to spend it with you. I promise to show you the best within me."

John stopped there and Melissa stood relishing the moment. It was better than she could have hoped for. Her life was complete.

John's mother and Will both had their heads down and in an unexpected, unplanned motion, they both, in complete unison, crossed themselves. Melissa looked over at both of them incredulously, feeling a little uneasy at this strange connection. They looked at each other, then lifted their eyes to the sky.

They exchanged rings. Melissa looked up at John and they kissed each other. The union of souls was complete, well almost, Melissa mused.

Will turned to John's mother and said in a voice all could hear, "When a fig tree blossoms, it is evident what the season is." He smiled a radiant smile.

John's mother glowed with enthusiasm. She tapped Will's arm as though trying to remember something. She snapped her fingers. "A farmer sows seeds. Some fall along the path and are eaten by birds; some fall on rocky ground; others fall in the midst of thorns and are choked," She stopped and looked into Will's smiling eyes then to John and Melissa who were both now watching, "but some fall on good soil and bring forth good crops."

Will laughed and leaned over and embraced John's mother closely. "Having you say that confirms that Jesus is alive and well, and with us." He broke the embrace and looked into her eyes.

"It seemed like the right parable to use now ... I pray every day," John's mother said, barely able to contain her excitement.

"That's obvious by the glow in your eyes and your gentle presence."

John's mother bowed her head. "Lord bless and keep my son John and his wife Melissa, shine Your countenance upon them and give them peace and happiness."

Again they both crossed themselves.

She looked up at Will inquisitively.

"It was a wonderful prayer," he confirmed.

John and Melissa finished with the legalities and, as planned, went up to John's mother's house for a small reception. John had invited his helper Brent and Brent's girlfriend, Tamara. Some of the neighbors joined them in the celebration.

After some food and socializing, Melissa and Will took a walk around part of the land. She thanked him for being a part of her big day and expressed her disappointment at her expulsion from the family. She also told him about her friend Stephanie, who for some reason she could not stop thinking about. She figured it was because she had found her needle in a haystack.

They stopped by the pond. It was spring fed, lined with stone cut by John and his father, and bordered by a hedge sculptured in perfectly straight lines that sprouted colorful flowers around the base. Melissa sat down, took off her shoes, and dipped her feet in the water. The water was cold and clear making her feet appear unusually large and pale. Will sat down beside her and rolled up his pants, took off his socks, and also put his feet in the water.

"I miss my sister, I wish she was here today. I feel like I've been fighting something within me that I shouldn't be fighting." Melissa paused to gather her thoughts. "I love the smell of flowers in expensive perfumes."

She lifted her nose to the sky and inhaled. The scents made her feel warm. "I feel like such a hypocrite for wanting to have the nicer things in life, while preaching in the name of the homeless. It's guilt, I know it is." Melissa swirled her feet in the water watching the waves they made. She looked over at Will. He held his hands together and watched across the pond. She felt completely comfortable with him and his silence showed that he really wanted to understand her. "What do you think?"

He turned to her. "I don't know much about what happened to Stephanie, but she touched you deeply and that must have opened your heart as far as the homeless are concerned. After she died, you could see them in a whole new light. Maybe you thought the homeless were on the street because they chose not to accept the challenges of life, or maybe you didn't think of them at all. It makes no difference. You took up helping in the only way you knew how because it was something you needed to do. It gave some kind of meaning to the premature death of your friend, some kind of purpose for a completely unexplainable, painful event in your life. Your working with the homeless started off as a way to fix the hurt in your heart, but at some point, the work and ideal took on an energy of its own. Now that you're passing through the hurt, you realize that there's something real there for you, a way for you to make a difference. Even if you were to quit working for the homeless and start on something new, it wouldn't matter, because the more whole you are, and the better you have healed, the better off the world is for having you. You already know, even if not fully, that it's not only the homeless who need to be raised up, it's everybody. Your paintings are more a reflection of society than a reflection of the homeless." Will smiled.

Melissa contemplated what Will had said for a moment and needed to know: "You're a smart man, Will, but I have a difficult time with the life you've chosen. How can you not see through all that—?" Melissa restrained herself. It was none of her business and Will was becoming a friend, she had no right to judge him.

"It's because I do see through it, Melissa, don't you understand?" He paused for a moment. "When you took up your work with the homeless, could you paint effectively only from your apartment?"

"No, I had to be involved, to somehow be an integral part of the homeless situation, and because I was unwilling to become homeless, I did the next best thing: I served them. I think to better understand their situation."

"Yes, that's in part why I respect you. I, too, have immersed myself deeply in a system that must change. God must be seen through a different lens. All the creeds, doctrines, prayers were created to allow people of the past to identify with God. It was the only language available. I believe there is a dimension in life that is deeply spiritual, a dimension involving an interior journey, not an exterior one. The profession of academic theology has enslaved those theistic concepts of the past and passed them off in literal form. The Bible is a window into the spirit we all house within us, we must take off the blinds so that we can look at all new information with honesty. I'm afraid, with the growing skepticism of religious leaders, the most important message will die."

"What's that?" Melissa asked. It was strange, until now she had done most of the talking. It was a nice switch.

"God is not somewhere out there behind the clouds, or behind the universe in a land of nothingness. Don't get me wrong, God is real, as real as you and I sitting here talking, but He is here, too, inside both of us. Can't you feel it? It's that tug, that pull from deep within your soul telling you to search, to look inside, for if you dare to, you will find the meaning to life itself." Will's excitement gave Melissa energy.

She smiled. "Yeah, I feel that too, but I still can't subscribe to an institution that believes civilization will sink into moral anarchy without their behavior-controlling doctrines. Especially with what they've done throughout the years."

"You're not alone, there's a large group of intelligent people who feel a God presence and need direction toward it. I have taken it upon myself to guide those who are ready, to that light." Will spoke with power, persuasion.

Melissa's body tingled. He was so passionate, wonderful. "I understand what you're saying, but don't you want to live, to experience life?"

"What do you think I'm doing?"

"I guess, but what about a wife? You have so much to offer." She felt that he was bound by so many rules of conduct that surely he was denying himself the greatest reward of life, the full expression and reflection of himself through a woman's eyes.

"Yes, love, the essential power that deepens our relationships, the core element of every human being. I have that. There are many scientists out there who work tirelessly to find an all encompassing, unified theory to explain the universe, men and women who courageously look for medical answers for deadly diseases that take away our children, friends, and family. This is important, but it is also important to use this kind of systematic approach to the soul, that which gives us life itself. It's only through pure love that we can grow and the only reason humanity hasn't perished. That's why I'm needed to spread the word, so that we can live and grow in peace and tolerance." Will's voice held a conviction that Melissa aspired toward.

"You study science?"

"I do now, ever since I met Charlie. It was the only way I could relate to him. He taught me a great deal."

"Are you the Messiah?" She laughed.

"You flatter me," Will replied. "My goals are the same. His aim was to make people think for themselves, to find the Divine within them, to dispel anger and hatred, and spread love. That starts with the individual. In order to do that you must put yourself first, have constructive desires, and a healthy concept of your own worth."

"Doesn't that go against the system you believe in, don't they say put others first, be selfless?"

"I think that creates inner conflict and is, over all, bad for the person."

"Aren't you breaking some kind of religious code or law?"

Will placed his hand over his chin. "Well, we're told that we should follow the example of Jesus. He spoke with power unlike any other religious leader at the time. He and his disciples broke many religious laws. In fact, his whole experience on this earth tells us that we must die to old ways of thinking and aspire to meet the light within us."

"I agree." Melissa looked over toward the house. "We should probably socialize a little."

They both stood up. "Thank you," Melissa said as they started back. She thought for a moment, then turned to Will. "I bet he was sexy."

"Pardon?"

"Jesus, I bet he was sexy, all that virtue, good will, confidence."

Will let out a laugh. "You're something special, Melissa." He shook his head.

"Thanks. I still think you need a woman." Melissa was feeling energized, as if she could say anything to Will.

"Maybe one day." He bowed his head.

She wrapped her arm through his and squeezed tightly as they walked.

# Chapter 25

The canoe glided through the clear calm water. Only the softest sound of water being pushed back against the fiberglass could be heard as paddles dipped and rose from the lake. Melissa looked back at John.

"Well, what's the plan today?"

John had on a bucket hat with the faded image of a wolf on the front, a T-shirt, baggy shorts, and a smile so bright she could not tell if it was the morning sun reflecting off the lake that made her squint, or John's beaming face. He opened up the knapsack, pulled out a map and threw it to Melissa. "I want to make it to Burnt Island Lake by late tomorrow. We'll find a campsite, hang out for a few days, and then make our way back."

Melissa looked at the map. "What does 'P295' mean?"

"That'll be our first portage."

Melissa looked sideways at John. "295 feet?"

"Meters," John laughed. "Don't worry, you'll be fine." He dug his paddle into the water raising the front end slightly. The canoe continued to move forward.

She turned, held her paddle across the front of the canoe and took in the scenery, the trees.

After a few minutes John said, "This is where Tom Thomson drowned."

"Yeah, I was just thinking about him. Isn't he buried here somewhere?" By the look of the countryside they would be portaging up hill quite a bit.

"He was buried up on the hill over there. Close to a place called Mowat Lodge." John pointed to the right over Melissa's shoulder. "But his family dug him up and moved him closer to his home by Owen Sound."

"That's sad, it makes more sense for him to be here." The colors, shapes, and sky made Melissa think of Cézanne. 'Art is a harmony parallel to nature'. It had been years since she had thought of him, it was as if that saying had lain dormant in her mind, waiting patiently for a certain kind of beauty to bring it back to life.

"Maybe so, but his spirit is still here." The tone in John's voice was pure, there seemed to be no feeling save a profound sense of being alive.

"Yeah ..." Melissa breathed deeply, almost in a sigh. The ripples pushing away from the canoe in the water made her think of her presence here, not only at Algonquin, but also on earth. She felt somehow she made a wave similar to that which the canoe made in the water. Macdonald, Melissa thought. He was the one who trained Thompson and showed him to realize the best within him, to reflect the world through his own vision. Melissa looked around at the trees, every now and again passing a pine, shaped by the paintbrush of Tom Thompson. She took a deep breath, closed her eyes, and tried to reach a higher spiritual end.

John stopped paddling and was rustling with something behind Melissa. The canoe glided to a stop. The lake was so calm that the morning sun and fluffy white clouds were mirrored clearly. For a moment, Melissa could not discern between the sky and its reflected image. Pictures of the Group of Seven's work flew through her mind, exposing abstract values and the real world in direct, easy-to-understand ways. The lake seemed to take on the effect of watercolor paint. She dipped her paddle into the water to swirl the sky, like the sky in Van Gogh's "Wheatfield with Cypress Trees." Her vision narrowed when out through the whirling sky exploded a creature.

"AH!" Melissa screamed and shot up stiff, almost tipping the canoe.

John steadied the boat. "Easy, Melissa, it's only a Loon."

The bird let out a mournful wail, fluttered its wings spraying little beads of water on Melissa, and ducked down beneath the clouds.

Her heart was beating furiously. "Sorry, I just ..." She became more embarrassed as she realized the canoe had almost tipped over. She breathed deeply slowing her heart. "Is it common for a loon to come so close?" She turned, needing to see John. His face calmed her.

"It doesn't surprise me that it happens here. Algonquin is a haven for both animals and humans. I think because there's never any hunting here, they feel safe." John looked around. "More and more people are finding out about this place, it's not like it used to be."

Melissa followed John's eyes and saw at least ten other canoes.

"Don't worry though, at night we'll be very alone," John sighed. "When I first started coming up here there would be days without seeing a soul. It was just me and my father …"

The water was flat and the horizon wavy as they moved forward.

* * *

Department of Defense. The sign was plated to the wall like a shield. Charlie smiled, not the slightest bit nervous or anxious, well actually, a little anxious.

Charlie walked through the doors between two men. They directed him to a room that was bare of everything save the antiseptic feeling of sterility and a table with only two chairs. Charlie felt as though he was about to be deloused. The two men left the room.

A large well dressed man entered. He was probably in his early fifties with short black hair, a large deadpan face with a fat nose, and a streamlined mass of body. He reached out and shook Charlie's hand. His hand engulfed the whole of Charlie's, and he could feel the strength this man housed. Charlie knew that he did not squeeze tightly for fear of hurting his old feeble hand, but enough to let him know who was in charge. He dropped a file on the table and sat down.

"Mihaly Kolazar," He opened the file and shook his head, "you're quite a prodigy around here." He flipped through some pages.

Charlie smiled and said nothing, noticing that this man did not introduce himself.

"Where have you been?"

"Around."

"I've been through your file and can see nothing as to why you left us. You spoke to no one about wanting to leave. It says, in fact, that you were extremely pleased to be here and that you made many friends. There were many people worried about you. Not nice to leave your friends without a word."

"I'm kind of inconsiderate that way." There was no way he was going to make Charlie feel guilty after what they had done.

"We've heard many explanations." He flipped through at least ten pages. "Maybe you can enlighten me?"

"Well at that point in my life, I was only a young man, and until then had been shipped around to many places. After working with the brilliant men here in America, it dawned on me that I had never really experienced the kind of freedom the land promised. So I left to explore, you know, do some soul searching." Charlie shook his head. "I didn't realize that it would take over fifty-five years."

This large cynical man narrowed his eyes and looked at Charlie as though he wanted to strike him. He had probably fought in a couple of wars and worked his way up to where he was today, an elite officer. Charlie was not afraid. There was no way, no matter how much training this man had, that he could inflict a pain greater to him than Charlie had on himself. He seemed to realize this, stood up without a word, and walked out the door.

Charlie assumed that there would be other visitors, some kind and endearing, some malicious and strong. They would try to find the best way to extract the information they wanted. He was ready for this game.

\* \* \*

One thin line of sunlight was left over the trees in a sky that clouded over quickly. Melissa looked back at John nervously. The lake went from calm, to ripples on the verge of waves with white caps. Paddling became difficult as the wind pushed directly against them. John smiled, trying to reassure her that everything was fine. He opened the top of his knapsack and pulled out rain gear for Melissa.

"Here, put this on." He handed her the jacket and steadied the canoe as she put it on. When she was done he asked that she sit still as he pulled a tarp out to cover their knapsacks. He draped the tarp over the bags, tied it to the side of the canoe so the water would run off into the lake, and put on his own rain gear. He clapped his hands together. "Bring it on!" he shouted as he grabbed his paddle that lay across the boat in front of him. *Nimbostratus clouds,* John thought, *rain will be heavy.*

Melissa looked back at him. "Should I be worried?"

"I'll take care of you."

"Yeah, I know but ..."

John got the feeling here of man versus nature and the more nature tormented the situation, the better the challenge. It was a primitive instinct, a need he could now fulfill, the need to protect his love. Somehow in the city he had always felt that on this level, it was she who protected and guided him. It was an insecurity that some part of him was not fulfilling the role he was supposed to. Now the more the weather acted as the antagonist, the more he could fill that role. He paddled hard, winning this battle. Beyond the sheet of rain was a yellow tag pinned to a tree. They were at the first portage. Melissa climbed out of the canoe and stood, not knowing what to do. Without delay, John emptied the canoe's contents, strapped a pack on Melissa, and told her to follow him.

John hoisted the canoe over his shoulder and started up the path while Melissa followed. On his way back to get his knapsack he noticed that her thin body looked weak under the weight of the pack. The expression of awe had left her face. He smiled, gave her a positive "You're almost there," and hurried back for the rest of the gear. They made it to the other side at almost the same time. She threw the sack down and let out an exhausted breath of air. John knew her spirit was down because her body was tired. They stood under the cover of the trees to catch their breath.

John slapped his arm. "Ah! Tiny Vampire got me." He pulled his hand away exposing a mutilated mosquito in a smear of blood. Expressionless, he flicked the dead insect away and said, "Bet he doesn't have the guts to do that again."

Melissa struggled to keep a stoic face, but failed and her smile betrayed her. She shook her head. "Think you're funny, don't you?"

"And so do you."

"I'm just smiling to humor you."

"I'm okay with that, you can humor me any time." John pushed the canoe into the water and loaded up the gear.

He decided that they would stop at the island on Joe Lake. It would have been better to make it a little further because of the long portages the next day to get to Burnt Island, but the rain was coming down hard and he wanted to get camp set up. He could see that Melissa was done for the day. They paddled up to the island on the southeast side where a well-maintained campsite was laid out. He wedged the canoe between two rocks and held the boat steady as Melissa climbed out.

"Careful, the rocks are slippery," John cautioned.

"I can see that," Melissa snapped.

John said nothing. Melissa looked displeased as he unloaded the gear from the canoe.

\* \* \*

Melissa could barely see across the lake because of the rain. The only indication that there were trees on the other side was the slightly darker tone between the ground and the sky. John first tied a ten by ten foot tarp to four trees, giving enough height to stand underneath. Relief spread over Melissa while taking off her rain suit and clothes. She stood in just her underwear as the warm air brushed across her body. John refused her offer to help, and went about setting up camp, first taking the canoe out of the water and flipping it upside down. Melissa took a deep breath, feeling better to be out of the suffocating rain suit. The pine needle ground was lined, like veins, with roots that were difficult to avoid. With her foot she searched out a soft spot to rest comfortably. Finally, she found a place and eased into a sitting position.

She watched John as he worked. His motions were fluid and calculated. This was his environment, where he was most at home. All this time he had been in her realm, the city, exposed to the essence of who she was. The tent went up quickly and he walked over to her. His faced beamed, stimulating a hesitant smile in return.

"How can you be so happy?" Melissa narrowed her eyes.

"Because I choose to be. It helps to have you in my life."

"I didn't mean in that way …" She stopped wondering exactly what she did mean.

The motion of John removing his shirt sent a flash of heat through her tired body. He opened the side pack on his knapsack and pulled out a collapsible shovel. He went back and channeled a small trench around the tent. Melissa watched as the muscles in his back contracted and expanded while he worked. The rain dripping from the pine tree above made little beads of water over his whole body. She ran her hand across her bare stomach.

John finished and sat down beside her. He pulled out a bag from his pack. It was filled with nuts, dried fruits, and some other objects Melissa could not recognize. His skin was moist and alluring. The feeling in her heart moved south as her stomach growled. Melissa ran her hand across his leg and into the bag that was strategically positioned, as though John had drawn her there. She fiddled around in the bag for longer than she needed and quickly pulled out a handful, then she ate each morsel one at a time while staring him straight in the eyes.

The lake dimpled with rain and the sky was a darkening gray.

"What time do you think it is?"

John looked up as if accounting for the day. "I'd say it's about six."

"Six!" Melissa postured firmed as the whole day flashed before her mind.

John laughed.

"I feel like I've been up here a week already."

"That's normal for your first time. You'll find by the end of the trip it went by too quickly." John put his arm around her.

"I find that hard to believe." Melissa thought of the next few days and longed for her dry, comfortable apartment. Her shoulders sagged and her amorous feeling had all but disappeared.

"Trust me—"

"If I didn't trust you, do you think I'd be here in the middle of nowhere with you? I'm getting the feeling this is some kind of test for me."

A serious look spread over John's face. "No, not a test ..." John's lips curled down and his eyes thinned.

The honesty on his face made Melissa feel bad for saying that. This place was in his heart. It was time she started sharing in his experiences, became enthusiastic about his passions.

"... of all the times I've been here, I'm most excited about this one because—"

"There's no need to explain." Melissa placed her finger on his lips. "I'm sorry, I guess I'm just tired."

"That's all right, I understand, it isn't the nicest day, but I promise the sun will shine this week, it always does." John inched closer to Melissa and brushed his bare arm against her breast.

"It doesn't matter." She slid her arm around his neck, pulled his face to hers and kissed him naturally. With her lips pressed against his, she could feel her strength returning. She broke the embrace. "I want to help you."

John's eyes looked a million miles away. "I think you just did."

Melissa smiled knowingly. "I mean with things around here."

John clapped his hands. "Lets make dinner, I'm starved." He pulled a pack close to him and started to unload its contents.

"Me, too."

"Great," John began, "one sweet red pepper." He handed it to Melissa with a knife. "Sliced." She began slicing it on a plastic plate. "One cup of mushrooms sliced." He wielded a knife between his fingers and began to enthusiastically slice as he whistled.

Melissa felt a tingle up her spine as she, too, was beginning to get into the spirit. The rain only added to the ambience now. There they were in a rainstorm cooking dinner. The tarp overhead resounded like a million thumbtacks had fallen from the sky. A wonderful feeling of accomplishment ran through her veins at just being outside. A different side of her was opening. The pepper had been sliced. "Now what?"

"I guess we should start the noodles. I collected some lake water earlier, we'll need about four cups." John lit a stove he had set up.

Melissa stirred the noodles as John pulled out another stove. He unfolded it, attached another cylinder of propane, and fired it up. "Why didn't you just run a gas line here?" His resourcefulness was curious. The packs didn't seem to provide enough room for the things he pulled out.

"My father always told me that just because you're out in the woods camping, doesn't mean your food should taste like wood." He crushed a garlic clove and threw it into the sizzling butter. As it started to brown he added the mushrooms and peppers. His hands moved as though he were some creative master, a chef extraordinaire.

Melissa stirred for about fifteen minutes. She lifted a noodle to her mouth and pressed her lips against it, sensitive to its texture. "Hmm, I don't know if it's done yet." John watched as she caressed the underside of the noodle with the tip of her tongue, pressed her lips against it, paused, lifted her head and let it slide into her mouth. She chewed slowly.

"Is it done?" John showed no emotion, as though that was regular practice in testing pasta.

"Yes, it is." She was determined to arouse John if it took all night. Melissa had control of this libidinous game and she would make him surrender to her. It was time to seal this marriage.

"Good, let's eat." John watched as Melissa drained the pot and placed two plastic plates beside him. He poured the mushrooms and peppers over the noodles, mixed them in, and dished out equal portions onto the plates. Melissa went to grab one. "Hold on." He pulled open a zip lock bag. "We're not quite done yet: Parmesan cheese and pine nuts." He sprinkled some over each plate. Again she went to grab the plate, her mouth in an uncontrolled fit of salivation. "Not yet!" John exclaimed. He dug deeply into his pack and pulled out a canteen and two cups. After filling both, he handed one to Melissa.

Discerningly, she sniffed. Heat ran through her body. "Wine!" She sniffed again and lifted her chin. "Australian." She took a small taste. "Wolf Blass, yellow label. My favorite!"

John lifted his cup to her. "Here's to our lives together."

"This is perfect, you've made everything so …" She looked out over the lake at the falling rain and returned his smile. "If I weren't so hungry, I'd—"

John lifted his plate and began to eat. Melissa did the same. The rain was steady, businesslike and seemed to take on the sound of the vegetables sautéing. When she caught John's glance, Melissa would run her tongue across her upper lip. He pretended not to acknowledge it, but the small gleam in his eyes showed he was aware of her flirtatious advances. He was a full participant in this playful game. She would be the heat that opened up his passion; all she had to do was turn it up.

"That was wonderful." Melissa placed her plate down, drank the rest of her wine in one gulp, and threw the cup as though shattering it against a fireplace. Her body felt warm all over. She stood up and walked out from under the tarp, feeling more relaxed and free. She found a place where the rain came down unhindered by the trees and allowed it to wash over her. The tips of her fingers moved slowly up her stomach, across her breasts, then tilting her head to the sky. Pressing the water from her hair with her hands, she sent the most seductive look she could John's way. She knew her underwear would be totally transparent by now and wondered if the rain running over her body aroused John as much as she had been aroused by him earlier. As he stood up and approached, it was obvious that it did.

Standing in front of her, he stripped off his shorts, and unclasped her bra. He slid his hands around her waist and lowered her panties to her knees. John lifted her from under her arms while his foot rose up between her legs, forcing her panties to fall to the ground. She could feel that he did not have to strain to lift her. He held her at eye level.

She wrapped her arms around his neck and swung her legs around his stomach locking her feet at his tailbone imploring him, with all her feeling, to lower her. Her body shook as his self-assured smile showed that he could wait. She bit down hard on her lip and her eyes opened wide showing John that *she* surrendered. If it weren't for the cool rain running over her body she would have surely burst into flames. He slid one hand down her back under her buttocks and held her as the other hand slid down the other side. When properly positioned he lowered her slowly, savoring the moment. Her heart felt as if it had stopped beating, then burst open pushing blood to all extremities, cleansing her soul. His still presence engulfed her whole being and she could not tell where she ended and he began. Then he moved, sending her hips into orbit, and she could feel the intense mast of heat pillaring into her body. As she lifted her head, her mouth opened allowing the rain to fall over her lips and onto her tongue. She felt more natural and alive than ever. Her head lowered and their eyes met. The past and future were unimportant, she was in the moment, the abstract universe defining itself clearly through John's eyes. A vibrant pulse of energy ran through her body, heightening her physical awareness. Melissa, at once, understood her love, as her body, emotions, and intellect crashed together like a symphony in its final phrase. She rubbed her face alongside John's as a cat would against a hard surface. His face was tense and she pressed hard against the sharp lines, gliding from one side to the other. Their slick bodies and Melissa's spherical pelvic rotations forced John to grip tightly so that she wouldn't slip through his fingers. His hands were strong and covered the whole of her buttocks and part of her thighs. If not for the short blunted nails he would have pierced her skin. She felt his fingers press through her flesh touching the bone. For a million years or for one second, she could not determine how long it lasted ...

# Chapter 26

It was a small one room flat, a small bed, two chairs, a television, a bathroom with stand-up shower, and a window encased in bars. A jail disguised as a hotel, Charlie thought as he looked out over the compound. The design was similar to that of the Plex, where all units could watch the common area. Charlie was free to enter and leave his little apartment as he wished and on one occasion did. It was uncomfortable to be in the common area, it felt like he was being watched. He hadn't left the unit since. Now he observed a man sitting on a bench smoking a cigarette, a political prisoner, same as Charlie. What was his story? How many places like this were there?

The front door resonated with a knock.

Charlie opened the door and was met by a mid-sized man, dressed casually, thin, making his legs and arms appear too long, an inch maybe two under six feet. He was by no means a military man like the ones before him. The Department of Defense had tried different tactics to get Charlie to talk. There was nothing to say to those men.

"Hello my name is Leonard Miles, would it be alright if I came in and talked with you for a while?"

"Polite, how refreshing." Charlie opened his hand, moved out of the way, and gestured Leonard to enter. "Yes, please come in."

Leonard slipped off his shoes and walked into the living room.

"You may sit anywhere you like." Charlie noticed that Leonard was looking at the two chairs. Leonard had barely said a word, but Charlie knew he was refined by the way he carried himself. The stress wrinkles between his eyes showed that he was often in deep thought. His pale skin and emaciated body showed that he had never done physical labor. Charlie sat down after him. "Psychiatrist? Psychotherapist?"

"Psychiatrist." He smiled and opened his book.

"A doctor, good, I've been looking for an intelligent conversation. It's not been easy to find one around here."

Dr. Miles looked up. "Very well, Mr. Kolazar, lets get started, I—"

"Please, call me Charlie."

"As you wish, Charlie. You have many people wondering where you've been all these years."

"I *told* them where I've been." Charlie opened his hands in mock astonishment.

"You can understand their reluctance to accept that you lived on the street for over fifty years." The doctor looked down at his notepad. "It says here that you disappeared shortly after the bombs were dropped. Is that why you left?"

"Wow, it took over a dozen interviews and somebody finally pinpointed it."

"There's no need for sarcasm. I won't pretend I'm here for any other reason than to analyze you and determine if your story is true. Maybe you were working for another government. You were privy to information that the U.S. still deems top secret—"

"Yes, that's it, the Russians were hiding me out in a soup kitchen in Toronto." Charlie shook his head. "And the information I was privy to way back then is common knowledge today. Other countries have that capability. Your government gives away technology to build allies and enemies. That's not why I'm here."

Dr. Miles leaned back in his chair and scratched his head with his pen. "It seems we got off on the wrong foot, can we start again?"

"Absolutely, my apologies. Here I finally have somebody intelligent to talk with, and I've been rude." Charlie thought about Melissa and Will. It was important for Melissa's safety that they believe he had not been working on physics at all over the years.

"Good. Now, why did you run?"

"I wasn't willing to be a part of a machine that subjugates intelligence into violence."

"Don't you think a free nation should arm itself in the most efficient way possible and use those arms to protect the people?"

Charlie held his forefinger up. "First of all, dropping those bombs was not primarily a glorious military action that saved lives, as the men in power would have liked the nation to believe. It was a diplomatic maneuver aimed at intimidating Russia, it was to satisfy a national ego and prove that America was morally superior to the Japanese, it was justification for spending two billion dollars of the people's money; it was revenge for Pearl Harbor. Over two hundred thousand innocent lives in mere seconds. It should never have happened. Do I think a nation, that ensures the unhindered development of its citizens, should protect itself against aggressors?" Charlie could feel his eyes narrow. "Yes! By what ever force necessary. But it was the president's intention to provoke the Japanese into attacking them so that they could justify sending tens of thousands of people to war. When they died on foreign battlefields it helped solve the burgeoning unemployment problem, taking stress off his administration, and diverting focus from their inept ability to run the country. Recovering an economy is better achieved by removing controls and regulations, setting people free, rather than killing them or taxing them to death." Charlie shook his head. "If we're going to talk, lets tell it like it is."

Dr. Miles wrote something down on his pad. He looked up and opened his arms. "So there's no hope now?"

"No." Charlie could see where this conversation was going.

"Do you feel there is imminent danger under the current system?" Leonard's eyes creased.

"Of course."

"To whom, you or society?"

"Is there a difference? Society as a whole suffers upon the infringement of a single person's rights."

The doctor said nothing for a moment and studied the last answer. His eyes widened. "So you're transient. Is that what you thought life would be like as a child?"

"Actually, I never really considered it." Charlie thought now that the universe was no less astounding watching it from the streets. In fact, with Joanne, Melissa, and Will it had become more vibrant and alive. "I couldn't live in your world any longer, I was a creator, not a destroyer."

Dr. Miles pen became a constant flow of movement. "Do you feel responsible for what happened?" He was relaxed, his free arm loose with his hand resting, open palm toward Charlie, on his leg.

"I realize that what little input I had was not necessary to complete the project, but it put my light out, my wanting to strive for higher knowledge disappeared. Why bother? All the world's colors changed to gray at that time for me, neither bright nor dull." Charlie drew a deep breath and exhaled in a sigh. "Nobody really has any control."

"So your behavior and thought processes have become handicapped as a result?"

"Yes, they're very good at sublimating creativity into stagnation." Charlie let his shoulders drop, and tried to look lethargic.

"That must have been difficult. It says here, and even by your own admission, you were a very ambitious man. Were you right in shutting down your mind? It doesn't seem natural." Leonard's voice took on a twinge of disbelief. "Can you justify your present position in life?"

Charlie shot forward and pointed his finger. "Can you justify yours?"

Dr. Miles' body firm and his open hand clenched. "Me! I'm successful and have found my place in this world and—"

"Are as much to blame for the state of affairs in this country as anybody, probably more so." Charlie could see the doctor's face redden as his brow wrinkled.

"You have some nerve saying that." Dr. Miles took a deep breath as though trying to compose himself.

"Let's cut the Freudian crap before you bring my mother into it. My guess is on your notepad there you have 'Apathy, Widespread', maybe even 'Local' written in big bold letters at least three times."

Dr. Miles pulled his notepad close to his chest.

Charlie shook his head. "Close your book and let's talk."

Slowly, the doctor closed the pad and put it on the table in front of him, then leaned back in his chair and opened his arms. His face was confident, interested, stern.

Charlie began, "Most people in this world are trapped. By that I mean their happiness has been subjugated to some higher cause or pseudo-goodness and very few escape to live vibrant, exciting lives. Even you, of the intellectual group of society, part of the few who set the rules and standards per se, are working for smooth talking men with mediocre minds. Men who think that people by nature are bad, must be controlled, and that force is moral in maintaining that control."

"I personally don't believe that, I think in essence that the individual is good. Just look into a baby's eyes, there's no evil there. But then again, I still have hope," Dr. Miles cut.

"Yes, I can still see life in your eyes, but it's dwindling. You still have hope but you continue to give the despots the tools to destroy humanity."

The doctor pointed to himself. "I'm doing this? You don't even know me!"

"Don't get me wrong, you're probably not malicious, but throughout the ages it's always been the philosophers and elite who gave a small group of people control over a larger group. Through manipulation, the government has made the good seem bad and the bad seem good. The reason it has been so easy to do is because our mentality is still steeped heavily in the vestiges of a primitive time. It's an automatic following system that allows control. Most are contented and consider themselves lucky not to be in a worse situation, such as a third world country. The leaders are always pointing to something worse to justify their malevolent actions, and the philosophers talk in vague nonsense giving the elite language that is colorful and admired, and has the appearance of being valid, but really means nothing. Rhetoric that has nothing to do with reality." Charlie paused. He could tell that the doctor had something to say.

"Yes, I've read the theory of consciousness as a break in evolution. The right hemisphere of the brain guided man through auditory and visual hallucinations attributed to gods and rulers. Until about three thousand years ago when it broke down under external pressures of society becoming more complex, and man, in order to survive, reorganized his mind to become an introspective organism." Leonard shrugged his shoulders. "Even if that's true, that was a long time ago and we've come a long way since then."

"Have we? Instead of the controlling voices in our head, we've given that power to a small group. So it's not graves, idols, and statues that guide the masses now, it's living, breathing men of power that have assumed that authority under the title, 'The voice of the people'. Only sixty years ago, through Divine Providence, Hitler, in his clear and insistent voice, ushered millions of people to their death. He assumed that lost voice of control."

Dr. Miles leaned forward. "So you've identified this."

"No, not me, and I would probably have never known it if I hadn't quit working and studied other areas. Look into people's eyes, the vast majority have lost their happiness. Contrary to popular belief, it's not natural to lose our childlike awe as we grow older. This universe is so astounding! Our seventy-five years, give or take, in this world is not nearly enough time for us to become so quickly bored with it. Life, the greatest gift bestowed on us, has been infected with indifference. The natural essence of life is to forge ahead and become the most that is possible from within.

"As an example, think of a sperm en route to the egg, the would-be fertilizer of life. How far do you think it would get giving only a fraction of its potential? And then it has to fight innumerable obstacles to grow within the womb. When you think of the possible things that could go wrong, it's surprising that anybody makes it into the world at all. Then after fighting all those challenges he is thrown out into the world and until the age of around five is so inspired with life that people are in awe of so pure a light.

"The average person's face illuminates with joy at the sight of a baby. After a year or so he tries to walk. Have you ever watched a baby try to walk?" He paused so Leonard could acknowledge his question. "It's incredible. The baby will fall numerous times but continues to try because walking is something he has chosen, albeit sub-consciously, to accomplish. He has set no limits on himself yet. The universe to that baby is all-inspiring, and although unfamiliar with it, he knows by trial and error that it is an intelligible universe. His experiments prove that a ball will roll a cube will not, that gravity is his obstacle to standing upright and works in direct proportion with his mass. Then the astounding feat of learning to speak ... it's an incredible breakthrough! All things, up until about the age of five, are limitless. And then we all know what happens." Charlie raised his eyebrows in search for a response.

"School?" Leonard replied.

"Good, I'm glad to see you're following along here. And what happens with school?" Charlie leaned forward.

"Children are graded mainly on two intelligences, mathematical-logical and linguistic, then classified subjectively, often to the hindrance of the brighter, more creative students. More and more students are graduating with substandard levels of reading and writing ... there's nothing groundbreaking here. It's a problem that needs attention and you may not be aware of it but there are many people out there making a difference in the way our children are taught." The doctor's voice seemed slightly agitated. "And I've busted my butt to get to where I am today. I had to break through many personal barriers. Unlike you, I wasn't naturally endowed with genius and worked hard, *toward my potential*, to be where I am today. I'm paid well, and I make what difference I can. I know there are things wrong with the world, but I didn't run from it." His eyes filled with insolence. "Man has come a long way and there's work to do, but you can't help change it if you run away and hide yourself on the street. If you want to change things you must stand up and be counted. There's no guidebook on life, so we have to move ahead and work with what we have. But you, an intelligent, once creative man, have taken away from people a needed contribution. What a waste." Dr. Miles flicked his hand and shook his head.

*He's good,* Charlie thought. He wanted to stand up for himself and shout, 'I haven't been wasting my time. My mind is not of today's mentality, it's of tomorrow's and will be expressed!' But he didn't express it and remained calm. He let out a smile to release his inner tension. Optimism raced through him that all he had done over the years would indeed find its place in the world, seeds that would break to the surface and fill the entropy of common thought. His life had meaning. He continued, "But there *is* a guide book on life and it's inductive in nature which is naturally embedded in every individual. It has to be honestly identified. Only then can valuable creation begin, creation conducive to the well being of the individual and therefore society as a whole. Watching your world from the streets, how could I not give up? What a sad state of affairs." Charlie studied the doctor for a moment, then continued:

"Your lethargic, mandatory education system does more to slow down the cognitive ability of the student than to train and allow it to mature into its natural healthy state. Science is taught without a foundation of essential principals. I've read your high school texts books and they are more obscure than the outdated books I had in my youth, although there are many colorful pictures on every page; pictures replacing meaningful text, in science? Had I been in your country and forced to go to public school here, I would have been *dumbed down* and not known the first thing about physics, or worse, considered eccentric and labeled selfish for wanting to express my creativity when other children weren't *lucky* enough to be naturally endowed. Pictures have to be in your texts books, though, because high school students can't read well and would soon become frustrated with any form of learning. That's because reading is taught in the same fashion where the science of phonetics is considered irrelevant, and math is force-fed then regurgitated without telling the student why patterns are necessary and useful in life. Wonderful discoveries in any field have been scarce and far between as a result. This day and age requires self-responsibility and self-reliance not conformity and obedience if the world stands a chance at all. Which it doesn't. Instead of setting the child free, mandatory education has done more to paralyze the students' critical faculty. Your society pushes them through school and thrusts them out into the world without showing them how to use that magnificent tool naturally endowed to them: their mind."

"Okay, it's wrong, so how do we change the system?" The doctor asked, seemingly willing to play along.

"It's not possible. Even if there were solutions, they would not be made available. The system, so ingeniously designed, creates individuals that can't think independently, leaving any figure of authority with good language skills a natural leader, regardless of intention or principals. Meanings and concepts are altered through flowery speeches to manipulate the masses, which is easy because they have already been matured by the education system for political indoctrination. The assault on children's minds through mandatory education is criminal and has all the characteristics of a totalitarian society."

"I don't believe that and I'd say you're too far removed from society to have a valid assessment."

Charlie smiled. "Actually, I didn't identify this, it's been identified many times in the past and is now being lobbied by heroic people who are shunned, ostracized … really, when you look at the overall picture, I'm insignificant to the numbers of brilliant men who have been jailed, stifled and slaughtered over the ages. There is no greater evil than a government that enslaves its own people and sucks the life out of them for a greater cause: society."

"Isn't that what America fights for? Isn't democracy worth a fight?" Dr. Miles seemed more at ease and deeply interested.

"That's just another concept that's been obscured. Democracy is another form of control. It's a social system that gives the majority unlimited rule. So any group of people can do anything as long as it's the majority, even murder. It's not the basis of the American system. America is a constitutional republic first, not a pure democracy. It was meant to limit the government, not the citizens. At one time it was a land where man could develop his genius and reap the rewards of that, but now his genius has become the property of the state, taken by force if necessary, and that's rationalized in the name of the common good. So the atom became the ultimate tool of destruction first, instead of an endless source of power to serve mankind. The atom, to this day, is in a losing fight to solve many of the energy problems this world faces.

"The founding fathers established the first system to give rise to the individual. It was the first nation in history where man had the right to life, liberty, and the pursuit of happiness. Men of action appeared out of everywhere to build a monumental country. The genius of the founding fathers was that they formed a practical system that protected man from every kind of tyranny. It was a model country born with the guarantee of individual rights, protected for any and all individuals whether strong or weak, rich or poor. Everybody had a chance now to become a self-made scientist, artist, inventor, or entrepreneur without birth predetermining what an individual's occupation would be. A whole new era had begun in America of self-determinism. Any and everything of value in this country is a result of that kind of freedom. That's why progress was so slow until men were free to develop. Electricity had always been here but it took freedom for a man to harness that into a light bulb. But now the business, political, and educational structures have feverishly worked to stagnate the would-be creators into pessimism and dysfunction."

"I don't believe that." Dr. Miles shrugged his shoulders. "Nobody told me I had to be a psychiatrist, and I'm paid in direct proportion to my worth. Maybe a little underpaid, but I accept that."

"Yes, but you're locked in a system that uses your intelligence to further their bogus livelihoods. Not so different from the elite harboring the scholars away in the dark ages to work solely for them. That's what they tried to do with me."

"How do you mean?"

"You've been sent here because you're considered the best in your field, or as close as they could afford, to see if I've been working. More specifically, to see if maybe I completed the theorem that showed such promise for replacing tritium with a cheap, easy-to-manufacture material, among other things I had been working on." Charlie stopped to let that sink in. "And although I came back without resistance, I had no choice in the matter."

The doctor stared fixedly into Charlie's eyes.

"America has become so left-brained, analytical, filled with regulations that no one can see through the cluster of confusion. The country is swimming in an ocean of rules that have nothing to do with the protection of the people. In all the countries where I've lived, the need to control the people for the sake of a few parasites has taken precedence over everything. But the American constitution is the only one that spells out in black and white that above all else the individual's life must be protected in his pursuit of happiness. I must say when I came over I was inspired by life, but my happiness was not to use my genius for destructive purposes, so I ran to the streets to get my liberty. The constitution had been changed to read, albeit between the lines, that you have the right to life, liberty, and the pursuit of happiness, unless the government wants something from you, at which point they have the right to override the constitution. The Decree for the Protection of the People and the State of March 1933, gave Hitler written permission to deviate from the

Constitution of Germany at his sole discretion. At that time it was a 'democracy'. Of course there's no written permission here in the states, but lawyers have obscured the true essence of the Constitution. What started off as a heroic venture has now been buried under decades of misrepresentation. The philosophy of the founding fathers must be rediscovered and fixed at its root. The constitution had a virtuous beginning built on a shaky foundation. The job is not complete." Charlie stopped, feeling that his words were about to breathe optimism.

"Maybe you should have done that instead of wasting your life as a vagrant." Dr. Miles pointed his finger at Charlie.

*He's really good*, Charlie thought again. It was another attempt to draw out information about his work habits. "No, I was never a man of philosophy, especially of a sociopolitical type. In fact, it was only when I hit the streets that I had had enough time on my hands to read the constitution and the philosophies of the world. It wasn't until then that I realized science could not survive without a reality-based philosophy. A scientist must be a philosopher and a philosopher a scientist ... I couldn't do both," Charlie lied, as he had in fact been doing both for years from the street.

Charlie shook his head. The face of the young boy he had seen with his father walking out of Sick Children's Hospital appeared before him. It was the fuel that ignited the anger he had embraced so tightly all these years. His fear of any centralized government using his genius for destructive purposes was scary enough to keep him on the fringes of society, but it frightened him even more that his discoveries, once brought forward for mankind, would not be used at all. The doctor now sat in front of him, not as a person, but as the embodiment of all that was wrong with the world. He would let his anger free. It was time to make Dr. Miles believe that he had lost all hope and in turn, protect Melissa.

"You know I had never really planned to remain hidden forever," Charlie started passively. "I decided I would come back if one test of humanity was passed. Really until it happened, there was no reason for me to go back to work." Charlie took a deep breath. "I met a man while studying medicine in the late thirties: the most brilliant man I had ever known, and I had come to know many. He set the foundation that should have broken out and triggered a chain reaction of research, clinical treatment and the beginnings of an entirely new health system. I was still optimistic until the bombs were dropped that it would come to fruition. I understand that new ideas and theories often take some time before being accepted by the general population. History has demonstrated that clearly. But when I saw this great microscope and how it could isolate any disease's electromagnetic pattern, I knew that it was the beginning of a new era in medicine. This man discovered a painless, inexpensive cure for cancer and many others diseases. In the thirties! But his discovery was suppressed because of corrupt politics and medical profiteering—"

"You are paranoid," the doctor said.

"Am I? I get so angry when I think about the lives that could have been saved since that discovery ... you goddamn sons-of-bitches!"

The doctor leaned back at Charlie's shouting at him. "Take it easy, Charlie. You're directing your hatred at me, I don't even know what you're talking about."

"Take it easy? Take it easy!" Venom spewed from his mouth. "This man discovered a way to end all diseases but he was silenced because the establishment has always put power and money ahead of innocent lives. In his story stands the greatest criminal act of all time and illustrates all my points clearly. The rapid, painless, and free of side effects cure, yes cure, for all diseases without damaging healthy cells, tissues or organs was available in the nineteen-thirties, but deliberately suppressed for no other reason than it would have put the elite pill-pushing power hungry parasites at the top, out of business!" Charlie's anger became feral. "Doctors and scientists have been harassed, persecuted, and murdered for using therapy that threatened the profits of the pharmaceutical industry because disease is especially profitable for them. It had been proven effective on terminally ill patients—"

"This is crazy, I don't believe the medical community would ignore a harmless method to eliminate disease, pain and suffering. I can't accept that."

"Well don't rush off to the library to look up Dr. Rife—the most intelligent, benevolent, and honest man I had ever met—his name has been wiped from all the history books."

"I think you've been misguided and are sorely disillusioned by your pessimism of life. I'm not familiar with Rife's work and I've been in the medical field for years."

"Exactly my point! Rife discovered through his great microscope that disease organisms have their own unique electromagnetic pattern. He isolated those patterns, modified them, and used them to kill the microbes that produced them, by the millions without damage to healthy tissue.

The patience, time, study and sheer persistence that went into his findings is the very thing that's destroyed in the mind of the individual today. There is a cure for what conventional medicine calls incurable but it threatens the drug medicine industry; there is a cure for a bizarrely insane world that is feasted upon by the parasitical elite, but that threatens their very existence. All are no better than the mob, actually they are worse because they all claim to be working in the interest of humanity while dooming millions of people to ugly, premature deaths. In 1971 Dr. Royal Raymond Rife died a penniless and broken man. His works were never recognized. I'm penniless, broken, and unrecognized; what the hell's the difference? Was I wrong not to try?"

"Yes, of course you were." Dr. Miles picked up his notepad.

"You should *not* have to worry about malevolent politics in the act of discovery!" he yelled. He eased his tone and finished with, "Time is catching up to humanity. It won't be long now."

"I disagree. You could have helped this world." Dr. Miles stood.

"No, I would only have sped up the inevitable."

"I'm sorry you feel that way. In my eyes, you've wasted your one and only life as a vagrant."

Charlie stood up. They both walked to the door. "Actually, it wasn't so bad. There were only two things to worry about, food and shelter. It was a simple life, not too much stress. I fared okay."

Dr. Miles extended his hand. "Nice to meet you, Charlie."

Charlie shook his hand.

He left the apartment and Charlie reflected on the entire discussion and was confident that he hadn't given him reason to be suspicious of his work.

* * *

Melissa was happy to be close. The thick clouds finally broke midafternoon, allowing sunrays to break through and wash warmth over the tips of the trees. Methodically, the light weaved itself into the crevices until it was able to penetrate the whole of the forest. By the time John and Melissa had reached the well-illuminated Burnt Island Lake, the sun was sinking in the sky leaving only the tail end of the day to bask in its warmth. John took them to a campsite that was spacious and well laid out. It was a long hard day of paddling and portaging. Melissa helped set up the campsite, feeling quite proficient at this now, while John prepared dinner over an open fire. The sun went from yellow, to orange, to red as it sank lower toward the horizon. Slight ripples in the water reflected a shimmering golden line toward their campsite, creating an aqua-mirage of fire and love. They sat together after dinner and talked.

John looked into Melissa's eyes. She could see a sadness she had never seen in him before.

He continued to speak. "... and as I sat and watched his life slip away, a part of me died." For the first time John was speaking of his father's death. "He died in my arms before the ambulance could get there." His head bowed and he wiped under his eyes. "And they were there within minutes. It was so fast."

Melissa moved over and hugged him.

"I didn't know what to feel. My chest tightened as I thought, 'He's gone.' It was my first exposure to death. Well, my grandparents, but I was young and I think my parents shielded me from that. There were no tears for my father; I was frozen. Then my mother walked into the room and I knew it was she I had to take care of, be strong for. Ever since then I never let it surface. It seemed the more the feeling arose, the more I had to push it down. Then I got so scared to let it show, I'm not sure why, but the feeling seemed to gain strength buried inside and I was afraid ..." John broke Melissa's grip. His eyes were filled with grief. "He'll never be back, it's over for good. Melissa, I miss him so much ..." He pulled her close again.

Melissa stroked his back. "It's okay, John, let it out. Let him live again."

After a few moments Melissa broke the embrace and kissed him on the lips, then the forehead and the cheeks until she covered the whole of his face and neck. She pulled him close again. "You're so strong, I love you more than you can imagine."

John breathed deeply and looked Melissa directly in the eyes with no attempt to hide his pain. She felt a need to protect him. "I haven't been up here since he died, like somehow I knew I would have to come to terms with it here. I had all kinds of excuses: too busy at work, building a relationship with you, but they were all lies. I just couldn't deal with it, that's why I needed you to be here."

The sun was dropping quickly toward the tree line and the water was now like a sheet of glass, mirroring the shadow of the trees, only a whisper of a breeze brushing across Melissa's face remained. The tumultuous weather had ceased and order had been restored.

Melissa looked around the campsite. "I get a very strong feeling of your father here. I wish I'd met him personally."

"Oh yeah, you'd have loved him. He'd have loved you, too."

Melissa moved around John's back and began massaging his shoulders.

"He taught me everything I know, how to canoe, camp, work with wood. He was an expert carpenter. Did you know that people from all over the county would come to him for advice on building things? My father was very generous with information, with everything actually. He always said what goes around comes around. Sometimes I would get upset that he was spending so much time working for other people and not with me. 'Be patient my son, you'll have your turn.' He never let me down. It seemed every year we would come here, sometimes for two weeks at a time. Every year, I tried to impress him with mastering a new paddle stroke, getting a fire going in the rain, setting up camp in record time. When he looked at me, Melissa, his face beamed with pride. I think I miss that more than anything, the way he looked at me …" John turned sideways to see Melissa. "I think that's what scared me most with you, I felt so alone and afraid. It wasn't even a year after he died that we got together and you, in a way, replaced that void. I know it doesn't make sense, but when you stopped looking at me like you used to … everything kind of arose for me."

Melissa stopped massaging but made sure her hands never left John's shoulders. "Yeah, I know, but you know what, I never really lost admiration or love for you, and I always thought we'd be together forever. Well, except for that brief time that you initiated. I took you for granted, that was my mistake, even looked down on you in some ways. That was a shortcoming of mine, not yours. Even before we met, I lived for you."

"I understand that. You've shown me that … especially coming here with me."

The sun had buried itself behind the trees. Two loons swam by, looked at John and Melissa and kept going into the dusk, leaving a fan of gentle waves behind them.

"Ouch!" John shouted, his body trying to escape Melissa's grip.

Melissa laughed. "Sorry." She rubbed more gently. "I guess I'm getting stronger, living off the land and all." His shoulders felt nice under her touch. She was the happiest and most fortunate person in the world.

# Chapter 27

Charlie was happy that he had given no cause for suspicion about his work habits. He figured that his diagnosis would consist of severe post-traumatic stress disorder, anxiety, and anger resulting in his alienation from society. Thoughts of Melissa occupied most of his time these days; it was a healthy distraction. His eyes became heavy.

Mozart's Symphony Number 31 rose to life in Charlie's mind as he walked toward a white diffused light. Black and white Serroka birds flew by in front of him fluttering their wings as harmony caressed his soul. He was light and happy. He walked through a wall of light into an area of trees, mountains, and shrubs. It was his home. The garden was filled with dark, rich soil and a girl was on her knees digging in the ground, nurturing life bringing forth the most beautiful flowers he had ever seen. There was a stork sitting on the pole over her. Was that his sister? No, he thought excitedly as he approached. She turned and Charlie was lost for words to describe the feelings that arose at the sight of Joanne's clean, healthy, smiling face.

"I knew you would come." Joanne's tone was soft.

"I'm sorry, Joanne." Charlie kneeled and looked at Joanne, begging forgiveness.

"No, I should be sorry, I could've trusted you." She smiled, her face beaming, her lips curled upwards easily, her eyes glistening like a child in awe of everything. "This is your home, it's beautiful." She lifted her head and graciously waved her hand in front of herself adding more depth and color to the landscape. "The mountains are still, yet move like waves across the horizon."

"Yes, yes!" Charlie exclaimed. "There's so much I can show you, teach you."

"No, it's I who can teach you now, but there's no time for that, you have to go." Joanne's eyes were infinite, glowing.

"No, I can't, I want to stay." Charlie could feel a pull from behind as Joanne, the mountains, and his home gradually became smaller separating him with distance. "Joanne …"

"Thank you, Charlie, for everything. I love you. See you soon …" Her voice was filled with the ardor of youth as it trailed off.

He was pulled back through the white light and sent spiraling through time and space. His form elongated, then snapped back at the change of speed.

His eyes flew open. He got up and struggled to find the light switch. Melissa, he had to get a message to Melissa.

\* \* \*

John looked back at Melissa and felt content. She had made this place a part of her and had helped him come to terms with his father's death. He noticed that she had looked up from her sketchbook right at him. He turned around and looked out over the lake. The sun was rising and the thick mist from the perfectly calm water was dispersing. The sound of crickets and the occasional loon call were the only things to break the silence. John felt completely relaxed. He looked back again. She was a fair distance away, twenty feet maybe, but he could see her eyes. They showed she was far away: A distant place, maybe another universe located deep within her.

"I knew you would love it here," he said, projecting his voice.

She looked at him as though her trance was broken. "Oh, John, it's beautiful, everything's been perfect."

"Lets go for a swim." John removed his shorts and shirt. Without a stitch of clothing on, he turned around. "Are you coming?"

She jumped up, removed her clothing, and stood beside him.

He felt a peaceful, high energy standing there beside Melissa. When John looked at her something was different. It was a deep feeling of confidence, awareness within him. He could feel his mouth curl into a smile as he lifted himself from the rock and dove through the white mist and into the dark soft mine of Algonquin water. The wetness surrounded him like a protective gel, as though he was back in the womb with love energy all around him. He remained still and let the feeling envelope him. He felt the beating of his heart, rhythmic, strong. He could hear the water break just before Melissa swam up from underneath him and climbed onto his back. He pulled her to the surface.

They swam, playfully touching and splashing each other. After about twenty minutes, they got out, wrapped themselves in a big fleece blanket and stared out over the lake. Silent and motionless, they watched the shadow from the trees behind them shrink on the water as the sun rose higher in the sky. The mist over the water had completely dispersed.

"I have all kinds of new ideas to raise the quality of life for homeless people," Melissa said.

"Oh, like?" John wanted to be supportive, but knew his voice didn't project confidence.

"I've been thinking. Harris funded the Group of Seven, which subsequently put Canadian artists on the world map. They, as a group, showed the strength and beauty of this land. Without him the group would never have formed. He had the organizational skills and, of course, the money. I'm thinking of forming a group myself. I could rent a warehouse and we could work as a team to put homelessness on the map, awaken the sleeping conscience of the world. I could teach, chisel away like a sculptor, the true essence of other artists, like McDonald did with Thompson." Melissa's voice grew animated. "We could sell our work and start education programs to eradicate the homeless problem by instilling confidence. Charlie opened my eyes where they're concerned and I have a better understanding now. I would put some of the paintings in the shelters to show hope. By using teaching as an avenue, I think I could learn a lot and help in a way I never dreamed. Well, what do you think?"

John did not say anything. He wasn't sure what he wanted to say.

Melissa held him a little more tightly. "Don't worry, I promise not to take you for granted. I want you to tell me if I'm not giving you enough time. It's you who's most important to me."

"That doesn't concern me as much as ..." John could not think of how he wanted to express himself. Melissa watched, as if waiting for him to say something. "I don't know, it's like the loon we saw on the first day, or the rabbit and weasel this morning, the beaver that slapped its tail on the water to distract us from closing in on its dam, and Rocky our chipmunk friend. They all just live and do what comes naturally to them ..." John thought of the talk he had had with her father and how he had said she would want to spread her wings and that her work with the homeless was just a phase. John felt that he might have been right about that. She was so talented.

Melissa continued to look at John as though she didn't understand. A Gray Jay with its white forehead and collar, boldly flew right in front of them chirping and singing, its gray feathered wings graciously flitting to keep it gliding smoothly. "You see how beautiful and natural it is for a bird to flutter by and sing. It doesn't sing because it's trying to tell us something, or because it needs to share wisdom, it sings because of the song within." John paused. "You have a beautiful song inside you, Melissa, be true to that. Express it in a way most suited to your true self. I guess I'm just worried that you put a lot of pressure on yourself because of what happened to Stephanie. You can't blame yourself for that."

Melissa did not respond right away. She looked around and after a moment said, "Yeah, I know, but I do really miss her." She smiled and snuggled up even closer to John, their bare bodies absorbing into each other under the blanket. "That was beautiful, what you said about my song. I do feel I'm being true to my song, though, I want to make a difference and help people. Everything good in my life, John, is a result of dealing with the homeless, you, Charlie, Will. How can I turn my back on something that's given me so much? Spiritually, Stephanie gave me more than I ever gave her. I'm willing to give more of myself now. I just have to learn how to do it with proper balance. And I feel my work is about to take off, double, maybe even triple in price."

"You have my support in whatever you decide, I want you to know that. You can choose any dream you want to." John looked out over the lake.

"I hope Charlie's okay," Melissa said.

"I hope so, too," John replied.

Melissa leaned over and kissed him on the cheek. "I've decided where I want to go next year on our first anniversary."

"I'll pick a different route next time."

It was their last day, and they spent it talking, relaxing, touching, watching. They had to leave early the next morning, as John had a meeting with Matthew about some more work. Melissa suggested that they all meet at her place. She wanted to show Matthew some of her work and assure him that she would fulfill her promise to paint him a building for his wall as payment for allowing her to use his building. She could also pack up some essential things she would need to start living with John. The sun seemed to race across the sky. As usual, time went by too quickly here for John.

\* \* \*

"Well, can we expect some answers from him? Has he been working?" The Defense Secretary, Harold Weaver, sat at a table across from Dr. Leonard Miles.

"He won't work for the government. He'd rather die than work for the U.S. or any government for that matter," Dr. Miles replied.

"Has he been working, Leonard?"

"He says no," Leonard began, "but I'm sure he's been doing something."

"Why do you say that?"

"He can sure make you think. Very intelligent …" Leonard narrowed his eyes. "He doesn't give much credit to Freud's psychoanalysis, which left him open to errors. Errors, I mean, if his objective was to make me believe he hasn't been working." Leonard's back straightened and he looked quite proud of himself.

"What do you mean?" Harold asked.

"Well, my diagnoses is that he suffers from apathy among other things, all of which he agreed with. Collective apathy is a cover for social despair, inertia disengagement from the political and social process of society. It's the result of widespread loss of hope."

Harold tapped his pen on the table and rubbed his face. "So that only tells us that yes, he could have taken to the streets to escape."

"That's what he would like us to believe, and he thinks he's accomplished that goal. As I spoke to him, I found out that at one time he did indeed lose hope, but has at some point regained it, maybe even on a subconscious level." Leonard shifted his head and squinted his eyes as though giving deep thought to his last statement.

"So he cured himself of apathy, what does that prove?" Harold was feeling anxious, he hated the way Leonard always took the long way around to get to an explanation.

"Emotions fuel our lives, without desire there is really no motivation to live. I've had extensive experience with apathy and have found creativity to be the only antidote. It gives purpose to living, for all of us, and we all express it in different ways. In Mr. Kolazar's case, you can be pretty sure he wasn't basket weaving all these years."

"What if it was just recently that he found hope? There wouldn't be much work. After all he eluded capture for over fifty-five years. Why had he allowed himself to be caught now?" Harold let out a breath of air.

"That I don't know, maybe it had something to do with the homeless girl who died. Although it's my opinion that he recovered that part of him a long time ago; somebody suffering from widespread apathy living on the streets would not become old. The streets are a dangerous place. To live there for fifty-five years is quite a feat, a feat that requires ambition to survive. Some of my patients, in a very hospitable environment, must be force fed and given drugs to keep them alive."

"Thanks for your help." Harold waved a dismissive hand.

Leonard left the room. Harold sent for Agent Peters.

He walked in. "Yes, sir."

"Have a seat." Harold thought for a moment. "Good work, bringing Mihaly Kolazar back."

"Thank you, sir."

"Now I want you to release him."

Fred shook his head. "Pardon me?" he asked, his voiced filled with astonishment.

"I want you to let him go and follow him. I want to know if he's been working on anything and if he has, I want that work. Send some men to Toronto and have them talk to anybody who knows him. This is highly secret and I want no stone unturned in this pursuit."

"Sir," Fred cut in, "all my men are tied up at the moment, and I don't—"

"No excuses, you find a way. I don't care if you have to send the I.R.S. up there. They've been the toughest of the bunch lately, anyway. You found out he was in Toronto because he had come forward in an investigation. Start there. And when you follow him back, don't keep the same men on the job all the way. Switch them periodically he's not a stupid man. I want this cleared up pronto. I have more important things to do than chase phantom theorems."

"Yes, sir." Fred stood up and left the room in a dutiful manner.

* * *

An agent informed Charlie that he had every right to decline the invitation back to the states. And that now he was free to decide whether he wanted to stay or to leave. When, on his request, Charlie was given a plane ticket to Toronto, taken to the airport, and told that he was on his own, he couldn't help but feel suspicious. He would be sensitive to people following him.

The flight back was smooth. When he got off the plane and cleared customs, he had the same feeling as when he sat out in the common area in the compound. They didn't believe him and now wanted him to lead them to his work. He had to get a message to Melissa. His heart all of a sudden pulsed in rapid succession. He clutched his chest and fell to the ground. *Not now, it's too soon ...*

# Chapter 28

The pleasant rejuvenating feeling inspired by the last week didn't last long after Melissa opened the door to her apartment.

"John!" she gasped, unable to believe her eyes.

The place was a shambles. John walked by her and turned on the light. "Stay here." He carefully walked over the books that had been strewn all over the floor and across the stairs. "Nobody here."

Melissa was immobilized as she stared at her apartment. There was not one book remaining on the shelves and all of the paintings had been ripped off the walls and torn apart as though somebody was looking for something hidden in them. She was in shock, unable to formulate any words.

John picked up the phone and went to close the front door when it swung open knocking his hand back. Two men barged in, grabbed the phone from John's hand, and threw him to the ground. John tried to get up but one of the men stepped on his chest. Melissa instinctively went to help John. The second of the two men grabbed her by the arms, forced her to the futon and made her sit down. His hands were big and strong. She struggled against him.

"Stay where you are!" the man yelled at Melissa as she tried to get back up.

The other man picked John up by the throat with ease and threw him down beside Melissa. "Don't move!" He walked over and closed the front door.

The two men were large, well over six feet tall and solid, probably nearing two hundred and fifty pounds. There was one with thick straight blonde hair and a wide ridged face, the other had dark hair cut to a stubble, army style. He had a longer face with a chiseled nose and flaring nostrils. Both wore suits.

"Now, just cooperate and nobody will get hurt," said the blonde one as his face constricted with a haunting direct-gaze. There was no life in those eyes, but there was immense power. "We know Charlie stayed here and we're looking for the package he left with you. Where is it?"

"I don't know what you're talking about," Melissa shot back defiantly.

"Listen, little girl, this is no game." The chisel nosed man walked over, grabbed John by the hair, and pulled him off the futon.

John threw a punch into the man's stomach. He didn't flinch other than his nostrils seemed to thin even more as air rushed out. He took his other hand and closed it around John's throat. John gasped for air and his face turned beet red.

"Okay, stop! We haven't seen him, we don't even know him that well, and he didn't give me anything. Please let him go! We just got back from our honeymoon. We don't know anything," Melissa pleaded.

The man dropped John down onto the futon beside Melissa. He coughed and gasped for breath. Melissa looked into his eyes and caressed his face. She feared for their lives.

The phone rang twice successively.

"That means there's somebody downstairs." The militant, blonde haired man picked up the phone. "What number do you push to allow access?"

Melissa said nothing and threw as evil a look as she could manage toward both men.

The man approached with the phone in his hand. His eyes narrowed and his lips pursed.

"Four, the number is four," Melissa shouted before he got too close. "Bastards," she said under her breath.

The two men stood by the door.

"If it's him, we'll drag him in here to talk," the chisel nosed man said. "If we have to use the girl as a tool to get information, then so be it. We'll see how well they really know him." He opened his eyes widely while looking at Melissa. He had unusually small irises that were a dull gray.

The door resonated with a knock. The blonde man answered while the other stood behind.

"I'm looking for John and Melissa." Melissa could hear Matthew in the hallway. She had almost forgotten that John had called him on the way home to arrange a meeting here.

"Get in here." The man pulled Matthew inside by his collar and closed the door. "Well, it's definitely not him."

"Oh, no," Melissa said. Matthew had always seemed quite big, but seemed so small in comparison to these thugs.

Matthew knocked the man's hand off his shirt. "What the hell do you think you're doing?" He looked at Melissa and noticing her fear, said, "They're not welcome here I take it."

Melissa shook her head no.

"I think it's time you guys left." Matthew's tone was even, not raised, but powerful.

In a split second the militant blonde man threw a punch that landed in Matthew's stomach. He fell to the floor by his feet. It seemed Matthew was no more than a fly that needed to be swatted by this abusive man. Matthew curled inward, holding his stomach. He looked badly hurt. Then, seemingly out of nowhere, his foot shot out, landing right in the crease of the towering man's knee causing him to start falling. Matthew rolled out of the way, lifted his leg straight up, like an axe, and brought it down on the man's head sending it smashing into the floor.

From that moment it was all a blur to Melissa.

Matthew was on his feet; she did not see him get up. The other man lunged toward him and all she could hear were a series of blows being exchanged. She could not see anything clearly, it all happened in a split second. Then they were still. The man with small gray eyes stood there motionless, staring at Matthew. She couldn't figure it out until the man's knees buckled and he fell to the ground. Matthew remained motionless. A flash of heat ran through Melissa's body as she looked into his eyes. There it was, the look of the tiger, he was fierce, strong, alive. A visible energy radiated around his body.

Both men struggled to get up. It was strange, but Matthew stood there not even looking at them, but Melissa felt he knew. He was looking at Melissa but he was aware of the whole room, she could sense that. The two men were standing upright, still dazed. In the blink of an eye, Matthew had one man pinned up against the door with his foot on his neck while holding the windpipe of the other man with his two forefingers and thumb. He was a human vise. For some reason it didn't look unnatural for him to be in this position, his leg stretched almost straight up over his head. He seemed bigger now. There was still no visible emotion in Matthew as his free hand roamed the pockets of these men. He came out with two small guns, one from each man. Matthew threw them on the floor. "John, grab those and hold onto them."

John jumped up and grabbed the guns.

Matthew released both men and stood before them. He looked around the room. "You guys do this?"

There was no answer.

The chisel nosed man rubbed his neck where Matthew's foot had been. Attempting to surprise Matthew, he flung his hand out to strike him in the face. Matthew deflected the strike and swung around behind him. He kicked him behind the knees causing the man to cave, grabbed him around the neck with both arms, and began to squeeze. Within seconds, he released the man and he fell to the floor, unconscious. The blonde haired man was still struggling for breath.

"Tell me who you are and what you're doing here or I'll close your throat this time." Matthew's tone was low but penetrating.

"We're looking for a man named Charlie and a package he left, we thought he might be here."

"Why?"

"I don't know, we were just told that he might be here. We know the girl had contact with him." The man coughed, still trying to regain his full breath.

Matthew turned to Melissa. "Do you know Charlie?"

Melissa was still in shock. "Yes but … I haven't seen him in a long time."

"Good enough for me, is that good enough for you?" Matthew turned back to the blonde man.

"Yes."

"How about you?" Matthew looked at the other man who was shaking his head and seemed dazed now as he got up.

He looked at Matthew as if wondering where he was. "What?"

"Just say yes," the blonde man said. The militant man said nothing.

Matthew moved toward him as though ready to strike him.

"Okay, yes."

"Now leave before I get angry," Matthew said.

The chisel nosed man opened the door and both of them backed out, not once releasing Matthew from their sight.

"Somebody want to explain to me what this is all about?" Matthew locked the door behind the men.

Melissa told him about Charlie, how he had been instrumental in catching Joanne's abuser, and how he had been taken away not long ago. She noticed that Matthew had a small cut above his left eye that seemed almost the same shape as the pale scar over the other eye.

John assured both Melissa and Matthew that he was okay, although there was a noticeable handprint around his neck. Melissa slowly made her way upstairs and picked up her painting "A Vision of Hope" and noticed it had been sliced three times, destroyed beyond repair. She couldn't say anything as she stared blankly into John's eyes. She could feel the three slits transfer and open a wound deep within her. John watched from the lower level, his posture and face showing concern. She didn't know how to feel, whether she should cry, be angry, sad. Then a strong feeling of violation pierced her; it was incomprehensible that anybody could do this. She could not grasp the evil that could wreak such destruction. Her shoulders rolled forward and she exhaled. She felt like she was losing an important part of who she was as pain rippled through the shadows of her soul.

"I don't think you should stay here." Matthew looked at John.

"We'll talk at my place," John said.

John made his way past the books and paintings on the floor up to Melissa. "Come on, let's go."

Reluctantly, she stood up and John directed her down the stairs.

"Charlie!" she shouted. "We have to find Charlie."

\* \* \*

Somehow Charlie had managed to slow his heart. He knew he had suffered a heart attack and time was short. He had to see Will, to tell him to relay a message to Melissa.

Charlie was not worried about leading the men to the church where Will was. He had, over the time he was in Toronto, never disclosed any of his work to him. When they had spoken it was always philosophy, never directly what he was working on.

He opened one of the front doors of the church. As he walked in he felt his body twitch and his heart began to race again. This was it. His legs felt weak and he had to have a seat before he fell over. *I need to speak to Will before ... where is he? Damn! Where is he?*

\* \* \*

Matthew told John and Melissa that he would check the Plex for Charlie. Melissa showed him her sketch of him that was torn and bore the mark of a footprint. On the way out of her apartment, she had picked it up off the floor. Matthew recommended that they stay put and not open the door for anybody as he left the apartment.

Three hours had passed without word from Matthew.

Melissa got up from the couch. "I'm going to look for him."

John pulled her down. "You're not going anywhere." He knew this was going to be difficult, but he would tie her up if he had to. He could see that her emotions were getting the better of her.

"You can't tell me what I can or can't do!"

John took a breath and continued to hold her arm. "You're not going anywhere tonight, Melissa. If you think for one minute that I'm letting you go, you're sadly mistaken."

"I have to find him." She bolted up, breaking free from John's grip.

He ran up and stood in front of the door. "Listen, Melissa, what if you do go out and find him and those men follow you? I know you're not concerned about yourself right now, but what about Charlie? Is that what you want? You don't think they are waiting for you, hoping that you'll take them right to him? How would you feel then?" John could see that she was thinking. Her eyes glossed over with a look of realization. Her whole body slouched with hopelessness. "Now let's just go over and have a seat."

The phone rang.

"Hello," John answered.

"He's not here, John. I'm going to come back to your place." Matthew's voice was firm.

"See you in a bit." John hung up the phone and sat down beside Melissa.

They waited in silence for Matthew to come back.

Melissa noticed on the table the mail that John had picked up before finding her place torn apart. It had seemed, at the time, strange to have so much. She sifted through the pile, throwing all advertisements off to the side. But there were three that piqued her interest from London, Paris, and Glasgow, her largest galleries. Strange. Did they want more work? It was always she who contacted them when she had something to send. She dug her fingernail into the corner and tore open the envelope of the first, then the second and the third. She could not believe her eyes. They all informed her that her work was no longer wanted and would be refused if she tried to send anything. She would be paid the last of what they owed her, and she was not to contact them in any way again.

It all made sense to her now, what support her father was taking away from her. All the galleries that paid large sums of money were in cities where her father did a lot of business. It was he, not she who had given her art its worth. It was all a lie.

\* \* \*

Matthew came back and agreed to stay the night. He decided to help find Charlie the next day. Melissa wondered what interest he had in this, but felt more comfortable with him being there. She held John tightly throughout the night. Her mind was preoccupied with Charlie and she hoped he was safe. It was all that was left.

Visions of her apartment flashed through her mind as a razor blade making a slow incision through her heart. Treading wearily through a devastated and alien land, she drifted in and out of dreams wondering what was real and what wasn't.

The next morning they all sat around trying to decide the next step.

"Check your messages," John suggested to Melissa. "Maybe he's called."

Melissa checked her messages and discovered she had one from Will. She was to call him immediately. She offered to come down to the church at his request for a meeting. Will said he would come to John's.

They waited for an hour. Not one word was spoken between them. Matthew used John's bedroom to make phone calls.

* * *

When Will arrived he greeted Melissa with a solemn smile. He shook John's hand and introduced himself to Matthew.

"Melissa, I think we should speak alone," he said, looking toward Matthew and John.

"Have you seen Charlie? How is he?"

Will looked at both Matthew and John again.

"Come on, John, I'd like to discuss a business proposal with you." Matthew took the lead and they both left the apartment.

"What's wrong? Why do they have to wait outside? Where's Charlie? I have to see him." Melissa spoke quickly, her mind, body and spirit not ready for what Will had to say. His expression showed he did not bring good news.

"Sit down, Melissa." Will directed her over to the couch. He sat down and held her hands. She sat wide-eyed, not willing to believe anything bad. She could not take more bad news now. "It's about Charlie. He came to my church two days ago—"

"Where is he? Does he want to see me?" Melissa perked up.

"Please, Melissa, let me finish." This was obviously very difficult for him. "When I came out and saw him sitting in a pew he looked hurt as though he had been crippled—"

"Did they hurt him? Those bastards, what did they do to him?"

"Melissa, please let me finish. He was suffering from a heart attack. I quickly sat down beside him. He did not want any form of help. I tried to get up to call an ambulance but he pulled me down. He said he didn't have much time and needed me to relay information to you. I promised I would—"

"Where is he? What hospital? I have to go see him." Melissa stood up.

"Melissa, Charlie died in my arms." His eyes filled with tears.

"No, that's not true, you're lying to protect him." Melissa pulled her arm away. "Why are you trying to hurt me this way? It's not true, it can't be true." Melissa would not believe it, even from Will. She thought he must be lying to protect him.

Will got up and walked over to Melissa. She backed away as if he could infect her somehow. They had gotten to him and now he wanted her to turn on Charlie. Will was in on it. She backed to the wall.

"I'm sorry, Melissa." He moved closer and put his hands on her shoulders.

Melissa pushed him away. "When's the funeral?" she asked coldly. Her body rejected the hurt, it was too much in such a short time.

"Day after tomorrow, but you can't come. That's part of the reason I came here today." Will's eyes showed a deep pain.

"Oh that's great, that's just like your church to push me away. Maybe you can invite Edward Woodrow." Melissa felt malicious. She needed to deflect the pain.

Will's eyes filled with tears again. "Please don't, Melissa, there's a reason."

"I'm sure there is, it's because you and your church are so narrow minded it would be blasphemy to have me, an atheist, come into it." She felt like hurting him.

Will bowed his head and breathed in heavily for a second or two. A tear fell from his eye to the ground. He looked up at Melissa who was looking directly at him. She felt no sympathy, no pain, nothing at all.

His lips pursed and he looked as though he was summoning all his strength. "When I spoke to Charlie in his dying minutes he told me exactly how he wanted the service to go. You and John were not to attend. He knew he was dying and felt that if they linked you to him you would be in danger. They will come to his funeral, and if you're there it will lead them to believe you're closer than you want them to believe. Please don't come, it was one of Charlie's last wishes. Promise me that right now,

Melissa. He wanted me to hear you say it." Will stood as if ready to take more abuse. She said nothing. "Melissa, you have to promise me."

"Fine! I promise I won't come to the funeral. Are you happy?" Melissa shot back.

"Yes, your word is good with me and Charlie." Will bowed his head as though he was about to lose control of his feelings. He took a deep breath.

"Is that it?" Melissa snarled.

It took a moment for Will to answer. He took another deep breath. "Melissa …" His voice cracked.

"Don't you have a funeral to get ready for?" Melissa's jaw clenched as she waved the back of her hand for Will to leave.

"Yes, I suppose I do." Will started walking to the door. As he grabbed the handle he turned back. His eyes still filled with tears. "I'm sorry, Melissa." He opened the door and hesitated, like he was going to turn around, but he didn't and left the apartment.

Matthew and John walked in.

Melissa looked at both of them. "Well, we should have nothing to worry about now, Charlie's dead."

"Oh, Melissa, I'm sorry." John rushed to her side.

She pushed him away. "It's okay, I'm fine. In fact it's good because now we don't have to worry about it any longer." Her voice was strong and cold.

John's face contorted with worry, Matthew showed no expression.

Melissa looked at Matthew. "Thanks for your help, but I don't think we need it any longer. We've wasted enough of your time." She walked over to the door and held it open for him.

"When you sort through things here, give me a call. I want to fill you in more on the project," Matthew said to John.

He walked to Melissa and stopped. "Melissa, if you need anything give me a call." His tone was businesslike, his face strong, a true warrior.

"Thank you. I'm fine, really." Melissa closed the door after Matthew walked out. "See, that's the way to be, strong." Nothing could penetrate her now. She had given her feelings away and did not want them back.

# Chapter 29

Father Bower stood behind the podium, the light reflecting off the statue of Jesus illuminating him from behind. "… and Charlie was a good man. May God show him access to heaven and may his soul rest in peace."

There were about fifty people in attendance at Charlie's funeral; most were homeless. Out of the fifty there were maybe ten that actually knew Charlie. The rest knew that there would be refreshments and sandwiches after the service. It was perfect, Will thought, just as Charlie wanted.

"Charlie had often come to me with questions about my beliefs and had very strong beliefs himself. I got to know him quite well and discovered that he was quite the creative person." Will looked around the room taking in all in attendance. He noticed six men at the back of the room dressed in suits. They stood out like wolves in a heard of sheep. *They must be the ones Charlie was talking about.* Will could see two making notes while the others looked around as though taking inventory of who was there.

"Now I would like to give the floor to Kelly, one of Charlie's closest friends." Will gestured toward her to come up.

Kelly stood up and walked up to the lectern. She looked around and smiled. "You know, Charlie wanted people to think he hated them, but I saw him with Joanne." Kelly's clothes were old and ragged, she had made no attempt to freshen up before coming here. "That was Charlie, a grumpy old man. But, he took care of Joanne and put back a sense of humanity into her soul. Actually, I think it was the other way around." Kelly laughed. "He was always carving something, his hands were always busy. He said carving wood was like carving patterns in your brain." She laughed again. "Yep, it got to a point where he was finishing at least one little sculpture a week, some weeks two." Kelly pulled something out of her pocket. She held it up. "He made me this one and told me every time I felt like I needed a fix to get through the day, I should hold it in my hand until the feeling went away. And it really worked. Well, that's what

I told him anyway." Kelly smiled and looked up to the roof. "Hey, Repellent, you better be saving a spot for me, wherever the hell you are." Kelly looked around the room. "Yep, I don't see it being too long before they're packing dirt on my face." Her countenance turned serious as she looked around the room. She stepped down, walked down the aisle and right out of the church.

Will continued with the service, interpreting verses from the Bible. Through scripture he showed the light that was Charlie. Charlie would have liked his service, Will mused. He noticed that the men didn't stay long after Kelly had spoken. One man actually followed her out the door. Will finished with the service and they all went downstairs for coffee and refreshments. Only one of the suited men came down, he looked around quickly and then left.

Will was happy that he had fulfilled Charlie's wish. Now he gave comfort to these men and women. After everybody had cleared out and he had cleaned up, he went back up to the church. He knelt before Jesus and prayed for Melissa. He reproached himself for letting her hurt him when he had told her of Charlie's death. It was true that he loved Charlie, too, but he should have been strong for Melissa. He understood her pain and felt that he had failed her somehow. He should not have broken down, and he should have gone back to console her, but he admitted that he could not bear to look into her eyes one more time that day. He felt weak and prayed for strength. Suddenly, all of his healing tools seemed inadequate ... Was he really worthy of his position?

\* \* \*

The whole trip, the elated feelings, her unification with John and the foundation they had begun for their marriage, all the new ideas that had come to her, ideas of how to make her work more effective, came spiraling down into the hopeless pursuit of an illusion. Melissa realized now that she had never been grounded and had not only strived toward goals that she could never attain, but goals unattainable in this world. Her artwork was not prodigious; it was not even very good. She was no better than a common criminal, taking money for a value that never existed. Anton Strand was right, she rode on the shoulders of her father's bank account. Without it, she was nothing. Her mood became melancholic, and her spirit had all but left her. Her life was meaningless. She had never really helped anybody. In fact, since she had started her mission, the homeless situation had worsened. She was part of the problem, not the solution. The future came caving in and an overwhelming sense of dread surrounded her. One by one recent events flashed before her mind's eye: Charlie dying, the letters from the galleries, her ripped-through apartment, her ruined painting 'A Vision of Hope', Stephanie's piercing eyes. Like dark storm clouds those thoughts continued to roll in. A white heat flashed through her like a bolt of lightning. She felt dirty and used, by what and why she did not know, but somehow she deserved it. Her body slouched forward in her chair as if her spine had vanished.

The sun began to sink and the room darkened. There was no reason to get up and turn on the light. She was separating somehow. Her visions fragmented and took on different sizes. She could not pull them together. Her glowing colors, high energy, and fluid motion were only a mask to cover the vileness, the grotesque flesh of living affliction. A group of biochemicals chained to the soul of a wretched body. She was a violation of all that was good and true and she represented all that had happened to her over the last year.

Guilt was now the driving force of all the events of her wrongdoing throughout her life. Her early dissociation from her family came first: what right did she have? The self-absorption where Stephanie was concerned: she must have said something wrong to make her run. She had killed her! Then the painting that hurt many good people ... She could form no logical thoughts and her power of integration was gone. Her mind had lost all abilities, save the systematic torture it bestowed. One emotion crawled out from the darkest part of her soul a stood clearly before her: Shame.

* * *

"There's no question that he's dead," Mark Edwards said, looking at Harold Weaver.

Harold looked at Leonard but directed his question to Mark, "Did you see the death certificate?"

"Yes, sir, the evidence is overwhelming."

"Who was at the funeral?" Harold asked. Leonard's full attention was on a piece of wood in front of him. Was he even listening? There was a mirror on the wall behind where Leonard sat and Harold noticed that the gray in his own hair had woven itself between the black and overpowered the last bit of youth in his appearance. He turned back to Mark.

"About fifty homeless people. Some got up and spoke on his behalf." Mark explained the funeral in full detail. "They spoke of Charlie's carvings and how he was consistently, almost neurotically, chiseling out ... ," He paused as he looked at a piece of paper in front of him, "spaces in the mind." He had obtained three carvings of Charlie's, all for less than twenty dollars. Leonard continued to analyze the one little statue, turning it, flipping it upside-down, squinting his eyes and pursing his lips.

"Thank you, Mark. You can go now." Harold looked over the report Mark had left with him. He had spoken to all the agents and they all reported the same things. All his companions were homeless and nobody ever saw him working on anything other than his woodcarvings.

"Well, what do you think?" Harold asked Leonard.

Leonard smiled as he shrugged his shoulders. "Well, it's not basket weaving." He played with the carving. "I suppose it could be considered creative therapy. They're actually quite nice, very emotional expressions on the faces."

"So could he have been doing these all this time?"

"It's unlikely, but possible." Leonard held the piece up in front of his face. "What a waste of a mind." He shook his head.

"Thank you." Harold frowned and waved his hand indicating that the meeting was over.

Leonard left the room. Harold thought about his predicament with defense. He needed more money. His phone rang.

"Yes, what is it?" He did not want to be disturbed.

"Jason Walburg is here to see you," his secretary answered.

"Send him in."

Deputy Defense Secretary Jason Walburg walked in and sat down.

"What can I do for you?"

"I have good news." Jason placed a file on the table.

Harold rubbed his face. "What is it?" He didn't pick up the file.

"The President has asked our nuclear weapons scientists to find out how quickly they could restart nuclear test explosions under the Nevada desert." Jason looked at the file on the table. "And he's willing to direct thirty billion dollars towards defense right away. That's the largest peacetime increase in defense spending since the 1980s. He also stated that there would be no limit to funding necessary programs, stressing that the safety and potency of the American arsenal can be assured only by periodically detonating randomly selected warheads."

Harold shook his head. "This is what we've been saying all along."

"Yes, sir, but with the rising threat coming from China, he's had second thoughts about ratifying the treaty of a permanent global ban on nuclear testing." Jason raised his eyebrows.

"We should expect some resistance to this," Harold said.

"Yes, sir. I'm sure Britain, France, and even some of our scientists, will argue that underground tests are unnecessary and could provoke a new nuclear arms race."

"Are we supposed to fall behind China? They continue to test. And unlike China, which is willing to initiate force, the sole purpose of our posturing to be the strongest is to deter the use of nuclear weapons. Russia is also becoming a threat, terrorism is escalating … We must maintain the upper hand or the world will fall under the heading 'Dictatorship' and human rights will no longer exist anywhere." Harold could feel his face flush.

"Yes, sir," Jason said as though he had heard that speech numerous times. But why now? "Sir, what exactly did you put in that report of yours that made the President change his mind?"

Harold let out a half smile and thought about his long letter that finished with:

*… and, sir, the inhaler your daughter uses for her asthma has the capacity to hold enough Botulinal Toxin, the most lethal substance known, to kill millions of people. There is no effective detection, or proven vaccine for this biological weapon and can be safely transported as an aerosol. Small seed cultures can produce large quantities of biological weapons cheaply, making the stakes high for countries where nuclear weapons are not options. Our nuclear arsenal, an area that only needs attention by way of funds to remain the strongest in the world, must be in place so that our attention can be directed to biological and chemical warfare …*

Harold answered, "Just the reality of things. Lets get started."

"Yes, sir." Jason got up and left the room.

\* \* \*

It had been six days since Charlie's funeral and Melissa had not left the apartment once. She sat deadened on the couch as though she had been struck on the head by a large rubber mallet. Painful ripples coursed through her veins and subsided. Numbness followed, then settled over her like a thick heavy blanket. There was nothing to think, nothing to feel, nowhere to go. Her wrathful aspersions silenced leaving only an empty space of defeat. She could almost feel scar tissue growing over her soul. There were only small spaces of vulnerability left. Good, she thought, it was about time she grew up.

John stayed with her for three days feeding her, holding her hand, watching over her. Then he had to get back to work, as Matthew had urgent business to take care of. John called Melissa every two hours to make sure she was okay. The one time she didn't answer, he rushed home fearing the worst. She didn't feel like answering, was all she said as though it was no big deal.

This morning before leaving for work he threatened that if she didn't eat the food he had prepared, he was going to check her into a hospital where they would feed her intravenously and put her on drugs. "You can't afford to lose another ounce!" he shouted before he left. She only shrugged her shoulders in response.

It had been an hour since he last called. It was midday and the sun, as usual, caught the corner of the window and shone its light upon Melissa's face. It would slowly move across the pane and disappear into the afternoon and then night … She would wait, drifting in and out of sleep to see it rise again the next morning, sitting, watching, and wondering why it kept coming up. What was the point? The shadows that moved across the room with the sun's movement became more real than the forms that threw them. There was no different feeling between night and day. Everything was dull.

She felt more like an outsider than ever. In her lethargic state she would experience little flares of light thrown by a minuscule flicker in her soul, glimpses of hope through her arid mind. In those flashes, feelings and memories arose of how she used to be. The world could be remade and she was the vein of expression to pursue that noble goal. It was her duty to interpret and set free a world bound by chains. She was in tune and her disposition to ecstasy gave passionate expression to her art. She would celebrate the light with persistent observation and was free to create without bounds or limits, something so entirely personal, a fingerprint in time, intelligible for all to understand. Those flashes came sporadically without warning as blazing pulses of energy and joy. But, without exception, they lasted for only a fleeting second and were then extinguished by the dark faceless demon that continued to usher her more deeply into a black mass of hopelessness. Why had her inspiration, her muse, asked so much of her?

She thought of Stephanie, Joanne, and Charlie. She had come to rationalize that they were better off dead. Charlie was right to run to the streets. At least he had protected his soul. She had been too naïve, a soul turned outward for all to tear and rip open. She had not shielded it, and now it was beyond repair. All the world's beauty had died in her and her friends. They were too good for this world! The world could not recognize such wonder and she had been foolish to believe it could. Her mouth was dry and she had the urge to throw up. Her body convulsed to rid herself of something she could not name. Acids from her stomach climbed up in the back of her throat. Her body calmed after one last uncontrolled heave. There was only one course of action now.

It took all of her energy to stand up and walk out the front door. She got on the elevator and made her way to the roof. Seventeen stories up, she stood along the ledge as the wind pushed against her back. She looked down and was not afraid. There was no feeling save a familiar energy. It was the same force that seemingly lifted her from the roof after dropping the painting of Joanne, except this time it was drawing her toward the ground. Her toes and the balls of her feet hung over the edge of the building as the wind whispered by her ear. It made a hollow sound that changed in pitch as it picked up speed. She felt lightheaded and dizziness set in. Her balance started to waver and the rush of the wind at her back began to overpower any resistance. She could feel her body moving forward.

In that moment, her awareness peaked as though this would be the last time she would see anything. Each and every window in the building across the street stood before her as shining entities of shimmering yellow turning, in swirls, to ruddy pools connected to nothing. The buildings lay in succession across the horizon and stood on their own in her vision, having no meaning other than that she saw them, and saw them clearly. She could no longer feel her body, time was non-existent, and her conceptual capacity was diminishing. In some form of defense the remaining cognitive ability struggled to reason with what was going on. Reality was fading, and control of her actions, thoughts, and feelings was gone. Everything in sight had more definition than ever before. It was as if a dam broke open and flooded her mind with sensory perceptions, dreamlike abstractions floating in her vision. She drifted forward, toward the abyss, as a languorous funeral ballad reverberated in her head. A sunflower stood before her, a Van Gogh sunflower …

"Come to your senses, Child! You have work to do." The thunderclap of sound shocked her.

Melissa's posture firmed and she leaned back. She felt like she was spiraling back from a distant place as the city before her snapped together like a puzzle. The buildings, streets, houses explicably tied together to furnish people who form society.

"Charlie, you're alive!" She turned around quickly. His voice had resonated so clearly that she felt surely he was standing right behind her. There was nobody there. Her body contorted with a paroxysmal shiver. Where had he gone? She was positive he had been there. She scanned every corner of the building top as if he was hiding behind the whistling wind. She stopped and ran her hand over her body as though exploring a new terrain. Was she dreaming? She went back to where she had been standing and now saw the whole building across the street. Windows, like eyes to the soul, showed her the interior as her mind channeled through the heating system down to the foundation where it all began. Her thoughts fused together and she understood the concept of that building. It was not a collection of bricks, steel, glass, and concrete as she had just perceived in her heightened awareness, it was a symbol of the heroic effort of man and what he was capable of, what she was capable of.

She could almost see the dark cloud surrounding her soul disintegrate like the mist over the Algonquin water dispersing from the sun's filaments of warmth. His voice was so clear, so real ... she had to go see Will. She went down and changed the message on the answering machine to tell John that she was fine and would be back soon. She also left a note in case he came running home before listening to the message.

She left the apartment feeling she had seen a reality different from the one she was in now, as if somehow there was a parallel world that ran along side this one. She shook her head and thought, *I'm going mad!*

\* \* \*

Walking to the church, Melissa was in awe of how clearly she could see everything. The sky was so blue, the clouds smoky white, the people so vivid ... A pain shot through her body at the thought of painting. Everything she saw, abstract and concrete, produced a deeply emotional experience within and her natural response would be to put those images onto a surface for all to see. But she couldn't. Just the thought of painting opened a wound she thought had scarred over within her. It was painful to accept the fact that she wouldn't be able to continue. She wasn't strong enough to expose herself in that way again. She walked into the church.

The stained glass windows seemed more colorful and the channel of sunlight reflected Jesus in a different way than the last time she had been there. Melissa slid into a seat. She hoped Will there today.

The discomfort she had felt when she was last in the church ran through her body and disappeared. All the peaks and valleys of her feelings over the last year flashed over her senses and went away. She didn't know what to think or feel any longer. She looked up at Jesus and marveled at the craftsmanship. She felt the love, care, and power of the artist's work. That artist had had a deep connection with the spirit in which it was made. Melissa felt better knowing there was somebody else in the world that gave their heart and soul to their work. She wondered if that person had suffered the same fate she had. Her head fell forward and she felt like crying.

Warmth spread over her right shoulder immobilizing her. She could not lift her head or move in any way. Her eyes were open but she could not see anything. It was as if all her senses were shut down save the feeling on her right shoulder. It felt like a hand, a large hand. Slowly, the warmth spread down across her shoulder through her arm and torso. The feeling kept radiating down to her legs, then feet. The hand was heavy on her shoulder and at first the picture of Will flashed through her mind. The feeling was the same as when he touched her hand in the shelter, but immeasurably more powerful. Charlie had once touched her on that shoulder when he was in her apartment. In a white flash, as if that dying flicker of light in her soul burst open into a sun fire, the benevolent face of Jesus opened in front of her. She stood face to face with her spirit. It was the place where great things arise, the seed of profound wisdom. A universal sense of harmony surrounded her. With all her strength she tried to lift her head and turn around to see who was applying this pressure, but she was powerless.

Like waves, the warm healing sensation flowed through her body. It passed through countless times, taking away her pain. The scar tissue she envisioned around her soul broke away and dissipated. In her mind she wanted to fight this as she was becoming more open, vulnerable. She felt like a reptile crawling out of its skin.

A coolness set in on her shoulder as the heaviness of the hand disappeared. Her vision came back and she gained control. She looked up at the statue of Jesus, which strangely, seemed to be smiling at her. She did not want to turn around to see who was behind her, fearing ...

Slowly, her head involuntarily turned and she was right, there was nobody there. *I'm going crazy,* she thought. She sat for a moment feeling revived. The face of Edward Woodrow flashed before her mind and she could not feel hatred. Some force within her wanted to, but she couldn't. She could see in his eyes that something had gone wrong with him. His soul stood broken before her and she felt sad for him, but also hopeful. It was not something she could explain other than that on the deepest level he could be helped. A sense of warmth and power ran through her veins and she was regaining her strength. The words of Will rang through her head, *I hope one day you will find forgiveness in your heart, for when you do, you will understand the hidden source of power it inspires.* All hatred had left her heart, a feeling she used to think protected her somehow. She realized now that it had only caged her. She looked around the church and smiled. Her eyes widened as a single thought entered her head: *John.*

* * *

She rushed to the apartment, fearing he probably had the whole police force out looking for her. She opened the door and he was sitting on the couch looking out the window, the note she had written clenched in his hand. He turned his head to Melissa. He was so worried, she thought. What had she done to him? She walked over to where he was and stood in front of him. He looked at her as if not knowing what to do. She had thwarted all his advances over the last couple of weeks. He had tried everything and now looked helpless. Sheepishly, she opened her arms inviting a hug, unsure if he would. He stood up and carefully put his arms around her. Her body quivered at the feel of his embrace. It was comfortable and she felt starved for his affection. Her hands made their way around his back and she held tightly. John's hold was delicate, as if afraid to hurt her.

"I'm sorry, John," was all she could say as, for the first time since ... Stephanie, tears released and fell down her face.

It was at least five minutes before she could stop crying. Gently, she pushed him away and looked into his eyes. How lovely it was to see him again. Her hand caressed his cheek and around his eyes. "Oh my, look at the lines I've deepened on your face."

He pulled her close. "Oh, Melissa, I was so worried about you. I thought you might ..." He didn't finish.

She took a deep breath and tried unsuccessfully to keep the tears from pouring down her face again. "I'm fine now, John, I've come through it."

She continued to hold him for a few minutes, then broke the embrace. She looked up at him and smiled. "I'm starved, can we go get something to eat?"

John laughed as he brushed a tear from his eye. "I don't know, you're getting kind of heavy."

She laughed. "You're so smooth, you know exactly what to say to make a girl feel good."

Melissa picked a Greek restaurant. They ordered and talked. Melissa could tell she looked horrible. John's eyes were full of concern. She tried to eat but could barely swallow. She assured him it was because her body could not accept too much right now. Over the next while, she would work hard to get her energy back so that they could dine over a bottle of wine again. A promise she would not forget. They continued in silence. When they caught each other's glance they would hold it for a couple of seconds without saying anything, nothing needed to be said.

Melissa and John spent the rest of the day together. They spoke mostly about Charlie, and Melissa was starting to come to terms with his death. John was of great help and knew exactly what to say to make her feel better. She felt terrible about how she had treated Will. He must hate her, she thought. John was reassuring, being his normal comforting self. She never left his side once they returned to the apartment and she fell asleep in his arms. She had not told him about being up on the roof and hearing Charlie's voice or of the feelings she had had in the church. She could not come to terms with everything herself and John had been through enough. It was her job to get better now. If John had had any doubt that he was important in her life, it would be dispelled over the next little while. She needed him more than anything. John was and always would be most important in her life.

\* \* \*

Melissa could feel the energy returning to her body. She had slept well for the first time in weeks and was feeling more grounded. Her mission today was to find Will. She wasn't sure what she was going to say, but she had to see him. John had a busy day ahead of him. He told Melissa all about work and future prospects with Matthew's company. Melissa was happy for him. Before leaving for the day he told Melissa that when she was up to it, Matthew wanted to speak with her.

Melissa left immediately after John to find Will. She had gone to the church, three shelters he frequented, and found herself at City Hall sitting on a bench, watching people walk by in front of her. It was lunch hour and there were many people passing by. Her mind wandered. She was worried about her kitchen, there wasn't much money left now and she would have to close it and the hotline.

"Mind if I sit down?"

She didn't look over. "Sure, sit where you like." A moment had passed and she thought about all the people who would be on the streets. Hopelessness began again to spread across her body. Then with a startling realization she turned. "Will!"

He smiled his usual infectious smile. "Hi, Melissa."

With unfettered emotion she threw her arms around him and squeezed tightly. "I've been looking all over for you."

"I heard."

She leaned back to look into his eyes. They were deeper and more caring than ever. "I'm sorry ..." As the words fell from her mouth she realized words could never convey the regret she felt for treating him the way she had. "You're the most kind and understanding man I know and I ..." Tears ran down her cheeks.

Will grabbed her hand. "There's no need for apology, in fact I was out of line losing my composure the way I did. I'm supposed to be strong and helpful in times of need, and I failed you."

Melissa dried her face with her palm. "What was it you told me one time?" She pursed her lips and squinted her eyes trying to recall the exact words. "Ah, so it is with the good."

Will looked toward the ground, as though being humbled by her saying that. He lifted his head and looked her over. "You look terrible. You lose any more weight and you'll disappear."

"Yeah, I know, I put worry lines on John's face that I fear may be permanent." She looked discerningly into his eyes. "Will, I think I'm going crazy."

Will laughed and said nothing.

"I'm hearing voices and feeling things that aren't there." She told him of the events of yesterday with apprehension.

"It was the stress, Melissa. You heard Charlie's voice because your mind and body had an overload of external pressures that you could not deal with all at once. Actually, what really happened was you turned your mind over to a higher authority. In your case it was Charlie. He had had such a strong impact on your life and because you valued his opinion and what he said, he came back to you. Your body didn't want to die so you manufactured an authority figure to pull you back. No other voice at that time could have had such an impact on you. I believe it was your own natural resistance to dying."

Melissa thought about what Will had said. "Have you ever heard voices?"

"Yes, and many people have, actually probably most people at some point in their life. Children have imaginary friends that are very real to them. Charlie believed it a vestige of primitive man." Will chuckled and shook his head.

Melissa was surprised. "What are you saying, you believe in evolution?"

"Yes, of course. Melissa, I don't evade the truth." Will thought for a moment. "I have a degree in psychology, and study Neuro-Linguistic Programming. I'm where I am right now because of that. I could see that information was traveling faster than the ability of nations to use that knowledge in a way that protects people. Charlie understood that and, in fact, that's why he took to the streets. In our world there is only one way to transcend safely to the next evolution. You see, my voices told me to take to the spirit as a means of benevolence. Jesus is my guide." Will paused. "He preached an unbreakable code of moral values to live by and how to move beyond, in any time. His work is not done yet."

It was the right moment. Melissa cut in, "Now there's something I can relate to. You understand that I'm more secular in view, and I have opened my mind a little of late toward your views, but there is one thing I can't adhere to. I can agree that Jesus was a man men should emulate, but he didn't die for his own sins, did he?" Melissa asked as her spirit strengthened.

Will shook his head no and smiled.

"He died for the sins of humanity. Two thousand years and what's changed? Nothing. We need people of virtue here. We're still sacrificing the virtuous for the savages that run this planet. I can't agree with the spirit of the good being sacrificed and never could. That would be like you sacrificing yourself so that Edward Woodrow may be free. I've lost my bitter hatred for him, but why should you or anybody else die for the sins of others?"

"Jesus stood up for what he believed and looked his accusers in the eye." Will paused.

"So are you condoning what he allowed to happen to him?" Melissa now had the internal space to ask these questions without the unsolicited wave of hatred rising up in her blood.

"Are you ready to go there with me?" Will looked over Melissa. "I've wanted to talk with you about this from the first day we met, and we did start on your wedding day ... but now might not be—"

"No, no. I'm ready." Melissa looked into his eyes. They were so deep and seemed to hold a power beyond his own. She could use some of that power right now.

"Okay. Jesus allowed himself to be crucified because he had no other choice. Once exposed to God you realize that there is nothing that can hurt you, the essential you that is. So he stood face to face with his accusers to show humanity, in tangible terms, what we should be fighting. His death portrayed the fight between good and evil. This fight continues today."

Melissa thought of Charlie. "This is what Charlie ran from."

"Yes, but he actually didn't run, he embraced it. It was only on the last day while he was dying that I fully understood his plight. He believed his work could not be used until humanity gets past the nuclear decision threshold. He thinks it's you and your kind who will bring it forward. He was so pessimistic about life before you came along. He had a brief moment of light with Joanne, but of course her death only made it worse." Will smiled as his eyes shifted up. "But then you came along. You have no idea how much energy you gave him. He worked for many years from the streets, not because he thought he was doing this great service for humanity. He had a strong connection between his existence and his true nature. When you have that connection, Melissa, there is no other way you can be."

"Yeah, I know it."

"Yes you do." Will smiled like he had seen it in her long ago. "He told me on his final day that he fully expected his work to die in lock boxes never to be seen by anybody, the ink well faded before anybody could read it. Then you came along and he realized that his work would come to be known. He told me when he had seen your painting, 'A Vision of Hope', that he knew it was you who would figure out how the key worked. In his last gasping breaths he felt the God force and his life had meaning. It was you who showed him that."

Melissa's shoulders rolled forward. "How could I show him that? I don't even believe in God and can't."

"But you do, Melissa, don't you see that?"

There was no feeling of anger or need to lash out at Will but Melissa still felt no connection. "No, Will, I'm sorry, I still don't."

"That's only because of the way you're looking. You're seeing through the lens of the past, old theology."

"Yes, but as much as I believe in Jesus as a virtuous man, he was not born from immaculate conception, Mary was not a virgin …" Melissa felt like going on step by step to disintegrate the whole belief system, but Will was not stupid, he knew everything she would say.

"It's the power structure that is the problem Melissa. They're protecting the system because the system protects them and they think people need the system more than they need the truth. The church has always resisted new knowledge. They, through different men over the years, preached against medical intervention because it took away God's will; 'who are we to stand in the way of God if he decides to take one of his flock away? It is His will.' But it was also His will to cherish and protect life and we were given this wonderful tool to do that: the mind. In the past the Almighty power took sides between human conflicts allowing the slaughter of certain groups of people. But this spirit, in my belief, does not condone ethnic cleansing and has, in old terms, become impotent. Science has overpowered the old metaphor of who God was. The metaphors have to be adjusted and the Bible should not be taken so literally, and used as more of a window than a sword, a vehicle to find the power of Jesus within each and every one of us. Personally, Melissa, I don't subscribe to a God who embodies the worst of our tribal and political hatreds."

"I don't understand, then who do you—?"

"Good, Melissa, you've lost all the apprehension in your voice. I will never ask you to believe in something against your will, but you're now showing that you're able to listen without prejudice. A true gateway to understanding and personal growth." Will grabbed her hand. "I believe in Christ, he had more of a God presence than anybody in history or even today. But at that time language was too limited to describe Him accurately.

"So with the limited avenue of language, namely concept-forming, on which to take the teachings of Jesus, theism was born. It was a language of a pre-modern, pre-scientific world that would not allow for change as the world changed. But Jesus had tried to change that by giving the peasants the tools to free themselves. He knew, as do you, that change is more likely possible for those not flourishing in this world. You see, like Jesus had seen, that the less fortunate a person is, the more likely he'll be to grasp onto change, and if able to harness it, will be happier and more fulfilled than people trapped in the 'normalcy' of society that have everything to lose by change. In the spirit of Jesus, Melissa, is the answer, and always has been, to transcend into the future with peace and understanding. And that means seeking guidance from within as Jesus taught, that a higher power exists, but within each and every one of us and by walking in His presence, we can take the leap of faith to the new world. Indeed only the person can do that for himself."

Melissa could feel the spirit of Will and could see that there was something very alive in him as he spoke. It would have been scary, she thought, had her hand not been receiving a power she could not describe. Will was not holding tightly but energy radiated through her body as he spoke. It was even, direct, endless; the universal endorphin she sought. "How?" she asked.

"By understanding where this magnificent spirit lies and then garnering its power. First this spirit was found externally as it could only be found. You see, in the Old Testament God was found through external events, real and imagined. In much the same way as you found Charlie on the building. God came to man in voices and visions manufactured by the right hemisphere of the brain and heard by the left. Men built idols, tombs, and gave this voice total authority. It was the only place this spirit could have been found for them. Then as the brain organized into conscious terms, those Gods vanished and man was now to aspire to a 'oneness' with Him. The voices fell silent. But man still housed this spirit and needed direction toward it. Then came a man who found a bridge."

"Jesus." Melissa's body tingled all over.

"Yes. This was where God resided now. The intensity of God within him was so great that people called him His son and put the spirit of God in human form, and He was! And as much as He tried to pave a new road to God, people because of limited ability at the time, described His life in terms of ancient expectations. But it is clear to me that this was not His goal. His goal was to show people the spirit within themselves. He spoke in parables in order to get people to think for themselves, that it wasn't only Him who housed this spirit, it was everybody, no exception. He knew that God was not to be found outside any longer. People had to look within, that God was a universal presence supporting all life. As Jesus destroyed the old ways of viewing God, so must we. But it's not this spirit that has changed. It's us, and how we describe His light. The reformation of Christianity must happen soon or that spirit will die with the old creeds and doctrines, which, to me, have been interpreted to fit a self-serving political context. There's a burgeoning group of people in search for spiritual relief with nowhere to turn. Humanity has reached 'The dark night of the soul'.

"That's my goal, that's what my voices told me. Form the church of tomorrow in such a way that this spirit may manifest within the individual to lift humanity past this stage in history, and all others. A new Bible must be written with real life characters to lead and show the most peaceful way to live using all the lessons Jesus taught. But instead of one man like Jesus leading, this document must show people how to lead themselves. That's what Jesus tried to do. But now we have more information available of human nature, medicine, science to do the job again as the four men that did it for a different era." Will stopped and continued to hold Melissa's hand. "You have the ability to help in this goal, to become a real life character in the quest for peace. Your spirit can help lead in the same way Jesus' did. We can help change the worldview, and bring everything into focus to make sense of the ideas around us. You, with your paintings, have already put a magnifying glass on some most important areas. You need not change anything about yourself, just continue to look at nature honestly and beauty will be the result. I believe we all meet God when we've achieved our highest good, He is the essence of the purest of hearts ... you may give that any name you wish."

"No," Melissa could feel a tear well in her eye, "I can't help. I've discovered that I'm not nearly worth what I thought I was. I'm going to have to give up my work with the homeless because it was not my paintings that made money it was my father's influence. If it weren't for John I would have no sense of worth. My money will dry up soon, I don't have a job and have never had a job, and ..." She could not continue. If it weren't for Will's hand on hers she would surely drop back into depression.

Will released her hand and put his arm around her. "You will come through this, Melissa. I've worked with many people who have suffered depression and it takes a while to heal. But if you think about it, how could a person of no worth have so many wonderful people love her? Stephanie, Charlie, John, John's mom ..."

She looked up feeling insecure. Her voice quivered. "You?"

"If it were possible, more than all of them. Even your family, Melissa, will come to realize that it's more important to have you in their life than to be worried about position. Don't give up on them. Also, it was never money that gave your art worth."

"Maybe, but you can't feed people with a collection of colorful images on canvas." She paused. "It's hard. I just feel like I'm so needy. I need you, I need John, I need Charlie ..." Her eyes filled with tears and she turned and threw her arms around Will. "Why did he have to die?" Will said nothing and held her tightly. "I need him so badly. I need him to tell me what to do." After a few moments she released her grip. "I'm sorry."

Will's smile started small and gradually spanned the width of his face.

Melissa dried her eyes with her sleeve and looked incredulously at Will. "What?"

"He's got a list."

"Pardon?"

"Charlie has a list for you. After one year, not before, you are to take his work from the secured areas it's in. You're to organize it the way he has stipulated in the book he gave to me, and study it. He could not emphasize enough that if you're threatened in any way that you're to give up his work without any kind of fight. 'She is not a spirit to be sacrificed!' he said." Will continued to smile. "He was sorry to keep you away from his funeral and knew you would be upset at that, so his last wish was for you to take his ashes and spread them over his homeland in the Carpathian Mountains. He's left a detailed map. It doesn't have to be done right away." Will laughed.

"What are you laughing at?" Melissa's heart was lighter now.

"When Charlie was making the transition from this world, he laughed with a defiant air and said, 'Why should it matter when she takes my ashes there? I will already be there, I'm on my way right now.' Then a calm serene look overspread his face and his eyes glowed with the fire of light." Will paused. His look became serious and his eyes deep. "I saw it, Melissa." He spoke to her as an excited friend. "It was like Charlie kept his body alive and his eyes open just so that I could see it."

"What? What did you see?" The sense of lightness spread throughout her body. She had forgotten everything that had weighed her down over the last year. What did he see?

"It was as if I could see his soul leaving. He stopped functioning. With a furious jolt followed by his body becoming completely lifeless I knew his heart and mind had stopped. But his eyes were still windows to his soul that continued to live. I looked deeper and deeper into his eyes and could see his soul leaving. I was struck at the time by this incredible event. Now, of course, I realize that I had manufactured in my mind what I saw from my own expectations."

"What was it?"

"I saw his essence spiraling down, I don't know how to explain it." Will stopped. "I got a similar feeling when I saw the painting of Joanne you dropped from the building. It was the transition point where Joanne lost her life and ended up in the bus shelter. Actually, you have great leaps in all your work that I've seen, and like most this time the transition was to somewhere great. Energy passed through me like he had surfaced on some other side, giving life to a new universe and the words 'Let there be light!' resounded in my mind in Charlie's voice. It was as clear as day. Then at the very next moment he was gone, mind and spirit."

"Wow, that's incredible," Melissa said without knowing what else to say.

"Yeah. He gave so much life and I feel like it was only a beginning with him. You're the one to keep him alive here Melissa, and I'm here to help you."

They both sat in silence for over five minutes. "I need to go for a walk." Melissa leaned over and kissed Will on the cheek.

"You know what I think?"

Melissa said nothing, letting her expression inquire.

"I think it's about time you came to one of my sermons."

"I feel like I've already been to them all." She laughed and walked away.

# Chapter 30

Melissa waited on a comfortable leather chair on the wall beside Suzanne's desk. She had built up enough strength to see Matthew, today. Not knowing what he wanted left her feeling a little uneasy, but like the last time she was here, the people in the building inspired energy. They performed their duties in a businesslike manner, but there was no sense of boredom. A vision of a car engine came to life in her mind, she could not determine why. There were only a few occasions she had even seen an engine and she knew little about how one worked. It was at John's farm where she had watched him tune up and fix his van. He had tried to explain how things worked, but he had always distracted her with warm sensual feelings.

Matthew stuck his head out of his door and signaled Melissa over. Uneasiness set in again as she walked into his office. As usual his face showed no sign of emotion.

"How are you, Melissa?"

"I'm better. Things have been difficult, but I have John to help me through. I'll be fine," Melissa said, her voice soft, her words honest. Matthew's stoic demeanor was not as intimidating as the last time she had been in this office. "I'm sorry for involving you."

"First of all, never apologize for things that aren't your fault. Second, never apologize." Matthew squinted his eyes as if studying Melissa. "I want you to know that I haven't forgotten that I owe you a painting for letting me use your building … it's just that I'm not ready to go there right now. Maybe there is something else I could do for you."

Melissa explained how her father had disowned her and that her work wasn't worth as much as she thought it was. Once she began talking it seemed she couldn't stop. She told him everything. How her soup kitchen would have to be closed down, the feelings she had for Charlie. Matthew sat silently taking everything in. "I don't know why, I guess I don't feel worthy," Melissa said.

Matthew swiveled his chair and looked out the window, his left hand cupped under his chin. The silence did not make Melissa feel uncomfortable. Her feelings for Matthew were strong. It was growing respect. The way he had taken control of the situation in her apartment had been incredible.

He turned back to her. "Phil was foolish for disowning you."

"You know my father?" Melissa's posture firmed.

"Yes, he's a brilliant trader but he sleeps with parasites."

"I beg your pardon!" Melissa stood up.

Matthew let out a half smile. "Excuse my frankness, I just meant that ingratiating politicians doesn't serve society the way he thinks it does."

"I'm sorry, but I didn't like that 'frankness'. And my father does a lot of good in the world," Melissa said defensively.

"Have a seat and let's get down to the business at hand." Matthew's voice was sharp.

Melissa sat down on her own terms.

"You owe me a painting for letting you use my building. It doesn't seem that you're able to live up to your end of the bargain."

"It's not that I don't want to, I was just hoping maybe there could be another way to pay." Melissa's head sank as insecurity overwhelmed her again. "I'm not sure how, I'm almost out of money."

"This is a predicament. Looks like you need a job."

"What?"

"Well it seems to me that at the time you offered me a painting, your art was selling for anywhere between ten and twenty thousand dollars. Now I'm a fair man and certainly don't expect you to pay me that much. Although, I did assume you would put your heart and soul into a piece for me." Matthew looked on the verge of a victory. It made Melissa feel uncomfortable. "Now even if I were to charge you half of what your work was worth, you would owe me at least five thousand dollars."

"I can't afford that. I don't know how I can make it up to you." Melissa had never gone back on an agreement and she wouldn't now. "Tell me what I can do to clear my debt."

"Well it looks like you need a job and I'm having a difficult time lately finding competent people."

"You're offering me a job? I've never had a job. Of what value would I be to you?" Melissa was feeling stronger. The thought of working for Matthew thrilled and scared her.

"Well the fact that you've never had a job is good. I won't have to shed a bunch of bad habits before I teach you the business. And your value is for me to decide. Now if you come to an agreement on my terms, I will consider it payment for the painting."

Melissa felt uneasy again.

"You will work for me for no fewer than two years. You will be paid in direct proportion to your value, which won't be much at first. I will provide you with a base salary that will grow exponentially with the skills you learn, providing you learn and apply them. My staff, you will find, is incredibly helpful." Matthew pulled out a piece of paper and handed it to Melissa.

Melissa read it over. It had everything he just said on it with a place for a signature at the bottom. She thought about the people in this building and how lively and confident they looked. With everything that had happened, she really needed a job. "Do you want me to sign this?"

"Do you accept my terms?"

"Yes, I would love to work for you," Melissa replied with hesitant enthusiasm.

Matthew smiled. "That will change, you'll come to hate me."

"I don't think I could ever hate you, you've helped so much." Melissa signed the paper.

Matthew laughed as she went to hand him the contract. "No, that's for you to keep, to look at when you feel like quitting. Your word is good enough for me." Matthew extended his hand as he stood up.

"I'm not a quitter." Melissa shook his hand.

"I'm sure of that. See you Monday morning, seven sharp." Matthew indicated that the interview was over with a dismissive wave of his hand.

On the way out Melissa looked back. "Just so you know, I appreciate and will keep up my end of the agreement, but if for some reason things don't work out, you can keep the painting I dropped from your building. I assume you have it?"

Matthew nodded yes.

"Even if we go with the lower number, appraised value at the time we made the agreement, being ten thousand dollars, it would be worth much more because of its size. Especially in a market where size seems to outweigh quality." Melissa smiled. "That will be my collateral, if you agree of course?"

"Yes, of course. I'll take into account the storage fees if I have to give it back."

"I'm sure you will." Melissa smiled.

He waved the back of his hand for her to leave. "Monday, be here at seven."

Melissa smiled at everybody as she passed by on her way out of the building. She couldn't wait to tell John about her job. He was going to be so proud. She stopped and picked up some dinner and a bottle of red wine.

When she got home she reflected on what a fortunate person she was. John loved her, Will had become a good friend, and she had known Charlie, if only for a brief time. It had not been a year since Joanne had died and Melissa had grown in leaps and bounds. She was a better person now. John's place was nice she thought as she looked around. She would be comfortable living there. Taking a deep breath of air made her feel good to be alive. Melissa decided that she would call her sister tomorrow. If her father didn't want her in the family, maybe Camille still did. Her mother must miss her. Easing into the couch, she drifted off into sleep.

Floating through space feeling buoyant and free, Melissa could see the earth coming toward her. The beautiful blue oceans mesmerized her as she drifted over the atmosphere. The year was 2091. A sense of euphoria danced through her, the world was still here, vibrant. She was omniscient. Over the last ninety years the world had secured itself as an integral part of the benevolent universe. Humanity had overcome the need to start wars; hunger and starvation were a thing of the past; each person had touched his internal power and love swept through the world, seemingly overnight. No longer did people subjugate themselves to any higher causes and society was reorganized so that the most competent people in the arts, science, business, and medicine naturally rose to the top. Cures for all diseases had been found and longevity was doubled. People never lost their happiness, creativity flourished, and everybody could rise, unhindered by oppressive forces, as high as their desire and capability lifted them. Melissa had banded with like-minded individuals and formed a coalition that had never stopped growing once it had started. Her whole body shook as she felt a presence within her. She looked up and there was Charlie's face among the stars. "Well done, Melissa." Joanne's face rested easily beside Charlie's. They were soul-mates. That was it, the key. Charlie gave the world a creative intelligence and Joanne a pureness of heart. Using the mind to its full capacity with a pureness of heart automatically eradicated hatred and jealousy and allowed civilization to flourish. That was what must be realized in every individual.

Melissa woke as John entered the room. He was carrying a large object in one hand wrapped in plain brown paper, in the other a large bunch of Tiger Lily's. She stretched her arms, still somewhat in her dream. "What's that?" She yawned.

"A present for me and you!" John replied with the excitement of a young boy. "And, of course, flowers for you from me." He held out the Lily's.

Melissa was wide-awake now. "Who's it from?" She rubbed her hands together allowing John's giddiness to rub off on her. "My father maybe?" she said, hopefully.

"I'm not sure. It was left with the superintendent of the building for us." John began to open the card. "No, not your father."

"What, who's it from?" Melissa grabbed the card and read it:

Dear John and Melissa,
    I wanted to wait until you came back from your honeymoon before giving you this. The unity of your souls is such a positive light and I am proud to know the both of you. You have added so much to my life in such a short time that I thought it only right to reciprocate. I know the both of you have suffered a great deal of pain lately and have sustained damaging blows. This present is in response to that. Melissa, I want to give back a piece of your soul. This is as much for you as well John because I know when Melissa is strong, you are happy. I look forward to many times together and think you should both get your butts down to one of my sermons.
With much love and respect,
Will

Melissa looked at John, her bottom lip pulled back by her top teeth. John was still smiling. "Well, should I open it?"

Melissa could not respond, she could only nod her head yes. She watched as John peeled away the brown paper. She knew what it was, the size, shape ... Her heart momentarily stopped. It was her painting, "A Life Cycle." She was in shock and could barely breathe. This was as generous a gesture as she had ever known. She looked at John whose eyes had glossed over slightly. She jumped up and hugged him soaking his shirt with her tears and laughing.

After what seemed like hours, Melissa was able to compose herself. She looked around the room for a place to hang the painting. Her glance stopped at the wall in the dinning room. She looked into John's eyes and could feel her face rise into a smile. "I've found the perfect place." Confidently, Melissa pulled a nail from a toolbox and hung the painting on the wall where there was already a hole made. It was off centered and not at the right height, but it was perfect. Looking around the room she wondered what else he had tried to rearrange in the apartment.

They drank wine and stared at the painting in between staring into each other's eyes. John was a reflection of everything Melissa was, a tangible manifestation of her soul.

"I've discovered a way to save the world." Melissa smiled derisively.

"Can it wait until after dinner? I'm getting hungry," John replied with a pleasing voice.

"Sure, but this can't."

Melissa leaned over and embraced him in a kiss. They made love in the living room, then moved to the bedroom tightly embraced as puzzle pieces that formed the picture of sensuality and pleasure. While on the bed, John's muscular body moved gracefully, evoking more energy and passion than Melissa had ever experienced. He was more than the tiger; he was the embodiment of everything she revered as good. They slipped night clothes over their warm naked bodies, went to the kitchen to make dinner to refuel and give them the energy to spend the rest of the night in exquisite rapture.

The Beginning